THE JOHN HARVARD LIBRARY

Bernard Bailyn

Editor-in-Chief

THE DUKE OF STOCKBRIDGE

A ROMANCE OF SHAYS' REBELLION

By

EDWARD BELLAMY

Edited by Joseph Schiffman

THE BELKNAP PRESS OF
HARVARD UNIVERSITY PRESS
Cambridge, Massachusetts
1962

Distributed in Great Britain by Oxford University Press, London

Library of Congress Catalog Card Number 62–17215
Printed in the United States of America

CONTENTS

EDWARD BELLAMY:
REALIST AND UTOPIAN

I

Edward Bellamy is renowned as the author of *Looking Backward*,[1] the classic industrial utopian novel which helped shape our modern world. At the turn of the century, *Looking Backward* and intellectual America were as inseparable as the McGuffey Reader and the classroom, the Bible and the home.

Though *Looking Backward* is avowedly utopian (Henry George viewed it as "a castle in the air, with clouds for its foundation" [2]), it rose from Bellamy's apprenticeship in the school of historical and literary realism. Though imperceptible, realism is the taproot of the novel's power to exalt earthbound man to aspire to a higher social life. Bellamy's youthful ardor for tearing away romantic trappings to present facts in unrelieved reality transmuted the well-grounded fears of his own time into utopianism for all time. The linkage between realism and utopianism can be glimpsed in several of his writings as a young man, but is particularly manifest in his neglected historical novel, *The Duke of Stockbridge*, published eight years before *Looking Backward*.

II

The Duke of Stockbridge first appeared as a serialized novel in a small-town newspaper, the *Berkshire Courier* of Great Barrington, Massachusetts.[3] Printed in 1879, it re-

---

[1] Boston, 1888.
[2] Quoted in Charles Albro Barker, *Henry George* (New York, 1955), p. 540.
[3] Vol. XLV, No. 1. On file at the Berkshire Athenaeum, Pittsfield, Mass.

flected a mood of national soul-searching stimulated by centennial celebrations of American Independence held in a time of economic distress, industrial conflict resembling rebellion,[4] and exposés of corruption in political, professional, and social life. Pointedly reverting to an earlier troubled time, 1786, *The Duke of Stockbridge* dealt with a revolt of debtor-farmers. In introducing the novel to their readers, the editors of the *Berkshire Courier* drew a parallel between post-Revolutionary and post-Civil War America:

. . . the experience of business depression which we are now passing through, furnishes the closest of historical parallels. . . . The same confusion in the currency, the same destruction of commerce, the same paralysis of industry, are now, as then, the result of a war. . . . And in the deep, popular discontent . . . we have evidence enough that debt, poverty, and non-employment have lost none of their maddening influence upon the hearts and brains of working-men. The parallel extends even to the very schemes and theories by which the agitations of today, encourage and delude their followers, most of which are merely the revamped ideas of Shays and his lieutenants. . . .[5]

Displaying traditional fear of "the poor, ignorant masses," the *Berkshire Courier* editors planned to parade the bedraggled Shaysites as symbols of a threat to the republic — standard treatment for that time. Two books had helped form the conventional attitude of fear and hatred toward Shaysites: George Richards Minot's *The History of the Insurrections in Massachusetts,* published in 1788 just two years after the rebellion, and Ralph Ingersoll Lockwood's novel, *The Insurgents,* published in 1835. Minot, imputing to Shaysites the anarchism of the incendiary "malcontent," established an attitude which dominated American historiography for over a century, influencing the work of Hannah Adams, John Marshall, Timothy Pitkin, and Richard Hil-

---

[4] Robert V. Bruce, *1877: Year of Violence* (Indianapolis, 1959).
[5] January 1, 1879, p. 2.

dreth. Lockwood's novel begins with sober insight into the causes of the rebellion only to conclude with a lurid depiction of Shaysites aflame with destructive passion.

But the novelist chosen by the *Berkshire Courier* was to pioneer in an unforeseen path. Always suspicious of mass attitudes, Bellamy rejected interpretations based on Minot and Lockwood; undertaking original research, he visited the Berkshire area, scene of the bloodiest fighting in the rebellion. There, as the editor of the *Berkshire Courier* explained, "by means of meagre local histories, family records, town and country archives and popular traditions, still . . . to be gathered up," [6] Bellamy developed a fresh interpretation of the causes of the insurrection. Identifying most of his historical characters by their actual names (Timothy Edwards, Perez Hamlin, Abner Rathbun, Abe Konkapot, *et al.*), and placing them in their actual geographic settings (Stockbridge, Great Barrington, Sheffield), the novelist wove a tale faithful to events.

Bellamy unearthed a rigid social structure in colonial Stockbridge, a "social antipodes" carried over from Europe. Squire Woodbridge, Squire Sedgwick, and Squire Edwards (son of Jonathan Edwards), all men of considerable property, are the "selectmen," the political, economic, and moral rulers of the village. "The back room [of Squire Timothy Edwards' store] is, in a sense, the Council-chamber, where the affairs of the village are debated and settled by these magnates, whose decisions the common people never dream of anticipating or questioning." [7] But, soon after the Revolution, the social structure is put under severe stress. Because of post-Revolutionary impoverishment, "hewers of wood and drawers of water, mechanics, farm-laborers, and farm-

---

[6] *Ibid.*

[7] *The Duke of Stockbridge*, Chap. I. Concerning the absence of "freedom of speech or press as a meaningful condition of life" during the colonial and revolutionary period, see Leonard W. Levy, *Legacy of Suppression* (Cambridge, 1960).

ers" [8] begin to grumble and question. In *The Duke of Stockbridge* Shays' Rebellion is not a matter of odious lawlessness; it is the product of economic and social forces.

Bellamy goes behind abstract slogans, vividly sketching the bitterness of the poor. A sore-pressed farmer says, ". . . we tho't we wuz big pertaters, agoin to fight fer lib'ty. Wall, we licked the redcoats, and we got lib'ty, I s'pose; lib'ty ter starve, that is ef we don' happin to git sent tew jail fus." [9] The reader is taken inside a debtor's prison to witness the heart-breaking sufferings of the imprisoned. Many of them are honored veterans of the Revolution, and they have been greatly altered by their experience in the war: ". . . the army of the revolution had been for its officers and [the] more intelligent element, a famous school of democratic ideas." [10] Bellamy recognized the educative leaven of the American Revolution, its role in sharpening the struggle between European ideas of class rule and American ideals of equality.

The debtors, with no hope of legal succor, tremble on the brink of rebellion. In Bellamy's book the Shaysites are not in favor of "anarchy and treason"; they are forced into rebellion in an attempt to keep their farms and themselves free. Looking for a leader, the rebels of Stockbridge choose Perez Hamlin, an ex-captain in the Revolutionary Army, who had returned home to find his brother dying in a debtor's jail and his family in danger of losing their farm to creditors. Rallied by Perez, the debtors march to a popular tune of the Stamp Act period:

> With the beasts of the wood, we will ramble for food,
> And lodge in wild deserts and caves;
> And live as poor Job on the skirts of the globe,
> Before we'll submit to be slaves, brave boys,
> Before we'll submit to be slaves.[11]

[8] *The Duke of Stockbridge*, Chap. II.
[9] *Ibid.*
[10] *Ibid.*, Chap. XIV.
[11] *Ibid.*, Chap. XXII.

When the peace-loving villagers tire of the turmoil, Shays' Rebellion is doomed. Undisciplined vandals and rogues among the Shaysites alienate the public by their acts, while the creditor class, enjoying superior leadership, offer concessions to the debtors which "practically cut the ground out from under the rebellion." [12]

So authentic and convincing was Bellamy's account that the editors of the *Berkshire Courier*, in following the serialized novel from week to week, experienced a conversion in attitude toward the Shaysites and all that they symbolized. Whereas the editors, upon introducing *The Duke of Stockbridge* to their readers, had expressed fear of "the maddening influence" of Shaysite thought and emotion, they eventually placed responsibility for the rebellion upon the pillars of colonial society:

Mr. Bellamy has seen more clearly than many historians and not a few political economists where to place the blame for the cruel misery that he depicts. He does not forget the principle that to whom much is given from them much is required. While never permitting us to sympathize with the crude notions, dissolute ways and bloody designs of the armed mob, he does not let us lose sight of the facts that these are but the outgrowths of an ignorance and despairing poverty that the more favored families, and even the christian [sic] church, had taken absolutely no pains to alleviate. No helping hand was extended to keep the ruined head of a household from the tax collector's or creditor's clutches; the laws, themselves a disgrace to humanity, were left to fulfil their blind and merciless course. Such men as Timothy Edwards and Parson West did not devise the prison pens, but neither did they unearth and expose their horrors to the public gaze. The theology of Calvin, Edwards and Hopkins was ably discussed but the religion of Jesus was never preached. . . . The story is a sad one, but its lesson is one that we all . . . may study with profit.[13]

In his concern with economic, social, and moral factors, Bellamy showed himself to be in advance of most of the

[12] *Ibid.,* Chap. XXIII.
[13] *Berkshire Courier,* July 2, 1879, p. 4.

formal historians of his time. Even John Bach McMaster, the father of social history in America, treated the rebellion as primarily a military matter,[14] and John Fiske, the most popular American historian of Bellamy's day, although aware of the heavy burden of taxation upon the farmers, emphasized the violent aspects of the rebellion.[15]

Bellamy's most illuminating observation, startling for his time, concerned the economic origin of the Constitution of the United States. In his novel the creditors of Stockbridge hunger for news from the Constitutional Convention meeting in Philadelphia. Squire Sedgwick expresses his hope that the way will be paved "for a stronger government . . . one that will guarantee us not only against foreign invasion but domestic violence and insurrection also." [16] Bellamy prefigured the development of one of the most useful tools of modern scholarship, the economic interpretation of history. When Charles Beard published *An Economic Interpretation of the Constitution* in 1913, it fell like a bombshell in academic circles.[17]

[14] *A History of the People of the United States* (New York, 1885), I, 280–281.

[15] *Critical Period of American History* (Boston, 1888), pp. 179–186.

[16] *The Duke of Stockbridge*, Chap. XIX. Here Bellamy is telescoping events; the Constitutional Convention did not convene until May, 1787, several months after Shays' Rebellion.

[17] To be sure, the economic interpretation of the Constitution was original with neither Bellamy nor Beard. "The fact was well known . . . to the men of the late eighteenth century," as Earl Latham, ed., remarks in *The Declaration of Independence and the Constitution* (Boston, 1949), p. 118. However, Beard's detailed exposition of this viewpoint is described as revolutionary by Max Lerner. See his essay, "Beard's Economic Interpretation of the Constitution," in *Books That Changed Our Minds*, edited by Malcolm Cowley and Bernard Smith (New York, 1939), pp. 145–162.

There are no grounds for assuming that Professor Beard ever read, or even heard of, *The Duke of Stockbridge*. However, like millions of his generation, Beard was an enthusiastic reader of *Looking Backward*. See his discussion of the book in *The Rise of American Civilization* (New York, 1945), New Edition, II, 443. In 1935, when Beard was asked to list "the twenty-five books of the preceding half century which had most influenced the thought and action of the world," he ranked *Looking Backward* as the second most important book. See Arthur E. Morgan, *Edward Bellamy* (New York, 1944), p. ix.

Twentieth-century research has authenticated Bellamy's approach. Since the appearance in 1926 of James Truslow Adams' *New England in the Republic*, contemporary historians have reinterpreted Shays' Rebellion in terms corroborating the central theme of *The Duke of Stockbridge*.[18] Recently, Samuel Eliot Morison has proclaimed *The Duke of Stockbridge* "one of the greatest historical novels. Based on extensive research, it gives a more accurate account of the causes and events of Shays' Rebellion than any of the formal histories do." [19]

For demonstrating how Shays' Rebellion helped produce the "more perfect union," Bellamy deserves the type of recognition accorded his contemporaries, Moses Coit Tyler, John Bach McMaster, and Edward Eggleston, each acclaimed for broadening American historiography.

What forces prompted young Bellamy, formally untrained as an historian, to make such a valuable contribution? The answer can be found in his experiences as a newspaperman working in the raw New England mill area during the Gilded Age.

III

Edward Bellamy was born March 26, 1850, into the family of a Baptist minister in Chicopee Falls, Massachusetts. Although he ultimately rejected traditional church worship, he retained a religious-ethical regard for the welfare of his fellow men. This was the chief motive for his lifelong study of history and literature.

Bellamy's devotion to the study of history began at an early age in the mood of youthful idealism which was to remain his outstanding characteristic. In one of his earliest

---

[18] For examples, see Marion L. Starkey, *A Little Rebellion* (New York, 1955); Robert J. Taylor, *Western Massachusetts in the Revolution* (Providence, 1954).

[19] In a letter to the editor, August 23, 1961.

compositions, written when he was eleven years old, he defended man's desire for constructive change:

. . . It is not Treason when the subjects of an unjust oppressive and tyrannical Government revolt for they do not owe allegiance to a Government that oppresses them. It is not Treason but self defence and defence of the rights of men. If it becomes a crime then Washington Kosciusko Koosuth [Kossuth] and other brave defenders of their country and their coontrys [sic] rights will become criminals.[20]

Here we recognize the long foreground of *The Duke of Stockbridge.*

Influenced by Civil War tales glorifying soldierly heroism, young Bellamy longed for a military career in the belief that it would afford opportunity for high-minded service, but he failed the physical requirements for admission to West Point. Disconsolate, he enrolled for a course in literature at Union College, but soon left on a tour of Europe as companion to a wealthy cousin. Abroad, he became aware of "man's inhumanity to man" and upon his return home he recognized, as he later explained, even in his own "comparatively prosperous village, the same conditions in course of progressive development." [21] The industrial sores of a typical nineteenth-century mill town festered in nearby Chicopee — child labor, crowded tenements, epidemics, unemployment, low wages, long hours of work, and strikes.[22]

But Bellamy did not concern himself with these problems immediately. Instead, he studied law "under the sordid and selfish necessity," as he phrased it, of earning a livelihood.[23] Admitted to the Massachusetts bar, he abandoned law as a career after handling only one case, which forced the eviction

---

[20] Bellamy Collection, MS45M-551 (22), Houghton Library, Harvard.

[21] The posthumous collection, *Edward Bellamy Speaks Again!* (Kansas City, 1937), pp. 217 ff.

[22] Vera Shlakman, "Economic History of a Factory Town: A Study of Chicopee, Massachusetts," *Smith College Studies in History*, XX, 1–4 (Oct. 1934–July 1935).

[23] *Edward Bellamy Speaks Again!*, p. 221.

of a widow for inability to pay her rent. This was not law as the idealistic Bellamy had imagined it, "the arguing of great constitutional questions, the chivalrous defense of the widow and the orphan against their oppressors. . . ." [24]
Undertaking newspaper work in 1871, Bellamy served on William Cullen Bryant's *New York Evening Post,* but soon returned to Springfield to work as editorial writer and book reviewer for the *Springfield Daily Union.* As a newspaperman Bellamy was pained by the human cost of the Industrial Revolution. In an editorial for the *Springfield Daily Union* he wrote of child labor in the mills:

What . . . shall we say of the children of this misery? . . . Any day at noon you can see them in dingy flocks, hovering along the sidewalks between their boarding place and 'the yard.' . . . The mere sight of them; so old and worn and miserable to look at, yet so young, is proof enough that a great wrong exists somewhere among us which is inflicting a vast amount of barbarity, a positive cruelty of monstrous proportions upon these children and others like them in New England. . . ." [25]

These children were on Bellamy's mind when he mounted the lecture platform of the Chicopee Village Lyceum in 1872 to deliver a public address, apparently his first, entitled "The Barbarism of Society." Lamenting the "slavery" of poor laborers, he asked: "Have the ardent longings of the lovers of men been toward an unattainable felicity? Are the aspirations after liberty, equality, and happiness implanted in the very core of our hearts for nothing?" [26]
The genesis of his social gospel can be traced in his edi-

[24] Quoted from Bellamy's unfinished, unpublished, semi-autobiographical novel, "Eliot Carson," Bellamy Collection, Binder 2.
[25] "Overworked Children in Our Mills," June 5, 1873, p. 2. Many of Bellamy's newspaper contributions, unsigned, have been identified and collected by his daughter, Mrs. Marion Bellamy Earnshaw, and by his grandson, Bellamy Earnshaw. More recently, a trained scholar has identified many more of Bellamy's unsigned newspaper contributions. See Sylvia E. Bowman, *The Year 2000* (New York, 1958).
[26] *Edward Bellamy Speaks Again!,* pp. 218-221.

torials and in his reviews of books by such authors as John Richard Green, Victor Hugo, Hippolyte Taine, Henry James, and Ivan Turgenev. Bellamy was particularly impressed by Green's *A Short History of the English People*. Published in 1874, Green's book represented a complete break with traditional concepts of historiography, moving away from an obsession with kings, politics, and wars toward a concern with "constitutional, intellectual and social advance in which we read the history of the nation itself." Reviewing the book for the *Springfield Daily Union*, Bellamy praised it as "remarkably spicy history without the usual sanguinary seasoning." [27] Years later, in drawing up a reading list for his son, Bellamy listed Green's book first.[28]

As book reviewer and editorial writer, Bellamy called upon historians and historical novelists to write of events with more attention to their causes and results rather than to the bloodshed involved. He praised Victor Hugo for treating the French Revolution as the birth of a new world rather than a civil war, so that "this savagery appear[s] to us but a type of the tremendous contest of ideas, of the past and the future, of feudality and democracy, of medievalism and the nineteenth century." [29] Echoing Green's contempt for "drum and trumpet history," Bellamy allied himself with the new school of literary realism.

IV

Published in 1879, the same year as Henry George's *Progress and Poverty*, *The Duke of Stockbridge* was a token of what Oscar Cargill has termed "the social revolt," the birth in America of "a new literature, conscious of wrong in the world" and dedicated to its obliteration.[30]

---

[27] May 22, 1875, p. 6.
[28] "Paul Bellamy's Notebook," Bellamy Collection.
[29] In his review of the historical novel, *Ninety-Three*, in the *Springfield Daily Union*, April 3, 1874, p. 6.
[30] Preface to *The Social Revolt* (New York, 1933), p. 3.

When Edward Bellamy began his literary career in the 1870's, the domestic sentimentalists were America's most popular authors. In 1872, the year of Bellamy's "Barbarism of Society" address, Edward Payson Roe wrote the first of his seventeen best-selling novels, *Barriers Burned Away*. In this story of a rural lad determined to succeed in Chicago by honest means, Roe attempted to prove that "there was an agreeable relationship between solvency in this world and salvation in the next." Before tasting success, however, the hero, Dennis Fleet, must overcome many barriers — social, religious, amatory, and physical. Through it all he is sustained by a firm faith which he articulates clearly:

Neither do I want position and money for low, selfish purposes. My ends are the best and purest, for I am seeking my own honest living and the support of my mother and sisters. . . . Take heart, Dennis Fleet: God is on your side in the struggle for an honest success in this life as truly as in your fight against sin and the devil.[31]

Fortified by such faith, our "true knight" triumphs over all barriers, and finds love, fortune, and happiness.

Bellamy was not so certain that solvency and salvation are related, nor that virtue always brings fair repute. His "Duke," guided by love of family and fellow man, adopts a social gospel and suffers the stigma of a pariah. Unlike Dennis Fleet, he is unable to overcome barriers to fulfillment. His courageous altruism cannot avert the loss of home, family, romantic love, even life itself; his fate indicates that the wages of virtue may be death.

Bellamy subtitled his realistic novel *A Romance of Shays' Rebellion*. Although he never defined "romance," it would appear that he interpreted it much as William Gilmore Simms and Nathaniel Hawthorne had done. To both Simms

[31] New York, 1886, pp. 52–53. For an account of Roe's career, see Alexander Cowie, *The Rise of the American Novel* (New York, 1948), pp. 439–446.

and Hawthorne, a romance permitted "latitude" from the confinements of either the "known" or the "probable." For Simms a romance helped embody the ethos of a culture; for Hawthorne it helped reveal "the truth of the human heart." [32] In *The Duke of Stockbridge* Bellamy seems to be writing a romance in both senses, a union of the social and the psychological. He succeeded in capturing the ethos of colonial culture but failed in depicting the psychology of love.

In their bizarre relations as lovers, Perez Hamlin and Desire Edwards are the least satisfying characters in *The Duke of Stockbridge*. Conceived by Bellamy as incarnations of the class system of colonial Massachusetts, they fail to achieve credibility as people. Their barren, posed relationship is characteristic of the wooden fictional lovers of Bellamy's time. While Scott had invigorated the historical novel by giving it verisimilitude, he had retained the insipid lovers of sentimental romance. His American disciples, Cooper and Simms, were no more successful in bringing them to life. The school of historical romance generally created lovers as puppets to be finally united in bliss despite their affiliations with mutually antagonistic forces. To Bellamy's credit as a realist, he at least refused to contrive a happy ending.

Furthermore, he refused to ignore sexual drives. Although the Genteel Tradition forbade realistic depiction of erotic desire, Bellamy communicates Perez' passion to the reader. The architect of "the new realism" in American prose fiction, William Dean Howells, opposed the introduction of "certain facts of life which are not usually talked of before young people, and especially young ladies." In Howells' fictional world, a pre-marital kiss augured evil. [33] Against such a back-

---

[32] See Simms, Preface to *The Yemassee* (New York, 1835); Hawthorne, Preface to *The House of the Seven Gables* (Boston, 1851).

[33] See Howells, *Criticism and Fiction* (New York, 1891), p. 147; Kenneth E. Eble, "Howells' Kisses," *American Quarterly*, IX (Winter 1957), 441–447.

ground of literary repression, how can Perez ever forget that Desire once offered him "her red lips"? Writing for the *Berkshire Courier,* a newspaper designed for a "cordial welcome in all families and at all firesides," Bellamy reassured his readers: "There were men here whom neither lines of bayonets nor walls of stone would have turned back, but not one of them was bold enough to lay a forcible hand upon the veil that covered a woman's breast. They were Americans." [34] And yet, despite the Victorian sexual safeguards so prominently displayed in Chapter XX, "Two Critical Interviews," the reader identifies with Perez, buffeted by the heat and frost of Desire's "imperious magnetism."

In its mixture of realism and romanticism, the Perez Hamlin-Desire Edwards affair was an unfortunate act of condescension on the part of the author toward the mass literary taste of his time. In real life there was no Desire Edwards,[35] and Perez Hamlin was married.[36] By fabricating their relationship, the only major ingredient in his novel without foundation in fact or legend, Bellamy was exercising his prerogative as a romancer, though he would have been better advised to adhere to realism. Treatment of Perez as a married man would probably have resulted in a more mature love story compatible with a realistic account of rebellion.

As a relatively inexperienced novelist, Bellamy used the traditional story-telling techniques of his time. The modern reader (unless he be an enthusiast of Victoriana) may wince at Bellamy's awkward shifts in fictional point of view, his authorial intrusions for purposes of observation, essay, or historical perspective; his euphemisms, interpolated rhetori-

[34] *The Duke of Stockbridge,* Chap. X.
[35] See William H. Edwards, comp., *Timothy and Rhoda Ogden Edwards of Stockbridge, Mass. and Their Descendants* (Cincinnati, 1903), pp. 22–30 for a listing of Edwards' six daughters.
[36] See Box 160538, Records of the Massachusetts Supreme Judicial Court, Suffolk County Courthouse, Boston.

cal questions and exclamatory emphases; his use of such stock characters from sentimental novels as the rapacious creditor, the inhuman jailor, the altruistic soldier, the fainting heroine, the servile Negro; and his occasional preference for the panoramic rather than the scenic or graphic. Although many of these fictional devices can be found in Fielding, Scott, Cooper, Hawthorne, Melville, Thackeray, Charlotte Brontë, Dickens, and Trollope,[37] Bellamy handled them rather mechanically in *The Duke of Stockbridge,* the result of inexperience and haste (he was simultaneously serializing another novel, *Dr. Heidenhoff's Process,* an augury of the modern psychiatric approach to emotional problems).

Although he was writing for weekly serial publication and was expected to end each installment on a note of climax or impending doom ("the cliff-hanger technique"), Bellamy's chapters often lack crescendo. Still in the apprentice stage, he achieved little variety; the development of poetic vision and consummate rhetoric, the use of deft analogy, parable, Socratic argument, tragic irony, and personification, qualities which help make *Looking Backward* a classic, were to be developed later.

Despite its flaws as a work of art, *The Duke of Stockbridge* possesses power to stir and inform readers by virtue of Bellamy's ability in special areas of literary craft — the analysis and dramatization of social discord, the depiction of human character in its mixture of nobility and oddity, pride and force of leadership — important elements for the success of an historical novel of rebellion.

Bellamy is especially gifted in the expression of social grievance through dialogue. A few lines of conversation etch the bitterness of insolvent war veterans toward sheriffs and lawyers:

[37] See John T. Winterich, "Speaking of Books," *New York Times Book Review,* August 20, 1961, Section 7, p. 2; Herbert Ross Brown, *The Sentimental Novel in America, 1789–1860* (Durham, 1940).

"Wat I can't make aout is that the lawyers and sheriffs sh'd git so dern fat a pickin our bones, seein ez ther's sech a dern leatle meat ontew us," said Abner.

"There's as much meat on squirrels as bears if you have enough of em," replied Hubbard. "They pick clean, ye see, an take all we've got, an every little helps."

"Yas," said Abner, "they do pick darned clean, but that ain't the wust on't, fer they sends our bones tew rot in jail arter they've got all the meat orf." [38]

With the ability of the true novelist to allow expression for various social types, Bellamy has Jabez, the Tory, rebuke the complaining veterans in incisive terms:

"Ef I don' furgit," [Jabez] said at length, "that's 'baout the way I talked wen the war wuz a goin on, an if I rekullec, ye, Peleg, an ye, Abner Rathbun and Meshech Little, thar on the floor, tuk arter me with yer guns and dorgs caze ye said I wuz a dum tory. An ye hunted me on Stockbridge mounting like a woodchuck, an ye'd a hed my skelp fer sartin ef I hadn't a been a durn sight smarter'n ye ever wuz."

"Jabez," said Abner, "I hope ye don' hev no hard feelin's. Times be changed. Let by gones be by gones."

"Mos' folks ud say I hed some call to hev hard feelin's. Ye druv me ter hide in caves, an holes, fer the best part o' tew year. I dass'n come hum tew see my wife die, nor tew bury on her. Ye confiscated my house and tuk my crops fer yer derned army. Mos' folks ud sartingly say ez I hed call tew hev hard feelin's agin' ye. But gosh, I hain't, an wy hain't I? Caze ye hev been yer own wust enemies; ye've hurt yerselves more ner ye hev me, though ye didn't go fer ter dew it. Pooty nigh all on ye, as fit agen the King, is beggars naow, or next door tew it. Everybudy hez a kick fer a soldier. Ye'll fine em mosly in the jails an the poor-haouses. Look at you fellers as wuz a huntin me. Ther's Meshech on the floor, a drunken, worthless cuss. Thar ye be, Abner, 'thout a shillin in the world, nor a foot o' lan', yer dad's farm gone fer taxes. An thar be ye, Peleg. Wal Peleg, they dew say, ez the neighbors sends ye in things." [39]

[38] *The Duke of Stockbridge*, Chap. II.
[39] *Ibid.*

Bellamy's hero, the Duke of Stockbridge, is the most articulate of the rebels. His exchange with Parson West over the relevance of Christian ethics is memorable as an expression of the theme of the novel. The parson is urging Perez not to whip his captive selectmen:

[Perez asks,] "These men [the selectmen], if they had succeeded in their plan last night, would have whipped me, and a score of others to-day. Would you have protested against that?"
[Parson West answers,] "That is different. They would have proceeded against you as criminals, according to law."
"No doubt they would have proceeded according to law" replied Perez, with a bitter sneer. "They have been proceeding according to law for the past six years here in Berkshire, and that's why the people are in rebellion. I'm no lawyer, but I know that Perez Hamlin is as good as [Squire] Jahleel Woodbridge, whatever the parson may think, and what he would have done to me, shall be done to him."
"That is not the rule of the gospel," said the minister, taking another tack. "Christ said if any man smite you on the right cheek, turn to him the other also."
"If that is your counsel, take it to those who are likely to need it. I am going to do the smiting this time, and it's their time to do the turning." [40]

Many of the minor characters, with their individualistic mixtures of oddity and nobility, have imaginative appeal — the simple, idealistic Abner Rathbun, the self-centered, devoted Resignation Ann Poor, the flinty, courageous Marthy Bement are but three in a memorable gallery of rural New England portraits. Bellamy's masterly illumination of each one's individual make-up through group interaction in Chapter X, "Great Goings on at Barrington Continued," recalls the art of Dickens, his favorite novelist.

Despite Bellamy's clear disapproval of the social views of the Stockbridge selectmen, he dramatizes their courage in the face of hostility and danger with telling effect. Squire

[40] *Ibid.*, Chap. XVIII.

Woodbridge's pointed scrutiny of his fellow worshipers in church, after his public humiliation, makes for a sharp vignette. Squire Sedgwick gently trotting his horse toward "the onrushing, hooting multitude," when they expected him to flee in terror before them, symbolizes the force of character which enabled the pillars of colonial society to endure widespread rebellion and to reëstablish governmental authority.

Like Squire Woodbridge and Squire Sedgwick, Perez Hamlin possesses the power to disarm the opposition by tactics of surprise, a characteristic of inspired leadership. When Perez orders Little Pete to beat his drums just as the imperious Squire Woodbridge begins a public address, he wins the confidence of the disaffected, who are in need of leadership. In this scene Bellamy effectively contrasts three different social types of that period: the proud selectman accustomed to respectful audiences, the recently discharged Army officer, shocked by the fact that military victory has brought disaster to his family and friends, the Hessian drummer, marginal to New England society, who "had never learned to respect or fear anything not in uniform." The interaction of these three against the background of a tense, vacillating audience makes Chapter VII, "The First Encounter," vivid and convincing.

Even in defeat Captain Hamlin is able to nonplus the enemy by a surprise maneuver. His use of a yarn-beam disguised as a cannon in Chapter XXV, "A Game of Bluff," contributes a bit of welcome humor in an otherwise grim struggle. In the story of the yarn-beam Bellamy beguiles the reader with an artful adaptation of an old Berkshire legend illustrative of the cunning of New England farmers.

The Duke of Stockbridge is rich in the sensory delights of New England. Written when the local-color movement in America was reaching its zenith, the novel portrays the unique character of colonial-revolutionary Western Massachusetts in its distinctive vernacular speech, mores, folkways,

proverbial lore, and superstitious beliefs. Bellamy's understanding of the churchly nature of that society provides rare
insight into its traditions of Sabbath-breaking, its use of
meetin-seed and theological puns.

For writing a vigorous, realistic novel in an age of senti-
mentalism, Bellamy merits acclaim as a pioneer in American
fictional realism, along with such contemporaries as John
W. DeForest, Albion W. Tourgée, William Dean Howells,
Mark Twain, and Henry James.

For all his fidelity to realism, Bellamy's eyes were upon a
brighter horizon. He wrote of an age when two cultures were
in conflict, the colonial and the revolutionary, the first dying,
the other emerging. His defeated band of Shaysites march
victoriously toward a better day, the reaffirmation of the
American dream of equalitarian ideals and the pursuit of
happiness. This dream was nurtured by Bellamy amidst bleak
surroundings.

V

Living in a provincial town, indifferent to neighbors, lacking intellectual companionship (except for occasional correspondence with William Dean Howells), Edward Bellamy
fashioned an imaginative inner life of stewardship over suffering mankind everywhere. Nondescript in appearance —
medium in height, careless in dress, reserved in manner, his
drooping brown mustache resembling a million others in
that age — only the concerned, faraway gaze of his eye be-
tokened the thoughtful turbulence within caused by "the
unspeakable abomination of the actual universe." [41]

Bellamy's marriage to Emma Sanderson, who was reared
in his parental home as a foster sister and ward of the family,
reflected two of his salient traits, a "home-bound pattern" of
life [42] and a solicitude for the deprived. Mrs. Edward Bellamy,

[41] "Eliot Carson."
[42] Morgan's apt phrase, *Edward Bellamy*, p. 148.

who outlived her husband by many years, offered the few, intimate glimpses we have of Edward Bellamy's emotional make-up. Speaking with me in 1950, she painted a picture of her husband as a lonely man who confined himself to his immediate family and books: "We lived quietly with few close friends. My husband actually discouraged visitors. Sometimes he would cry out, 'Emma, please put out that light in the hall. Quick, or else someone may see it and call on us!' He seemed to want all his time for reading, thinking, or just sitting quietly at home."

While Mrs. Bellamy talked about her husband, one could not help recalling how closely he resembled his own fictional character, Edna Damon, who "had never particularly shone in city society. To do so involved for her too much affectation of interest in people . . . too much looking wise when she did not understand, too much smiling at remarks that made her feel sad, too much simulation of agreement when she vehemently disagreed, too much silence when she wanted to cry out." [43]

Mrs. Bellamy spoke of her husband's personal concern over the spectre of poverty and travail in the eighties:

He often seemed disturbed, concerned with a heavy problem. And he simply couldn't eat. That had been characteristic of him in all the time I knew him. . . . He would sit at the dinner table, and after carving generous slices of meat for the whole family, call out, "Mary, please bring me a glass of milk and a raw egg!" Or he would take a tumbler of whiskey. Underneath my husband's chronic refusal to eat lay a deep disturbance of spirit, I believe. I am sure he was haunted by thoughts of other people's problems, especially the poor.

Perez Hamlin and his footsore debtors were still marching.

By 1886, Bellamy had a son and a daughter; 1886 was also "the year of ten thousand strikes" [44] and violence at

[43] "Eliot Carson."
[44] Allan Seager, *They Worked for a Better World* (New York, 1939), p. 108.

Haymarket. Chronically feeble in health and unsure of his future as a free-lance writer, the solicitous husband and father could recognize his problem of insecurity written large in the lives of others: everyone "constantly turned to catch the whispers of a spectre at his ear, the spectre of Uncertainty. 'Do your work never so well,' the spectre was whispering, — 'rise early and toil till late, rob cunningly or serve faithfully, you shall never know security. Rich you may be now and still come to poverty at last. Leave never so much wealth to your children, you cannot buy the assurance that your son may not be the servant of your servant, or that your daughter will not have to sell herself for bread.' " [45] In parodying Benjamin Franklin's maxim, "Early to bed . . . ," Bellamy highlighted the pervading fear of his time — poverty.

At that time, the western world was beset by a host of complex problems: urban housing, policing, sanitation; social anonymity, spiritual deprivation, rootlessness; the hiatus in ethics resulting from the inapplicability of older, neighborly values to an impersonal, corporate society; the unequal apportionment of wealth and the emergence of hostile classes — problems rendered painfully acute by the inability of most nineteenth-century governments to deal with them. Pope Leo XIII in his historic encyclical, *The Condition of Labor*, warned the world: ". . . all agree, and there can be no question whatever, that some remedy must be found, and quickly found, for the misery and wretchedness which press so heavily at this moment on the large majority of the very poor . . . given over, isolated and defenseless, to the . . . greed of unrestrained competition . . . a yoke little better than slavery itself." [46]

Beginning work on *Looking Backward* as "a mere fairy tale of social perfection," Bellamy's deepest personal and

---

[45] *Looking Backward*, p. 453.

[46] From the official translation, reprinted in Henry George, *The Land Question* (Garden City, 1891), pp. 109–111.

social concerns transformed it into a "vehicle of a definite scheme of industrial reorganization." [47] Within the family circle, Bellamy often referred to his utopian novel as "a sugar-coated pill" intended as a cure for the deep-seated ills of the world.

Looking Backward opens on a night in 1887. Julian West, a troubled young Bostonian, summons a mesmerist to help him overcome insomnia. Falling into deep slumber at last, he awakes 113 years later to find himself in a wondrous Boston, a "new fraternal civilization" which incarnates "the solidarity of the race and the brotherhood of man." Competition is no longer the law of the land. Instead, a new principle has been introduced, national cooperation, and this has exalted all social activities.

In place of the laissez-faire policies of the Gilded Age, the new paternalistic state maintains an economy of abundance in which all citizens, even those infirm and insane, share equally. Pledged to the commonweal, society offers everyone suitable employment in the industrial army, retires workers at the age of forty-five, assures women independence, cooks meals in public kitchens, cleans clothes in public laundries, arranges centralized shopping, educates everyone to rising standards of personal refinement and culture, and pipes elevating talk and music into private parlors. All these changes have been introduced gradually and peaceably, without rancor or violence, solely by force of a change in public opinion. Class warfare, abhorred as a base weapon unworthy of man, has been consigned to the unhappy past.

Bellamy's utopian novel became one of the most widely-discussed books of the late nineteenth century. Along with Mark Twain, many literary men found *Looking Backward* "fascinating." [48] It generated a host of utopian and anti-

[47] *Edward Bellamy Speaks Again!*, p. 202.
[48] Quoted in Roger B. Salomon, *Twain and the Image of History* (New Haven, 1961), p. 39, n. 9.

utopian novels around the turn of the century, among them *Caesar's Column* by Ignatius Donnelly, *News from Nowhere* by William Morris, *When the Sleeper Wakes* by H. G. Wells, *The Iron Heel* by Jack London, and *A Traveler from Altruria* and *Through the Eye of the Needle* by William Dean Howells.[49] As the Dean of American Letters, Howells observed that Bellamy "revived throughout Christendom the faith in a millennium." [50]

From every area of thought and activity Bellamy attracted youthful devotees, among them John Dewey in philosophy and education, William Allen White in journalism, Eugene V. Debs in labor, Walter Rauschenbusch in religion, and Thorstein Veblen in economics and social psychology; through these men, each to become a seminal figure in his special field, Bellamy profoundly influenced the American mind.

Encouraged by the response of his readers, Bellamy threw himself into political activity, campaigning for Nationalism,[51] the name he gave to the social system described in *Looking Backward*. Gathering his financial and physical resources, he launched into a five-year period of writing and organizing for the Nationalist Party. Although millions of Americans had been encouraged by *Looking Backward* to hope for a utopian society, Bellamy found that few were disposed to engage in the political and social activity required to bring it into reality. Disheartened, depleted in financial reserves, and weakened in health, he was forced to give up his Nationalist crusade. But the dream of a happier society did not waste away; in 1897, he summoned his last remnants of energy to publish *Equality*,[52] the sequel to *Looking Back-*

[49] See W. Arthur Boggs, "*Looking Backward* at the Utopian Novel, 1888–1900," *Bulletin of the New York Public Library*, LXIV (June 1960), 329–336.

[50] Prefatory Sketch to Edward Bellamy, *The Blindman's World and Other Stories* (Cambridge, 1898), p. vi.

[51] See John Hope Franklin, "Edward Bellamy and the Nationalist Movement," *New England Quarterly*, XI (Dec. 1938), 739–772.

[52] New York, 1897.

ward. This was his final book. Soon after publishing it he died in his Chicopee Falls home, a victim of tuberculosis and possible cancer of the throat. He was forty-eight.

VI

The seeds of realism in Bellamy's utopianism are bearing fruit today as the major part of the world incorporates his chief ideas — comprehensive social welfare schemes, planned cities, large-scale industrial organization, and technologically oriented societies. Bellamy helped plant the seeds for what Frederick Lewis Allen has called "the big change" in American life, "the democratization of our economic system, or the adjustment of capitalism to democratic ends." [53] Indisputably, Bellamy's widely-read novel helped create an hospitable climate for Theodore Roosevelt's Square Deal, Woodrow Wilson's New Freedom, and Franklin D. Roosevelt's New Deal. And so manifest is his influence abroad that an international team of scholars has recently documented his enduring impact on twelve countries.[54]

To those dismayed by such tendencies, Bellamy seems more a prognosticator than a utopian. Despite shifts in critical evaluations of Bellamy's role, however, he remains what he has always been for millions of readers, a social evangelist. His eloquent insistence upon society's responsibility for each individual's welfare inspired the *New York Times* to comment editorially upon the occasion of Bellamy's centenary in 1950:

. . . he was able to persuade other men to look at the evils of the world and . . . to hope that some day they might be eradicated, to work to find some program for their eradication, and not to accept with smugness any belief that a world where children can starve and stunt could be the best of all possible

---

[53] *The Big Change* (New York, 1952).
[54] Sylvia E. Bowman, ed., *Edward Bellamy Abroad: An American Prophet's Influence* (New York, 1962).

worlds. Therein, and not in any specific program, lay his greatest influence.[55]

To Bellamy, the American dream of the brave new world, the holy commonwealth, the land of the free, the melting pot, the good neighbor was all so real that he exalted it into a religion.

We find in Edward Bellamy a unique and original mind, friutful in both the reality of history and the dream of utopia. In the sanguine age that gave birth to scientific history, he founded his millennial faith on the past, "History the magical: that basic faith of the modern world, that through History man is saved, all problems are resolved, all dilemmas removed, all tears wiped away." [56]

Bellamy's faith in history may seem naive to our contemporaries who have endured the agony of Buchenwald, Hiroshima, and Budapest. And yet, as *The Duke of Stockbridge* demonstrates, resistance to oppression, with all its discord and turbulence, does lead to the correction of wrongs. His lifelong literary endeavor, in its realism and utopianism, limns man's unique power to progress through pain. As long as man is man by virtue of his difficulties, a doer and a dreamer, a realist and a visionary, he will respond with warmth to Edward Bellamy's realism and utopianism.

Joseph Schiffman

Dickinson College
January 1, 1962

[55] March 25, 1950, p. 12.

[56] Ernest Lee Tuveson's phrase in *Millennium and Utopia: A Study in the Background of the Idea of Progress* (Berkeley and Los Angeles, 1949), p. 201.

NOTE ON THE TEXT

The Duke of Stockbridge was published in book form in 1900, after Bellamy's death. The person chiefly responsible for publication was the Reverend Francis Bellamy, cousin to the novelist, editor of *Youth's Companion,* and best known today for his authorship of the original Pledge of Allegiance to the Flag. Recalling the historical novel as it had appeared in the *Berkshire Courier,* Francis Bellamy asked Edward Bellamy's widow for the manuscript, but none could be found. Mrs. Bellamy had disposed of much of her husband's library and papers and could only suggest that a search be made of the attic. There, old copies of the *Berkshire Courier* containing the serialized novel were found. After editing it, Francis Bellamy persuaded Silver, Burdett and Company to publish it in book form.

Until preparation of the present edition was undertaken, nobody had apparently investigated the nature and extent of Francis Bellamy's role as editor; no known check had been made of the original newspaper version against the book. Collation of the two texts reveals that Francis Bellamy revised extensively throughout the novel in paragraphing, punctuation, capitalization, tense, vocabulary, spelling, and chapter titles, sometimes deleting and altering whole sentences or varying their time sequence. Several of these changes were necessitated by the fact that Edward Bellamy, under the pressure of meeting weekly deadlines, obviously wrote hurriedly; other changes appear to reflect differences in personal taste between author and editor.

Desire for propriety led to further editorial changes. Francis Bellamy brought the New England dialect closer to standard speech, corrected several instances of poor grammatical usage (particularly on the part of Perez Hamlin and

Jonathan Edwards), and expurgated an occasional recognition of sexual desire.

The text here used is the first printing of Edward Bellamy's novel almost exactly as he himself wrote it for the *Berkshire Courier*. The attempt to offer an authentic text has posed a number of difficult problems, stemming principally from the fact that Edward Bellamy published his novel as a newspaper serial, never as a finished volume. Book publication, with its more leisurely publishing pace, would have offered him greater scope for consistency in his use of the vernacular. Since the original manuscript is not extant, it is impossible to ascertain the author's responsibility in the baffling variety of vernacular usages; perhaps the newspaper editor and the typesetter contributed their share. Since the *Berkshire Courier* was generally well-edited, however, one can surmise that Bellamy's haste caused most of the inconsistencies. Hard-pressed for time, he was probably unable to check his manuscript carefully. Furthermore, since his handwriting was characteristically cryptic, the typesetters must often have resorted to improvisation.

In the face of these imponderables, the present editor has attempted to maintain Bellamy's own spelling and punctuation in the non-vernacular sections, except where they vary from usages prescribed by the edition of *Webster's International Dictionary* in widespread use during Bellamy's time (the edition of 1897 comprising the issues of 1864, 1879, and 1884). Thus, in this text one will find several spellings now obsolete, such as "hight," "every one," and "to-night." All questionable spellings have been checked in *Webster's*. In some cases, punctuation was altered when it was patently in error.

In the newspaper version, the same word occasionally appears with and without the hyphen. Here again it was decided to rely on *Webster's*; thus "bar-room" becomes "barroom," "living room" becomes "living-room." The same collation was made in cases of questionable capitalization, so that one finds "Continental army" and "bill of rights," for example, in the present text.

For the vernacular it was decided to retain the original spellings in almost all cases, except for obvious typographical errors, but to make as consistent as possible the punctuation of these words. Thus one will note that in some places "you" is spelled "ye" and in other places "yew." These have been kept as reflecting the likely intention of the author to indicate variance in speech. When, however, the same word is punctuated differently, as in "callate," or "cal'late" (calculate), the apostrophe has been dropped where it seemed that there were no two ways of pronouncing the word. The apostrophe and lack of apostrophe for "wen" and "we'n" (when) have been maintained as a possible indication of some difference in pronunciation. In some cases the apostrophe has been made consistent throughout the text, as with "agin' " (against), and for most negatives. In nearly all cases the usage adopted for this edition is the one most frequently used by the author himself. In a few cases spelling has been made consistent in the vernacular, for example "hes" (have) has been rendered "hez."

That Bellamy intended to vary the vernacular is unquestionable. The diction of Resignation Ann Poor differs as markedly from Prudence Fennell's as Paul Hubbard's from Meschech Little's. Bellamy underlines these distinctions in the debate by Peleg, Abner, and Obadiah over the proper pronunciation of "piano" — is it "pianner," "peeanner," or "pianny"?

Bellamy himself seemed undecided concerning the use of an apostrophe after the vernacular form of words that end in "in" (ing) and after "an" (and) and before "em" (them). Since a plethora of apostrophes was found in the original, apostrophes for these three forms have been dropped for the comfort of present-day readers. However, in plural forms of "ing," the apostrophe has been retained (in some cases it had to be inserted), as in "doin's," and "goin's on."

Only three or four words have been added to the original, in two cases to clarify the text and in one case to supply a word that was obviously dropped by the typesetter. These words are carried within brackets.

The number has been supplied for "Chapter Fifth" and the number corrected for "Chapter Twentieth," originally mislabeled "Chapter Nineteenth." Chapters nine and sixteen were untitled in the original; for these chapters titles were taken from Francis Bellamy's *The Duke of Stockbridge,* the only instances of borrowing from that edition.

The introductory material for this edition of *The Duke of Stockbridge* has been drawn in part from the following publications of mine, with the kind permission of the publishers:

"Edward Bellamy's Religious Thought," *PMLA* (Publications of the Modern Language Association of America), LXVIII (September 1953), 716–732; "Edward Bellamy's Altruistic Man," *American Quarterly,* VI (Fall 1954), 195–209; "Editor's Introduction," *Edward Bellamy: Selected Writings on Religion and Society,* No. 11 of the American Heritage Series, The Liberal Arts Press Division of the Bobbs-Merrill Company, 1955; "Mutual Indebtedness: Unpublished Letters of Edward Bellamy to William Dean Howells," *Harvard Library Bulletin,* XII (Autumn 1958), 363–374; "Introduction," Edward Bellamy, *Looking Backward,* Harper & Brothers, 1959.

I should also like to record my gratitude to the following people for various acts of helpfulness in making this edition possible: the late Mrs. Edward Bellamy, Sylvia E. Bowman, Mrs. Marion Bellamy Earnshaw, Mrs. Janet M. Edwards, Alfred N. Hartshorn, Nancy J. Loughridge, Roger E. Nelson, R. G. Newman, Charles C. Sellers, Mrs. Barbara N. Vianey, Mrs. Graham D. Wilcox, and particularly Oscar Cargill, under whom I first began research into the thought of Edward Bellamy.

THE DUKE OF STOCKBRIDGE

CHAPTER FIRST

THE MARCH OF THE MINUTE MEN

The first beams of the sun of August 17, 1777, were glancing down the long valley, which opening to the East, lets in the early rays of morning, upon the village of Stockbridge. Then, as now, the Housatonic crept still and darkling around the beetling base of Fisher's Nest, and in the meadows laughed above its pebbly shoals, embracing the verdant fields with many a loving curve. Then, as now, the mountains cradled the valley in their eternal arms, all round, from the Hill of the Wolves, on the north, to the peaks that guard the Ice Glen, away to the far south-east. Then, as now, many a lake and pond gemmed the landscape, and many a brook hung like a burnished silver chain upon the verdant slopes. But save for this changeless frame of nature, there was very little, in the village, which the modern dweller in Stockbridge would recognize.

The main settlement is along a street lying east and west, across the plain which extends from the Housatonic, northerly some distance, to the foot of a hill. The village green or "smooth" lies rather at the western end of the village than at the center. At this point the main street intersects with the county road, leading north and south, and with divers other paths and lanes, leading in crooked, rambling lines to several points of the compass; sometimes ending at a single dwelling, sometimes at clusters of several buildings. On the hill, to the north, somewhat separated from the settlement on the plain, are quite a number of houses, erected there during the recent French and Indian wars, for the sake of being near the fort, which is now used as a parsonage by Reverend Stephen West, the young minister. The streets are all very wide and grassy, wholly without shade trees, and bordered generally by rail fences or stone walls. The houses, usually separated by wide intervals of meadow, are rarely over a story and a half in height. When painted, the color is usually red, brown, or yellow, the effect of which is a certain picturesqueness wholly outside any design on the part of the practical minded inhabitants.

Interspersed among the houses, and occurring more thickly in the south and west parts of the village, are curious huts, as much like wigwams as houses. These are the dwellings of the Christianized and civilized Stockbridge Indians, the original possessors of the soil, who live intermingled with the whites on terms of the most utter comity, fully sharing the offices of church and town, and fighting the battles of the Commonwealth side by side with the white militia.

Around the green stand the public buildings of the place. Here is the tavern, a low two-story building, without porch or piazza, and entered by a door in the middle of the longest side. Over the door swings a sign, on which a former likeness of King George has, by a metamorphosis common at this period, been transformed into a soldier of the revolution, in Continental uniform of buff and blue. But just at this time its contemplation does not afford the patriotic tipler as much complacency as formerly, for Burgoyne is thundering at the passes of the Hoosacs, only fifty miles away, and King George may get his red coat back again, after all. The Tories in the village say that the landlord keeps a pot of red paint behind the door, so that the Hessian dragoons may not take him by surprise when they come galloping down the valley, some afternoon. On the other side [of] the green is the meeting-house, built some thirty years ago, by a grant from government at Boston, and now considered rather old-fashioned and inconvenient. Hard by the meeting-house is the graveyard, with the sandy knoll in its south-west corner, set apart for the use of the Indians. The whipping-post, stocks, and cage, for the summary correction of such offences as come within the jurisdiction of Justice Jahleel Woodbridge, Esquire, adorn the middle of the village green, and on Saturday afternoon are generally the center of a crowd assembled to be edified by the execution of sentences.

On the other side [of] the green from the meeting-house stands the store, built five years before, by Timothy Edwards, Esquire, a structure of a story and a half, with the unusual architectural adornment of a porch or piazza in front, the only thing of the kind in the village. The people of Stockbridge are scarcely prouder of the divinity of their late shepherd, the famous Dr. Jonathan Edwards, than they are of his son Timothy's store. Indeed, what with Dr. Edwards, so lately in their midst, Dr. Hopkins, down at Great Barrington, and Dr. Bellamy, just over the State line in Bethlehem, Connecticut, the people of Berkshire are decidedly more familiar with theologians than with storekeepers, for when Mr. Edwards built his store in 1772, it was the only one in the county.

At such a time it may be readily inferred that a commercial occupation serves rather as a distinction than otherwise. Squire Edwards is moreover chairman of the selectmen, and furthermore most of the farmers are in his debt for supplies, while to these varied elements of influence, his theological ancestry adds a certain odor of sanctity. It is true that Squire Jahleel Woodbridge is even more brilliantly descended, counting two colonial governors and numerous divines among his ancestry, not to speak of a rumored kinship with the English noble family of Northumberland. But instead of tending to a profitless rivalry the respective claims of the Edwardses and the Woodbridges to distinction have happily been merged by the marriage of Jahleel Woodbridge and Lucy Edwards, the sister of Squire Timothy, so that in all social and political matters, the two families are closely allied.

The back room of the store is, in a sense, the Council-chamber, where the affairs of the village are debated and settled by these magnates, whose decisions the common people never dream of anticipating or questioning. It is also a con-vivial center, a sort of clubroom. There, of an afternoon, may generally be seen Squires Woodbridge, Williams, Elisha Brown, Deacon Nash, Squire Edwards, and perhaps a few others, relaxing their gravity over generous bumpers of some choice old Jamaica, which Edwards had luckily laid in, just before the war stopped all imports.

In the west half of the store building, Squire Edwards lives with his family, including, besides his wife and children, the remnants of his father's family and that of his sister, the widowed Mrs. President Burr. Young Aaron Burr was there, for a while after his graduation at Princeton, and during the intervals of his arduous theological studies with Dr. Bellamy at Bethlehem. Perchance there are heart-sore maidens in the village, who, to their sorrow, could give more particular in-formation of the exploits of the seductive Aaron at this period, than I am able to.

Such are the mountains and rivers, the streets and the houses of Stockbridge as the sun of this August morning in the year 1777, discloses them to view. But where are the people? It is seven, yes, nearly eight o'clock, and no human being is to be seen walking in the streets, or travelling in the roads, or working in the fields. Such lazy habits are certainly not what we have been wont to ascribe to our sturdy fore-fathers. Has the village, peradventure, been deserted by the population, through fear of the Hessian marauders, the threat of whose coming has long hung like a portentous cloud, over the Berkshire valley? Not at all. It is not the fear of man, but the fear of God, that has laid a spell upon the place. It is the Sabbath, or what we moderns call Sunday, and law and con-science have set their double seal on every door, that neither man, woman nor child, may go forth till sunset, save at the summons of the meeting-house bell. We may wander all the way from the parsonage on the hill, to Captain Konkapot's hut on the Barrington road, without meeting a soul, though the windows will have a scandalized face framed in each seven by nine pane of glass. And the distorted, uncouth and variously colored face and figure, which the imperfections of the glass give the passer-by, will doubtless appear to the horrified spectators, but the fit typical representation of his inward depravity. We shall, I say, meet no one, unless, as we pass his hut by Konkapot's brook, Jehoiachim Naunumpetox, the Indian tithing man, spy us, and that will be to our exceeding discomfiture, for straightway laying implacable hands upon us, he will deliver us to John Schebuck, the constable, who will grievously correct our flesh with stripes, for Sabbath-breaking, and cause us to sit in the stocks, for an ensample.

But if so mild an excursion involve so dire a risk, what must be the desperation of this horseman who is coming at a thundering gallop along the county road from Pittsfield? His horse is in a foaming sweat, the strained nostrils are filled with blood and the congested eyes protrude as if they would leap from their sockets to be at their goal.

It is Squire Woodbridge's two story red house before which the horseman pulls rein, and leaving his steed with hanging head and trembling knees and laboring sides, drags his own stiffened limbs up the walk and enters the house. Almost instantly Squire Woodbridge himself, issues from the door, dressed for church in a fine black coat, waistcoat, and knee-breeches, white silk stockings, a three-cornered black hat and silver buckles on his shoes, but in his hand instead of a Bible, a musket. As he steps out, the door of a house further east opens also, and another man similarly dressed, with brown woolen stockings, steps forth with a gun in his hand also. He seems to have interpreted the meaning of the horseman's message. This is Deacon Nash. Beckoning him to follow, Squire Woodbridge steps out to the edge of the green, raises his musket to his shoulder and discharges it into the air. Deacon Nash coming up a moment later also raises and fires his gun, and e'er the last echoes have reverberated from the mountains, Squire Edwards, musket in hand, throws open his store door and stepping out on the porch, fires the third gun.

A moment ago hundreds of faces were smiling, hundreds of eyes were bright, hundreds of cheeks were flushed. Now there is not a single smile or a trace of brightness, or a bit of color on a face in the valley. Such is the woful change wrought in every household, as the successive reports of the heavily-charged pieces sound through the village, and penetrate to the farthest outlying farmhouse. The first shot may well be an accident, the second may possibly be, but as the third inexorably follows, husbands and wives, brothers and sisters, parents and sons, look at each other with blanched faces, and instantly a hundred scenes of quiet preparation for meeting, are transformed into the confusion of a very different kind of preparation. Catechisms are dropped for muskets, and Bibles fall unnoticed under foot, as men spring for their haversacks and powder-horns. For those three guns summon the minute men to be on the march for Bennington. All the afternoon before, the roar of cannon has faintly sounded from the northward, and the people knew that Stark was meeting Baum and his Hessians, on the Hoosac. One detachment of Stockbridge men is already with him. Does this new summons mean disaster? Has the dreaded foe made good his boasted invincibility? No one knows, not even the exhausted messenger, for he was sent off by Stark, while yet the issue of yesterday's battle trembled in the balance.

"It's kinder suddin. I wuz in hopes the boys wouldn' hev to go, bein as they wuz a fightin yisdy," quavered old Elnathan Hamlin, as he trotted about, helplessly trying to help, and only hindering Mrs. Hamlin, as with white face, but deft hands, and quick eyes, she was getting her two boys ready, filling their haversacks, sewing a button here, tightening a buckle there, and looking to everything.

"Ye must tak keer o' Reub, Perez. He ain't so rugged 'zye be. By rights, he orter ha stayed to hum."

"Oh, I'm as stout as Perez. I can wrastle him. Don't fret about me," said Reuben, with attempted gayety, though his boyish lip quivered as he looked at his mother's face, noting how she did not meet his eye, lest she should lose her self-control, and not be able to do anything more.

"I'll look after the boy, never fear," said Perez, slapping his brother on the back. "I'll fetch him back a General, as big a man as Squire Woodbridge."

"I dunno what 'n time I shall dew 'bout gittin in the crops," whimpered Elnathan. "I can't dew it 'lone, nohow. Seems though my rheumatiz wuz wuss 'n ever, this las' spell o' weather."

"There goes Abner Rathbun, and George Fennell," cried Perez. "Time we were off. Good-bye mother. There! There! Don't you cry, mother. We'll be back all right. Got your gun, Reub? Good-bye father. Come on," and the boys were off.

In seeming sympathy with the sudden grief that has fallen on the village, the bright promise of the morning has given place in the last hour to one of those sudden rain storms to which a mountainous region is always liable, and a cold drizzle is now falling. But that does not hinder every one who has friends among the departing soldiers, or sympathy with the cause represented, from gathering on the green to witness the muster and march of the men. All the leading men and the officials of the town and parish are there, including the two Indian selectmen, Johannes Metoxin and Joseph Sauquesquot. Squire Edwards, Deacon Nash, Squire Williams and Captain Josiah Jones, brother-in-law of Squire Woodbridge, are going about among the tearful groups, of one of which each soldier is a centre, reassuring and encouraging both those who go, and those who stay, the ones with the promise that their wives and children and parents shall be looked after and cared for, the others with confident talk of victory and speedy reunions.

Squire Edwards tells Elnathan, who with Mrs. Hamlin
has come down to the green, that he needn't fret about the
mortgage on his house, and Deacon Nash tells him that he'll
see that his crops are saved, and George Fennell, who, with his
wife and daughter, stands by, is assured by the Squire, that
they shall have what they want from the store. There is not
a plough-boy among the minute men who is not honored to-
day with a cordial word or two, or at least a smile, from the
magnates who never before have recognized his existence.

And proud in her tears, to-day, is the girl who has a sweetheart among the soldiers. Shy girls, who for fear of being
laughed at, have kept a secret of their inclinations, now
grown suddenly bold, cry, as they talk with their lovers, and
refuse not the parting kiss. Desire Edwards, the Squire's
daughter, as she moves among the groups, and sees these
things, is stirred with envy and thinks she would give anything
if she, too, had a sweetheart to bid good-bye to. But she is
only fifteen, and Squire Edwards' daughter, moreover, to
whom no rustic swain dares pretend. Then she bethinks herself that one has timidly, enough, so pretended. She knows
that Elnathan Hamlin's son, Perez, is dreadfully in love with
her. He is better bred than the other boys, but after all he is
only a farmer's son, and while pleased with his conquest as a
testimony to her immature charms, she has looked down upon
him as quite an inferior order of being to herself. But just
now he appears to her in the desirable light of somebody to
bid good-bye to, to the end that she may be on a par with the
other girls whom she so envies. So she looks about for Perez.

And he, on his part, is looking about for her. That she, the
Squire's daughter, as far above him as a star, would care
whether he went or stayed, or would come to say good-bye to
him, he had scarcely dared to think. And yet how deeply has
that thought, which he has scarcely dared own, tinged all his
other thinking! The martial glory that has so dazzled his
young imagination, how much of its glitter was but reflected

from a girl's eyes. As he looks about and not seeing her, says, "She does not care, she will not come," the sword loses all its sheen, and the nodding plume its charm, and his dreams of self-devotion all their exhilaration.

"I came to bid you good-bye, Perez," says a voice behind him.

He wheels about, red, confused, blissful. Desire Edwards, dark and sparkling as a gypsy, stands before him with her hand outstretched. He takes it eagerly, timidly. The little white fingers press his big brown ones. He does not feel them there; they seem to be clasping his heart. He feels the ecstatic pressure there.

"Fall in," shouts Captain Woodbridge, for the Squire himself is their captain.

There is a tumult of embraces and kisses all around. Reuben kissed his mother.

"Will you kiss me, Desire?" said Perez, huskily, carried beyond himself, scarcely knowing what he said, for if he had realized he never would have dared.

Desire looked about, and saw all the women kissing their men. The air was electric.

"Yes," she said, and gave him her red lips, and for a moment it seemed as if the earth had gone from under his feet. The next thing he knew he was standing in line, with Reub on one side, and George Fennell on the other and Abner Rathbun's six feet three towering at one end of the line, while Parson West was standing on the piazza of the store, praying for the blessing of God on the expedition.

"Amen," the parson said, and Captain Woodbridge's voice rang out again. The lines faced to the right, filed off the green at quick step, turned into the Pittsfield road, and left the women to their tears.

CHAPTER SECOND

NINE YEARS AFTER

Early one evening in the very last of August, 1786, only three years after the close of the Revolutionary war, a dozen or twenty men and boys, farmers and laborers, are gathered, according to custom, in the big barroom of Stockbridge tavern. The great open fireplace of course shows no cheery blaze of logs at this season, and the only light is the dim and yellow illumination diffused by two or three homemade tallow candles stuck about the bar, which runs along half of one side of the apartment. The dim glimmer of some pewter mugs standing on a shelf behind the bar is the only spot of reflected light in the room, whose time-stained, unpainted woodwork, dingy plastering, and low ceiling, thrown into shadows by the rude and massive crossbeams, seems capable of swallowing up without a sign ten times the illumination actually provided. The faces of four or five men, standing near the bar, or lounging on it, are quite plainly visible, and the forms of half a dozen more who are seated on a long settle placed against the opposite wall, are more dimly to be seen, while in the back part of the room, leaning against the posts or walls, or lounging in the open doorway, a dozen or more figures loom indistinctly out of the darkness.

The tavern, it must be remembered, as a convivial resort, is the social antipodes of the back room of Squire Edwards' "store." If you would consort with silk-stockinged, wigged, and silver shoe-buckled gentlemen, you must just step over there, for at the tavern are only to be found the hewers of wood and drawers of water, mechanics, farm-laborers, and

farmers. Ezra Phelps and Israel Goodrich, the former the
owner of the new gristmill at "Mill Hollow," a mile west of
the village, the other a substantial farmer, with their cordu-
roy coats and knee-breeches, blue woolen hose and steel shoe
buckles, are the most socially considerable and respectably
attired persons present.

Perhaps about half the men and boys are barefooted, according to the economical custom of a time when shoes in
summer are regarded as luxuries not necessities. The costume
of most is limited to shirt and trousers, the material for which
their own hands or those of their women-folk have sheared,
spun, woven and dyed. Some of the better dressed wear
trousers of blue and white striped stuff, of the kind now-a-
days exclusively used for bed-ticking. The leathern breeches
which a few years before were universal are still worn by a
few in spite of their discomfort in summer.

Behind the bar sits Widow Bingham, the landlady, a buxom, middle-aged woman, whose sharp black eyes have lost
none of their snap, whether she is entertaining a customer
with a little pleasant gossip, or exploring the murky recesses
of the room about the door, where she well knows sundry
old customers are lurking, made cowards of by consciousness
of long unsettled scores upon her slate. And whenever she
looks with special fixity into the darkness there is soon a
scuttling of somebody out of doors.

She pays little or no attention to the conversation of the
men around the bar. Being largely political, it might be expected to have the less interest for one of the domestic sex,
and moreover it is the same old story she has been obliged to
hear over and over every evening, with little variation, for a
year or two past.

For in those days, throughout Massachusetts, at home, at
the tavern, in the field, on the road, in the street, as they rose
up, and as they sat down, men talked of nothing but the hard
times, the limited markets, and low prices for farm produce,

the extortions and multiplying numbers of the lawyers and
sheriffs, the oppressions of creditors, the enormous, grinding
taxes, the last sheriff's sale, and who would be sold out next,
the last batch of debtors taken to jail, and who would go next,
the utter dearth of money of any sort, the impossibility of
getting work, the gloomy and hopeless prospect for the coming winter, and in general the wretched failure of the triumph
and independence of the colonies to bring about the public
and private prosperity so confidently expected.

The air of the room is thick with smoke, for most of the
men are smoking clay or corncob pipes, but the smoke is
scarcely recognizable as that of tobacco, so largely is that ex-
pensive weed mixed with dried sweet-fern and other herbs,
for the sake of economy. Of the score or two persons present,
only two, Israel Goodrich and Ezra Phelps, are actually drinking anything. Not certainly that they are the only ones disposed to drink, as the thirsty looks that follow the mugs to
their lips, sufficiently testify, but because they alone have
credit at the bar. Ezra furnishes Mrs. Bingham with meal
from his mill, and drinks against the credit thus created, while
Israel furnishes the landlady with potatoes on the same understanding. There being practically almost no money in circulation, most kinds of trade are dependent on such arrange-
ments of barter. Meshech Little, the carpenter, who lies
dead-drunk on the floor, his clothing covered with the sand,
which it has gathered up while he was being unceremonious-
ly rolled out of the way, is a victim of one of these arrange-
ments, having just taken his pay in rum for a little job of
tinkering about the tavern.

"Meshech hain't hed a steady job sence the new meetin-
haouse wuz done las' year, an I s'pose the critter feels kinder
diskerridged like," said Abner Rathbun, regarding the prostrate figure sympathetically. Abner has grown an inch and
broadened proportionally, since Squire Woodbridge made

him file leader of the minute men by virtue of his six feet three, and as he stands with his back to the bar, resting his elbows on it, the room would not be high enough for his head, but that he stands between the cross-beams.

"I s'pose Meshech's fam'ly 'll hev to go ontew the taown," observed Israel Goodrich. "They say ez the poorhouse be twicet ez full ez 't orter be, naow."

"It'll hev more intew it fore 't hez less," said Abner grimly.

"Got no work, Abner? I hearn ye wuz up Lenox way a lookin fer suthin to dew," inquired Peleg Bidwell, a lank, loose-jointed farmer, who was leaning against a post in the middle of the room, just on the edge of the circle of candle-light.

"A feller ez goes arter work goes on a fool's errant," responded Abner, dejectedly. "There ain' no work nowhar, an a feller might jess ez well sit down to hum an wait till the sheriff comes arter him."

"The only work as pays now-a-days is pickin the bones o' the people. Why don't ye turn lawyer or depity sheriff, an take to that, Abner?" said Paul Hubbard, an undersized man with a dark face, and thin, sneering lips.

He had been a lieutenant in the Continental army, and used rather better language than the country folk ordinarily, which, as well as a cynical wit which agreed with the embittered popular temper, gave him considerable influence. Since the war he had been foreman of Colonel William's iron-works at West Stockbridge. There was great distress among the workmen on account of the stoppage of the works by reason of the hard times, but Hubbard, as well as most of the men, still remained in West Stockbridge, simply because there was no encouragement to go elsewhere.

"Wat I can't make aout is that the lawyers an sheriffs sh'd git so dern fat a pickin our bones, seein ez ther's sech a dern leatle meat ontew us," said Abner.

"There's as much meat on squirrels as bears if you have enough of em," replied Hubbard. "They pick clean, ye see, an take all we've got, an every little helps."

"Yas," said Abner, "they do pick darned clean, but that ain't the wust on't, fer they sends our bones tew rot in jail arter they've got all the meat orf."

" 'Twas ony yesdy Iry Seymour sole out Zadkiel Poor, ez lives long side o' me, an tuk Zadkiel daown tew Barrington jail fer the res' what the sale didn't fetch," said Israel Goodrich. "Zadkiel he's been kinder ailin like fer a spell back, an his wife, she says ez haow he can't live a month daown tew the jail, an wen Iry tuk Zadkiel orf, she tuk on reel bad. I declare for't, it seemed kinder tough."

"I hearn ez they be tew new fellers a studyin law intew Squire Sedgwick's office," said Obadiah Weeks, a gawky youth of perhaps twenty, evidently anxious to buy a standing among the adult circle of talkers by contributing an item of information.

Abner groaned. "Great Crypus! More blood-suckers. Why, they be ten lawyers in Stockbridge taown a'ready, an they warn't but one wen I wuz a boy, an thar wuz more settlers 'n they be naow."

"Wal, I guess they'll git nuff to dew," said Ezra Phelps. "I hearn as haow they's seven hundred cases on the docket o' the Common Pleas, nex' week, mos' on em fer debt."

"I hearn as two hundred on em be from Stockbridge an the iron-works," added Israel. "I declare for 't Zadkiel 'll hev plenty o' kumpny daown tew jail, by the time them suits be all tried."

"By gosh, what be we a comin tew?" groaned Abner. "It doos seem zif we all on us mout z'well move daown tew the jail to onc't, an hev done with 't. We're baown to come to 't fuss or las'."

Presently Peleg Bidwell said, "My sister Keziah's son, by

her fuss husban's been daown tew Bosting, an I hearn say ez haow he says ez the folks daown East mos'ly all hez furniter from Lunnon, and the women wears them air Leghorn hats as cos ten shillin lawful, let alone prunelly shoes an satin stockins, an he says as there ain't a ship goes out o' Bosting harbor ez don' take more'n five thousan paound o' lawful money outer the kentry. I callate," pursued Peleg, "that's jess what's tew the bottom o' the trouble. It's all long o' the rich folks a sendin money out o' the kentry to git theirselves fine duds, an that's wy we don' git more'n tuppence a paound fer our mutton, an nex' ter nothin fer wheat, an don't have nothin to pay taxes with nor to settle with Squire Edwards, daown ter the store. That's the leak in the bar'l, an times won't git no better till that's plugged naow, I tell yew."

"If't comes to pluggin leaks ye kin look nigher hum nor Bosting," observed Abner. "I hearn ez Squire Woodbridge giv fifty pound lawful fer that sorter tune box ez he'z get fer his gal, an they doos say ez them cheers o' Squire Sedgwick's cos twenty pound lawful in the old kentry."

"What dew they call that air tune box?" inquired Israel Goodrich. "I've hearn tell but I kinder fergit. It's some Frenchified soundin name."

"It's a pianner," said Obadiah.

"I guess peeanner's nigher right," observed Peleg critically. "My gal hearn the Edwards gal call it peeanner."

"They ain't nuther of ye in a mile o' right. 'Tain't pianner, an 'tain't peeanner; it's pianny," said Abner, who on account of having once served a few weeks in connection with a detachment of the French auxiliaries, was conceded to be an authority on foreign pronunciation.

"I hain't got no idee on't, nohow," said Israel shaking his head. "I hearn it a goin ez I wuz a comin by the store. Souns like ez if it wuz a hailin ontew a lot o' milk pans. I never suspicioned ez I should live tew hear sech a n'ise."

"I guess Peleg's baout right," said Abner. "Thar won't be no show fer poor folks, 'nless they is a law agin' sendin money aouter the kentry."

"I callate that would be a shuttin of the barn door arter the hoss is stole," said Ezra Phelps, as he arrested a mug of flip on its way to his lips, to express his views. "There ain' no use o' beginnin to save arter all's spent. I callate guvment's got ter print a big stack o' new bills ef we're a goin to git holt o' no money."

"Ef it's paper bills as ye're a talkin baout," said Abner grimly, "I've got quite a slew on em tew hum, mebbe a peck or tew. I got em fer pay in the army. They're tew greasy tew kindle a fire with, an I dunno o' nothin else ez they're good for. Ye're welcome to em, Ezry. My little Bijah assed me fer some on em tew make a kite outer thuther day, an I says tew him, says I, 'Bijah, I don' callate they'll do nohow fer a kite, for I never hearn of a Continental bill a goin up, but ef yer want a sinker fer yer fish line they're jess the thing.' "

There was a sardonic snicker at Ezra's expense, but he returned to the charge quite undismayed.

"That ain't nuther here nor there," he said, turning toward Abner and emphasizing his words with the empty mug. "What I asses yew is, wan't them bills good fer suthin wen they wuz fuss printed?"

"They wuz wuth suthin fer a wile," assented Abner.

"Ezackly," said the other, "that's the nater o' bills. Allers they is good fer a wile and then they kinder begins to run daown, an they runs daown till they ain't wuth nuthin," and Ezra illustrated the process by raising the mug as high as his head and bringing it slowly down to his knees. "Paounds an shillins runs daown tew by gittin wored off till they's light weight. Every kine o' money runs daown, on'y it's the nater o' bills to run daown a leetle quicker nor other sorts. Naow I says, an I ain't the ony one ez says it, that all guvment's got to dew is tew keep a printin new bills ez fass ez the old ones gits run daown. Times wuz good long in the war. A feller could git baout what he assed fer his crops an he could git any wages he assed. Yer see guvment wuz a printin money fass. Jess's quick ez a bill run daown they up and printed another one, so they wuz allers plenty. Soon ez the war wuz over they stopped a printin bills and immejetly the hard times come. Hain't that so?"

"I dunno but yew be right," said Abner, thoughtfully, "I never thort on't ezzackly that way," and Isaiah Goodrich also expressed the opinion that there was "somethin into what Ezry says."

"What we wants," pursued Ezra, "what we wants, is a kine o' bills printed as shall lose vally by reglar rule, jess so much a month, no more no less, cordin ez its fixed by law an printed on tew the bills so'z everybody'll understan an nobody'll git cheated. I hearn that's the idee as the Hampshire folks went fer in the convenshun daown tew Hatfield this week. Ye see, ez I wuz a sayin, bills is baoun tew come daown anyhow ony if they comes daown regler, cordin tew law, everybody'll know what t'expect, and nobody won' lose nothin."

"Praps the convenshun what's a sittin up tew Lenox'll rekummen them bills," hopefully suggested a farmer who had been taking in Ezra's wisdom with open mouth.

"I don' s'pose that it'll make any odds how many bills are printed as far's we're concerned," said Hubbard, bitterly. "The lawyers'll make out to git em all pretty soon. Ye might's well try to fat a hog with a tape worm in him, as to make folks rich as long as there are any lawyers round."

"Yas, an jestices' fees, an sheriff fees is baout ez bad ez lawyer's," said Israel Goodrich, whose countenance was beginning to glow from the influence of his potations. "I tell you wesh'd be a dern sight better off 'f'all the courts wuz stopped. Most on ye is young fellers, 'cept you Elnathan Hamlin, thar. He'll tell ye, ez I tell ye, that this air caounty never seen sech good times, spite on'ts bein war times, ez long fur '74 to '80, arter we'd stopped the King's courts from sittin an afore we'd voted for the new constitution o' the state, ez we wuz durn fools fer doin of, ef I dew say it. In them six year thar warn't nary court sot nowhere in the caounty, from Boston Corner tew ole Fort Massachusetts, an o' course thar warn't no lawyers an no sheriffs ner no depity sheriffs nuther, tew make every debt twice as big with ther darnation fees. They warn't no sheriffs sales, nuther, a sellin of a feller outer house'n hum an winter comin on, an thar warn't no suein an no jailin of fellers fer debt. Folks wuz keerful who they trusted, ez they'd orter be allers, for ther warn't no klectin o' debts nohow, an ef that warn't allers jestice I reckin 'twas as nigh jestice as 'tis to klect bills swelled more'n double by lawyers' and sheriffs' and jestices' fees ez they doos naow. In them days ef any feller wuz put upon by another he'd jess got tew complain tew the slectmen or the committee, an they'd right him. I tell yew rich folks an poor folks lived together kinder neighborly in them times an 'cordin tew scripter. The rich folks warn't a grindin the face o' the poor, an the poor they wuzn't a hatin an a envyin o' the rich, nigh untew blood, ez they is naow, ef I dew say it. Yew rekullec them days, Elnathan, warn't it jess ez I say?"

"Them wuz good times, Israel. Ye ain't sayin nothin more'n wuz trew," said Elnathan in a feeble treble, from his seat on the settle.

"I tell you they wuz good," reiterated Israel, as he looked around upon the group with scintillating eyes, and proceeded to hand his mug over the bar to be refilled.

"I hearn ez haow the convenshun up tew Lenox is a goin tew 'bolish the lawyers an the courts," said a stalwart fellow of bovine countenance, named Laban Jones, one of the discharged iron-works men.

"The convenshun can't 'bolish nothin," said Peleg Bidwell,

gloomily. "It can't do nothin but rekommen the Gineral Court way daown tew Bosting. Bosting is too fer orf fer this caounty, nor Hampshire nuther, tew git no considerashin. This eend o' the state ull never git its rights till the guvment's moved outer Bosting tew Worcester where't uster be in war times."

"That's so," said Ezra Phelps, "everybody knows as these tew counties be taxed higher nor the other eend o' the state."

"Hev yew paid up ye taxes fer las' year, Peleg?" inquired Abner.

"No, I hain't, nor fer year afore, nuther. Gosh, I can't. I could pay in pertaters, but I can't pay in money. Ther ain't no money. Klector Williams says as haow he'd hafter sell me out, an I s'pose he's goin ter. It's kinder tough, but I don' see zi kin dew nothin. I callate to be in the jail or poorhouse, afore spring."

"I dunno o' nobody roun here, as haz paid ther taxes fer las year, yit," said Israel. "I callate that more'n half the farms in the caounty 'll be sole fer taxes afore spring."

"I hearn as how Squire Woodbridge says taxes is ten times what they wuz afore the war, an its sartain that they ain't one shillin intew folks' pockets tew pay em with whar they wuz ten on em in them days. It seems dern curis, bein as we fit agin the redcoats jest tew git rid o' taxes," said Abner.

"Taxes is mosly fer payin interest ontew the money what govment borrowed tew kerry on the war. Naow, I says, an I ain't the on'y one in the caounty as says it, nuther, ez debts orter run daown same ez bills does, reglar, so much a month, till they ain't nuthin leff," said Ezra Phelps, setting down his mug with an emphatic thud. "S'poosn I borrers money of yew, Abner, an built a haouse, that haouse is boun tew run daown in vally, I callate, 'long from year tew year. An it seems kinder rees'nable that the debt sh'd run daown 's fass as the haouse, so's wen the haouse gits wored aout, the debt 'll be, tew. Them things ez govment bought with the

money it borrered, is wore aout, an it seems kinder rees'nable that the debts should be run daown tew. A leetle orter a
been took orf the debt every year, instead o' payin interes
ontew it."

"I guess like 's not ye hev the rights on't, Ezry. I wuzn't
a thinkin on't that air way, ezzactly. I wuz a thinkin that if
govment paid one kine o' debts 't orter pay t'other kine. I
fetched my knapsack full o' govment bills hum from the war.
I callate them bills wuz all on em debts what the govment
owed tew me fur a fightin. Ef govment ain't a goin tew pay me
them bills, an 'tain't, 'it don' seem fair tew tax me so 's it kin
pay debts it owes tew other folks. Leastways seems 's though
them bills govment owes me orter be caounted agin the
taxes instead o' bein good fer nothin. It don't seem ez if 'twas
right, nohaow."

"Leastways," said Peleg, "if the Gineral Court hain't a
goin ter print more bills 't orter pass a lor, seein thar ain't
no money in the kentry, so 'z a feller's prop'ty could be tuk
by a fair valiation fer what he owes, instead o' lettin the
sheriff sell it fer nothin and sendin a feller tew jail fer the
balince. Wen I giv Squire Edwards that air leetle morgidge
on my farm, money wuz plenty, an I callated tew pay it up
easy; an naow thar ain't no money, an I can't git none, if I
died for 't. It's jess zif I 'greed tew sell a load o' ice in January,
an a thaw come an thar wan't no ice leff. Property's wuth 's
much 'z ever I callate, an 't orter be good fer debts instead
o' money, 'cordin to a far valiation."

"Mr. Goodrich, how did you go to work to stop the King's
courts in '74? Did you hang the justices?" inquired Paul
Hubbard, arousing from a fit of contemplation.

"Nary bit," replied Isaiah, "there warn't no need o' hangin
nobody. 'Twas a fine mornin in May, I rekullec jess zif 'twas
yes'day, wen the court was a goin tew open daown tew
Barrington, an abaout a thousan men on us jess went daown
an filled up the court haouse, an woudn' let the jedges in, an

wen they see 'twan't no use, they jess give in quiet 's lambs, an we made em sign their names tew a paper agreein not tew hold no more courts, an the job wuz done. Ye see the war wuzn't farly begun an none o' the King's courts in th' uther caounties wuz stopped, but we callated the court mout make trouble for some o' the Sons o' Liberty, in the caounty if we let it set."

"I callate 't ain't nothin very hard tew stop a court, 'cordin tew that," said Peleg Bidwell.

"No, 'tain't hard, not ef the people is gen'ally agin' the settin on it," said Isaiah.

"I s'pose ef a thousan men sh'd be daown tew Barrington nex' week Tewsday, they could stop the jestice fr'm openin the Common Pleas, jess same ez yew did," said Peleg, thoughtfully.

"Sartain," said Isaac, "sartain; leastways 's long ez the militia warn't aout, but gosh, they ain't no sense o' talkin baout sech things! These hain't no sech times ez them wuz, an folks ain't what they wuz, nuther. They seems kinder slimpsy; hain't got no grit."

During this talk, Elnathan had risen and gone feebly out.

"Elnathan seems tew take it tew heart baout leavin the ole place. I hearn ez how Solomon Gleason 's goin ter sell him aout pooty soon," Abner remarked.

"I guess t'ain't so much that as 'tis the bad news he's heerd baout Reub daown tew Barrington jail," said Obadiah Weeks.

"What's abaout Reub?" asked Abner.

"He's a goin intew a decline daown to the jail."

"I wanter know! Poor Reub!" said Abner, compassionately. "He fout side o' me tew Stillwater, an Perez was t'other side. Perez done me a good turn that day, ez I shan't furgit in a hurry. Gosh, he'd take it hard ef he hearn ez haow Reub wuz in jail! I never seed tew fellers set more store by another 'n he did by Reub."

"Wonder ef Perez ain't never a comin hum. He hain't been back sence the war. I hearn his folks had word a spell ago, ez he wuz a comin," said Peleg.

"Gosh!" exclaimed Abner, his rough features softening with a pensive cast, "I rekullec jess zif 'twar yes'dy, that rainy mornin wen we fellers set orf long with Squire Woodbridge fer Bennington. Thar wuz me, 'n Perez, an Reub, an Abe Konkapot, 'n lessee, yew went afore, didn't ye, Peleg?"

"Yas, I went with Cap'n Stoddard," replied that individual.

"Thar we wuz; all a stannin in line," pursued Abner, gazing right through the ceiling, as if he could see just the other side of it the scene which he so vividly recalled, "an Parson West a prayin, an the wimmin a whimperin, an we nigh ontew it; fer we wuz green, an the mothers' milk warn't aouter us. But I bet we tho't we wuz big pertaters, agoin to fight fer lib'ty. Wall, we licked the redcoats, and we got lib'ty, I s'pose; lib'ty ter starve, that is ef we don' happin to git sent tew jail fus," and Abner's voice fell, and his chin dropped on his breast, in a sudden reaction of dejection at the thought of the bitter disappointment of all the hopes which that day had made their hearts so strong, even in the hour of parting.

"I callate we wuz a dern sight better orf every way under the King, 'n we be naow. The Tories wuz right, arter all, I guess. We'd better a let well nuff l'one, an not to a jumped aouter the fryin-pan intew the fire," said Peleg, gloomily.

As he ended speaking, a medium sized man, with a pasty white, freckled complexion, bristly red hair, a retreating forehead and small, sharp eyes, came forward from the dark corner near the door. His thin lips writhed in a mocking smile, as he stood confronting Peleg and Abner, and looking first at one and then at the other:

"Ef I don' furgit," he said at length, "that's 'baout the way I talked wen the war wuz a goin on, an if I rekullec, ye, Peleg, an ye, Abner Rathbun and Meshech Little, thar on the floor, tuk arter me with yer guns and dorgs caze ye said I wuz a dum Tory. An ye hunted me on Stockbridge mounting like a woodchuck, an ye'd a hed my skelp fer sartin ef I hadn't been a durn sight smarter 'n ye ever wuz."

"Jabez," said Abner, "I hope ye don' hev no hard feelin's. Times be changed. Let by gones be by gones."

"Mos' folks ud say I hed some call to hev hard feelin's. Ye druv me ter hide in caves, an holes, fer the best part o' tew year. I dass'n come hum tew see my wife die, nor tew bury on her. Ye confiscated my house and tuk my crops fer yer derned army. Mos' folks ud sartingly say ez I hed call tew hev hard feelin's agin' ye. But gosh, I hain't, an wy hain't I? Caze ye hev been yer own wust enemies; ye've hurt yerselves more ner ye hev me, though ye didn't go fer ter dew it. Pooty nigh all on ye, as fit agen the King, is beggars naow, or next door tew it. Everybudy hez a kick fer a soldier. Ye'll fine em mosly in the jails an the poorhaouses. Look at you fellers as wuz a huntin me. Ther's Meshech on the floor, a drunken, worthless cuss. Thar ye be, Abner, 'thout a shillin in the world, nor a foot o' lan', yer dad's farm gone fer taxes. An thar be ye, Peleg. Wal Peleg, they dew say, ez the neighbors sends ye in things."

Jabez looked from one to the other till he had sufficiently enjoyed their discomfiture and then he continued:

"I ain't much better orf'n ye be, but I hain't got nothin ontew my conscience. An wen I looks roun' an sees the oppresshin, and the poverty of the people, and how they have none tew help, an the jails so full, an the taxes, an the plague o' lawyers, an the voice o' cryin as is goin up from the land, an all the consekences o' the war, I tell ye, it's considabul satisfacshin to feel ez I kin wash my hans on't." And, with a glance of contemptuous triumph around the circle, Jabez turned on his heel and went out. The silence was first broken by Ezra Phelps, who said quietly:

"Wal, Jabez ain't fur from right. It's abaout so. Some says the King is callatin to try to git the colonies back agin fore

long. Ef he doos I guess he'll make aout, fur I don't bleeve ez
a kumpny o' men could be raised in all Berkshire, tew go an
fight the redcoats agin, if they wuz to come to-morrer." And
a general murmur of assent confirmed his words.

"Wal," said Abner, recovering speech, "live an larn. In
them days wen I went a gunnin arter Jabez, I uster to think ez
thar wuzn't no sech varmint ez a Tory, but I didn't know
nothin bout lawyers, and sheriffs them times. I callate ye
could cut five Tories aout o' one lawyer an make a dozen
skunks aout o' what wuz leff over. I'm a goin hum."

This was the signal for a general break-up. Israel, who had
fallen into a boozy slumber on the settle, was roused and
sent home between his son and hired man, and presently the
tavern was dark save for the soon extinguished glimmer of
a candle at the upstairs window of Widow Bingham's apartment. Meshech was left to snore upon the barroom floor and
grope his way outdoors as best he might, when he should
return to his senses. For doors were not locked in Stockbridge
in those days.

CHAPTER THIRD

THE TAVERN-JAIL AT BARRINGTON

Peleg's information, although of a hearsay character, was correct. Perez Hamlin was coming home. The day following the conversation in the barroom of Stockbridge tavern, which I have briefly sketched in the last chapter, about an hour after noon, a horseman might have been seen approaching the village of Great Barrington, on the road from Sheffield. He wore the buff and blue uniform of a captain in the late Continental army, and strapped to the saddle was a steel hilted sword which had apparently experienced a good many hard knocks. The lack of any other baggage to speak of, as well as the frayed and stained condition of his uniform, indicated that however rich the rider might be in glory, he was tolerably destitute of more palpable forms of wealth.

Poverty, in fact, had been the chief reason that had prevented Captain Hamlin from returning home before. The close of the war had found him serving under General Greene in South Carolina, and on the disbandment of the troops he had been left without means of support. Since then he had been slowly working his way homewards, stopping a few months wherever employment or hospitality offered. What with the lack and insecurity of mails, and his frequent movements, he had not heard from home for two or three years, though he had written. But in those days, when the constant exchange of bulletins of health and business between friends, which burdens modern mail bags, was out of the question, the fact perhaps developed a more robust quality of faith in the well-being of the absent than is known in these timid and anxious days. Certain it is that as the soldier rides along, the smiles that from time to time chase each other across his bronzed face, indicate that gay and tender anticipations of the meeting now only a few hours away, leave no room in his mind for gloomy conjectures of possible disaster. It is nine years since he parted with his father and mother; and his brother Reub he has not seen since the morning in 1778, when Perez, accepting a commission, had gone south with General Greene, and Reub had left for home with Abner and Fennell, and a lot of others whose time had expired. He smiles now as he thinks how he never really knew what it was to enjoy the fighting until he got the lad off home, so that he had not to worry about his being hit every time there was any shooting going on. Coming into Great Barrington, he asked the first man he met where the tavern was.

"That's it, over yonder," said the man, jerking his thumb over his shoulder at a nondescript building some way ahead.

"That looks more like a jail."

"Wal, so 'tis. The jail's in the ell part o' the tavern. Cephe Bement keeps 'em both."

"It's a queer notion to put em under the same roof."

"I dunno 'bout that, nuther. It's mostly by way o' the tavern that fellers gits inter jail, I calc'late."

Perez laughed, and riding up to the tavern end of the jail, dismounted, and going into the barroom, ordered a plate of pork and beans. Feeling in excellent humor he fell to conversing over his modest meal with the landlord, a big, beefy man, who evidently liked to hear himself talk, and in a gross sort of way, appeared to be rather good natured.

"I saw a good many red flags on farmhouses, as I was coming up from Sheffield, this morning," said Perez. "You haven't got the smallpox in the county again, have you?"

"Them wuz sheriff's sales," said the landlord, laughing uproariously, in which he was joined by a seedy, red-nosed character, addressed as Zeke, who appeared to be a hanger-on of the barroom in the function of echo to the landlord's jokes.

"Ye'll git uster that air red flag ef ye stay long in these parts. Ye ain't so fer from right arter all, though, fer I guess mos' folks 'd baout as leeve hev the smallpox in the house ez the sheriff."

"Times are pretty hard hereabouts, are they?"

"Wal, yes, they be baout ez hard ez they kin be, but ye see it's wuss in this ere caounty 'n 'tis 'n mos' places, cause ther warn't nary court here fer six or eight year, till lately, an no debts wuz klected 'n so they've kinder piled up. I callate they ain't but dern few fellers in the caounty 'cept the parsons, 'n lawyers, 'n doctors ez ain't a bein sued ted-day, 'specially the farmers. I tell you it makes business lively fer the lawyers an sheriffs. They're the ones ez rides in kerridges these days."

"Is the jail pretty full now?"

"Chock full, hed to send a batch up ter Lenox las' week, an got em packed bout's thick's they'll lay naow, like codfish in a bar'l. Haow in time I'm a gonter make room fer the fellers the court'll send in nex' week, I d'now, derned if I dew. They'd orter be three new jails in the caounty this blamed minit."

"Do you expect a good many more this week?"

"Gosh, yes. Why, man alive, the Common Pleas never had ez much business ez this time. I callate they's nigh onter seven hundred cases tew try."

"The devil! Has there been a riot or a rebellion in the county? What have they all done?"

"Oh they hain't done nothin," replied the landlord, "they ain't nothin but debtors. Dern debtors, I don' like to hev the jailin of em. They hain't got no blood intew em like Sabbath-breakers, an blasphemers, an rapers has. They're weakly, pulin kinder chaps, what thar ain't no satisfaction a lockin up an a knockin roun'. They're dreffle deskerridgin kind o' fellers tew. Ye see we never git rid on em. They never gits let aout like other fellers as is in jail. They hez tew stay till they pays up, an naterally they can't pay up 's long ez they stays. Genally they goes aout feet foremost, when they goes aout at all, an they ain't long lived."

"Why don't they pay up before they get in?" queried Perez.

"Whar be ye from?" asked the landlord, staring at him.

"I'm from New York, last."

"I thort ye could't be from roun' here, nowheres, to as' sech a queschin. Why don' they pay their debts? Did ye hear that Zeke? Why, jess caze they ain' no money in the kentry tew pay em with. It don' make a mite o' odds haow much propty a feller's got. It don' fetch nothin tew a sale. The credtor buys it in fer nothin, an the feller goes to jail fer the balance. A man as has got a silver sixpence can amos buy a farm. Some folks says they orter be a law makin propty a tender fer debts on a far valiation. I dunno, I don' keer, I hain't no fault tew find with my business, leastways the jail end on't."

Finishing his dinner, Perez asked for his score, and drew a large wallet from his pocket, and took out a roll of about five thousand dollars in Continental bills.

"Hain't ye got no Massachusetts bills? They ain't wuth but one shillin in six but that's suthin, and them Continental bills ain't wuth haouse room. Gosh durn it. I swow, ef I'd a known ye hadn't nothin but them, I wouldn't a guv ye a drop to drink nor eat nuther. Marthy say only this morning, 'Cephas,' says she, 'rum 's rum an rags is rags, an don' ye give no more rum fer rags.' "

"Well," said Perez, "I have nothing else. Government thought they were good enough to pay the soldiers for their blood; they ought to pay landlords for their rum."

"I dunno nothin baout bein soldiers, an I dunno ez I or any other man's beholden to ye for't, nuther. Ye got paid all twat wuth if ye didn't git paid nuthin; fur's I kin reckon, we wuz a durn sight better orf under Ole King George 's we be naow. Ain' that baout so, Zeke?"

"Well," said Perez, "if you won't take these, I can't pay you at all."

"Well" said Bement crossly, "thar's the beans an mug o' flip. Call it a thousand dollars, an fork over, but by gosh, I don' git caught that way again. It's downright robbery, that's wot it is. I say ain't ye got no cleaner bills nor these?"

"Perhaps these are cleaner," said Perez, handing him another lot. "What odds does it make?"

"Wal, ye see, ef they be middlin clean, I kin keep kaounts on the backs on em, and Marthy finds em handy wen she writes to her folks daown tew Springfield. Tain't fuss class writin paper, but it's cheaper'n other kinds, an that's suthin in these times."

Having satisfied the landlord's requirements, as well as possible, Perez walked to the door and stood looking out. The ell containing the jail, coming under his eye, he turned and said, "You spoke of several hundred debtors coming before the court next week. It don't look as if you could get over fifty in here."

"Oh ye can jam in a hundred. I've got nigh that naow, and thay's other lockups in the caounty," replied the land-lord. "But ef they wuz a gonter try to shet up all the debtors, they'd hev tew build a half a dozen new jails. But bless ye, the mos' on em won't be shet up. Ther creditors 'll git jedg-ments agin' em, an then they'll hev rings in their noses, an kin dew wot they likes with em caze ef they don' stan raoun' they kin shove em right intew jug ye see."

"You don't mean to say there's much of that sort of slavery," ejaculated Perez.

"I'd now baout slavery ezzackly, but thar's plenty o' that sort o' thing fer sartin. Credtors mosly'd ruther dew that way, caze they kin git suthin aout a feller, an ef they sen em tew jail it's a dead loss. They makes em work aout ther debt and reckons ther work tew baout wat they pleases. They is some queer kinder talk baout wat kind er things they makes em stan sometimes rather'n go ter jail. Wal, all I says is that a feller ez hez got a good lookin gal hed better not git a owin much in these ere times. I hain't said nothin, hev I, Zeke?'' and that worthy answered his wink with a salacious chuckle.

"Have you any debtors from Stockbridge?" asked Perez, suddenly.

"A hull slew on em," replied Bement. "I've got one more'n I shall hev much longer, tew."

"Who be that?" asked Zeke.

"Wal, I callate George Fennell won't hole out much longer."

"Fennell; George Fennell! George Fennell is not in this jail," cried Perez.

"Wal, naow," said Bement, imperturbably, "perhaps ye know better'n I dew."

"But, landlord, he's my friend, my comrade, I'd like to see him," and the young man's countenance expressed the liveliest concern.

The landlord seemed to hesitate. Finally he turned his head and called, "Marthy", and a plump, kitten-like little woman appeared at a door, opening into the end of the bar, whereupon, the landlord, as he jerked his thumb over his shoulder to indicate their guest, remarked:

"He wants ter know if 'ee kin be let ter see George Fennell. Says he's his fren, an uster know him to the war."

Mrs. Bement looked at the officer and said, "Wal, my husbun don' genally keer to hev folks a seein the pris'ners, coz it makes em kinder discontented like." She hesitated a little and then added, "But I dunno's 'twill dew no harm Cephas, bein as Fennell won' las' much longer anyhow."

Thus authorized, Bement took a bundle of keys from a hook behind the bar, and proceeded to unlock the padlock which fastened an iron bar across a heavy plank door, in the middle of one of the sides of the room. As he threw open the door, a gust of foul stenches belched forth into the room, almost nauseating Perez. The smell of the prison was like that of a pig sty. The door had opened into a narrow corridor, dimly lit by a small square grated window at the further end, while along either side were rows of strong plank doors opening outward, and secured by heavy, oaken bars, slipped across them at the middle. The muggy dog-day had been very oppressive, even out of doors; but here in the corridor, it was intolerable. To breathe in the horrible concoction of smells, was like drinking from a sewer; the lungs, even as they involuntarily took it in, strove spasmodically to close their passages against it. It was impossible for one unaccustomed to such an atmosphere, to breathe, save by gasps. Bement stopped at one of the doors, and as he was raising the bar across it, he said:

"Thar ain' on'y one feller 'sides Fennell in here. He's a Stockbridge feller, too. The cell ain' so big's the others. Genally thar's three or four together. I'll jess shet ye in, an come back for ye in a minit."

He opened the door, and as the other stepped in, it was closed and barred behind him. The cell was about seven feet square and as high. The floor was a foot lower than the corridor, and correspondingly damper. It must have been on or below the level of the ground, and the floor, as well as the lower end of the planks which formed the walls, was black with moisture. The cell was littered with straw and every kind of indescribable filth, while the walls and ceiling were mildewed and spotted with ghastly growths of mould, feeding on the moist and filthy vapors, which were even more sickening than in the corridor.

Full six feet from the floor, too high to look out of, was a small grated window, a foot square, through which a few feeble, dog-day sunbeams, slanting downward, made a little yellow patch upon the lower part of one of the sides of the cell. Sitting upon a pile of filthy straw, leaning back against the wall, with his face directly in this spot, one of the prisoners was half-sitting, half-lying, his eyes shut as if asleep, and a smile of perfect happiness resting on his pale and weazened face. Doubtless he was dreaming of the time, when, as a boy, he played all day in the shining fields, or went blackberrying in the ardent July sun. For him the river was gleaming again, turning its million glittering facets to the sun, or, maybe, his eye was delighting in the still sheen of ponds in Indian summer, as they reflected the red glory of the overhanging maple or the bordering sumach thicket.

The other prisoner was kneeling on the floor before the wall, with a piece of charcoal in his hand, mumbling to himself as he busily added figures to a sum with which the surface above was already covered. As the door of the cell closed, he looked around from his work. Like the man's on the floor, his face had a ghastly pallor, against which the dirt with which it is stained, shows with peculiarly obscene effect, while the beards and hair of both had grown long and matted and were filled with straw. So completely had their miserable condition disguised them, that Perez would not have known in the dim light of the cell that he had ever seen either before.

The man who had been kneeling on the floor, after his first look of dull curiosity, began to stare fixedly at Perez, as if he were an apparition, and then rose to his feet. As he did so, Perez saw that he could not be Fennell, for the latter was tall, and this man was quite short. Yes, the reclining man must be George, and now he noted as an unmistakable confirmation, a scar on one of the emaciated hands lying on his breast. "George," he said, stepping to his side. As he did so he passed athwart the bar of sunshine that was falling on the man's countenance. A peevish expression crossed his face, and he opened his eyes, the burning, glassy eyes of the consumptive. For a few seconds he looked fixedly, wonderingly, and then said half dreamily, half inquiringly, as if he were not quite certain whether it were a man or a vision, he murmured:

"Perez?"

"Yes, it is I, George," said the soldier, his eyes filling with compassionate tears. "How came you in this horrible place?"

But before Fennell could answer the other prisoner sprang to the side of the speaker, clutching his arm in his claw-like fingers, and crying in an anguished voice:

"Perez; brother Perez. Don't you know me?"

At the voice Perez started as if a bullet had reached his heart. Like lightning he turned, his face, frozen with fear, that was scarcely yet comprehended, his eyes like darts. From that white filthy face in its wild beast's mat of hair, his brother's eyes were looking into his.

"Lord, God in Heaven!" It was a husky, struggling voice, scarcely more than a whisper in which he uttered the words. For several seconds the brothers stood gazing into each other's countenances, Reuben holding Perez' arm and he half shrinking, not from his brother, though such was the attitude, but from the horror of the discovery.

"How long" he began to ask, and then his voice broke. The emaciated figure before him, the face bleached with the ghastly pallor which a sunless prison gives, the deep sunken eyes looking like coals of fire, eating their way into his brain, the tattered clothing, the long unkempt hair and beard, prematurely whitening, and filled with filth, the fingers grown claw-like and blue, with prison mould, the dull vacant look and the thought that this was Reuben, his brother; these things all filled him with such an unutterable, intolerable pity, that it seemed as if he should lose his head and go wild for very anguish of heart.

"I 'spose I'm kinder thin and some changed, so ye didn't know me," said Reuben, with a feeble smile. "Ye see I've been here a year, and am going into a decline. I sent word home to have father ask Deacon Nash if he wouldn't let me go home to be nussed up by mother. I should get rugged again if I could have a little o' mother's nussin. P'raps ye've come to take me home, Perez?" And a faint gleam of hope came into his face.

"Reub, Reub, I didn't know you was here," groaned Perez, as he put his arm about his brother, and supported his feeble figure.

"How come ye here, then?" asked Reuben.

"I was going home. I haven't been home since the war. Didn't you know? I heard o' George's being here, and came in to see him, but I didn't think o' you're being here."

"Where have ye been, Perez, all the time? I callated ye must be in jail, somewheres, like all the rest of the soldiers."

"I had no money to get home with. But how came you here, Reub? Who put you here?"

"'Twas Deacon Nash done it. I tried to start a farm arter the war, and got in debt to Deacon for seed and stock, and there wasn't no crop, and the hard times come. I couldn't pay, and the Deacon sued, and so I lost the farm and had to come here."

"Why didn't father help you? He ain't dead is he?"

Almost any misfortune now seemed possible to Perez.

"No, he ain't dead, but he ain't got nothin. I spose he's sold out by this time. Sol Gleason had a mortgage on the place."

"How much was your debt, Reub?"

"Nineteen pound, seven shilling and six-pence. 'Least-ways, the debt was nine pound, and the rest was lawyers', justices' and sheriffs' fees. I callate they'll find them figgers cut into my heart, when I'm dead."

And then he pointed to the sums in charcoal, covering the walls of the cell.

"I callated the interest down to how much a minute. I

allers liked cipherin, ye know, Perez, and I have a great deal of time here. Ye see, every day, the interest is a penny and twenty-six twenty-sevenths of a farthin. The wall round me gits that much higher and thicker every day." He stepped closer up to the wall, and pointed to a particular set of figures.

"Here's my weight, ye see, ten stone and a fraction," and then observing Perez' pitiful glance at his emaciated form, he added, "I mean when I come to jail. Dividin nineteen pound, seven and six, by that, it makes me come to thrippence happenny a pound, 'cording to the laws o' Massachusetts, countin bones and waste. Mutton ain't wuth but tuppence, and there's lots o' fellers here for sech small debts, that they don't come to mor'n a farthin a pound, and ye see I'm gittin dearer, Perez. There's the interest one way, and I'm a gittin thinner the other way," he added with a piteous smile.

"Perez," interrupted Fennell, in a feeble, whimpering voice, as he weakly endeavored to raise himself from the floor, "I wish you'd jess give me a boost on your shoulders, so I kin see out the winder. Reub uster to do it, but he ain't stout enough now. It's two months since I've seen out. Say, Perez, won't ye?"

"It'll do him a sight o' good, Perez, if ye will. I never see a feller set sech store by trees and mountings as George does. They're jess like medicine to him, an he's fell off faster'n ever since I hain't been able to boost him up."

Perez knelt, too much moved for speech, and Reub helped to adjust upon his shoulders the feeble frame of the sick man, into whose face had come an expression of eager, excited expectation. As the soldier rose he fairly tottered from the unexpected lightness of his burden. He stepped beneath the high, grated window, and Fennell, resting his hands on the lintel, while Reub steadied him from behind, peered out. He made no sound, and finally Perez let him down to the floor.

"Could you see much?" asked Reub, but the other did not answer. His gaze was afar off as if the prison walls were no barrier to his eyes, and a smile of rapturous contemplation rested on his face. Then with a deep breath he seemed to return to a perception of his surroundings, and in tones of irrepressible exultation he murmured:

"I saw the mountains. They are so," and with a waving, undulating gesture of the hand that was wonderfully eloquent, he indicated the bold sweep of the forest clad Taghcanic peaks. The door swung open, and the jailer stood there.

"Time's up," he said sharply.

"What, you're not going now? You're not going to leave us yet?" cried Reuben, piteously.

Perez choked down the wrath and bitterness that was turning his heart to iron and said, humbly.

"Mr. Bement, I should like to stay a few minutes longer. This is my brother. I did not know he was here."

"Sorry for't," said Bement, carelessly. "Don' see as I kin help it, though. S'posed like nuff he was somebuddy's brother. Mout's well be your'n ez anybuddy's. I dunno who ye be. All I knows is that ye've been here fifteen minutes and now ye must leave. Don' keep me waitin, nuther. Thay ain' nobuddy tendin bar."

"Don't make him mad, Perez, or else he won't let ye come again," whispered Reuben, who saw that his brother was on the point of some violent outburst. Perez controlled himself, and took his brother's hands in his coming close up to him and looking away over his shoulder so that he might not see the pitiful workings of his features which would have negatived his words of comfort.

"Cheer up, Reub," he said huskily, "I'll get you out. I'll come for you," and still holding his grief-wrung face averted, that Reuben might not see it, he went forth, and Bement shut the door and barred it.

CHAPTER FOURTH

THE PEOPLE ASK BREAD
AND RECEIVE A STONE

As Captain Hamlin, leaving behind him Great Barrington and its tavern-jail, was riding slowly on toward Stockbridge, oblivious in the bitter tumult of his feelings, to the glorious scenery around him, Stockbridge Green was the scene of a quite unusual assemblage. Squire Sedgwick, the town's delegate, was expected back that afternoon from the county convention, which had been sitting at Lenox, to devise remedies for the popular distress, and the farmers from the outlying country had generally come into the village to get the first tidings of the result of its deliberations.

Seated on the piazza of the store, and standing around it, at a distance from the assemblage of the common people, suitably typifying their social superiority, was a group of the magnates of Stockbridge, in the stately dress of gentlemen of the olden time, their three-cornered hats resting upon powdered wigs, and long silk hose revealing the goodly proportions of their calves. Upon the piazza sits a short, portly gentleman, with bushy black eyebrows and a severe expression of countenance. Although a short man he has a way of holding his neck stiff, with the chin well out, and looking downward from beneath his eyelids, upon those who address him, which, with his pursed up lips, gives a decided impression of authority and unapproachableness. This is Jahleel Woodbridge, Esquire.

Parson West is standing on the ground in front of him, his silver headed cane tucked under one arm. His small person — he is not an inch over five feet tall — is as neatly dressed as if just taken out of a band-box, and his black, shining hose encase a leg and ankle which are the chaste admiration of the ladies of the parish, and the source, it is whispered, of no small complacency to the good man himself.

"What think you," he is saying to Squire Woodbridge, "will have been the action of the convention? Will it have emulated the demagogic tone of that at Hatfield, do you opine?"

"Let us hope not, Reverend Sir," responded the Squire, "but methinks it was inexpedient to allow the convention to meet, although Squire Sedgwick's mind was on that point at variance with mine. It is an easier matter to prevent a popular assembly than to restrain its utterances, when assembled."

"I trust," said the parson, looking around upon those standing near, "that we have all made it a subject of prayer, that the convention might be Providentially led to devise remedies for the inconveniences of the time, for they are sore, and the popular discontent is great."

"Nay, I fear 'tis past hoping for that the people will be contented with anything the convention may have done, however well considered," said Dr. Partridge. "They have set their hearts on some such miracle as that whereby Moses did refresh fainting Israel with water from the smitten rock. The crowd over yonder will be satisfied with nothing short of that from the convention," and the doctor waved his hand toward the people on the green, with a smile of tolerant contempt on his clean-cut, sarcastic, but not unkindly face.

"I much err," said Squire Woodbridge, "if the stocks and the whipping-post be not the remedy their discontent calls for. I am told that seditious and disorderly speech is common at the tavern of evenings. This presumption of the people to talk concerning matters of government, is an evil that has greatly increased since the war, and calls for sharp castigation. These numskulls must be taught their place or t'will shortly be no country for gentlemen to live in."

"A letter that I had but a day or two ago from my brother at Hatfield," said Dr. Partridge, "speaks of the people being much stirred up in Hampshire, so that some even fear an attempt of the mob to obstruct the court at Northampton, though my brother opined that their insolence would not reach so far. One Daniel Shays, an army captain, is spoken of as a leader."

Timothy Edwards, Esquire, a tall sharp featured man, with a wrinkled forehead, had come to the door of his store while the doctor was talking. I should vainly try to describe this stately merchant of the olden time, if the reader were to confound him, ever so little in his mind's eye, with the bustling, smiling, obsequious, modern storekeeper. Even a royal customer would scarcely have presumed so far as to ask this imposing gentleman, in powdered wig, snuff-colored coat, waistcoat and short clothes, white silk stockings and silver-buckled shoes, to cut off a piece of cloth or wrap up a bundle for him. It may be taken for granted that commercial enterprise, as illustrated in Squire Edwards' store, was entirely subservient to the maintenance of the proprietor's personal dignity. He now addressed Dr. Partridge:

"Said your brother anything of the report that the Tories and British emissaries are stirring up the popular discontent, to the end that reproach may be brought on the new government of the States, by revealing its weakness as compared with the King's?"

"Nay, of that he spoke not."

"For my part, I do fully believe it," resumed Edwards, "and, moreover, that this is but a branch of the British policy, looking toward the speedy reconquering of these States. It is to this end, also, that they are aiming to weaken us by drawing all the money out of the country, whereby, meanwhile, the present scarcity is caused."

"Methinks, good sir," replied the doctor, "the great expense of the war, and the public and private debts made thereby, with the consequential taxes and suits at law, do fully explain the lamentable state of the country, and the disquiet of the people, though it may be that the King has also designs against us."

"Nay," said the parson, in tones of gentle reproof, "these all be carnal reasons, whereby if we seek to explain the judgments of God, we do fail of the spiritual profiting we might find therein. For no doubt these present calamities are God's judgment upon this people for its sins, seeing it is well known that the bloody and cruel war now over, hath brought in upon us all manner of new and strange sins, even as if God would have us advertised how easily that liberty which we have gained may run into licentiousness. Sabbath-breaking and blasphemy have come in upon us like a flood, and the new and heinous sin of card-playing hath contaminated our borders, as hath been of late brought to light in the cases of Jerubbabel Galpin and Zedekiah Armstrong, who were taken in the act, and are even now in the stocks. And thereby am I reminded that I had purposed to improve this occasion for the reproof and admonition of them that stand by."

And thereupon the parson saluted the gentlemen and sedately crossed the green toward the stocks, around which was a noisy crowd of men and boys. As the parson approached, however, a respectful silence fell upon them. There was a general pulling off of hats and caps, and those in his path stood obsequiously aside, while the little children, slinking behind the grown folks, peeped around their legs at him. The two hobbledehoys in the stocks, loutish farmer's boys, had been already undergoing the punishment for about an hour. Their backs were bent so that their bodies resembled the letter U laid on its side, and their arms were strained as if they were pulling out of the sockets. All attempted bravado, all affectation of stoical indifference, all sense even of embarrassment, had evidently been merged in the demoralization of intense physical discomfort, and the manner in which they lolled their heads, first on one side and then on the other, was eloquent of abject and shameless misery. Standing directly in front of these hapless youths, and using them as his text, the parson began to admonish the people in this wise:

"It would seem the will of God to permit the adversary to try the people of Stockbridge with divers new and strange temptations, not known to our fathers, doubtless to the end, that their graces may shine forth the more clearly, even as gold tried in the fire hath a more excellent lustre, by reason of its discipline.

"I have examined myself with fasting, to see if any weakness or laxity in my office, as shepherd of this flock, might be the occasion of this license given to Satan. And it behooveth you, each in his own soul, and in his own household, to make inquisition lest some sin of his or theirs, bring this new temptation of card-playing, upon our people, even as the wedge of fine gold which Achan took and hid in his tent, did mightily discomfit the host of Israel with the plagues of the Lord. For even as for the sin of Adam, we are all justly chargeable, so for the sins of one another, doth the justice of God afflict us, so that we may find our account in watching over our brethren, even as over ourselves.

"And you, whom Satan hath led away captive," pursued the reverend orator, addressing himself to the young men in the stocks, "be ye thankful that ye have not been permitted to escape this temporal recompense of your transgression, which, if proved, may save you from the eternal flames of hell, Reflect, whether it be not better to endure for a season, the contempt and the chastisement of men, rather than to bear the torments and jeers of the devil and his angels forever."

"Behold," said the minister, holding up the pack of cards

taken from the prisoners, "with what instruments Satan doth tempt mankind, and consider how perverse must be the inclination which can be tempted by devices that do so plainly advertise their devilish origin. At times Satan doth so shrewdly mask his wiles that if it were possible the very elect might be deceived, but how evidently doth he here reveal his handiwork."

He held up some of the court cards.

"Take note of these misshaped and deformed figures, heathenishly attired, and with no middle parts or legs, but with two heads turned diverse ways. These are not similitudes of man, who was made in the image of his Maker, but doubtless of fiends, revealed by Satan to the artificers who do his work in the fabrication of these instruments of sin. Mark these figures of diamonds and hearts, and these others, which I am told do signify spades and clubs. How plainly do they typify ill-gotten riches and bleeding hearts, violence and the grave. Wretched youths, which of ye tempted the other to this sin?"

"Je assed me to dew it," whimpered Zedekiah.

"Kiah, he assed me fust," averred Jerubbabel.

"No doubt ye are both right," said the minister sternly. "When two sin together, Satan is divided in twain, and the one half tempteth the other. See to it that ye sin not again on this wise, lest a worse thing come upon you."

Scarcely had the parson turned away, when a shout from some boys who had gone to the corner to watch for the coming of the Squire, announced his approach, and presently he appeared at the corner, riding a fine gray horse, and came on at an easy canter across the green. He was a tall, broad-shouldered, finely-proportioned man of about forty, with a refined face, frank and open, but rather haughty in expression, with piercing black eyes; a man in whose every gesture lay conscious power and obvious superiority. As he rode by the silent crowd, he acknowledged the salutations of the people with a courteous wave of the hand, but drew rein only when he reached the group of dignitaries about the store. There he dismounted and shook hands with the parson, who has rejoined the party, with Dr. Partridge, Squire Edwards and Squire Woodbridge.

"What news bring you from the convention? I trust you have been Providentially guided. I have not failed to remember you in my prayers," said the parson.

"For which I am deeply grateful, Reverend Sir," replied Sedgwick. "And truly I think your prayers have been effectual. The blessing of God has been manifestly upon the convention. Berkshire has not been disgraced, as have been the lower counties, by a seditious and incendiary body of resolutions on the part of her delegates. There were not wanting plenty of hot-heads, but they were overruled. I am convinced such might also have been the issue in the other counties, had the gentlemen put themselves forward as delegates, instead of leaving it all in a fit of disgust to the people."

"Was there any action taken in favor of the plan for the emission of bills, which shall systematically depreciate!" inquired Squire Woodbridge.

"Such a resolution was introduced by Thomas Gold of Pittsfield, a pestilent fellow, but we threw it out."

"What was the action on reduction of expenses of suits at law?" inquired Dr. Partridge.

"Again nothing," replied Sedgwick. "In a word, we refused to yield to any of the demands of the malcontents, or to hamper the Legislature with any specific recommendations. You know that we Berkshire people, thanks to our delay in recognizing the State authority, have an evil repute at Boston for a mobbish and ungovernable set. It seemed that this was a good opportunity, when the conventions of all the other counties were sending up seditious petitions, to make the moderation of our conduct such a contrast that there might be an end of such talk in the future."

Meanwhile, as it became apparent to the crowd on the green that they were not likely to be vouchsafed any information unless they asked for it, a brisk disputation, conducted in an undertone, so that it might not reach the ears of the gentlemen, arose as to who should be the spokesmen.

"I jess ez leeve go 's not," said Jabez Flint, the Tory, "only they wouldn' hev nothin tew say ter me ez wuz a Tory."

"Ef I were ten year younger, I'd go in a minute," said Israel Goodrich, "but my jints is kinder stiff. Abner, thar, he'd orter go, by rights."

"Why don' ye go, Abner? Ye ain't scairt o' speakin tew Squire, be ye!" said Peleg.

"I ain't scairt o' no man, and ye know it 's well 's ye wanter know. I'd go in a jiffey, only bein a young man, I don' like tew put myself forrard tew speak for them as is older."

"Why don' ye go yerself, Peleg, if ye be so dretful brave!" inquired Israel Goodrich.

"That's so, Peleg, why don' ye go?"

"I ain't no talker," said Peleg. "Ther's Ezry, he'd orter go, he's sech a good talker."

But Ezra swallowed the bait without taking the hook. "Tain't talkin ez is wanted, it's assin. Any on ye kin dew that 's well 's I," he discriminated.

The spirit of mutual deference was so strong that it is doubtful how long the contest of modesty might have continued, had not Laban Jones suddenly said:

"Ef none on ye dasn't ass what the convenshin has did, I'll ass myself. I'm more scairt o' my hungry babbies an I be o' the face o' any man."

Raising his stalwart figure to its full height, and squaring his shoulders as if to draw courage from a consciousness of his thews and sinews, Laban strode toward the store. But though he took the first steps strongly and firmly, his pace grew feebler and more hesitating as he neared the group of gentlemen, and his courage might have ebbed entirely, had not the parson, glancing around and catching his eye, given him a friendly nod. Laban thereupon came up to within a rod or two of the group, and taking off his cap, said in a small voice:

"Please we'd like ter know what the convenshin has did?"

Sedgwick, who had his back to him, turned quickly, and seeing Laban, said in a preëmptory tone:

"Ah! Laban, you may tell your friends that the convention very wisely did nothing at all," and as he said this he turned to finish something that he was saying to Squire Woodbridge. Laban's jaw fell, and he continued to stand stock still for several moments, his dull features working as he tried to take in the idea. Finally, his consternation absorbing his timidity he said feebly:

"Nothin? Did you say, Squire?"

Sedgwick wheeled about with a frown, which however, changed into an expression of contemptuous pity as he saw the genuineness of the poor fellow's discomfiture.

"Nothing, Laban," he said, "except to resolve to support the courts, enforce the laws, and punish all disorderly persons. Don't forget that last, Laban, to punish all disorderly persons. Be sure to tell your friends that. And tell them, too, Laban, that it would be well for them to leave matters of government to their betters and attend to their farms," and as Laban turned mechanically and walked back Sedgwick added, speaking to the gentlemen about him:

"I like not this assembling of the people to discuss political matters. We must look to it, gentlemen, or we shall find that we have ridded ourselves of a king only to fall into the hands of a democracy, which I take it would be a bad exchange."

"Sir," said Edwards, "you must be in need of refreshment, after your ride. Come in, sir, and come in gentlemen, all.

We shall discuss the Providential issue of the convention more commodiously within doors, over a suitable provision of Jamaica."

The suggestion seemed to be timely and acceptable, and one by one the gentlemen, standing aside with ceremonious politeness to let one another precede, entered the store, Parson West leading, for it was neither according to the requirements of decorum, or his own private tastes, that the minister should decline a convivial invitation of this character.

"What d'ee say, Laban?"

"What did they dew?"

"Did they 'bolish the loryers?"

"Wat did they dew baout more bills, Laban, hey?"

"What did they dew baout the taxes?"

"Why don't ye speak, man?"

"What's the matter on ye?" were some of the volley of questions with which the people hailed their chop-fallen deputy on his return, crowding forward around him, plucking his sleeves and pushing him to get his attention, for he regarded them with a dazed and sleep-walking expression. Finally he found his voice, and said:

"Squire says ez haow they didn' dew nothin."

There was a moment's dead silence, then the clamor burst out again.

"Not dew nothin?"

"What d'ye mean, Laban?"

"Nothin baout the taxes?"

"Nothin baout the loryers?"

"Nothin baout the sheriffs' fees?"

"Nothin baout jailin for debt?"

"Nothin baout takin prop'ty tew a valiation, Laban?"

"Nothin baout movin govment aout o' Bosting?"

"Nothin, I tells ye," answered Laban, in the same tone of utter discouragement. "Squire says ez haow the convenshin hain't done nothin 'cept tew resolve that ez courts sh'd go on an the laws sh'd be kerried aout an disorderly folks sh'd be punished."

The men looked from one to another of each other's faces, and each wore the same blank look. Finally Israel Goodrich said, nodding his head with an expression of utter dejection at each word:

"Wal, I swow, I be kinder disappinted."

There was a space of silence.

"So be I," said Peleg.

Presently Paul Hubbard's metallic voice was heard.

"We were fools not to have known it. Didn't we elect a General Court last year a purpose to do something for us, and come to get down to Bosting didn't the lawyers buy em up or fool em so they didn't do a thing? The people won't git righted till they take hold and right themselves, as they did in the war."

"Is that all the Squire said, Laban, every word?" asked Israel, and as he did so all eyes turned on Laban with a faint gleam of hope that there might yet be some crumb of comfort. Laban scratched his head.

"He said suthin baout govment bein none o' our business an haow we'd a better go hum an not be loafin roun'."

"Ef govment hain't no business o' ourn I'd like tew know what in time we fit the King fer," said Peleg.

"That's so, wy didn' ye ass Squire that queschin?" said Meshech Little.

"By gosh," exclaimed Abner Rathbun, with a sudden vehemence, "ef govment ain't no business o' ourn they made a mistake when they teached us that fightin was."

"What dew ye mean?" asked Israel half timorously.

"Never mind wat I mean," replied Abner, "on'y a wum 'll turn wen it's trod on."

"I don' bleeve but that Laban's mistook wat the Squire

said. Ye ain't none tew clever, ye know, yerself, Laban, and I callate that ye didn' more'n half understan' wat Squire meant."

It was Ezra Phelps who announced this cheering view, which instantly found general favor, and poor Laban's limited mental powers were at once the topic of comments more plain spoken than flattering. Paul Hubbard, indeed, shook his head and smiled bitterly at this revulsion of hopefulness, but even Laban himself seemed eager to find ground for believing himself to have been, in this instance, an ass.

"Ye see the hull thing's in a nutshell," said Abner. "Either Laban's a fool, or else the hull caounty convenshin o' Berkshire is fools an wuss, an I callate it's Laban."

Perhaps the back room of the store lacked for Sedgwick, a comparatively recent resident of Stockbridge, those charms of familiarity it possessed for the other gentlemen, for even as Abner was speaking, he came out alone. As he saw the still waiting and undiminished crowd of people, he frowned angrily, and mounting his horse, rode directly toward them. Their sullen aspect, which might have caused another to avoid them, was his very reason for seeking an encounter. As he approached, his piercing eye rested a moment on the face of every man, and as it did so, each eye, impelled by a powerfull magnetism, rose deferentially to his, and every cap was pulled off.

"What is it, Ezra?" he demanded sharply, seeing that Ezra wanted to address him.

"If you please, Squire," said Ezra, cap in hand, "Laban's kinder stupid, an we callate he muster got what ye said tuther eend to. Will ye kindly tell us what the convenshin did?"

Stopping his horse, Sedgwick replied, in a loud, clear voice.

"The convention declared that the laws shall be enforced, and all disorderly persons punished with the stocks and with lashes on the bare back."

"Is that all?" faltered Ezra.

"All!" exclaimed Sedgwick, as his eye rested a moment on every face before him. "Let every one of you look out that he does not find it too much."

And now he suddenly broke off in a tone of sharp command, "Disperse and go to your houses on the pains and penalties of Sabbath breaking. The sun is down," and he pointed to the last glimmer of the yellow orb as it sank below the mountains. The people stood still just long enough to verify the fact with a glance, that holy time had begun, and instantly the green was covered with men and boys swiftly seeking shelter within their doors from the eye of an angry Deity, while from the store hastily emerged Squire Woodbridge, Dr. Partridge and the parson, and made their several ways homeward as rapidly as dignity would permit.

Perhaps ten minutes later, Captain Perez Hamlin might have been seen pricking his jaded horse across the deserted green. He looked around curiously at the new buildings and recent changes in the appearance of the village, and once or twice seemed a little at loss about his route. But finally he turned into a lane leading northerly toward the hill, just at the foot of which, beside the brook that skirted it, stood a weather-beaten house of a story and a half. As he caught sight of this, Perez spurred his horse to a gallop, and in a few moments the mother, through her tears of joy, was studying out in the stern face of the man, the lineaments of the boy whose soldier's belt she had buckled round him nine years before.

CHAPTER FIFTH

THAT MEANS REBELLION!

Elnathan was the only one of the family who went to church the following day. Mrs. Hamlin was too infirm to climb the hill to the meeting-house, and Perez' mood was more inclined to blood-spilling than to God's worship. All day he walked the house, his fists clenched, muttering curses through his set teeth, and looking not unlike a lion, ferociously pacing his cage. For his mother was tearfully relating to him the share of the general misery that had fallen to their lot, as a family, in the past nine years, how Elnathan had not been able to carry on his farm, without the aid of the boys, and had run behind, till now, Solomon Gleason the schoolmaster, had got hold of the mortgage, and was going to turn them into the street, that very week. But all this with the mother, as with the brother, was as nothing, compared with Reuben's imprisonment and sickness unto death.

It was Mrs. Hamlin, who did most of the talking, and much of what she said fell unheeded on Perez' ears, as he walked unceasingly to and fro across the kitchen. For his mind was occupied with all the intensity of application, of which it was capable, with the single point, — how he was to get Reuben out of jail. Even the emergency, which would so soon be raised, by the selling out of the homestead, and the turning of the family into the street, was subordinated, in his mind, to this prime question. The picture of his brother, shaggy-haired and foul, wallowing in the filth of that prison sty, and breathing its fetid air, which his memory kept constantly before him, would have driven him distracted, if for a moment he had allowed himself to doubt that he should somehow liberate him, and soon. He had told his mother nothing of the horrible condition in which he had found him. Under no circumstances must she know of that, not even if worst came to worst, and so even while he shuddered at the vision before his mind's eye, he essayed to speak cheerfully about Reuben's surroundings, and his condition of health. When she told him that Deacon Nash had refused to let him come home to be nursed back to health, Perez had to comfort her by pretending that he was not so very badly off where he was, and would doubtless recover.

"Nay, Perez," she said, "my eyes are dim, come close to me, that I may read your eyes. You were ever tender to your old mother, and I fear me, you hide somewhat lest I should disquiet myself. Come here my son." The brave man's eyes, that had never quailed before the belching artillery, had now ado indeed. Such sickness at heart behind them, such keen mother's instinct trying them before.

"Oh, Perez! My boy is dying! I see it."

"He is not, I tell you he is not," he cried hoarsely, breaking away from her. "He is well. He looks strong. Do you think I would lie to you? I tell you he is well and getting better."

But after that she would not be comforted. The afternoon wore on. Elnathan came from meeting, and at last, through the open windows of the house, came the cry, in children's voices.

"Sun's down! Sun's down!"

From the upper windows, its disc was yet visible, above the crest of the western mountains, and on the hilltops, it was still high Sabbath; but in the streets below, holy time was at an end. The doors, behind which, in Sabbatical decorum, the children had been pent up all day long, swung open with a simultaneous bang, and the boys with a whoop and halloo, tumbled over each other into the street, while the girls tripped gaily after. Innumerable games of tag, and "I spy," were organized in a trice, and for the hour or two between that and bed time, the small fry of the village devoted themselves, without a moment's intermission, to getting the Sabbath stiffening out of their legs and tongues.

Nor was the reawakening of the community by any means confined to the boys and girls. For soon the streets began to be alive with groups of men and women, all in their Sunday best, going to make social calls. In the majority of Stockbridge households, the best clothes, unless there chanced to be a funeral, were not put on oftener than once a week, when the recurrence of the Sabbath made their assumption a religious duty, and on this account it naturally became the custom to make the evening of that day the occasion of formal social intercourse. As soon, too, as the gathering twilight afforded some shield to their secret designs, sundry young men with liberally greased hair, their arms stiff in the sleeves of the unusual and Sunday coat, their feet, accustomed to the immediate contact of the soil, encased in well larded shoes, might have been seen gliding under the shadows of friendly fences, and along bypaths, with that furtive and hangdog air which, in all ages, has characterized the chicken-thief and the lover.

In front of the door of Squire Sedgwick's house is drawn up his travelling carriage, with two fine horses. On the box is Sol, the coachman, one of the Squire's negro freedmen, whose allegiance to the Sedgwick family was not in the least shaken by the abolition of slavery in the state by the adoption of the bill of rights six years before.

"I dunno noffin bout no Bill Wright," was Sol's final dismissal of the subject.

"Drive to Squire Woodbridge's house, Sol," said Sedgwick, as he stepped into the carriage.

Woodbridge was at the gate of his house, apparently about starting on his usual evening visit to the store, when the carriage drove up. Sedgwick alighted, and taking the other a little aside, said:

"It is necessary for me to start tonight for Boston, where I have some important cases. I regret it, because I would rather be at home just now. The spirit among the people is unruly, and while I do not anticipate serious trouble, I think it is a time when gentlemen should make their influence felt in their communities. I have no doubt, however, that the interests of Stockbridge and of the government are entirely safe in your hands as selectman and magistrate."

"I hope, sir, that I am equal to the duties of my position," replied Woodbridge, stiffly.

"Allow me again to assure you that I have not the smallest doubt of it," said Sedgwick, affably, "but I thought it well to notify you of my own necessary departure, and to put you on your guard. The bearing of the people on the green last evening, of which I saw more than you did, was unmistakably sullen, and their disappointment at the refusal of the convention to lend itself to their seditious and impracticable desires, is very bitter."

"Undoubtedly the result of the convention has been to increase the popular agitation. I had the honor to represent to you before it was held that such would be its effect, at which time, I believe you held a different view. Nevertheless, I opine that you exaggerate the degree of the popular agitation. It would be natural, that being a comparatively recent resident, you should be less apt to judge the temper of the Stockbridge people, than we who are longer here."

A half humorous, half impatient expression on Sedgwick's face, was the only indication he gave that he had recognized the other's huffy and bristling manner.

"Your opinion, Sir," he replied, with undiminished affability, "tends to relieve my apprehensions. I trust the event will justify it.

"And how does Miss Desire, this evening?" he added,

saluting with doffed hat and a courtly bow, a young lady who had just come up, with the apparent intention of going in at the Woodbridge gate.

"I do but indifferent well, Sir. As well as a damsel may do in a world where gentlemen keep not their promises," she answered, with a curtsey, so saucily deep, that the crisp crimson silk of her skirt rustled on the ground.

"Nay, but tell me the caitiff's name, and let me be myself your knight, fair mistress, to redress your wrongs."

"Nay, 'tis yourself, Sir. Did you not promise you would come and hear me play my piano, when it came from Boston, and I have it a week already?"

"And I did not know it. Yes, now I bethink myself, Mrs. Sedgwick spoke thereof, but this convention has left me not a moment. But damsels are not political; no doubt you have heard nothing of the convention."

"Oh, yes; 'tis that all the poor want to be rich, and to hang all the lawyers. I've heard. 'Tis a fine scheme."

"No doubt the piano is most excellent in sound."

"It goes middling well, but already I weary me of my bargain."

"Are you then in trade, Miss Desire?"

"A little. Papa said if I would not tease him to let me go to New York this winter, he would have me a piano. I know not what came over me that I consented. I shall go into a decline ere spring. The ugly dress and the cowlike faces of the people, make me sick at heart, and give me bad dreams, and the horses neigh in better English than the farmers talk. Alack, 'tis a dreary place for a damsel! But, no doubt, I have interrupted some weighty discussion. I bid you good even, Sir," and, once more curtsying, the girl went up the path to the house, much to her uncle Jahleel's relief, who had no taste for badinage, and wanted to get on to the store, whither, presently he was on his way, while Sedgwick's carriage rolled off toward Boston.

About a mile out of Stockbridge, the carriage passed two men standing by the roadside, earnestly talking. These men were Perez Hamlin and Abner Rathbun.

"You remember the Ice-hole," said Perez, referring to an extraordinary cleft or chasm, of great depth, and extremely difficult and perilous of access, situated near the top of Little Mountain, a short distance from Stockbridge.

"Yes," said Abner, "I rekullec it, well. I guess you an I, Perez, air abaout the on'y fellers in taown, ez hev been clean through it."

"My plan is this," said Perez. "Kidnap Deacon Nash, carry him up to the Ice-hole, and keep him there till he makes out a release for Reub, then just carry down the paper to jail, get Reub out, and across the York State line, and send back word to Stockbridge where to find the deacon."

"But what'll we dew, ourselves?"

"Of course we shall have to stay in York. Why shouldn't we? There's no chance for a poor man here. The chances are that we should both be in jail for debt before spring."

"But what be I a goin to dew with my little Bijah? He's all I've got, but I can't leave him."

"My father and mother will take care of him, and bring him with em to York State, for I'm goin to get them right over there as soon as they're sold out. There's a chance for poor folks west; there's no chance here."

"Perez, thar's my fist. By gosh I'm with ye."

"Abner, it's a risky business, and you haven't got the call I've got, being as Reub isn't your brother. I'm asking a good deal of you Abner."

"Don' ye say nothin more baout it," said Abner, violently shaking the hand he still held, while he reassuringly clapped Perez on the back. "Dew ye rekullec that time tew Stillwater, when ye pulled them tew Britishers orfer me? Fer common doin's I don' callate ez two fellers is more'n my fair share in a scrimmage, but ye see my arm wuz busted, an if ye hadn't come along jess wen ye did, I callate the buryin squad would a cussed some on caount of my size, that evenin.

"But gosh all hemlock, Perez, I dunno wat makes me speak o' that naow. It wouldn' make no odds ef I'd never sot eyes onter ye afore. I'd help eny feller, 'bout sech a job es this ere, jess fer the fun on't. Risky! Yes it's risky; that's the fun. I hain't hed my blood fairly flowin afore, sence the war. It doos me more good nor a box o' pills. Jerewsalem, how riled deacon'll be!"

The two young men walked slowly back to the village, earnestly discussing the details of their daring enterprise, and turning up the lane, leading to the Hamlin house, paused, still conversing, at the gate. As they stood there, the house door opened, and a young girl came out, and approached them, while Mrs. Hamlin, standing in the door, said:

"Perez, this is Prudence Fennell, George Fennell's girl. She heard you had seen her father, and came to ask you about him."

The girl came near to Perez, and looked up at him with a questioning face, in which anxiety was struggling with timidity. She was a rosy cheeked lass, of about sixteen, well grown for her age, and dressed in coarse woolen homespun, while beneath her short skirt, appeared a pair of heavy shoes, which evidently bore very little relation to the shape of the feet within them. Her eyes were gray and frank, and the childishness, which the rest of her face was outgrowing, still lingered in the pout of her lips.

"Is my father much sick, sir?"

"He is very sick," said Perez.

The pitifulness of his tone, no doubt, more than his words, betrayed the truth to her fearful heart, for all the color ran down out of her cheeks, and he seemed to see nothing of her face, save two great terrified eyes, which piteously beseeched a merciful reply, even while they demanded the uttermost truth.

"Is he going to die?"

Perez felt a strong tugging at his heart strings, in which, for the moment, he forgot his own personal trouble.

"I don't know, my child," he replied, very gently.

"Oh, he's going to die. I know he's going to die," she cried, still looking through her welling eyes a moment, to see if he would not contradict her intuition, and then, as he looked on the ground, making no reply, she turned away, and walked slowly down the lane sobbing as she went.

"Abner, we must manage somehow to get George out too."

"Poor little gal, so we must Perez. We'll kidnap School-master Gleason 'long with deacon. But it's a pootty big job, Perez, two o' them and on'y two o' us."

"I'm afraid we're trying more than we can do, Abner. If we try too much, we shall fail entirely. I don't know. I don't know. There's the whole jail full, and one ought to come out as well as another. All have got friends that feel as bad as we do." He reflected a moment. "By the Lord, we'll try it, Abner. Poor little girl. It's a desperate game, anyway, and we might as well play for high stakes."

Abner went down the lane to the green, and Perez went into the house, and sat down in the dark to ponder the new difficulties with which the idea of also liberating Fennell complicated their first plan. Bold soldier as he was, practiced in the school of Marion and Sumter, in the surprises and stratagems of partisan warfare, he was forced to admit that if their project had been hazardous before, this new feature made it almost foolhardy. In great perplexity he had finally determined to go to bed, hoping that the refreshment of morning would bring a clearer head and more sanguine mood, when there was a knock on the door. It was Abner looking very much excited.

"Come out! Come out! Crypus! Come out, I've got news."

"What is it?" said Perez eagerly, stepping forth into the darkness.

"That wuz a pootty leetle plan o' yourn, Perez."

"Yes, yes."

Abner, he knew had not come to tell him that, for his voice trembled with suppressed excitement, and the grip of his hand on his shoulder was convulsive.

"P'raps we could a kerried it aout, an p'raps we should a kerflummuxed. Ye've got grit an I've got size," pursued Abner. "Twuz wuth tryin on. I'm kinder sorry we ain't a gonter try it."

"What the devil do you mean, Abner? not going to try it?"

"No, Perez, we ain't goin tew try it, leastways, not the same plan we callated, an we ain't a goin tew try it alone," and he leaned over and hissed in Perez' ear:

"The hull caounty o' Berkshire 's a gonter help us."

Perez looked at him with horror. He was not drunk; he must be going crazy.

"What do you mean, Abner?" he said soothingly.

"Ye think I don' know wat I be a talkin baout, don' ye, Perez? Wal, jess hole on a minit. A feller hez jess got in, a ridin 'xpress from Northampton, to fetch word that the people in Hampshire has riz, and stopped the courts. Fifteen hundred men, with Captain Dan Shays tew ther head, stopped em. Leastways, they sent word to the jedges that they kinder wisht they wouldn't hole no more courts till the laws wuz changed, and the jedges, they concluded that the 'dvice o' so many fellers with guns, wuz wuth suthin, so they 'journed."

"That means rebellion, Abner."

"In course it doos. An it means the Lord ain't quite dead yit. That's wat it means."

"But what's that got to do with Reub and George?"

"Dew with em, why, man alive, don' ye unnerstan? Don' ye callate Berkshire folks haz got ez much grit ez the Hampshire fellers, an don' ye callate we haz ez much call to hev a grudge agin courts? Ye orter been daown tew the tavern tew see haow the fellers cut up wen the news come. T'was like a match dropping intew a powder bar'l. Tuesday's court day tew Barrington, an ef thar ain't more'n a thousand men on han with clubs an guns, tew stop that air court, wy, call me a skunk. An wen that air court's stopped, that air jail's a comin open, or it's a comin daown, one o' the tew naow."

CHAPTER SIXTH

PEREZ DEFINES HIS POSITION

We who live in these days, when press and telegraph may be said to have almost rendered the tongue a superfluous member, quite fail to appreciate the rapidity with which intelligence was formerly transmitted from mouth to mouth. Virgil's description of hundred tongued Rumor appeared by no means so poetical an exaggeration to our ancestors as it does to us. Although the express, bearing the news of the Northampton uprising did not reach Stockbridge tavern a minute before half-past seven in the evening, there were very few families in the village or the outlying farmhouses, which had not heard it ere bedtime, an hour and a half later. And by the middle of the following forenoon there was in all Southern Berkshire, only here and there a family, off on a lonely hillside, or in a hidden valley, in which it was not the subject of debate.

In Stockbridge, that morning, what few industries still supported a languishing existence in spite of the hard times, were wholly suspended. The farmer left his rowen to lie in the field and take the chances of the weather, the miller gave his mill-stream a holiday, the carpenter left the house half-shingled with rain threatening, and the painter his brush in the pot, to collect on the street corners with their neighbors and discuss the portentous aspect of affairs. And even where there was little or no discussion, to stand silently in groups was something. Thus merely to be in company was, to these excited men, a necessity and a satisfaction, for so does the electricity of a common excitement magnetize human beings, that they have an attraction for one another, and are drawn together by a force not felt at other times. There were not less than three hundred men, a quarter of the entire population of the town, on and about Stockbridge Green at ten o'clock that Monday morning, twice as many as had assembled to hear the news from the convention the Saturday preceding.

The great want of the people, for the most part, tongue-tied farmers, seemed to be to hear talk, to have something said, and wherever a few brisk words gave promise of a lively dialogue, the speakers were at once surrounded by a dense throng of listeners. The thirsting eagerness with which they turned their open mouths toward each one as he began to speak, in the hope that he would express to themselves some one of the ideas formlessly astir in their own stolid minds, was pathetic testimony to the depth to which the iron of poverty, debt, judicial and governmental oppression had entered their souls. They had thought little and vaguely, but they had felt much and keenly, and it was evident the man who could voice their feelings, however partially, however perversely, and for his own ends, would be master of their actions.

Abner was not present, having gone at an early hour over to Lenox furnaces, where he was acquainted, to carry the news from Northampton, if it should not have arrived there, and notify the workmen that there would be goings-on at Barrington, Tuesday, and they were expected to be on hand. Paul Hubbard, also, had not come down from West Stockbridge, although the news had reached that place last night. But from the disposition of the man, there could be no question that he was busily at work moulding his particular myrmidons, the iron-workers, into good insurrectionary material. There was no doubt that he would have them down to Barrington on time, whoever else was there.

In the dearth of any further details of the Northampton

uprising, the talk among the crowd on Stockbridge Green turned largely upon reminiscences and anecdotes of the disturbances at the same place, and at Hatfield four or five years previous. Ezra Phelps, who had been concerned in them, having subsequently removed from Hatfield to Stockbridge, enjoyed by virtue of that fact an oracular eminence, and as he stood under the shadow of the buttonwood tree before the tavern, relating his experiences, the people hung upon his lips.

"Parson Ely," he explained, "Parson Sam'l Ely wuz kinder tew the head on us. He wuz a nice sorter man, I tell yew. He wuz the on'y parson I ever seen ez hed any flesh in his heart for poor folks, 'nless it be some o' them ere Methody an Baptis preachers ez hez come in sence the war, an I callate they ain' reglar parsons nuther. Leastways, thuther parsons, they turned Parson Ely aout o' the min'stry daown to Somers whar he wuz, fer a tellin the poor folks they didn' git their rights. Times wuz hard four or five year ago, though they warn't so all-fired hard ez they be naow. Taxes wuz high 'nuff, an money wuz dretful skurce, an thar wuz lots o' lawin an suein o' poor folks. But gosh, ef we'd a known haow much wuss all them things wuz a going tew git, we sh'd a said we wuz well orf. But ye see we warn't so uster bein starved an cheated an jailed an knocked roun' then 's we be sence, an so we wuz kinder desprit, an a slew on us come daown from Hatfield tew Northampton an stopped the court, wen t'wuz gonter set in the spring o' '82. I callate we went tew work baout the same ez Dan Shays an them fellers did las' week. Wal, arter we'd did the job an gone hum agin, Sheriff Porter up an nabbed the parson, an chucked him inter jail. He was long with us ye see, though he warn't no more tew blame nor any of us. Wal, ye see, we callated t'wouldn't be ezzackly fa'r tew let parson git intew trouble fer befriendin on us, an so baout 300 on us went daown tew Northampton agin, and broke open the jail an tuk parson aout. The sheriff didn' hev nothin tew say wen we wuz thar, but ez soon ez we'd gone hum, he up an took three o' the parson's frens as lived to Northampton an chucked em inter jail fer tew hold ez sorter hostiges. He callated he'd hev a ring in the parson's nose that ere way, so 's he wouldn' dass dew nothin. Thar warn't no law nor no reason in sech doins, but 'twuz plantin time, leastways gittin on tew it, and he callated the farmers wouldn' leave ther farms, not fer nothin. But he mistook. Ye see we wuz fightin mad. Baout 500 on us tuk our guns an made tracks fer Northampton. Sheriff he'd got more'n a thousan milishy tew defend the jail, but the milishy didn' wanter fight, an we did, an that made a sight o' odds, fer wen we stopped night tew the taown an sent word that ef he didn' let them fellers aout o' jail we'd come an take em aout, he let em aout dum quick."

"Wat did they do nex?" inquired Obadiah Weeks, as Ezra paused with the appearance of having made an end of his narration.

"That wuz the eend on't," said Ezra. "By that time govment seen the people wuz in arnest, an quit foolin. Ginral Court passed a law pardnin all on us fer wat we'd done. They allers pardons fellers, ye see, wen ther's tew many on em tew lick, govment doos, an pooty soon arter they passed that ere tender law fer tew help poor folks ez hed debts so's prop'ty could be offered tew a far valiation instid o' cash."

"That air law wuz repealed sence," said Peleg. "Ef we hed it naow, mebbe we could git 'long spite o' ther being no money a cirkilatin."

"In course it wuz repealed," said Israel. "They on'y passed it caze they wuz scairt o' the people. The loryers an rich folks got it repealed soon ez ever they dasted. Gosh, govment don' keer nothin fer wat poor folks wants, 'nless they gits up riots. That's the on'y way they kin git laws changed, 's fur 's I see. Ain't that 'bout so Peleg?"

"Ye ain't fur outer the way, Isr'el. We hain't got no money, an they don' keer wat we says, but when we takes hole, an doos sumthin they wakes up a leetle. We can't make em hear us, but by jocks, we kin make em feel us," and Peleg pointed the sentiment with that cornerwise nod of the head, which is the rustic gesture of emphasis. "I callate ye've hit the nail on the head, Peleg," said a grizzled farmer. "We poor folks hez to git our rights by our hands, same ez we gits our livin."

But at this moment, a sudden hush fell upon the group, and from the general direction of the eyes, it was evidently the approach of Perez Hamlin, as he crossed the green toward the tavern, which was the cause thereof. Although Perez had arrived in town only at dusk on the preceding Saturday, and excepting his Sunday evening stroll with Abner, had kept within doors, the tongue of rumor had not only notified pretty much the entire community of his arrival, but had adorned that bare fact with a profuse embroidery of conjecture, as to his recent experiences, present estate, and intentions for the future.

An absence of nine years had, however, made him personally a stranger to most of the people. The young men had been mere lads when he went away, while of the elders, many were dead, or removed. As he approached the group around Ezra, he recognized but few of the faces, all of which were turned upon him with a common expression of curious scrutiny. There was Meshech Little. Him he shook hands with, and also with Peleg, and Israel Goodrich. Ezra had come to the village since his day.

"Surely this is Abe Konkapot," he said, extending his hand to a fine looking Indian. "Why Abe, I heard the Stockbridges had moved out to York State."

"You hear true," responded the smiling Indian. "Heap go. Some stay. No want to go."

"Widder Nimham's gal Lu, could tell ye 'bout why Abe don' want ter go, I guess," observed Obadiah Weeks, who directed the remark, however, not so much to Perez as to some

of the half-grown young men, from whom it elicited a responsive snicker at Abe's expense.

Indeed, after the exchange of the first greetings, it became
apparent that Perez' presence was a damper on the conversation. The simple fact was, the people did not recognize him
as one of them. It was not that his dress, although a uniform,
was better or costlier than theirs. The blue stockings were
threadbare, and had been often mended, and the coat, of the
same hue, was pitiably white in the seams, while the original
buff of the waistcoat and knee breeches had faded to a whitey
brown. But the erect soldierly carriage of the wearer, and
that neatness and trimness in details, which military experience renders habitual, made this frayed and time-stained uniform seem almost elegant, as compared with the clothes that
hung slouchily upon the men around him. Their faces were
rough, and unshaven, their hair unkempt, their feet bare, or
covered with dusty shoes, and they had generally left their
coats at home. Perez was clean shaven, his shoes, although they
barely held together, were neatly brushed, and the steel
buckles polished, while his hair was gathered back over his
ears, and tied with a black ribbon in a queue behind, in the
manner of gentlemen. But Israel Goodrich and Ezra also
wore their hair in this manner, while shoes and clean shaved
faces were occasional indulgences with every bumpkin who
stood around. It was not then alone any details of dress, but
a certain distinction in air and bearing about Perez, which
had struck them. The discipline of military responsibility,
and the officer's constant necessity of maintaining an aspect of
authority and dignity, before his men, had left refining marks
upon his face, which distinguished it as a different sort from
the countenances about him with their expressions of pathetic
stolidity, or boorish shrewdness. In a word, although they
knew old Elnathan Hamlin to be one of themselves, they
instinctively felt that this son of his had become a gentleman.

At any time this consciousness would have produced constraint, and checked spontaneous conversation, but now, just at the moment when the demarcation of classes was taking the character of open hostility, it produced a sentiment of repulsion and enmity. His place was on the other side; not with the people, but with the gentlemen, the lawyers, the parsons, and the judges. Why did he come spying among them?

Perez, without guessing the reason of it, began to be conscious of the unsympathetic atmosphere, and was about moving away, when Israel Goodrich remarked, with the air of wishing to avoid an appearance of churlishness.

"Lessee, Perez, ye've been gone nigh onter nine year. Ye muss find some changes in the taown."

Israel, as a man of more considerable social importance than the most of those who stood around, and being moreover, old enough to be Perez' father, had been less affected by the impulse of class jealousy than the others.

"I've been home only one day, Mr. Goodrich," said Perez quietly, "but I've noticed some changes already. When I went away, every man in town had a farm of his own. As far as I've seen since I've been back, a few rich men have got pretty near all the farms now, and the men who used to own em, are glad of a chance to work on em as hired hands."

Such a sentiment, expressed by one of themselves, would have called forth a shower of confirmatory ejaculations, but the people stared at Perez in mere astonishment, the dead silence of surprise, at hearing such a strong statement of their grievances, from one whose appearance and manner seemed to identify him with the anti-popular, or gentleman's side. So far as this feeling of bewilderment took any more definite form, it evidently inclined to suspicion, rather than confidence. Was he mocking them? Was he trying to entrap them? Even Israel looked sharply at him, and his next remark, after quite a silence, was on another subject.

"I s'pose ye know ez haow they've set the niggers free."

"Yes," replied Perez, "I heard of that when I was away, but I didn't know the reason why they'd set em free, till I got home."

"What dew ye callate 's the reason?"

"I see they've made slaves of the poor folks, and don't need the niggers any more," replied Perez, as quietly as if he were making the most casual remark.

But still the people stared at him and looked questioningly at each other, so bereft of magnetic force is language, though it express our inmost convictions, when we do not believe that the heart of the speaker beats in sympathy with what he says.

"I don' quite git yer idee. Haow dew ye make out that air 'bout poor folks bein slaves?" said Ezra Phelps dryly.

It was evident that any man who thought he was going to get at the real feelings of these rustics without first gaining their confidence, little understood the shrewd caution of the race.

"I make it out this way," replied Perez. "I find pretty much every rich man has a gang of debtors working for him, working out their debts. If they are idle, if they dispute with him, if they don't let him do what he pleases with them and their families, he sends them to jail with a word, and there they stay till he wants to let them out. No man can interfere between him and them. He does with em whatsoever he will. And that's why I call them slaves."

Now, Meshech Little was slightly intoxicated. By that mysterious faculty, whereby the confirmed drunkard, although absolutely impecunious, nevertheless manages to keep soaked, while other thirsty men can get nothing, he had obtained rum. And Meshech it was who, proceeding in that spirit of frankness engendered by the bottle, now brought about the solution of a misunderstanding, that was becoming painful.

"Wha' ye say, Perez, z'all right, but wha'n time be *yew* a sayin on it fer? Ye be dressed so fine, an a cap'n b'sides, that we callated ye'd take yer tod tew the store, long with the silk stockins, 'stid o' consortin with common folks like we be.''

There was a general sensation. Every mouth was opened, and every neck craned forward to catch the reply.

"Did you think so, Meshech? Well, you see you are mistaken. There's not a man among you has less cause to love the silk stockings, as you call them, than I have, and you Meshech ought to know it. Nine years ago, my brother Reub and I marched with the minute men. Parson and Squire Woodbridge, and Squire Edwards and all of em, came round us and said, 'We'll take care of your father and mother. We'll never forget what you are doing to-day.' Yesterday I came home to find my father and mother waiting to be sold out by the sheriff, and go to the poor house; and Reub, I found my brother Reub, rotting to death in Barrington jail.''

"By gosh, I forgot baout Reub, I declar I did,'' exclaimed Meshech, contritely.

"Give us yer hand,'' said Israel, "I forgot same ez Meshech, an I misdoubted ye. This be Ezra Phelps, ez owns the new mill.''

"Shake agin,'' said Peleg, extending his hand.

There was exhilaration as well as cordiality in the faces of the men, who now crowded around Perez, an exhilaration which had its source in the fact, that one whose appearance and bearing identified him with the gentlemen, was on their side. It filled them with more encouragement, than would have done the accession of a score of their own rank and sort. Brawn and muscle they could themselves supply, but for leadership, social, political and religious, they had always been accustomed to look to the gentlemen of the community, and from this lifelong and inherited habit, came the new sense of confidence and moral sanction, which they felt in having upon their side in the present crisis, one in whom they had instinctively recognized the traits of the superior caste.

"Hev ye hearn the news from Northampton, Perez?" asked Israel.

"Yes, and if you men are as much in earnest as I am, there'll be news from Barrington to-morrow," replied Perez, glancing around.

"Ef thar ain't, there'll be a lot on us disappinted, fer we be all a callatin tew go thar tew see," said Israel, significantly.

"We'll git yer brother aouter jail, fer ye, Perez, an ef thar's any fightin with the m'lishy, ye kin show us haow, I guess."

Meshech, as before intimated, was partially drunk, and spoke out of the fullness of his heart. But except for this one outburst, a stranger, especially one who did not know the New England disposition, and its preference for innuendo to any other mode of speech, in referring to the most important and exciting topics, would have failed entirely to get the idea that these farmers and laborers contemplated an act of armed rebellion on the morrow. He would, indeed, have heard frequent allusions to the probability there would be great goings on at Barrington, next morning, and intimations more or less explicit, on the part of nearly every man present, that he expected to be on hand to see what was done. But there was no intimation that they, themselves, expected to be the doers. Many, indeed, perhaps most, had very likely no distinct idea, of personally doing anything, nor was it at all necessary that they should have in order to ensure the expected outbreak, when the time should come. Given an excited crowd, all expecting something to be done which they desire to have done, and all the necessary elements of mob action are present.

THE FIRST ENCOUNTER

The next morning by six o'clock, a large number of persons had gathered on the green at Stockbridge, in consequence of an understanding that those intending to witness the goings on at Barrington, should rendezvous at the tavern, and go down together, whereby their own hearts would be made stronger, and their enemies the more impressed. A good many had, indeed, gone on ahead, singly, or in parties. Meshech Little, who lived on the Barrington road, said that he hadn't had a wink of sleep since four o'clock, for the noise of passing teams and pedestrians. Those who owned horses and carts, including such men as Israel Goodrich and Ezra Phelps, had preferred that mode of locomotion, but there were, nevertheless, as many as one hundred men and boys in the muster on the green. Perhaps a quarter of them had muskets, the others carried stout cudgels.

All sorts of rumors were flying about. One story was that the militia had been ordered out with a dozen rounds of cartridges, to defend the court and jail. Some even had heard that a cannon had been placed in front of the court house, and trained on the Stockbridge road. On the other hand, it was asserted that the court would not try to sit at all. As now one, and now another, of these contradictory reports prevailed, ebullitions of courage and symptoms of panic alternated among the people. It was easy to see that they contemplated the undertaking, on which they were embarking, not without a good deal of nervousness. Abner was going from group to group, trying to keep up their spirits.

"Hello," he exclaimed, coming across Jabez Flint. "Look a here, boys. Derned ef Jabez ain't a comin long with the res' on us. Wal, Jabez, I swow, I never callated ez I sh'd be a fightin long side o' ye. Misry makes strange bedfellers, though."

"It's you ez hez changed sides, not me," responded the Tory. "I wuz allers agin the state, an naow ye've come over tew my side."

Abner scratched his head.

"I swan, it doos look so. Anyhow, I be glad tew see ye tidday. I see ye've got yer gun, Jabez. Ye muss be keerful. Loryers is so derndly like foxes, that ye mout hit one on em by mistake."

There was a slight snicker at this, but the atmosphere was decidedly too heavy for jokes. However boldly they might discourse at the tavern of an evening, over their mugs of flip, about taking up arms and hanging the lawyers, it was not without manifold misgivings, that these law-abiding farmers found themselves on the point of being actually arrayed against the public authorities in armed rebellion. The absence of Israel Goodrich and Ezra Phelps, who were looked up to as the most substantial in estate and general respectability of those who inclined to the popular side, was moreover unfortunate, although it was supposed that they would be present at Barrington.

Meshech, indeed, in spite of the earliness of the hour, was full of pot-valor, and flourished his gun in a manner more perilous to those about him than to the state authorities, but his courage reeked so strongly of its source, that the display was rather discouraging than otherwise to the sober men around. Paul Hubbard, who had come down from the ironworks with thirty men or more, presently drew Abner aside and said:

"See here. It won't do to wait round any longer. We must start. They're losing all their grit standing here and thinking it over."

But the confabulation was interrupted by a cry of panic from Obadiah Weeks:

"Golly, here come the slectmen!"

"Hell!" exclaimed Hubbard, whirling on his heel, and taking in the situation with a glance, while Abner's face was expressive of equal consternation.

The local authorities had been so quiet the day before, that no interference on their part had been thought of.

But here in a body came the five selectmen, cane in hand, headed by Jahleel Woodbridge, wearing his most awful frown, and looking like the embodied majesty of law. The actions and attitudes of the crowd were like those of scholars interrupted by the entrance of the master in the midst of a scene of uproar. Those nearest the corners of the tavern promptly slunk behind it. Obadiah slipped around to the further side of the buttonwood tree before the tavern. There was a general movement in the body of the crowd, caused by the effort of each individual to slip quietly behind somebody else, while from the edges, men began to sneak homewards across the green, at a rate, which, had the warning been a little longer, would have left no assemblage at all by the time the selectmen arrived on the spot. Those who could not find shelter behind their fellows, and could not escape save by a dead run, pulled their hats over their eyes and looked on the ground, slyly dropping their cudgels, meanwhile, in the grass. There was not a gun to be seen.

With his head thrown back in the stiffest possible manner, his lips pursed out, and throwing glances like lashes right and left, Woodbridge, followed by the other selectmen, passed through the midst of the people, until he reached the stone step before the tavern door. He stepped up on this, and ere he opened his lips, swept the shame-faced assemblage before him with a withering glance. What with those who had pulled their hats over their eyes, and those who had turned their backs to him in anxiety to avoid identification, there was not an eye that met his. Abner himself, brave as a lion with his own class, was no braver than any one of them when it came to encountering one of the superior caste, to which he, and his ancestors before him, had looked up as their rulers and leaders by prescription. And so it must be written of even Abner, that he had somehow managed to get the trunk of the buttonwood tree, which sheltered Obadiah, between a part at least of his own enormous bulk, and Squire Woodbridge's eye. Paul Hubbard's bitter hatred of gentlemen, so far stood him in stead of courage, that it would not let him hide himself. He stood in plain view, but with his face half averted from Woodbridge, while his lip curled in bitter scorn of his own craven spirit. For it must be remembered that I am writing not of the American farmer and laborer of this democratic age, but of men who were separated but by a generation or two from the peasant serfs of England, and who under the stern and repressive rule of the untitled aristocracy of the colonies, had enjoyed little opportunity for outgrowing inherited instincts of servility.

And now it was that Perez Hamlin, who had been all this while within the tavern, his attention attracted by the sudden silence which had fallen on the people without, stepped to the door, appearing on the threshold just above Squire Woodbridge's head and a little to one side of him. At a glance he saw the way things were going. Already half demoralized by the mere presence and glance of the magnates, a dozen threatening words from the opening lips of Woodbridge would suffice to send these incipient rebels, like whipped curs, to their homes. He thought of Reub, and for a moment his heart was filled with grief and terror. Then he had an inspiration.

In the crowd was one known as Little Pete, a German drummer of Reidesel's Hessian corps, captured with Burgoyne's army. Brought to Stockbridge and quartered there as a prisoner he had continued to live in the town since the war.

Abner had somewhere procured an old drum for Pete, and with this hung about his neck, the sticks in his hands, he now stood not ten feet away from the tavern door. He spoke but little English, and, being a foreigner, had none of that awe for the selectmen, alike in their personal and official characters, which unnerved the village folk. Left isolated by the falling back of the people around him, Pete was now staring at these dignitaries in stolid indifference. They did not wear uniforms, and Pete had never learned to respect or fear anything not in uniform.

Having first brought the people before him, to the fitting preliminary stage of demoralization, by the power of his eye, Woodbridge said in stern, authoritative tones, the more effective for being low pitched,

"You may well" ——

That was as far, however, as he got. With the first sound of his voice, Perez stepped down beside him. Drawing his sword, which he had put on that morning, he waved it with a commanding gesture, and looking at little Pete, said with a quick, imperious accent:

"Drum!"

If a man in an officer's uniform, with a shining piece of steel in his hand, should order Pete to jump into the mouth of a cannon, he would no more think of hesitating, than the cannon itself of refusing to go off when the linstock was pulled. Without the change of a muscle in his heavy face, he raised the drumsticks and brought them down on the sheepskin.

And instantly the roll of the drum deafened the ears of the people, utterly drowning the imperious tones of the selectman, and growing louder and swifter from moment to moment, as the long unused wrists of the drummer recalled their former cunning.

Woodbridge spoke yet a few words without being able to hear himself. Then, his smooth, fleshy face purple with rage, he wheeled and glared at Hamlin. It did not need the drum to silence him now. He was so overcome with amazement and passion that he could not have articulated a word. But if he thought to face down the man by his side, he was mistaken. At least a head taller than Woodbridge, Perez turned and looked down into the congested eyes of the other with cool, careless, defiance.

And how about the people who looked on? The confident, decisive tone of Hamlin's order to the drummer, the bold gesture that enforced it, the fearless contempt for the village great man, which it implied, the unflinching look with which he met his wrathful gaze, and accompanying all these, the electrifying roll of the drum with its martial suggestions, had acted like magic on the crowd. Those who had slunk away came running back. Muskets rose to shoulders, sticks were again brandished, and the eyes of the people, a moment ago averted and downcast, rose defiantly. On every face there was a broad grin of delight. Even Paul Hubbard's cynical lips were wreathed with a smile of the keenest satisfaction, and he threw upon Perez one of the few glances of genuine admiration which men of his sardonic type ever have to spare for anybody.

For a few moments Woodbridge hesitated, uncertain what to do. To remain standing there, was impossible, with this crowd of his former vassals on the broad grin at his discomfiture. To retire was to confess defeat. The question was settled, however, when one of his official associates, unable longer to endure the din of the drum, desperately clapped both hands over his ears. At this the crowd began to guffaw uproariously, and seeing that it was high time to see about saving what little dignity he still retained, Woodbridge led the way into the tavern, whither he was incontinently followed by his compeers.

Instantly, at a gesture from Perez, the drum ceased, and his voice sounded strangely clear in the sudden and throbbing silence, as he directed little Pete to head the column, and gave the order to march. With a cheer, and a tread that shook the ground, the men set out. Perez remained standing before the tavern, till the last man had passed, by way of guarding against any new move by the selectmen, and then mounting his horse, rode along the column.

They were about half a mile out of Stockbridge, when Abner, accompanied by Paul Hubbard, approached Perez, and remarked:

"The fellers all on em says, ez haow ye'll hev tew be cap'n o' this ere kumpny. Thar's no use o' shilly-shallyin the business, we've got tew hev somebody ez kin speak up tew the silk stockins. Hain't that so, Paul?"

Hubbard nodded, but did not speak. It was gall and wormwood to his jealous and ambitious spirit, to concede the leadership to another, but his good sense forced him to recognize the necessity of so doing in the present case.

"Abner," replied Perez, "you know I only want to get Reub out. That's why I interfered when the plan looked like falling through. I don't want to be captain, man, I'd no notion of that."

"Nuther had I," said Abner, "till ye tackled the Squire, an then I see quick ez a flash that ye'd got ter be, an so'd all the other fellers. We sh'd a kerflummuxed sure's taxes, ef ye hadn't done jess what ye did. An naow, ye've got tew be cap'n, whether or no."

"Well," said Perez, "If I can do anything for you, I will. We're all in the same boat, I suppose. But if I'm captain, you two must be lieutenants."

"Yes, we're a gonter be," replied Abner. "Ye kin depend on us in a scrimmage, but ye muss sass the silk stockins."

Meanwhile the men, as they marched along the road in some semblance of military order, were eagerly discussing the recent passage between the dreaded Squire and their new champion. Their feeling about Perez seemed to be a certain odd mingling of respect, with an exultant sense of proprietorship in him as a representative of their own class, a farmer's son who had made himself as fine a gentleman as any of the silk stockings, and could face down the Squire himself.

"Did ye see haow Squire looked at Perez wen Pete begun tew drum?" observed Peleg. "I reckoned he wuz a gonter lay hans ontew him."

"Ef he had, by jimmeny, I b'leeve Cap'n would a hit him a crack ez would a knocked him inter the middle o' nex week," said Meshech.

"Oh, gosh, I ony wisht he hed," cried Obadiah, quite carried away at the wild thought of the mighty Squire rolling on the grass with a bloody nose.

"I allers hearn ez them Hamlin boys hed good blood intew em," observed a farmer. "Mrs. Hamlin's a Hawley, one o' them air River Gods, ez they calls em daown Hampshire way. Her folks wuz riled wen she tuk up with Elnathan, I hearn."

GREAT GOINGS ON AT BARRINGTON

As the company from Stockbridge surmounted the crest of a hill, about half way to Barrington, they saw a girl in a blue tunic, a brown rush hat, and a short gown, of the usual butternut dye, trudging on in the same direction, some distance ahead. As she looked back, in evident amazement at the column of men marching after her, Perez thought that he recognized the face, and on coming up with her, she proved to be, in fact, no other than Prudence Fennell, the little lass who had called at the house Sunday evening to inquire about her father down at the jail, and whose piteous grief at the report Perez was obliged to give, had determined Abner and him to attempt the rescue of George, as well as Reub, at whatever additional risk.

Far enough were they then from dreaming that two days later would find them leading a battalion of armed men, by broad daylight along the high road, to free the captives by open force. As readily would they then have counted on an earthquake to open the prison doors, as on this sudden uprising of the people in their strength.

As the men came up, Prudence stopped to let them pass by, her fresh, pretty face expressive of considerable dismay. As she shrunk closely up to the rail fence that lined the highway, she looked with timid recognition up at Perez, as if to claim his protection.

"Where are you going?" he asked kindly, stopping his horse.

"I'm going to see father," she said with a tremulous lip.

"Poor little lassie, were you going to walk all the way?"

"It is nothing," she said, "I could not wait, you know. He might die," and her bosom heaved with a sob that would fain break forth.

Perez threw himself from his horse.

"We are all going to the jail," he said. "You shall come with us, and ride upon my horse. Men, she shall lead us."

The men, whose discipline was not as yet very rigid, had halted and crowded around to listen to the dialogue, and received this proposition with a cheer. Prudence would far rather had them go on, and leave her to make her own way, but she was quite too much scared to resist as Perez lifted her upon his saddle. He shortened one of the stirrups, to support her foot, and then the column took up its march under the new captain, Perez walking by her side and leading the horse.

Had he arranged this stroke beforehand, he could not have hit on a more effective device for toning up the morals of the men. Those in whose minds the old misgivings as to their course had succeeded the sudden inspiration of Little Pete's drum, now felt that the child riding ahead lent a new and sacred sanction to their cause. They all knew her story, and to their eyes she seemed, at this moment, an embodiment of the spirit of suffering and outraged humanity, which had nerved them for this day's work. A more fitting emblem, a more inspiring standard, could not have been borne before them. But it must not be supposed that even this prevented, now and then, a conscience-stricken individual from stopping to drink at some brook crossing the road, until the column had passed the next bend in the road, and then slinking home cross-lots, taking an early opportunity after arriving to pass the store, so as to be seen and noted as not among the rioters. But whatever was lost in this way, if the defection of such material can be called a loss, was more than made up by the recruits which swelled the ranks from the farmhouses along the road. And so, by the time they entered Muddy Brook, a settlement just outside of Great Barrington, through which the road from Stockbridge then passed, they numbered full one hundred and fifty.

Muddy Brook was chiefly inhabited by a poor and rather low class of people, who, either from actual misery or mere riotous inclination, might naturally be expected to join in any movement against constituted authority. But instead of gaining any accession of forces here, the Stockbridge party found the place almost deserted. Even the small boys, and the dogs were gone, and apparently a large part of the able-bodied women as well.

"What be all the folks?" called out Abner to a woman who stood with a baby in arms at an open door.

"Over tew Barrington seein the fun. Thar be great dewins," she replied.

This news imparted valor to the most faint-hearted, for it was now apparent that this was not a movement in which Stockbridge was alone engaged, not a mere local revolt, but a general, popular uprising, whose extent would be its justification. And yet, prepared as they thus were, to find a goodly number of sympathizers already on the ground, it was with mingled exultation and astonishment that, on topping the high hill which separates Muddy Brook from Great Barrington, and gaining a view of the latter place, they beheld the streets packed, and the green in front of the court house fairly black with people.

There was a general outburst of surprise and satisfaction.

"By gosh, it looks like gineral trainin, or'n ordination."

"Looks kinder 'z if a good many fellers b'sides us hed business with the jestices this mornin."

"I'd no idee courts wuz so pop'lar."

"They ain't stocks nuff in Berkshire fer all the fellers as is out tidday, that's one sure thing, by gol."

"No, by Jock, nor Saddleback mounting ain't big nuff pil-

lory to hold em, nuther," were some of the ejaculations
which at once expressed the delight and astonishment of the
men, and at the same time betrayed the nature of their previous misgivings, as to the possible consequences of this day's
doings. Estimates of the number of the crowd in Barrington,
which were freely offered, ranged all the way from two thousand to ten thousand, but Perez, practiced in such calcula-
tions, placed the number at about eight or nine hundred men,
half as many women and boys. What gave him the liveliest
satisfaction was the absence of any military force, not indeed
that he would have hesitated to fight if he could not have
otherwise forced access to the jail, but he had contemplated
the possibility of such a bloody collision between the people
and militia, with much concern.

"There'll be no fighting to-day, boys," he said, turning to
the men, "you'd better let off your muskets, so there may be
no accidents. Fire in the air," and thus with a ringing salvo,
that echoed and reëchoed among the hills and was answered
with acclamations from the multitude in the village, the
Stockbridge battalion, with the girl riding at its head, entered Great Barrington, and breaking ranks, mingled with
the crowd.

"Bully, we be jess in time to see the fun," cried Obadiah
delightedly, as the courthouse bell rang out, thereby announc-
ing that the justices had left their lodgings to proceed to the
courthouse and open court.

"I declar for't," exclaimed Jabez, "I wonder ef they be gonter try tew hole court 'n spite o' all that crowd. Thar they
be sure's rates."

And, indeed, as he spoke, the door of the residence of Justice Dwight opened, and High Sheriff Israel Dickinson, followed by Justice Dwight and the three other justices of the
quorum, issued therefrom, and took up their march directly
toward the courthouse, seemingly oblivious of the surging
mass of a thousand men, which barred their way.

The sheriff advanced with a goose step, carrying his wand of office, and the justices strode in Indian file behind him. They were dressed in fine black suits, with black silk hose, silver buckles on their shoes, fine white ruffled shirts, and ponderous cocked hats upon their heavily powdered wigs. Their chests were well thrown out, their chins were held in air, their lips were judicially pursed, and their eyes were contemplatively fixed on vacancy, as if they had never for a moment admitted the possibility that any impediment might be offered to their progress. It must be admitted that their bearing worthily represented the prestige of ancient authority and moral majesty of law. Nor did the mob fail to render the tribute of an involuntary admiration to this imposing and apparently invincible advance. It had evidently been taken for granted that the mere assemblying and riotous attitude of so great a multitude, bristling with muskets and bludgeons, would suffice to prevent the justices from making any attempt to hold court. It was with a certain awe, and a silence interrupted only by murmurs of astonishment, that the people now awaited their approach. Perhaps had the throng been less dense, it might have justified the serene and haughty confidence of the justices, by opening a path for them. But however disposed the first ranks might have been to give way, they could not by reason of the pressure from behind, and on every side.

Still the sheriff continued to advance, with as much apparent confidence of opening a way as if his wand were the veritable rod wherewith Moses parted the Red Sea, until he almost trod on the toes of the shrinking first rank. But there he was fain to pause. Moral force cannot penetrate a purely physical obstacle.

And when the sheriff stopped, the justices marching behind him also stopped. Not indeed that their honors so far forgot their dignity as to appear to take direct cognizance of the vulgar and irregular impediment before them. It was the sheriff's business to clear the way for them. And although Justice Dwight's face was purple with indignation, he, as well as his associates, continued to look away into vacancy, suffering not their eyes to catch any of the glances of the people before them.

"Make way! Make way for the honorable justices of the Court of Common Pleas of the Commonwealth of Massachusetts!" cried the sheriff, in loud, imperative tones.

A dead silence of several moments followed, in which the rattling of a farmer's cart, far down the street, as it brought in a belated load of insurgents from Sheffield, was distinctly audible. Then somebody in the back part of the crowd, impressed with a certain ludicrousness in the situation, tittered. Somebody else tittered, then a number, and presently a hoarse haw haw of derision, growing momentarily louder, and soon after mingled with yells, hoots and catcalls, burst forth from a thousand throats. The prestige of the honorable justices of the Court of Common Pleas, was gone.

A moment still they hesitated. Then the sheriff turned and said something to them in a low voice, and they forthwith faced about and deliberately marched back toward their lodgings. In this retrograde movement the sheriff acted as rear guard, and he had not gone above a dozen steps, before a rotten egg burst on one shoulder of his fine new coat, and as he wheeled around an apple took him in the stomach, and at the same moment the cocked hat of Justice Goodrich of Pittsfield, was knocked off with a stone. His honor did not apparently think it expedient to stop just then to pick it up, and Obadiah Weeks, leaping forward, made it a prey, and instantly elevated it on a pole, amid roars of derisive laughter. The retreat of the justices had indeed so emboldened the more ruffianly and irresponsible element of the crowd, many of whom were drunk, that it was just as well for the bodily safety of their honors that the distance to their lodgings was no greater. As it was, stones were flying fast, and the mob was close on the heels of the sheriff when the house was gained, and as he attempted to shut the door after him, there was a rush of men, bent on entering with him. He knocked down the first, but would have been instantly overpowered and trampled on, had not Perez Hamlin, followed by Abner, Peleg, Abe Konkapot and half a dozen other Stockbridge men, shouldered their way through the crowd, and come to his relief. Where then had Perez been, meantime?

JUDGE DWIGHT'S SIGNATURE

As soon as the Stockbridge battalion had arrived on the green at Great Barrington, and broken ranks, Perez had directed Abner to pass the word to all who had friends in the jail, and presently a party of forty or fifty men was following him, as he led the way toward that building, accompanied by Prudence, who had not dismounted. The rest of them could attend to the stopping of the court. His concern was with the rescue of his brother. But he had not traversed over half the distance when the cry arose:

"They're stoning the judges!"

Thus recalled to his responsibilities as leader of at least a part of the mob, he had turned, and followed by a dozen men, had hurried back to the rescue, arriving in the nick of time. Standing in the open door of the house to which the justices had retired, the rescued sheriff just behind him in the hall, he called out:

"Stand back! Stand back! What more do you want, men? The court is stopped."

But the people murmured. The Great Barrington men did not know Perez, and were not ready to accept his dictation.

"We've stopped court to-day, sartin," said one, "but wot's to hender they're holden of it to-morrer, or ez soon's we be gone, an hevin every one on us in jail?"

"What do you want, then?" asked Perez.

"We want some sartainty baout it."

"They've got tew 'gree not ter hold no more courts till the laws be changed," were replies that seemed to voice the sentiments of the crowd.

"Leave it to me, and I'll get you what you want," said Perez, and he went down the corridor to the kitchen at the back of the house, where the sheriff had told him he would find the justices. Although the room had been apparently chosen because it was the farthest removed from the public, the mob had already found out their retreat, and a nose was flattened against each pane of the windows. Tall men peered in over short men's shoulders, and cudgels were displayed in a way not at all reassuring to the inmates.

Their honors by no means wore the unruffled and remotely superior aspect of a few minutes before. It must be frankly confessed, as regards the honorable Justices Goodrich of Pittsfield, Barker of Cheshire, and Whiting of Great Barrington, that they looked decidedly scared, as in fact, they had some right to be. It might have been supposed, indeed, that the valor of the entire quorum had gone into its fourth member, Justice Elijah Dwight, who, at the moment Perez entered the room, was being withheld by the combined strength of his agonized wife and daughter from sallying forth with a rusty Queen's arm to defend his mansion. His wig was disarranged with the struggle, and the powder shaken from it streaked a countenance, scholarly enough in repose no doubt, but just now purple with the three-fold wrath of one outraged in the combined characters of householder, host, and magistrate.

"Your honors," said Perez, "the people will not be satisfied without your written promise to hold no more courts till their grievances are redressed. I will do what I can to protect you, but my power is slight."

"Who is this fellow who speaks for the rabble?" demanded Dwight.

"My name is Hamlin."

"You are a disgrace to the uniform you wear. Do you know you have incurred the penalties of high treason?" exclaimed the justice.

"This is not the first time I have incurred those penalties in behalf of my oppressed countrymen, as that same uniform shows," retorted the other. "But it is not now a question of the penalties I have incurred, but how are you to escape the wrath of the people," he continued sharply.

"I shall live to see you hung, drawn and quartered for treason, you rascal," roared Dwight.

"Nay, sir. Do but think this man holds your life in his hands. Entreat him civilly," expostulated Madam Dwight.

"He means not so, sir," she added, turning to Perez.

"The fellers wanter know why in time that ere 'greement ain't signed. We can't keep em back much longer," Abner cried, rushing to the door of the kitchen a moment, and hurrying back to his post.

"Where are writing materials?" asked Justice Goodrich, nervously, as a stone broke through one of the window panes and feel on the table.

"I will bring them," said the young lady, Dwight's daughter.

"Do make haste, Miss," urged Justice Barker. "The mob is even now forcing an entrance."

"I forbid you to bring them. Remain here," thundered Dwight.

The girl paused, irresolute, pale and terrified.

"Go, Eliza," said her mother. "Disobey your father and save his life."

She went, and in a moment returned with the articles. Perez wrote two lines, and read them.

" 'We promise not to act under our commissions until the grievances of which the people complain are redressed.' Now sign that, and quickly, or it will be too late."

"Do you order us to sign?" said Barker, apparently willing to find in this appearance of duress an excuse for yielding.

"Not at all," replied Perez. "If you think you can make better terms with the people for yourselves, you are welcome to try. I should judge from the racket that they're on the point of coming in."

There was a hoarse howl from without, and Justices Goodrich, Barker and Whiting simultaneously grabbed for the pen. Their names were affixed in a trice.

"Will your honor sign?" said Perez to Dwight, who stood before the fireplace, silently regarding the proceedings. His first ebullition of rage had passed, and he appeared entirely calm.

"My associates may do as they please," he replied with dignity, "but it shall never be said that Elijah Dwight surrendered to a mob the commission which he received from his excellency, the governor, and their honors, the councillors of the Commonwealth."

"I admire your courage, sir, but I cannot answer for the consequences of your refusal," said Perez.

"For my sake sign, sir," urged Madam Dwight.

"Oh, sign, papa. They will kill you," cried Eliza.

"Methinks, it is but proper prudence, to seem to yield for the time being," said Goodrich.

"'Tis no more than the justices at Northampton have done," added Barker.

"I need not remind your honor that a pledge given under duress, is not binding," said Whiting.

But Dwight waved them away, saying merely, "I know my duty."

Suddenly Eliza Dwight stepped to the table and wrote something at the bottom of the agreement, and giving the paper to Perez said something to him in a low voice. But her father's keen eye had noted the act, and he said angrily:

"Child, have you dared to write my name?"

"Nay, father, I have not," replied the girl.

Even as she spoke there were confused cries, heavy falls, and a rush in the hall, and instantly the room was filled with men, their faces flushed with excitement and drink. The guard had been overpowered.

"Whar's that paper?"

"Hain't they signed?"

"We'll make ye sign, dum quick."

"We're a gonter tie ye up an give it to ye on the bare back."

"We'll give ye a dose o' yer own med'cin."

"I don' wanter hurt ye, sis, but ye muss git aout o' the way," said a burly fellow to Eliza, who, with her mother, had thrown herself between the mob and Justice Dwight, his undaunted aspect appearing to excite the special animosity of the rabble. The other three justices were huddled in the furthest corner.

"It's all right, men, it's all right. No need of any more words. Here's the paper," said Perez, authoritatively. A man caught it from his hand and gave it to another, saying,

"Here, Pete, ye kin read. Wot does it say?" Pete took the document in both hands, grasping it with unnecessary firmness, as if he depended in some degree on physical force to overcome the difficulties of decipherment, and proceeded slowly and with tremendous frowns to spell it out.

"We-promise-not-to-ak–under–our–c–o–m, –commishins –until-the-g–r–i–e –grievunces," —

"Wot be them?" demanded one of the crowd.

"That means taxes, 'n loryers, 'n debts, 'n all that. I've hearn the word afore," exclaimed another. "G'long Pete."

"Grievunces," proceeded the reader, "of-wich-the-people-complain."

"That's so."

"That's dern good. In course we complains."

"Is that writ so, Pete?"

"G'long, Pete, that ere's good."

"Complains," began the reader again.

"Go back tew the beginnin Pete, I los' the hang on't."

"Yes, go back a leetle, Pete. It be mos'z long ez a sermon."

"Shell I begin tew the beginnin?"

"Yes, begin tew the beginnin agin, so's we'll all on us git the hang."

"We–promise–not-tew-ak–under–our-commishins, - - until –the–g–r–grievunces–of - - wich–the–people - - complain, –are –r–e–d–r–redressed."

"Wot's redressed?"

"That's same ez 'bolished."

"Here be the names," pursued Pete.

"Charles Goodrich."

"He's the feller ez loss his hat."

"William Whiting."

"James Barker."

"Elijah Dwight."

"It's false," exclaimed Dwight, "my name's not there!"

But few, if any, heard or heeded his words, for at the moment Pete pronounced the last name, Perez shouted:

"Now, men, we've done this job, let's go to the jail and let out the debtors, come on," and suiting action to word he rushed out, and was followed pell-mell by the yelling crowd, all their truculent enthusiasm instantly diverted into this new channel.

The four justices, and the wife and daughter of Dwight, alone remained in the room. Even the people who had been staring in, with their noses flattened against the window panes, had rushed away to the new point of interest. Dwight stood steadfastly looking at his daughter, with a stern and Rhadamanthine gaze, in which, nevertheless, grief and reproachful surprise, not less than indignation, were expressed. The girl shrinking behind her mother, seemed more in terror than when the mob had burst into the room.

"And so my daughter has disobeyed her father, has told him a lie, and has disgraced him," said the justice, slowly and calmly, but in tones that bore a crushing weight of reproof.

"Add, sir, at least, that she has also saved his life," interposed one of the other justices.

"Oh, don't talk to me so, papa," cried the girl sobbing. "I didn't write your name, papa, I truly didn't."

"Do not add to your sin, by denials, my daughter. Did the fellow not read my name?" Dwight regarded her as he said this, as if he were somewhat disgusted at such persistent falsehood, and the others looked a little as if their sympathy with the girl had received a slight shock.

"But, papa, won't you believe me," sobbed the girl, clinging to her mother as not daring to approach him to whom she appealed. "I only wrote my own name."

"Your name, Eliza, but he read mine."

"Yes, but the pen was bad, you see, and my name looks so like yours, when it's writ carelessly, and the 'a' is a little quirked, and I wrote it carelessly, papa. Please forgive me. I didn't want to have you killed, and I quirked the 'a' a little."

The Rhadamanthine frown on Dwight's face yielded to a very composite expression, a look in which chagrin, tenderness, and a barely perceptible trace of amusement mingled. The girl instantly had her arms around his neck, and was crying violently on his shoulder, though she knew she was forgiven. He put his hand a moment gently on her head, and then unloosed her arms, saying, dryly,

"That will do, dear, go to your mother now. I shall see that you have better instruction in writing."

That was the only rebuke he ever gave her.

GREAT GOINGS ON AT BARRINGTON CONTINUED

When Perez and the men who with him were in the act of advancing on the jail, were so suddenly recalled by the cry that the people were stoning the judges, Prudence had been left quite alone, sitting on Perez' horse in the middle of the street. She had no clear idea what all this crowd and commotion in the village was about, nor even what the Stockbridge men had come down for in such martial array. She only knew that Mrs. Hamlin's son, the captain with the sword, had said he would bring her to her father, and now that he had run off taking all the other men with him, she knew not what to do or which way to turn. To her, thus perched up on the big horse, confused and scared by the tumult, approached a tall, sallow, gaunt old woman, in a huge green sunbonnet, and a butternut gown of coarsest homespun. Her features were strongly marked, but their expression was not unkindly, though just now troubled and anxious.

"I guess I've seen yew tew meetin," she said to Prudence. "Ain't you Fennell's gal?"

"Yes," replied the girl, "I come daown to see father." Prudence, although she had profited by having lived at service in the Woodbridge family, where she heard good English spoken, had frequent lapses into the popular dialect.

"I'm Mis Poor. Zadkiel Poor's my husban'. He's in jail over thar long with yer dad. He's kinder ailin, an I fetched daown some roots 'n yarbs as uster dew him a sight o' good, w'en he was ter hum. I thort mebbe I mout git to see him. Him as keeps jail lets folks in sometimes, I hearn tell."

"Do you know where the jail is?" asked the girl.

"It's that ere haouse over thar. It's in with the tavern."

"Let's go and ask the jailer if he'll let us in," suggested Prudence.

"I wuz gonter wait an' git Isr'el Goodrich tew go long an kinder speak fer me, ef I could," said Mrs. Poor. "He's considabul thought on by folks roun' here, and he's a neighbor o' ourn, an real kind, Isr'el Goodrich is. But I don' see him nowhar roun', an mebbe we mout's well go right along, an not wait no longer."

And so the two women went on toward the jail, and Prudence dismounted before the door of the tavern end, and tied the horse.

"I callate they muss keep the folks in that ere ell part, with the row o' leetle winders," said Mrs. Poor. She spoke in a hushed voice, as one speaks near a tomb. The girl was quite pale, and she stared with a scared fascination at the wall behind which her father was shut up. Timidly the women entered the open door. Both Bement and his wife were in the barroom.

"What dew ye want?" demanded the latter, sharply.

Mrs. Poor curtsied very low, and smiled a vague, abject smile of propitiation.

"If ye please, marm, I'm Mis Poor. He's in this ere jail fer debt. He's kinder pulin like, Zadkiel is, an I jess fetched daown some yarbs for him. He's been uster takin on em, an they doos him good, specially the sassafras. An I thort mebbe, marm, I mout git tew see him, bein ez he ain't a well man, an never wuz since I married him, twenty-five year agone come nex' Thanksgivin."

"And I want to see father, if you please, marm. My father's George Fennell. Is he very sick marm?" added Prudence eagerly, seeing that Mrs. Poor was forgetting her.

"I don' keer who ye be, an ye needn' waste no time o' tellin me," replied Mrs. Bement, her pretty blue eyes as hard as steel. "Ye couldn't go intew that jail not ef ye wuz Gin'ral Washington. I ain't goin ter hev no women folks a bawlin an a blubberin roun' this ere jail 's long's *my* husban' keeps it, an that's flat.

"I won't cry a bit, if you'll only let me see father," pleaded Prudence, two great tears gathering in her eyes, even as she spoke, and testifying to the value of her promise. "And—and I'll scrub the floor for you, too. It needs it, and I'm a good scrubber, Mrs. Woodbridge says I am."

"I'd take it kind of ye, I would," said Mrs. Poor, "ef ye'd let me in jess fer a minit. He'd set store by seein of me, an I could give him the yarbs. He ain't a well man, an never wuz, Zadkiel ain't. Ye needn't let the gal in. It don' matter 's much about her, an gals is cryin things. I'll scrub yer floor better'n she ever kin, an come to look it doos kinder need it," and she turned her agonized eyes a moment upon the floor in affected critical inspection.

"Cephas, see that crowd comin. What do they mean? Put them women out. G'long there, git out, quick! Shut the door, Cephas. Put up the bar. What ever's comin to us?"

Well might Mrs. Bement say so, for the sight that had caught her eyes as she stood confronting the women and the open door, was no less an one than a mass of nearly a thousand men and boys, bristling with clubs and guns, rushing directly toward the jail.

Scarcely had the women been thrust out, and the white-faced Bement dropped the bar into its sockets across the middle of the door, than there was a rushing, tramping sound before the house, like the noise of many waters, and a great hubbub of hoarse voices. Then came a heavy blow, as if with the hilt of a sword against the door, and a loud voiced called,

"Open, and be quick about it!"

"Don't do it, Cephas, the house is stout, and mebbe help'll come," said Mrs. Bement, although she trembled.

But Cephas, though generally like clay in the hands of his wife, was at this instant dominated by a terror greater than his fear of her. He lifted the bar from the sockets, and was instantly sent staggering back against the wall as the door burst open. The room was instantly filled to its utmost capacity with men, who dropped the butts of their muskets on the floor with a jar that made the bottles in the bar clink in concert.

Bement who had managed to get behind the bar, stood there with a face like ashes, his flabby cheeks relaxed with terror so they hung like dewlaps. He evidently expected nothing better than to be butchered without mercy on the spot.

"Good morning, Mr. Bement," said Perez, as coolly as if he had just dropped in for a glass of flip.

"Good morning sir," faintly articulated the landlord.

"You remember me, perhaps. I took dinner here, and visited by brother in the jail last Saturday. I should like to see him again. Will you be kind enough to hand me the keys, there behind you?" Bement stared as if dazed at Perez, looked around at the crowd of men, and then looked back at Perez again, and still stood gaping.

"Did ye hear the cap'n?" shouted Abner in a voice of thunder. Bement gave a start of terror, and involuntarily turned to take the bunch of keys down from the nail. But by the time he had turned, the keys were no longer there.

It had been easy to see from the first, that Mrs. Bement was made of quite different stuff from her husband. As she stood by his side behind the bar, although she was tremulous with excitement, the look with which she had faced the crowd was rather vixenish than frightened. There was a vicious sparkle in her eyes, and the color of her cheeks was concentrated in two small spots, one under each cheek bone. Just as her husband, succumbing to the inevitable, was turning to take the keys from their nail and deliver them over, she quietly reached behind him, and snatched them. Then, with a deft motion opening the top of her gown a little, she dropped them into her bosom, and looked at Perez with a defiant expression, as much as to say, "Now I should like to see you get them."

There was no doubt about the little shrew being thoroughly game, and yet her act was less striking as evidence of her bravery, than as testifying her confidence in the chivalry of the rough men before her. And, indeed, it was comical to see the dumbfounded and chop-fallen expression on their flushed and excited faces, as they took in the meaning of this piece of strategy. They had taken up arms against their government, and but a few moments before had been restrained with difficulty from laying violent hands upon the august judges of the land, but not the boldest of them thought it possible to touch this woman. There were men here whom neither lines of bayonets nor walls of stone would have turned back, but not one of them was bold enough to lay a forcible hand upon the veil that covered a woman's breast. They were Americans.

There was a dead silence. The men gaped at each other, and Perez himself looked a little foolish for a moment. Then he turned to Abner and said in a grimly quiet way:

"Knock Bement down. Then four of you swing him by his arms and legs and break the jail door through with his head."

"Ye wouldn' murder me, cap'n," gasped the hapless man. In a trice Abner had hauled him out from behind the bar, and tripped him up on the floor. Then three other men, together with Abner, seized him by the hands and feet, and half dragged, half carried him across the room to the door in the middle of one of the sides which opened into the jail corridor.

"Swing the cuss three times, so's ter git kinder a goin, an then we'll see w'ether his head or the door's the thickest," said Abner.

"Giv' em the keys, Marthy. They're a killin me," screeched Bement.

The woman had set her teeth. Her face was a little whiter, the red spots under her cheek bones were a little smaller and a little redder than before. That was all the sign she gave. Putting her hand convulsively over the spot on her bosom where the desired articles were secreted, she replied in a shrill voice:

"I shell keep the keys, Cephas. It's my dewty. Pray, Cephas, that I may hev strength given me ter dew my dewty."

"Ye won't see me killed 'fore yer eyes, will ye, give em the keys I tell ye," shrieked Bement, as they began to swing him, and Abner said:

"One."

The woman looked a bit more like going into hysterics, but not a whit more like yielding.

"Mebbe t'wont kill ye, an they can't bust the door, no-how. Mebbe they'll git tuckered 'fore long. If wust comes to wust, it's a comfort ter know ez ye're a perfesser in good stannin."

Bement had doubtless had previous experience of a certain tenacity of purpose on the part of his spouse, for ceasing to address further adjurations to her, he began to appeal for mercy to the men.

"Two," said Abner, as they swung him again.

Now, Mrs. Poor and Prudence, having been thrust out of the barroom just before the mob thundered up against the barred door, had been borne back into the room again by the rush when the door was opened, and it was Mrs. Poor who now made a diversion.

"Look a here, Abner Rathbun," she said. "W'at in time's the use of murd'rin the man? He hain't done nothin. It's the woman, as has got the keys. She wouldn' let me inter see Zadkiel, an I'm jess a itchin tew git my hands ontew her, an that's the trewth, ef I be a perfesser. You let the man alone. I'll git them keys, or my name ain't Resignation Ann Poor."

There was a general murmur of approval, and without waiting for orders from Perez, Abner and his helpers let Bement drop, and he scrambled to his feet.

Mrs. Bement began to pant. She knew well enough that she had nothing to fear from all the men in Massachusetts, but one of her own sex was a more formidable enemy. And, indeed, a much more robust person than the jailer's little wife, might have been excused for not relishing a tussle with the tall, rawboned old woman, with hands brown, muscular, and labor hardened as a man's, who now laid her big green sunbonnet on the counter, and stepping to the open end of the bar, advanced toward her. Mrs. Poor held her hands before her about breast high, at half arm's length, elbows depressed, palms turned outward, the fingers curved like a cat's claws. There was an expression of grim satisfaction on her hard features.

Mrs. Bement stood awaiting her, breathing hard, evidently scared, but equally evidently, furious.

"Give em the keys, Marthy. She'll kill ye," called out Bement, from the back of the room.

But she paid no attention to this. Her fingers began to curve back like claws, and her hands assumed the same feline attitude as Mrs. Poor's. It was easy to see that the pluck of the little woman extorted a certain admiration from the very men who had fathers, sons and brothers in the cells beyond. She was not a bit more than half as big as her antagonist, but she looked game to the backbone, and the forthcoming result was not altogether to be predicted. You could have heard a pin drop in the room, as the men leaned over the counter with faces expressive of intensest excitement, while those behind stood on tiptoe to see. For the moment everything else was forgotten in the interest of the impending combat. Mrs. Bement seemed drawing back for a spring. Then suddenly, quick as lightning, she put her hand in her bosom, drew out the keys, and throwing them down on the counter, burst into hysterical sobs.

In another moment the jail door was thrown open, and the men were rushing down the corridor.

END OF THE GOINGS ON AT BARRINGTON

Then, presently, the jail was full of cries of horror and indignation. For each cell door as it was unbarred and thrown open revealed the same piteous scene, the deliverers starting back, or standing quite transfixed before the ghastly and withered figures which rose up before them from dank pallets of putrid straw. The faces of these dismal apparitions expressed the terror and apprehension which the tumult and uproar about the jail had created in minds no longer capable of entertaining hope.

Ignorant who were the occupants of particular cells it was of course a matter of chance whether those who opened any one of them, were the friends of the unfortunates who were its inmates. But for a melancholy reason this was a matter of indifference. So ghastly a travesty on their former hale and robust selves, had sickness and sunless confinement made almost all the prisoners, that not even brothers recognized their brothers, and the corridor echoed with poignant voices, calling to the poor creatures:

"What's your name?" "Is this Abijah Galpin?" "Are you my brother Jake?" "Are you Sol Morris?" "Father, is it you?"

As they entered the jail with the rush of men, Perez had taken Prudence's hand, and remembering the location of Reuben's cell, stopped before it, lifted the bar, threw open the door and they went in. George Fennell was lying on the straw upon the floor. He had raised himself on one elbow, and was looking apprehensively to see what the opening of the door would reveal as the cause of this interruption to the usually sepulchral stillness of the jail. Reuben was standing in the middle of the floor, eagerly gazing in the same direction. Perez sprang to his brother's side, his face beautiful with the joy of the deliverer. If he had been a Frenchman, or an Italian, anything but an Anglo Saxon, he would have kissed him, with one of those noblest kisses of all, wherewith once in a lifetime, or so, men may greet each other. But he only supported him with one arm about the waist, and stroked his wasted cheek with his hand, and said:

"I've come for you Reub, old boy, you're free."

Prudence had first peered anxiously into the face of Reuben, and next glanced at the man lying on the straw. Then she plucked Perez by the sleeve, and said in an anguished voice:

"Father ain't here. Where is he?" and turned to run out.

"That's your father," replied Perez, pointing to the sick man.

The girl sprang to his side, and kneeling down, searched with straining eyes in the bleached and bony face, fringed with matted hair and long unkempt gray beard, for some trace of the full and ruddy countenance which she remembered. She would still have hesitated, but her father said:

"Prudy, my little girl, is it you?"

Her eyes might not recognize the lineaments of the face, but her heart recalled the intonation of tenderness, though the voice was weak and changed. Throwing her arms around his neck, pressing her full red lips in sobbing kisses upon his corpse-like face, she cried:

"Father! Oh Father!"

Presently the throng began to pour out of the jail, bringing with them those they had released. The news that the jail was being broken open, and the prisoners set free, had spread like wildfire through the thronged village, and nearly two thousand people were now assembled in front of and about the jail, including besides the people from out of town, nearly every man, woman and child in Great Barrington, not actually bedridden, excepting of course, the families of the magistrates, lawyers, court officers, and the wealthier citizens, who sympathized with them. These were trembling behind their closed doors, hoping, but by no means assured, that this sudden popular whirlwind, might exhaust itself, before involving them in destruction. And indeed the cries of pity, and the hoarse deep groans of indignation with which the throng before the jail received the prisoners as they were successively brought forth, were well calculated to inspire with apprehension, those who knew that they were held responsible by the public judgment for the deeds of darkness now being brought to light. It was now perhaps the old mother and young wife of a prisoner, holding up between them the son and husband, and guiding his tottering steps, that set the people crying and groaning. Now it was perhaps a couple of sturdy sons, unused tears running down their tanned cheeks, as they brought forth a white-haired father, blinking with bleared eyes at the forgotten sun, and gazing with dazed terror at the crowd of excited people. Now it was Perez Hamlin, leading out Reuben, holding him up with his arm, and crying like a baby in spite of all that he could do. Nor need he have been ashamed, for there were few men who were not in like plight. Then came Abner, and Abe Konkapot, stepping carefully, as they carried in their arms George Fennell, Prudence walking by his side, and holding fast his hand.

Nor must I forget to speak of Mrs. Poor. The big, raw-boned woman's hard-favored countenance was lit up with motherly solicitude, as she lifted, rather than assisted, Zadkiel, down the steps of the tavern.

"Wy don' ye take him up in yer arms?" remarked Obadiah Weeks, facetiously, but it was truly more touching than amusing, to see the protecting tenderness of the woman, for the puny little fellow whom an odd freak of Providence had given her for a husband, instead of a son.

Although Mrs. Poor movingly declared that "He warn't the shadder of hisself," the fact was, that having been but a short time in jail, Zadkiel showed few marks of confinement, far enough was he, from comparing in this respect, with the others, many of whom had been shut up for years. They looked, with the dead whiteness of their faces and hands, rather like grewsome cellar plants, torn from their native darkness, only to wither in the upper light and air, than like human organisms just restored to their normal climate. As they moved among the tanned and ruddy-faced people, their abnormal complexion made them look like representatives of the strange race of Albinos.

But saddest perhaps of all the sights were the debtors who found no acquaintances or relatives to welcome them as they came forth again helpless as at their first birth, into the world of bustle and sun and breeze. It was piteous to see them wandering about with feeble and sinewless steps, and vacant eyes, staring timidly at the noisy people, and shrinking dismayed from the throngs of sympathizing questioners which gathered round them. There were some whose names not even the oldest citizens could recall so long had they been shut up from the sight of men.

Jails in those days were deemed as good places as any for insane persons, and in fact were the only places available, so that, besides those whom long confinement had brought almost to the point of imbecility, there were several entirely insane and idiotic individuals among the prisoners. One of them went around in a high state of excitement declaring that it was the resurrection morning. Nor was the delusion altogether to be marvelled at considering the suddenness with which its victim had exchanged the cell, which for twenty years had been his home, for the bright vast firmament of heaven, with its floods of dazzling light and its blue and bottomless dome.

Another debtor, a man from Sheffield, as a prisoner of war during the revolution, had experienced the barbarities practiced by the British provost Cunningham at New York. Having barely returned home to his native village when he was thrust into jail as a debtor, he had not unnaturally run the two experiences together in his mind. It was his hallucination that he had been all the while a prisoner of the British at New York, and that the victorious Continental army had just arrived to deliver him and his comrades. In Perez he recognized General Washington.

"Ye was a long time comin, Ginral, but it's all right now," he said. "I knowd ye'd come at las', an I tole the boys not to git diskerridged. The redcoats has used us bad though, an I hope ye'll hang em, Gin'ral."

At the time of which I write, rape was practically an unknown crime in Berkshire, and theft extremely uncommon. But among the debtors there were a few criminals. These, released with the rest, were promptly recognized and seized by the people. The general voice was first for putting them back in the cells, but Abner declared that it would be doing them a kindness to knock them on the head rather than to send them back to such pigsties, and this view of the matter finding favor, the fellows were turned loose with a kick apiece and a warning to make themselves scarce.

In the first outburst of indignation over the horrible condition of the prison and the prisoners, there was a yell for Bement, and had the men, in their first rage, laid hands on him, it certainly would have gone hard with him. But he was not to be found, and it was not till some time after, that in ransacking the tavern, some one found him in the garret, hidden under a tow mattress stuffed with dried leaves, on which the hired man slept nights. He was hauled downstairs by the heels pretty roughly, and shoved and buffeted about somewhat, but the people having now passed into a comparatively exhilarated and good-tempered frame of mind, he underwent no further punishment, that is in his person. But that was saved only at the expense of his pocket, for the men insisted on his going behind the bar and treating the crowd, a process which was kept up until there was not a drop of liquor in his barrels, and scarcely a sober man in the village. Mrs. Bement, meanwhile, had been caught and held by some of the women, while one of the prisoners, a bestial looking idiot, drivelling and gibbering, and reeking with filth, was made to kiss her. No other penalty could have been devised at once so crushing to the victim, and so fully commending itself to the popular sense of justice.

There were about ten or fifteen of the released debtors whose homes were in or about Stockbridge, and as they could not walk any considerable distance, it was necessary to provide for their transport. Israel Goodrich and Ezra Phelps, as well as other Stockbridge men, had driven down in their carts, and these vehicles being filled with straw, the Stockbridge prisoners were placed in them. Israel Goodrich insisted that Reuben Hamlin and George Fennell, with Prudence, should go in his cart, and into it were also lifted three or four of the friendless prisoners, who had nowhere to go, and whose helpless condition had stirred old Israel's benevolent heart to its depths.

"The poor critters shell stay with me, ef I hev tew send my chil'n tew the neighbours ter make room fer em," he declared, blowing his nose with a blast that made his horses jump.

With six or seven carts leading the way, and some seventy or eighty men following on foot, the Stockbridge party began the march home about two o'clock. Full half the men who had marched down in the morning, chose to remain over in Barrington till later, and a good many were too drunk on

Bement's free rum to walk. Most of Paul Hubbard's iron-
workers being in that condition, he stayed to look after them,
and Peleg Bidwell had also stayed, to see that none of the
Stockbridge stragglers got into trouble, and bring them
back when he could. Abner walked at the head of the men.
Perez rode by Israel Goodrich's cart. They went on slowly,
and it was five o'clock when they came in plain view of
Stockbridge. The same exclamation was on every lip. It
seemed a year instead of a few hours only since they had
left in the morning.

"It's been a good day's work, Cap'n Hamlin, the best I
ever hed a hand in," said Israel. "I callate it was the Lord's
own work, ef we dew git hanged for't."

As the procession passed Israel's house, he helped out his
sad guests, and sent on his cart with its other inmates. All the
way back from Barrington, the Stockbridge company had
been meeting a string of men and boys, in carts and afoot,
who, having heard reports of what had been done, were
hastening to see for themselves. Many of these turned back
with the returning procession, others keeping on. This exo-
dus of the masculine element, begun in the morning, and
continued all day, had left in Stockbridge little save women
and girls and small children, always excepting, of course, the
families of the wealthier and governing classes, who had no
part nor lot in the matter. Accordingly, when the party
reached the green, there was only an assemblage of women
and children to receive them. These crowded around the
carts containing the released prisoners, with exclamations of
pity and amazement, and as the vehicles took different directions at the parting of the streets, each one was followed by
a score or two, who witnessed with tearful sympathy each
reunion of husband and wife, of brother and sister, of mother
and son. Several persons offered to take George Fennell, who
had no home to go to, into their houses, but Perez said that he
should, for the present, at least, lodge with him.

As Israel Goodrich's cart, containing Reuben and Fennell and Prudence, and followed by quite a concourse, turned up the lane to Elnathan Hamlin's house and stopped before the door, Elnathan and Mrs. Hamlin came out looking terrified. Perez, fearing some disappointment, had not told them plainly that he should bring Reuben home, and the report of the jail-breaking, although it had reached Stockbridge, had not penetrated to their rather isolated dwelling. So that it was with chilling apprehensions, rather than hope, that they saw the cart, driven slowly, as if it carried the dead, stop before their door, and the crowd of people following it.

"Mother, I've brought Reub home," said Perez, and a gaunt, wild-looking man was helped out of the cart, and tottered into Mrs. Hamlin's arms.

There was nothing but the faint, familiar smile, and the unaltered eyes, to tell her that this was the stalwart son whom the sheriff led away a year ago. Had she learned that he was dead, it would have shocked her less than to receive him alive and thus. Elnathan and she led him into the house between them. Ready hands lifted Fennell out of the cart and bore him in, Prudence following. And then Perez went in and shut the door, and the cart drove off, the people following.

Although the shock which Mrs. Hamlin had received was almost overwhelming, she had known, after the first moment, how to conceal it, and no sooner had the invalids been brought within doors and comfortably placed, than she began without a moment's delay, to bestir herself to prepare them food and drink, and make provision for their comfort. Tears of anguish filled her eyes whenever she turned aside, but they were wiped away, and her face was smiling and cheery when she looked at Reuben. But being with Perez a moment in a place apart, she broke down and cried bitterly.

"You have brought him home to die," she said.

But he reassured her.

"I have seen sick men," he said, "and I don't think Reub will die. He'll pull through, now he has your care. I'm afraid poor George is too far gone, but Reub will come out all right. Never fear mother."

"Far be it from me to limit the Holy One of Israel by my want of faith," said Mrs. Hamlin. "If it be the Lord's will that Reuben live, he will live, and if it be not His will, yet still will I praise His name for His great goodness in that I am permitted to take care of him, and do for him to the last. Who can say but the Most High will show still greater mercy to his servant, and save my son alive?"

As soon as the sick men were a little revived from the exhaustion of their journey, tubs of water were provided in the shed, and they washed themselves all over, Elnathan and Perez assisting in the repulsive task. Then, their filthy prison garments being thrown away, they were dressed in old clothing of Elnathan's, and their hair and matted beards were shorn off with scissors. Perez built a fire in the huge open fireplace to ward off the slight chill of evening, and the sick men were comfortably arranged before it upon the great settle. The elderly woman and the deft handed maiden, moved softly about, setting the tea table, and ministering to the needs of the invalids, arranging now a covering, now moving a stool, or maybe merely resting their cool and tender palms upon the fevered foreheads. Fennell had fallen peacefully asleep, but Reuben's face wore a smile, and in his eyes, as they languidly followed his mother's motions, to and fro, there was a look of unutterable content.

"I declar for 't," piped old Elnathan, as he sat in the chimney corner warming his fingers over the ruddy blaze, "I declar for 't, mother, the boy looks like another man a' ready. They ain't nothin like hum fer sick folks."

"I shan't want no doctor's stuff," said Reuben, feebly. "Seein mother round 's med'cin nuff fer me, I guess."

And Perez, as he stood leaning against the chimney, and looking on the scene, lit by the flickering firelight, said to himself, that never surely, in all his fighting had he ever drawn his sword to such good and holy purpose as that day.

Soon after nightfall the latchstring was pulled in a timid sort of way, and Obadiah Weeks stood on the threshold, waiting sheepishly till Mrs. Hamlin bade him enter. He came forward, toward the chimney, taking off his hat and smoothing his hair with his hand.

"It looks kinder good tew see a fire," he remarked, presently supplementing this by the observation that it was "kinder hot, though," and grinning vaguely around at every one in the room, with the exception of Prudence. He did not look at her, though he looked all around her. He put his hands in his pockets and took them out, rubbed one boot against the other, and examined a wart on one of his thumbs, as if he now observed it for the first time, and was quite absorbed in the discovery.

Then with a suddenness that somewhat startled Perez, who had been observing him with some curiosity, he wheeled round so as to face Prudence, and simultaneously sought in his pocket for something. Not finding it at first, his face got very red. Finally, however, he drew forth a little bundle and gave it to the girl, mumbling something about "Sassafras, thort mebbe 'twould be good fer yer dad," and bolted out of the room.

Nobody said anything after Obadiah's abrupt retirement, but when a few moments later, Prudence looked shyly around, with cheeks a little rosier than usual, she saw Perez regarding her with a slight smile of amusement. A minute after she got up and went over to Mrs. Hamlin, and laid the sassafras in her lap, saying:

"Don't you want this, Mrs. Hamlin? I'm sure I don't know what it's good for," and went back to her seat and sat down again, with a slight toss of the head.

Presently a medley of discordant sounds began to float up from the village on the gentle southerly breeze. There was a weird, unearthly groaning, as of a monster in pain, mingled with the beating of tin-pans. Perez finally went to see what it was. At the end of the lane he met Peleg Bidwell, and Peleg explained the matter.

"Ye see the boys hev all got back from Barrington, and they're pretty gosh darned drunk, most on em, an so nothin would do but they must go an rig up a hoss-fiddle an hunt up some pans, an go an serenade the silk stockins. They wuz a givin it tew Squire Woodbridge, wen I come by. I guess he won't git much sleep ter night," and with this information Perez went home again.

A FAIR SUPPLIANT

Dr. Partridge lived at this time on the hill north of the village, and not very far from the parsonage, which made it convenient for him to report promptly to Parson West, when any of his patients had reached that point where spiritual must be substituted for medical ministrations. It was about ten o'clock by the silver dialed clock in the living room of the doctor's house, when Prudence Fennell knocked at the open kitchen door.

"What do you want, child?" said Mrs. Partridge, who was in the kitchen trying to instruct a negro girl how to use her broom of twigs so as to distribute the silver sand upon the floor in the complex wavy figures, which were the pride of the housewife of that day.

"Please, marm, father's sick, and Mis Hamlin thinks he ought to have the doctor."

"Your father and Mrs. Hamlin? Who is your father, pray?"

"I'm Prudence Fennell, marm, and father's George Fennell. He's one of them that were fetched from Barrington jail yesterday, and he's sick. He's at Mis Hamlin's, please marm."

"Surely, by that he must be one of the debtors. The sheriff is more like to come for them than the doctor. They will be back in jail in a few days, no doubt," said Mrs. Partridge, sharply.

"No one will be so cruel. Father is so sick. If you could see him, you would not say so. They shall not take him to jail again. If Mr. Seymour comes after him, I'll tear his eyes out. I'll kill him."

"What a little tiger it is!" said Mrs. Partridge, regarding with astonishment the child's blazing eyes and panting bosom, while peering over her mistress's shoulders, the negro girl was turning up the whites of her eyes at the display. "There, there, child, I meant nothing. If he is sick, maybe they will leave him. I know naught of such things. But this Perez Hamlin will be hung of a surety, and the rest be put in the stocks and well whipt."

"He will not be hung. No one will dare to touch him," cried Prudence, becoming excited again. "He is the best man in the world. He fetched my father out of jail."

"Nay, but if you are so spunky to say 'no' to your betters, 'tis time you went. I know not what we are in the way to, when a chit of a maid shall set me right," said Mrs. Partridge, bristling up, and turning disdainfully away.

But her indignation, at once forgotten in terror lest the doctor might not come to her father, Prudence came after her and caught her sleeve, and said with tones of entreaty, supported by eyes full of tears:

"Please, marm, don't mind what I said. Box my ears, marm, but please let doctor come. Father coughs so bad."

"I will tell him, and he will do as he sees fit," said Mrs. Partridge, stiffly, "and now run home, and do not put me out with your sauce again."

An hour or two later, the doctor's chaise stopped at the Hamlins. Doctors, as well as other people, were plainer-spoken in those days, especially in dealing with the poor. Dr. Partridge was a kind-hearted man, but it did not occur to him as it does to his successors of our day, to mince matters with patients, and cheer them up with hopeful generalities, reserving the bitter truths to whisper in the ears of their friends outside the door. After a look and a few words, he said to Fennell:

"I can do you no good."

"Shall I die?" asked the sick man, faintly.

"You may live a few weeks, but not longer. The disease has taken too strong a hold."

Fennell looked around the room. Prudence was not present.

"Don't tell Prudy," he said.

As to Reuben, who was already looking much brighter than the preceding night, the doctor said:

"He may get well," and left a little medicine.

Perez, who had been in the room, followed him out of doors.

"Do you think my brother will get well?" he asked.

"I think so, if he does not have to go back to jail."

"He will not go back unless I go with him," said Perez.

"Well, I think it most likely you will," replied the doctor dryly. "On the whole, I should say his prospect of long life was better than yours, if I am speaking to Perez Hamlin, the mob captain."

"You mean I shall be hung?"

"And drawn and quartered," amended the doctor, grimly. "That is the penalty for treason, I believe."

"Perhaps," said Perez. "We shall see. There will be fighting before hanging. At any rate, if I'm hung, it will be as long as it's short, for Reub would have died if I hadn't got him out of jail."

The doctor gathered up the reins.

"I want to thank you for coming," said Perez. "You know, I s'pose, that we are very poor, and can't promise much pay."

"If you'll see that your mob doesn't give me such a serenade as it did Squire Woodbridge last night, I'll call it square," said the doctor, and drove off.

Now, Meshech Little, the carpenter, had gone home and to bed towering drunk the night before, after taking part as a leading performer in the aforesaid serenade to the Squire. His sleep had been exceedingly dense, and in the morning when it became time for him to go to his work, it was only after repeated callings and shakings, that Mrs. Little was able to elicit the first sign of wakefulness.

"You must get up," she expostulated. "Sun's half way daown the west post, an ye know how mad Deacon Nash'll be ef ye don' git don shinglin his barn tidday." After a series of heartrending groans and yawns, Meshech, who had tumbled on the bed in his clothes, got up and stood stretching and rubbing his eyes in the middle of the floor.

"By gosh, it's kinder tough," he said, "I wuz jess a dreamin ez I wuz latherin deakin. I'd jess swotted him one in the snout wen ye woke me, an naow, by gorry, I've got tew go an work fer the critter."

"An ye better hurry, tew," urged his wife anxiously. "Ye know ye didn't dew the fuss thing all day yis'dy."

"Whar wuz I yis'dy?" asked Meshech, in whose confused faculties the only distinct recollection was that he had been drunk.

"Ye went daown tew Barrington 'long with the crowd."

Meshech was in the act of ducking his head in a bucket of water, standing on a bench by the door, but at his wife's words he became suddenly motionless as a statue, his nose close to the water. Then he straightened sharply up and stared at her, the working of his eyes showing that he was gathering up tangled skeins of recollection.

"Wal, I swow," he finally ejaculated, with an astonished drawl, "ef I hadn't a furgut the hull dum performance, an here I wuz a gittin up an goin to work jess ez if court hadn't been stopped. Gosh, Sally, I guess I be my own man tidday, ef I hev got a bad tas in my mouth. Gorry, it's lucky I thort afore I wet my hed. I couldn't a gone tew sleep agin," and Meshech turned toward the bed, with apparent intention of resuming his slumbers.

But Mrs. Little, though she knew there had been serious disturbances the preceding day, could by no means bring her mind to believe that the entire system of law and public authority had been thus suddenly and completely overthrown, and she yet again adjured her husband, this time by a more dreadful name, to betake himself to labor.

"Ef ye don' go to work, Meshech, Squire Woodbridge 'll hev ye in the stocks fer gittin drunk. Deakin kin git ye put in any time he wants ter complain on ye. Ye better not rile him."

But at this Meshech, instead of being impressed, burst into a loud haw haw.

"Yes'dy mornin ye could a scart me outer a week's growth a talkin baout Squire, but, gol, ye'll have ter try suthen else naow. Wy don' ye know we wuz a serenadin Squire with a hoss-fiddle till ten o'clock las' night, an he didn' das show his nose outer doors.

"Gosh!" he continued, getting into bed and turning over toward the wall, "I'd giv considabul, ef I could dream I wuz lickin Squire. Mebbe I kin. Don' ye wake me up agin Sally," and presently his regular snoring proclaimed that he had departed to the free hunting grounds of dreamland in pursuit of his desired game.

Now Meshech's was merely a representative case. He was by no means the only workingman who that morning kept his bed warm to an unaccustomed hour. Except such as had farms of their own to work on, or work for themselves to do, there was scarcely any one in Stockbridge who went to work. A large part of the labor by which the industries of the community had been carried on, had been that of debtors working out their debts at such allowance for wages as their creditor-employers chose to make them. If they complained that it was too small, they had, indeed, their choice to go to jail in preference to taking it, but no third alternative was before them. Of these coolies, as we should call them in these days, only a few who were either very timid, or ignorant of the full effect of yesterday's doings, went to their usual tasks.

Besides the coolies, there was a small number of laborers who commanded actual wages in produce or in money. Although there was no reason in yesterday's proceedings, why these should not go to work as usual, yet the spirit of revolt that was in the air, and the vague impression of impending changes that were to indefinitely better the condition of the poor, had so far affected them also, that the most took this day as a holiday, with a hazy but pleasing notion that it was the beginning of unlimited holidays.

All this idle element naturally drifted into the streets, and collected in particular force on the green and about the tavern. By afternoon, these groups, reënforced by those who had been busy at home during the morning, began to assume the dimensions of a crowd. Widow Bingham, at the tavern, had deemed it expedient to keep the right side of the lawless element by a rather free extension of credit at the bar, and there was a good deal of hilarity, which, together with the atmosphere of excitement created by the recent stirring events, made it seem quite like a gala occasion. Women and girls were there in considerable numbers, the latter wearing their ribbons, and walking about in groups together, or listening to their sweethearts, as each explained to a credulous auditor, how yesterday's great events had hinged entirely on the narrator's individual presence and prowess.

Some of the youths, the preceding night, had cut a tall sapling and set it in the middle of the green, in front of the tavern. On the top of this had been fixed the cocked hat of Justice Goodrich, brought as a trophy from Great Barrington. This was the center of interest, the focus of the crowd, a visible, palpable proof of the people's victory over the courts, which was the source of inextinguishable hilarity. It was evident, indeed, from the conversation of the children, that there existed in the minds of those of tender years, some confusion as to the previous ownership of the hat, and the circumstances connected with its acquisition by the people.

Some said that it was Burgoyne's hat, and others that it was the hat of King George, himself, while the affair of the day before at Great Barrington, was variously represented as a victory over the redcoats, the Indians and the Tories. But, whatever might be the differences of opinion on these minor points, the children were uproariously agreed that there was something to be exceedingly joyful about.

Next to the hat, two uncouth-looking machines which stood on the green near the stocks, were the centers of interest. They were wooden structures, somewhat resembling saw-horses. Beside each were several boards, and close inspection would have shown that both the surface of the horses and one side of these boards, were well smeared with rosin. These were the horse-fiddles, contrived for the purpose of promoting wakefulness by night, on the part of the silk stockings. Given plenty of rosin, and a dozen stout fellows to each fiddle, drawing the boards to and fro across the backs of the horses, pressing on hard, and the resulting shrieks were something only to be imagined with the fingers in the ears. The concert given to Squire Woodbridge the night previous, had been an extemporized affair, with only one horse-fiddle, and insufficient support from other instruments. To judge from the conversation of the men and boys standing around, it was intended to-night to give the Squire a demonstration which should quite compensate him for the unsatisfactory nature of the former entertainment, and leave him in no sort of doubt as to the sentiments of the people toward the magistracy and silk stockings in general, and himself in particular. A large collection of tin-pans had been made, and the pumpkin vines of the vicinity had been dismantled for the construction of pumpkinstalk trombones, provided with which, some hundreds of small boys were to be in attendance.

Although the loud guffaws which from time to time were heard from the group of men and hobbledehoys about the horse-fiddles on the green, were evidence that the projected entertainment was not without comical features as they looked at it, the aspect of the affair as viewed by other eyes was decidedly tragical. Mrs. Woodbridge had long been sinking with consumption, and the uproar and excitement of the preceding night had left her in so prostrate a condition that Dr. Partridge had been called in. During the latter part of her aunt's sickness Desire Edwards had made a practice of running into her Uncle Jahleel's many times a day to give a sort of oversight to the housekeeping, a department in which she was decidedly more proficient than damsels of this day, of much less aristocratic pretensions, find it consistent with their dignity to be. The doctor and Desire were at this moment in the living-room, inspecting through the closed shutters the preparations on the green for the demonstration of the evening.

"Another such night will kill her, won't it, doctor?"

"I could not answer for the consequences," replied the doctor, gravely. "I could scarcely hazard giving her laudanum enough to carry her through such a racket, and without sleep she cannot live another day."

"What shall we do? What shall we do? Oh, poor Aunty! The brutes! The brutes! Look at them over there laughing their great horse laughs. I never liked to see them whipped before, when the constable whipped them, but oh I shall like to after this. I should like to see them whipped till the blood ran down," cried the girl, tears of mingled grief and anger filling her flashing eyes.

"I don't know when you are likely to have the opportunity," said the doctor, dryly. "At present they have the upper hand in town, and seem very likely to keep it. We may thank our stars if the idea of whipping some of us does not occur to them."

"My father fears that they will plunder the store and perhaps murder us, unless help comes soon."

"There is no help to come," said the doctor. "The militia are all in the mob."

"But is there nothing we can do? Must we let them murder Aunty before our eyes?"

"Perhaps," said the doctor, "if your Uncle Jahleel were to go out to the mob this evening, and entreat them civilly, and beg them to desist by reason of your aunt's sickness, they would hear to him."

"Doctor! Doctor! you don't know my uncle," cried Desire. "He would sooner have Aunt Lucy die, and die himself, and have us all killed, than stoop to ask a favor of the rabble."

"I suppose it would be hard for him," said the doctor, "and yet to save your aunt's life maybe—"

"Oh I couldn't bear to have him do it," interrupted Desire. "Poor Uncle! I'd rather go out to the mob myself than have Uncle Jahleel. It would kill him. He is so proud."

The doctor walked across the room two or three times with knitted brow and then paused and looked with a certain critical admiration at the face of the girl to which excitement had lent an unusual brilliance.

"I will tell you," he said, "the only way I see of securing a quiet night to your aunt. Just go yourself and see this Hamlin who is the captain of the mob, and make your petition to him. I had words with him this morning. He is a well seeming fellow enough, and has a bold way of speech that liked me well i' faith, though no doubt he's a great rascal and well deserves a hanging."

He paused, for Desire was confronting him, with a look that was a peremptory interruption. Her eyes were flashing, her cheeks mantled with indignant color, and the delicate nostrils were distended with scorn.

"Me, Desire Edwards, sue for favors of this low fellow! You forget yourself strangely, Dr. Partridge."

The doctor took his hat from the table and bowed low.

"I beg your pardon, Miss Desire. Possibly your aunt may live through the night, after all," and he went out of the house shrugging his shoulders.

Desire was still standing in the same attitude when a faint voice caught her ear, and stepping to a door she opened it, and asked gently, "What is it, Aunty?"

"Your uncle hasn't gone out, has he?" asked Mrs. Woodbridge, feebly.

"No, Aunty, he's in his study walking to and fro as he's been all day, you know."

"He musn't go out. I was afraid he'd gone out. Tell him I beg he will not go out. The mob will kill him."

"I don't think he will go, Aunty."

"Do you think they will make that terrible noise again tonight."

"I — I don't know. I'm afraid so, Aunt Lucy."

"Oh dear," sighed the invalid, with a moan of exhaustion, "it don't seem as if I could live through it again, I'm so weak, and so tired. You can't think, dear, how tired I am."

Desire went in and shook up the pillows, and soothed the sick woman with some little cares and then came out and shut the door. Her wide brimmed hat of fine leghorn straw with a blue ostrich plume curled around the crown, and a light cashmere shawl lay on the table. Perching the one a trifle sideways on her dark brown curls, which were gathered simply in a ribbon behind, according to the style of the day, she threw the shawl about her shoulders, and knocked at the door of her Uncle Jahleel's study, which also opened into the living-room, and was the apartment in which he held court, when acting as magistrate. In response to the knock the Squire opened the door. He looked as if he had had a fit of sickness, so deeply had the marks of chagrin and despite impressed itself on his face in the past two days.

"I'm going out for a little while," said Desire, "and you will go to Aunty, if she calls, won't you?"

Her uncle nodded and resumed his walking to and fro, and Desire, stepping out of the house by a back way, went by a path across the fields, toward Elnathan Hamlin's house.

The Hamlin house, like the houses of most of the poorer class of people, had but two rooms on the ground floor, a small bedroom and a great kitchen, in which the family lived, worked, cooked, ate and received company. There were two doors opening into the kitchen from without, the front door and the back door. On the former of these, there came a light tap. Now callers upon the Hamlins, in general, just pulled the latchstring and came in. Nobody tapped except the sheriff, the constable, the tax-collector and the parson, and the latter's calls had been rare since the family fortunes, never other than humble, had been going from bad to worse. So that it was not without some trepidation, which was shared by the family, that old Elnathan now rose from his seat by the chimney corner and went and opened the door. A clear, soft voice, with the effect of distinctness without preciseness, which betrays the cultured class, was heard by those within, asking, "Is Captain Hamlin in the house?"

"Do ye mean Perez?" parleyed Elnathan.

"Yes."

"I b'leve he's somewheres raound. He's aout doin up the chores, I callate. Did ye wanter see him?"

"If you please."

"Wal, come in won't ye, an sid down, an I'll go aout arter him," said Elnathan, backing in and making way for the guest to enter.

"It's the Edwards gal," he continued, in a feebly introductory manner, as Desire entered.

Mrs. Hamlin hastily let down her sleeves, and glanced, a little shamefacedly, at her linsey-woolsey short gown and coarse petticoat, and then about the room, which was a good deal cluttered up, and small blame to her, considering the sudden increase of her household cares. But it was, nevertheless, with native dignity that she greeted her guest and set her a chair, not allowing herself to be put out by the rather fastidious way in which Desire held up her skirts.

"Sid down," said Elnathan "an be kinder neighborly. She wants to see Perez, mother. I dunno what baout, I'm sure. Ef he's a milkin naow I s'pose I kin spell him so's he kin come in an see what she's a wantin of him," and the old man shuffled out the back door.

Desire sat down, calm and composed outwardly, but tingling in every particle of her body with a revulsion of taste at the vulgarity of the atmosphere, which almost amounted to nausea. But it may be doubted if her dainty attire, her air of distinction, and the refined delicacy of her flower-like face, had ever appeared to more advantage than as she sat, inwardly fuming, on that rude chair, in that rude room, amid its more or less clownish inmates. Prudence was very red in the face, and confused. As housemaid in Mr. Woodbridge's family, she knew Desire well, and felt a certain sort of responsibility for her on that account. She did not know whether she ought to go and speak to her now, though Desire took no notice of her. Reuben also had risen from his chair as she came in, and still stood awkwardly leaning on the back of it, not seeming sure if he ought to sit down again or not. Fennell, too sick to care, was the only self-possessed person in the room. It was a relief to all when the noise of feet at the door indicated the return of Elnathan with Perez, but the running explanations of the former which his senile treble made quite audible through the door, were less reassuring.

"Can't make aout what in time she wants on ye. Mebbe she's tuk a shine to ye, he, he, I dunno. Ye uster be allers arter her when ye wuz a young un."

"Hush father, she'll hear," said Perez, and opening the door came into the kitchen.

Desire arose to her feet as he did so, and their eyes met. He would have known her anywhere, in spite of the nine years since he had seen her. The small oval of the sparkling gypsy face, the fine features, so mobile and piquant, he instantly recognized from the portrait painted in undying colors upon his youthful imagination.

"Are you Captain Hamlin?" she said.

"I hope you remember Perez Hamlin," he answered.

"I remember the name," she replied coldly. "I am told that you command the — the men" — she was going to say mob — "in the village."

"I believe so," he answered. He was thinking that those red lips of hers had once kissed his, that August morning when he stood on the green, ready to march with the minute men.

"My Aunt Woodbridge is very sick. If your men make a noise again in front of my uncle's house, she will die. I came to — to ask" — she had to say it — "you to prevent it."

"I will prevent it," said Perez.

Desire dropped an almost imperceptible curtsey, raised the latch of the door and went out.

All through the interview, even when she had overheard Elnathan's confidences to Perez, at the door, her cheeks had not betrayed her by a trace of unusual color, but now as she hurried home across the fields, they burned with shame, and she fairly choked to think of the vulgar familiarity to which she had submitted, and the abject attitude she had assumed to this farmer's son. She remembered well enough that childish kiss, and saw in his eyes that he remembered it. This perception had added the last touch to her humiliation.

But Perez went out and wandered into the wood-lot and sat down on a fallen tree, and stared a long time into vacancy with glowing eyes. He had dreamed of Desire a thousand times during his long absence from home, but since his return, so vehement had been the pressure of domestic troubles, so rapid the rush of events, that he had not had time to once think of her existence, up to the moment when she had confronted him there in the kitchen, in a beauty at once the same, and so much more rare, and rich and perfect, than that which had ruled his boyish dreams.

Presently he went down to the tavern. The crowd of men and boys on the green received him with quite an ovation. Shaking hands right and left with the men, he went on to the tavern, and finding Abner smoking on the bench outside the door, drew him aside and asked him to see that there was no demonstration in front of Woodbridge's that evening. Abner grumbled a little.

"O' course I'm sorry for the woman, if she's sick, but they never showed no considerashun fer our feelin's, an I don' see wy we sh'd be so durn tender o' theirn. I shouldn't be naow, arter they'd treated a brother o' mine ez they hev Reub. But ye be cap'n, Perez, an it shel be ez ye say. The boys kin try ther fiddles on Squire Edwards instid."

"No. Not there, Abner," said Perez, quickly.

"Wy not, I sh'd like ter know. His wife ain't sick, be she?"

"No, that is I don't know," said Perez, his face flushing a little with the difficulty of at once thinking of any plausible reason. "You see," he finally found words to say, "the store is so near Squire Woodbridge's, that the noise might disturb Madam Woodbridge."

"She muss hev dum sharp ears, ef she kin hear much at that distance," observed Abner, "but it shell be as ye say, Cap'n. I s'pose ye've nothin agin our givin Sheriff Seymour a little mewsick."

"As much as you please, Abner."

A PRAISE MEETING

As a fever awakes to virulent activity the germs of disease in the body, so revolution in the political system develops the latent elements of anarchy. It is a test of the condition of the system. The same political shock which throws an ill-constituted and unsound government into a condition of chaos, is felt in a politically vigorous and healthful commonwealth, as only a slight disturbance of the ordinary functions. The promptness with which the village of Stockbridge relapsed into its ordinary mode of life after the revolt and revolution of Tuesday, was striking testimony to the soundness and vitality which a democratic form of government and a popular sense of responsibility impart to a body politic. On Tuesday the armed uprising of the people had taken place; on Wednesday there was considerable effervescence of spirits, though no violence; on Thursday there was still a number of loutish fellows loafing about the streets, wearing, however, an appearance of being disappointed that there was no more excitement, and no prospect of anything special turning up. Friday and Saturday, apparently disgusted at finding rebellion such a failure in elements of recreation, these had gone back to their farm-work and chores, and the village had returned to its normal quiet without even any more serenades to the silk stockings, to enliven the evenings.

A foreigner, who had chanced to be passing through Southern Berkshire at this time, would have deemed an informant practicing on his credulity who should have assured him that everywhere throughout these quiet and industrious communities, the entire governmental machinery was prostrate, that not a local magistrate undertook to sit, not a constable ventured to attempt an arrest, not a sheriff dared to serve a process or make an execution, or a tax-collector distrain for taxes. And yet such was the sober truth, for Stockbridge was in no respect peculiarly situated, and in many of the towns around, especially in Sheffield, Egremont, Great Barrington, and Sandisfield, an even larger proportion of the people were open sympathizers with the rebellion than in the former village.

In these modern days, restaurants, barrooms, and saloons, and similar places of resort, are chiefly thronged on Saturday evening, when the labors of the week being ended, the worker, in whatever field, finds himself at once in need of convivial relaxation, and disposed thereto by the exhilaration of a prospective holiday. Necessarily, however, Saturday evening could not be thus celebrated in a community which regarded it in the light of holy time, and, accordingly in Stockbridge, as elsewhere in New England at that day, Friday and Sunday evenings were by way of eminence the convivial occasions of the week. One of the consequences of this arrangement was that a "blue Saturday" as well as the modern "blue Monday," found place in the workingman's calendar. But the voice of the temperance lecturer was not yet heard in the land, and headaches were still looked upon as Providential mysteries.

The Friday following the "goings on at Barrington," the tavern was filled by about the same crowd which had been present the Friday evening preceding, and of whose conversation on that occasion, some account was given. But the temper of the gathering a week before had been gloomy, foreboding, hopeless and well-nigh desperate; to-night, it was jubilant.

"It's the Lord's doin's, an marvellous in our eyes, an that's all I kin say about it," declared Israel Goodrich, his rosy face beaming with benevolent satisfaction, beneath its crown of white hair. "Jess think whar we wuz a week ago, an whar we be naow. By gosh who'd a thought it? If one on ye had a tole me las' Friday night, what was a comin raound inside of a week, I should a said he wuz stark starin mad."

"We mout a knowed somethin wuz a gonter happin," said Abner. "It's allers darkest jess afore dawn, an 'twas dark nuff tew cut las' Friday."

"I declar for't," said Peleg Bidwell, "seem's though I never did feel quite so down-hearted like ez I did las' Friday night, wen we wuz a talkin it over. I'd hed a bad day on't. Sol Gleason'd been a sassin of me, an I dassn't say a word, fer fear he'd send me to jail, fer owin him, an wen I got home She wuz a cryin, fer Gleason'd been thar, an I dunno what he'd said tew her, and then Klector Williams he told me he'd hev tew sell the furnicher fer taxes, an by gosh, takin the hull together seemed 's though thar warn't no place fer a poor man in this ere world, and I didn' keer ef I lived much longer or not. An naow! Wal thay ain't no use o' tellin ye what ye know. I seen Gleason on the street yisday, an he looked like a whipped cur. He hed his tail atween his legs, I tell yew. I reckon he thort I wuz gonter lick him. It wuz 'Good mornin, Peleg,' ez sweet's sugar, an he didn't hev nothing tew say baout what I wuz a owin him, no; nor he didn't ass me nothin baout wy I hedn't been tew work fer him sence Tewsday."

After the haw-haw over Peleg's description had subsided, he added, with a grin,

"Klector Williams he hain't thort tew call baout them taxes, sence Tewsday, nuther. Hev any on ye seen nothin on him?"

"He hain't skurcely been outer his haouse," said Obadiah Weeks. "I on'y see him onct. It was arter dark, an he wuz a slippin over't the store arter his tod."

"I guess it muss be considabul like a funeral over't the store, nights," observed Abner, grinning. "Gosh I sh'd like ter peek in an see em a talkin on it over. Wal, turn about's fair play. They don' feel no wuss nor we did."

"Won't thar be no more klectin taxes?" inquired Laban Jones.

"I guess thar won't be much more klectin roun' here 'nless the klector hez a couple o' rigiments o' melishy tew help him dew it," replied Abner.

"I dunno, baout that," said Ezra Phelps. "Thar's more'n one way ter skin a cat."

"Thar ain't no way o' skinnin this ere cat 'cept with bago-nets," said Abner, decidedly, and a general murmur expressed the opinion that so far as the present company was concerned government would have to practice some preliminary phle-botomy on their persons before they would submit to any further bleeding of their purses by the tax-collector. Nothing pleased Ezra more than to get placed thus argumentatively at bay, with the entire company against him, and then discom-fit them all at a stroke. The general expression of dissent with which his previous remark was received, seemed actually to please him. He stood looking at Abner for a moment, without speaking, a complacent smile just curving his lips, and the sparkle of the intellectual combatant in his eye. To persons of Ezra's disputatious and speculative temper, such moments, in which they gloat over their victim as he stands within the very jaws of the logic trap which they are about to spring, are no doubt, the most delightful of life.

"Don't yew be in sech a hurry, Abner," he finally ejacula-ted. "Would ye mind payin yer taxes ef govment giv ye the money ter pay em with?"

"No. In course I wouldn't."

"Ezzackly. Course ye wouldn't. Ye'd be dum unreas'nable ef ye did. Wal, naow I callate that air's jess what govment's gonter dew, ez soon ez it gits the news from Northampton and Barrington. It's gonter print a stack o' bills, an git em inter cirk'lashun, an then we'll all on us hev suthin tew pay fer taxes, an not mind it a bit; yis, an pay all the debts that's a owin, tew."

"I hain't no objeckshun ter that," admitted Abner, frankly.

"Of course ye hain't," said Ezra. "Nobody hain't. Ye see ye spoke tew quick, Abner. All the kentry wants is bills, a hull slew on em, lots on em, an then the courts kin go on, an debts an taxes kin be paid, an everything'll be all right. I ain't one o' them ez goes agin' payin debts an taxes. I says let em be paid, ev'ry shillin, on'y let govment print nuff bills fer folks tew pay em with."

"I callate a couple o' wagon loads o' new bills would pay orf ev'ry morgidge, an mos' o' the debts, in Berkshire," said Israel, reflectively.

"Sartinly, sartinly," exclaimed Ezra. "That would be plenty. It don' cost nothin tew print em, an they'd pacify this ere caounty a dum sight quicker nor no two rigiments, nor no ten, nuther."

"That air's what I believe in," said Israel, beamingly, "peaceable ways o' settlin the trouble; bills instid o' bagonets. The beauty on't so fer is that thar hain't been no sheddin o' blood, nor no vi'lence tew speak of, ceppin a leetle shovin daown tew Barrington, an I hope thar won't be."

"I don't know about that," said Paul Hubbard. "Not that I want to see any killing, but there are some silk stockings in this here town that would look mighty well sticking through the stocks, an there are some white skins that ought to know how a whip feels, jist so the men that own em might see how the medicine tastes they've been giving us so many years."

There was a general murmur indicating approval of this sentiment, and several "that's sos" were heard, but Israel said, as he patted Hubbard paternally on the back:

"Let bygones be bygones, Paul. Them things be all over naow, an I callate thar won't be no more busin of poor folks. The lyin an the lamb be a gonter lie down together arter this, 'cordin tew scripter. I declar, it seems jiss like the good ole times 'long from '74 to '80, wen thar warn't no courts in Berkshire. Wen I wuz a tellin ye baout them times 'tother night, I swow I didn't callate ye'd ever have a chance to see em fer yerselves, leastways, not till ye got ter Heavin, an I guess that's a slim chance with most on ye. Jess think on't, boys. Thar ain't been nary sheriff's sale, nor a man tuk ter jail this hull week."

"Iry Seymour wuz a gonter sell aout Elnathan Hamlin this week, but somehow he hain't got tew it," said Abner, dryly. "I callate he heard some news from Barrington baout Tuesday."

"Iry mout's well give up his comishin ez depity sheriff an try ter git inter some honest trade," remarked Israel.

"Whar does Squire Woodbridge keep hisself these days? I hain't seen him skurcely this week," said Ezra Phelps.

"Yew don' genally see much of a rooster the week arter another rooster's gin him a darnation lickin on his own dung hill, an that's wat's the matter with Squire," replied Abner. Shifting his quid of tobacco to the other side of the mouth and expectorating across half the room into the chimney place he continued, reflectively:

"By gosh, I don' blame him, nuther. It muss come kinder tough fer a feller ez hez lorded it over Stockbridge fer nigh twenty year tew git put daown afore the hull village the way Perez put him daown Tuesday. Ef I wuz Squire, I shouldn't never wanter show myself agin roun' here."

"I be kinder sorry fer him," said Israel Goodrich. "I declar for't if I ain't. It muss be kinder tough tew git took daown so, specially fer sech a dreffle proud man."

"I hain't sot eyes on him on'y once sence Tewsday," said Peleg. "He looked right straight through me 'z ef he didn' see nothin. He didn' seem ter notice nobody ez he went along the street."

"By gosh, he'd notice ye quick nuff ef he could put ye in the stocks," observed Abner, grimly. "I tell yew he ain't furgut one on us that went daown ter Barrington, nor one on us ez wuz a serenadin him t'other night. Yew jess let Squire git his grip onto this ere taown agin ez he uster hev it an the constable an the whippin post won't hev no rest till he's paid orf his grudge agin' every one on us. An ef yew dunno that, yew dunno Squire Woodbridge."

The silence which followed indicated that the hearers did know the Squire well enough to appreciate the force of Abner's remarks, and that the contingencies which they suggested were inducive of serious reflections. It was Jabez Flint, the Tory, who effected a diversion by observing dryly,

"Yes, ef Squire gits his grip agin, some on us will git darnation sore backs, but he's lost it, an he ain't a gonter git it agin ez long ez we fellers keeps ourn. On'y 'twont dew ter hev no foolin, tain't no child's play we're at."

"I know one thing dum well" said Obadiah Weeks, "and that is I wouldn' like tew be in Cap'n Hamlin's shoes ef Squire sh'd git top agin. Jehosaphat, though, wouldn' he jess go fer the Cap'n. I guess he'd give him ten lashes ev'ry day fer a month an make him set in the stocks with pepper 'n salt rubbed in his back 'tween times, an then hev him hung ter wind up with, an he wouldn' be half sassified then."

"Warn't that the gol-darndest though, baout that Edwards gal agoin tew ass Perez to git the mewsic stopped? By gosh, I can't git over that," exclaimed Peleg, grinning from ear to ear. "I was a lyin awake las' night and I got ter thinkin bout it, an I begun snickering so's She waked up, and She says, 'Peleg,' seshee 'what in time be yew a snickerin at?' and I says I wuz a snickerin tew think o' that air stuck up leetle gal o' Squire Edwards daown on her knees tew Perez, a cryin an a assin him ef he wouldn' please hev the racket stopped. Yew sed she wuz ontew her knees, didn't yew, Obadiah?"

"Tell us all about it Obadiah, we wanter hear it agin," was the general demand.

"Ye see the way on't wuz this," said Obadiah, nothing loath. "She come in all a cryin an scairt like, and Perez he wuz thar an so wuz the res' o' the family, an the fuss thing she does, she gits down on the floor intew the sand with a new silk gown she hed on, and asses Perez to hev the hoss-fiddles stopped. An he said t'er fuss, as haow he wouldn't, said 'twas good nuff fur the silk stockings, and he pinted ter Reub an says for her tew see what they'd done ter his family. But she cried an tuck on, an says ez haow she wouldn't git up 'nless he'd stop the hoss-fiddles, an so he hed tew give in, an that's all I knows about it."

"Ye see Obadiah knows all baout it," said Abner. "He keeps kumpny with the Fennell gal, as is tew the Hamlins. He got it straight's a string, didn't ye, Obadiah?"

"Yes," said Obadiah, "it's all jess so. Thar ain't no mistake."

No incident of the insurrection had taken such hold on the popular imagination as the appeal of Desire Edwards to Perez for protection. It was immensely flattering to the vanity of the mob, as typifying the state of terror to which the aristocrats had been reduced, and all the louts in town felt an inch the taller, by reason of it, and walked with an additional swagger. The demand for the details of the scene between Perez and Desire was insatiable and Obadiah was called on twenty times a day to relate to gaping, grinning audiences just how she looked, what she did, and said, and what Perez said. The fact that Obadiah's positive information on the subject was limited to a few words that Prudence had dropped, made it necessary for him to depend largely on his imagination to satisfy the demands of his auditors, which accounts for the slight discrepancy between the actual facts as known to the reader and the popular version. After everybody had haw hawed and cracked his joke over Obadiah's last repetition of the anecdote, Peleg observed:

"I dunno's az a feller kin blame Perez fer givin intew her. The gal's derned hansum, though she be mos' too black complected."

"She ain't none tew black, not to my thinkin," said Widow Bingham, looking up from her knitting as she sat behind the bar, — the widow herself was a buxom brunette — "but I never did see anybuddy kerry ther nose quite so high in all my born days. She don't pay no more 'tension to common folks 'n if they wuz dirt under her feet."

"Whar's Meshech Little, ter night?" inquired Israel Goodrich, not so much interested as the younger men in the points of young women.

"He's been drunk all day," said Obadiah, who always knew everything that was going on.

"Whar'd he git the money?" asked some one.

"Meshech don' need no money tew git drunk," said Abner. "He's got a thirst ontew him as'll draw liquor aout a cask a rod orf, an the bung in, jess like the clouds draws water on a hot day. He don' need no money, Meshech don' tew git soaked."

"He hed some, he hed a shillin howsumever," said Obadiah. "Deacon Nash give it tew him fer pitchin rowen."

"I hain't been so tickled in ten year," said Israel, "ez I wuz wen Deacon come roun tidday a offerin a shillin lawful tew the fellers tew git in his rowen fer him. It must hev been like pullin teeth fer Deacon tew pay aout cash fer work seein ez he's made his debtors dew all his farmin fer him this five year, but he hed tew come tew 't, fer his rowen wuz a spilin, an nary one o' his debtors would lif a finger 'thout bein paid for 't."

"That air shillin o' Meshech's is the fuss money o' his'n I've seen fer flip in more'n a year," said Widow Bingham, "an thar be them, not a thousan mile from here, nuther, ez I could say the same on, more shame to em, for't, an I a lone widder."

The line of remark adopted by the widow, appeared to exert a depressing influence on the spirits of the company, and this, together with the information volunteered by Obadiah, that it was "arter nine," presently caused a general break-up.

PEREZ GOES TO MEETING

The very next day, as Squire Edwards and his family were sitting down to dinner, the eldest son Jonathan, a fine young fellow of sixteen, came in late with a blacked eye and torn clothes.

"My son," said Squire Edwards, sternly, "why do you come to the table in such a condition? What have you been doing?"

"I've been fighting Obadiah Weeks, sir, and I whipped him, too."

"And I shall whip you, sir, and soundly," said his father, with the Jove-like frown of the eighteenth century parent. "What have I told you about fighting? Go to your room, and wait for me there. You will have no dinner."

The boy turned on his heel without a word, and went out and up to his room. In the course of the afternoon, Squire Edwards was as good as his word. When he had come downstairs, after the discharge of his parental responsibilities, and gone into the store, Desire slipped up to Jonathan's room with a substantial luncheon under her apron. He was her favorite brother, and it was her habit thus surreptitiously to temper justice with mercy on occasions like the present. The lively satisfaction with which the youth hailed her appearance, gave ground to the suspicion that an empty stomach had been causing him more discomfort than a reproving conscience. As Desire was arranging the viands on the table she expressed a hope that the paternal correction had not been more painful than usual. The boy began to grin.

"Don't you fret about father's lickins," he said, "I'd just as lieve he'd lick me all day if he'll give me a couple o' minutes to get ready in. How many pair o' trowsers do you s'pose I've got on?"

"One, of course."

"Four," replied Jonathan, laying one forefinger by the side of his nose and winking at his sister. "I was sort of sorry for father, he got so tuckered trying to make me cry. Jimmeny, though, that veal pie looks good. I should hated to have lost that. You was real good to fetch it up.

"T'was only fair, though, this time," he continued, with his mouth full, "for t'was on 'count o' you I got to fightin."

"What do you mean?" said she.

"Why, Obadiah's been tellin the biggest set o' lies about you I ever heard of. He's been tellin em all over town. He said you went over to Elnathan Hamlin's, Wednesday, and got down on your knees to that Cap'n Hamlin, so's to get him not to have no more o' those horse-fiddles in front of Uncle's and our houses. You better believe I walloped him well, if he is bigger than me."

Jonathan, busy with eating, had not observed his sister's face during this recital, but now he said, glancing up:

"What on earth do you s'pose put such a lie into his head?"

"It isn't all a lie, Jonathan."

The boy laid down his knife and fork, and stared at her aghast.

"You don't mean you was over there?" he exclaimed.

Desire's face was crimson to the roots of her hair. She bowed her head.

"Wh-a-a-t!" said Jonathan, in a tone of utter disgust, tempered only by a remnant of incredulity.

"I didn't go on my knees to him," said Desire faintly.

"Oh, you didn't, didn't you? I believe you did," said the boy slowly, with an accent of ineffable scorn, rising to his feet and drawing away from his sister, as she seemed about to approach him.

Before the lad of sixteen, his elder sister, who had carried him in her arms as a baby, and been his teacher as a boy, stood like a culprit, quite abject. Finally she said:

"I didn't do it for myself. I did it for Aunt Lucy. The doctor said it would kill her if she was kept awake another night, and there was no other way to stop the mob. And so I did it."

"Was that the way?" said the boy, evidently staggered by this unexpected plea, and seeming quite at loss what to say.

"Yes," said Desire, rallying a little. "You might know it was. Do you think I'd do it any other way? I couldn't see Aunty die, could I?"

"No-o, darn it. I s'pose not," replied Jonathan slowly, as if he were not quite sure. His face wore a puzzled expression, the problem offered by this conflict of ethical obligations with caste sentiment being evidently too much for his boyish intellect. Evidently he had not inherited his grandfather's metaphysical faculty. Finally, with an air of being entirely posed, and losing interest in the subject, he sat down on the edge of his bed and abruptly closed the interview by observing:

"I'm going to take off some of these trowsers. They're too hot." Desire discreetly went out.

The only point in the observance of Sunday by the forefathers of New England, which is still generally practiced in these degenerate days, namely, the duty of sleeping later than usual that morning, was transgressed in at least one Stockbridge household on the Lord's Day following. Captain Perez Hamlin was up betimes and busy about house and barns. Since he had returned home he had taken the responsibility of all the chores about the place from the enfeebled shoulders of his father, besides supplying the place of man nurse to the invalids. This morning he had risen earlier than usual because he wanted to do up all the work before time for meeting.

It would have been easy for any one whose eye had followed him at his work, to see that his mind was preoccupied. Now he would walk about briskly, with head in the air, whistling as he went, or talking to the horse and cow, and anon bursting out laughing at his own absent-mindedness, as he found he had given the horse the cow's food, or put the meal into the water bucket. And again you would have certainly thought that he was fishing for the frogs at the bottom of the well instead of drawing water, so long did he stand leaning over the well-curb, before he bethought himself to loose his hold on the rope and let the ponderous well-sweep bring up the bucket.

He had not seen Desire Edwards since the Wednesday afternoon when she had called, but he knew he should see her at meeting. It was she who was responsible for the daydreaming way in which he was going about this morning, and for a good deal of previous daydreaming and night dreaming, too, in the last few days. The analogy of the tender passion to the chills and fever, had been borne out in his case by the usual alternations of complacency and depression. He told himself, that since he remembered so well his boyish courtship of her, she, too, doubtless remembered it. A woman was even more likely than a man to remember such things. Doubtless, she remembered too, that kiss she had given him. Her coming to him to ask his protection for her aunt, if she remembered those passages had some significance. She must have known that he would also remember them, and surely that would have deterred her from reopening their acquaintance had she found the reminiscences in question disagreeable. He assured himself that had it been wholly unpleasant for her to meet him, she would have been shrewd enough to devise some other way of securing the purpose of her visit. She had remained unmarried all the time of his absence, although she must have had suitors. Perhaps — well if this conjecture sounded a little conceited, be sure it was alternated with others self-depreciatory enough to balance it. But I have no space or need to describe the familiar process of architecture, by which with a perhaps for a keystone, possibilities for pillars, and dreams for pinnacles, lovers are wont to rear in a few idle hours, palaces outdazzling Aladdin's. I shall more profitably give a word or two of explanation to another point. Those familiar with the aristocratic constitution of New England society at this period, will perhaps deem it strange that the social gulf between the poor farmer's son, like Perez, and the daughter of one of the most distinguished families in Berkshire, should not have sufficed to deter the young man from indulging aspirations in that direction.

Perhaps, if he had grown up at home, such might have been the case, despite his boyish fondness for the girl. But the army of the revolution had been for its officers and more intelligent element, a famous school of democratic ideas. Perez was only one of thousands, who came home deeply imbued with principles of social equality; principles, which, despite finely phrased manifestoes and declarations of independence, were destined to work like a slow leaven for generations yet, ere they transformed the oligarchical system of colonial society, into the democracy of our day. It is true that, Paul Hubbard, Abner, Peleg, Meshech, and the rest, had been like Perez in the army, and yet the democratic impressions they had there received, now that they had returned home, served only to exasperate them against the pretensions of the superior class, without availing to eradicate their inbred instincts of servility in the presence of the very men they hated. Precisely this self-contemptuous recognition of his own servile feeling, operating on a morose temper, was the key to Hubbard's special bitterness toward the silk stockings. That Perez had none of this peasant's instinct, must, after all, be partly ascribed to the fact that his descent, by his mother's side, had been a gentleman's, and as Reuben had taken after Elnathan, so Perez was his mother's boy. He felt himself a gentleman, although a farmer's son. The air of dainty remoteness and distinction, which invested Desire in his imagination, was by virtue of her womanhood, solely, not as the representative of a higher class. He was penniless, she was rich, but to that sufficiently discouraging obstacle, no paralyzing sense of caste inferiority was added, in his mind.

Despite the dilatory and absent-minded procedure of the young man, by the time Prudence came out to call him in to the breakfast of fried pork and johnny-cake, the chores were done, and afterwards he had only to concern himself with his toilet. He stood a long time gazing ruefully at his coat, so sadly threadbare and white in the seams. It was his only one, and very old, but Prudence thought, when with a sigh he finally drew it on, that she had never seen so fine a soldier, and, indeed, the coat did look much better on than off, for a gallant bearing will, to some extent, redeem the most dilapidated attire.

Reuben had grown stronger from day to day, and though still weak, it was thought that he could well enough take care of George Fennell, during the forenoon, and allow the rest of the family to go to meeting. Perez had tinkered up the old cart, and contrived a harness out of ropes, by which his own horse could be attached to it, the farm horse having been long since sold off, and Mrs. Hamlin, who by reason of infirmities, had long been debarred from the privileges of the sanctuary, expected to be able by this means, to be present there this morning, to offer up devout thanksgiving for the mercy which had so wonderfully, in one week, restored her two sons to her.

It was half-past nine when the air was filled with a deep musical, melancholy sound, which appeared to come from the hill north of the village, where the meeting-house stood. It lasted, perhaps, five seconds, beginning with a long crescendo, and quivering into silence by an equally prolonged diminuendo. It was certainly an astonishing sound but none of the family appeared in the least agitated, Elnathan merely remarking:

"Thar's the warnin blow, Perez, I guess ye better be thinkin baout hitchin up." It were a pity indeed if the people of Stockbridge had not by that time become familiar with the sound of the old Indian conch-shell which since the mission church was founded at the first settlement of the town had served instead of a meeting-house bell. It may be well believed that strong lungs were the first requisite in sextons of that day. When an hour later the same dreary wail filled the valley once more with its weird echoes, the family was on its way to meeting, Mrs. Hamlin and Elnathan in the cart, and Perez with Prudence on foot. The congregation was now rapidly arriving from every direction, and the road was full of people. There were men on horseback with their wives sitting on a pillion behind, and clasping the conjugal waistband for security, families in carts, and families trudging afoot, while here and there the more pretentious members of the congregation were seen in chaises.

The new meeting-house on the hill had been built during Perez' absence, to supersede the old church on the green, with which his childish associations were connected. It had been erected directly after the close of the war and the effort in addition to the heavy taxation then necessary for public purposes, was such a drain on the resources of the town, as to have been a serious local aggravation of the distress of the times. According to the rule in church building religiously adhered to by the early New Englanders, the bleakest spot within the town limits had been selected for the meeting-house. It was a white barn-shaped structure, fifty feet by sixty, with a steeple, the pride of the whole countryside, sixty-two feet high, and tipped with a brass rooster brought from Boston, by way of weather vane.

Perez and Prudence separating at the door went to the several places which Puritan decorum assigned to those of the spinster and bachelor condition respectively, the former going into the right hand gallery, the other into the left, exceptions being however made in behalf of the owners of the square pews, who enjoyed the privilege of having their families with them in the house of God. Across the middle of the end gallery Dr. Partridge's square pew extended, so that by no means might the occupants of the two side galleries come within whispering distance of each other.

Obadiah Weeks, Abe Konkapot and Abner, who was a a widower and classed himself with bachelors, and a large number of other younger men whom Perez recognized as belonging to the mob under his leadership on Tuesday, were already in their seats. Fidgeting in unfamiliar boots and shoes, and meek with plentifully greased and flatly plastered hair, there was very little in the subdued aspect of these young men to remind any one of the truculent rebels who a few days before had shaken their bludgeons in the faces of the Honorable the Justices of the Common Pleas. As Perez entered the seat with them, they recognized him with sheepish grins, as much as to say, "We're all in the same box," quite as the occupants of a prisoner's dock might receive a fellow victim thrust in with them by the sheriff. Obadiah reached out his clenched first with something in it, and Perez putting forth his hand, received therein a lot of dried caraway seeds. "Thort mebbe ye hadn't got no meetin seed," whispered Obadiah.

Owing to the fact that nine years absence from home had weaned him somewhat from native customs, Perez had, in fact, forgotten to lay in a supply of this inestimable simple, to the universal use of which by our forefathers during religious service, may probably be ascribed their endurance of Sabbatical and doctrinal rigors to which their descendants are confessedly unequal. It is well known that their knowledge of the medicinal uses of common herbs was far greater than ours, and it was doubtless the discovery of some secret virtue, some occult theological reaction, if I may so express myself, in the seeds of the humble caraway, which led to the undeviating rule of furnishing all the members of every family, from children to grey heads, with a small quantity to be chewed in the mouth and mingled with the saliva during attendance on the stated ordinances of the Gospel. Whatever may be thought of this theory, the fact will not be called in question that in the main, the relaxation of religious doctrine and Sabbath observance in New England, has proceeded side by side with the decline in the use of meetin seed.

In putting all the young men together in one gallery, it may be thought that some risk was incurred of making that a quarter of disturbance. But if the tithingman, with his argus-eyes and long rod were not enough to insure propriety, the charming rows of maidens on the seats of the gallery directly opposite could have been relied on to complete the work. The galleries were very deep, and the distance across the meeting house, from the front seat of one to that of the other, was not over twenty-five feet. At this close range, reckoning girls' eyes to have been about as effective then as they are now-a-days, it may be readily inferred what havoc must have been wrought on the bachelors' seats in the course of a two hour service. After being exposed to such a fire all day, it was no wonder at all, quite apart from other reasons, that on Sunday night the young men found their ardor inflamed to a pitch at which an interview with the buxom enslaver became a necessity.

The singers sat in the front seat of the galleries, the bass singers in the front seat on the bachelors' side, the treble in the front seat on the spinsters' side, and the alto and tenor singers in the wings of the end gallery, separated by Dr. Partridge's pew. For, as in most New England churches at this date, the "old way," of purely congregational singing by "lining out," had given place to select choirs, an innovation however, over which the elder part of the people still groaned and croaked. On the back seats of the end gallery, behind the tenors and altos respectively sat the negro freedmen and freedwomen, the Pomps and Cudjos, the Dinahs and Blossoms. Sitting by Prudence, among the treble singers, Perez noticed a young Indian girl of very uncommon beauty, and refinement of features, her dark olive complexion furnishing a most perfect foil to the blooming face of the white girl.

"Who's that girl by Prudence Fennell?" he whispered to Abe Konkapot, who sat beside him. The young Indian's bronze face flushed darkly, as he replied:

"That's Lucretia Nimham."

Perez was about to make further inquiries, when it flashed on him that this was the girl, whom Obadiah had jokingly alluded to as the reason why Abe had lingered in Stockbridge, instead of moving out to York State with his tribe. She certainly was a very sufficient reason for a man's doing or not doing almost anything.

From his position in the gallery, Perez could look down on the main body of the congregation below, and his cheek flushed with anger as he saw his father and mother occupying one of the seats in the back part of the room, in the locality considered least in honor, according to the distinctions followed by the parish committee, in periodically reseating the congregation, or "dignifying the seats," as the people called it. Considerably nearer the pulpit, and in seats of correspondingly greater dignity, he recognized Israel Goodrich and Ezra Phelps, the two men of chiefest estate among the insurgents. Directly under and before the pulpit, almost beneath it, in fact, facing the people from behind a sort of railing, sat Deacon Nash. His brother deacon, no less an one than Squire Timothy Edwards, has not yet arrived.

As he looked over the fast filling house, for he and Prudence had arrived rather early, he met many eyes fixed curiously upon him. Sometimes a whisper would pass along a seat, from person to person, till one after another, the entire row had turned and stared intently at him. It was fame.

WHAT HAPPENED AFTER MEETING

There had been considerable discussion during the week as to whether Squire Woodbridge, in view of the public humiliation which had been put upon him, would expose himself to the curious gaze of the community by coming to meeting the present Sunday. It had been the more prevalent opinion that he would find in the low condition of Mrs. Woodbridge, who was hovering between life and death, a reason which would serve as an excuse for not "attending on the stated ordinances of the gospel," the present Sabbath. But now from those whose position enabled them to command a view of the front door of the meeting-house, rose a sibilant whisper, distinct above the noise of boots and shoes upon the uncarpeted aisles:

"Here he comes! Here comes Squire."

There were several gentlemen in Stockbridge who, by virtue of a liberal profession or present or past official dignities, had a claim, always rigorously enforced and scrupulously conceded, to the title of Esquire, but when "*The* Squire," was spoken of, it was always Jahleel Woodbridge whom the speaker had in mind. Decidedly, those who thought he would not dare to appear in public had mistaken his temper. His face, always that of a full-blooded man, was redder than common, in fact, contrasted with the white powder of his wig, it seemed almost purple, but that was the only sign he gave that he was conscious of the people's looks. He wore a long-skirted, straight-cut coat of fine blue cloth with brass buttons; a brown waistcoat, and small clothes, satin hose with ruffled white shirt and cuffs. Under one arm he carried his three-cornered hat and under the other his gold-headed cane, and walked with his usual firm, heavy, full-bodied step; the step of a man who is not afraid of making a noise, and expects that people will look at him. There was not the slightest deflection from the old-time arrogance in the stiff carriage of the head and eyes, nor anything whatever to show that he considered himself one jot or tittle less the autocrat of Stockbridge, than on the Sunday a week ago. Walking the whole length of the meeting-house, he opened the door of the big square pew at the right hand of the pulpit, considered the first in honor, and the only part of the interior of the meeting-house, save the pulpit and sounding-board, which was painted. One by one the numerous children who called him father, passed before him into the pew. Then he closed the door and sat down facing the congregation, and slowly and deliberately looked at the people. As his glance traveled steadily along the lines of seats, the starers left off staring and looked down abashed. After he had thus reviewed the seats below, he turned his eyes upward and proceeded to scan the galleries with the same effect.

So strong was the impression made by this unruffled and authoritative demeanor, that the people were fain to scratch their heads and look at one another in vacant questioning, as if doubtful if they had not dreamed all this, about the great man's being put down by Perez Hamlin, insulted by the mob, and reduced even now to such powerlessness that he owed the protection of his sick wife to the favor of the threadbare Continental captain up there in the gallery. To those conscious of having had a part in these doings, there was a disagreeably vivid suggestion of the stocks and whipping post in the Squire's haughty stare, against which even a sense of their numbers failed to reassure them. Of course the revolt had gained far too great headway to be now suppressed by anybody's personal prestige, by the frowns and

stares of any number of Squire Woodbridges, but, nevertheless, the impression which even after the events of the last
week, he was still able to make upon the people, by his
mere manner, was striking testimony to their inveterate habit
of awe toward him, as the embodiment of secular authority
in their midst.

Perez had been too long absent from home, and differed
too much in habits of thought, to fully understand the sentiments of the peasants round him for the Squire, and in truth
his attention was diverted from that gentleman ere he had
time to fully observe the effect of his entrance. For he had
scarcely reached his pew, when Squire and Deacon Timothy
Edwards came up the aisle, followed by his family. Desire
wore a blue silk skirt and close-fitting bodice, with a white
lace kerchief tucked in about her shoulders, and the same
blue plumed hat of soft Leghorn straw, in which we have
seen her before, the wide brim falling lower on one side
than the other, over her dark curls. As she swept up the
aisle between the rows of farmers and farmers' wives, the
contrast between their coarse, ill-fitting and sad-colored
homespun, and her rich and tasteful robes, was not more
striking than the difference between the delicate distinction
of her features and their hard, rough faces, weather-beaten
and wrinkled with toil and exposure, or sallow and hollow
cheeked with care and trouble. She looked like one of a
different order of beings, and indeed, it is nothing more
than truth to say that such was exactly the opinion which
Miss Desire herself entertained. The eyes of admiration with
which the girls leaning over the gallery followed her up the
aisle, were quite without a spark of jealousy, for they knew
that their rustic sweethearts would no more think of loving
her than of wasting their passion on the moon. She was meat
for their betters, for some great gentleman from New York
or Boston, all in lace and ruffles, some judge or senator, or,
greater still, maybe some minister.

To tell the whole truth, however, the admiring attention which her own sex accorded to Desire on Sundays, was rather owing to the ever varying attractions of her toilet, than to her personal charms. If any of the damsels of Stockbridge who went to bed without their supper Sunday night, because they couldn't remember the text of the sermon, had been allowed to substitute an account of Desire Edwards' toilet, it is certain they would not have missed an item. It was the chief boast of Mercy Scott, the Stockbridge seamstress, that Desire trusted her new gowns to her instead of sending to New York for them. From the glow of pride and importance on Miss Mercy's rather dried-up features, when Desire wore a new gown for the first time to church, it was perfectly evident that she looked upon herself as the contributor of the central feature of the day's services. At the quilting and apple paring bees held about the time of such a new gown, Miss Mercy was the center of interest, and no other gossip was started till she had completed her confidences as to the material, cost, cut and fit of the foreshadowed garment. It was with glistening eyes and fingers that forgot their needles, that these wives and daughters of poor hard-working farmers, drank in the details about rich eastern silks and fabrics of gorgeous tints and airy textures, their own coarse, butternut homespun quite forgotten in imagined splendors. In their rapt attention there was no tinge of envy, for such things were too far above their reach to be once thought of in connection with themselves. It was upon the fit of Desire's dresses, however, that Miss Mercy, with the instinct of the artist, grew most impassioned.

" 'Tain't no credit to me a fittin her," she would sometimes protest. "Thar's some figgers you can't fetch cloth tew, nohow. But, deary me, lands sakes alive, the cloth seems tew love her, it clings to her so nateral. An tain't no wonder ef it doos. I never see sech a figger. Why her ——." But Miss Mercy's audiences at such times were exclusively composed of ladies. She had no inflamable masculine imaginations to consider.

It was a very noticeable circumstance on the present Sunday, that all the persons in the meeting-house who looked at Desire as she walked up the aisle, proceeded immediately afterwards to screw around their necks and stare at Perez, thereby betraying that the sight of the one had immediately suggested the other to their minds.

The Edwards seat was the second in dignity in the meeting-house, being the one on the left of the pulpit, and ranking with that of the Sedgwicks, although as between the several leading pews the distinction was not considered so decided as to be odious. Having ushered his family to their place, Squire Edwards took his own official seat as deacon, beside Deacon Nash, behind the railing, below the pulpit and facing the people.

And now Parson West comes up the aisle in flowing gown and bands, his three-cornered hat under his arm, and climbs the steps into the lofty pulpit, sets the hour glass up in view, and the service begins. There is singing, a short prayer, and again singing, and then the entire congregation rises, the seats are fastened up that none may sit, and the long prayer begins, and goes on and on for nearly an hour. Then there is another psalm, and then the sermon begins. Up at Pittsfield to-day, you may be very sure that Parson Allen is giving his people a rousing discourse on the times, wherein the sin of rebellion is treated without gloves, and the duty of citizens to submit to the powers that be, and to maintain lawful authority even to the shedding of blood, are vigorously set forth. But Parson West is not a political parson, and there is not a word in his sermon which his hearers, watchful for anything of the kind, can construe into a reference to the existing events of the past week. It is his practice to keep several sermons on hand, and this might just as well have been prepared a thousand years before. It was upon the subject of the deplorable consequences of neglecting the baptism of infants.

If a parent truly gave up a child in baptism, it would be accepted and saved, whether it died in infancy or lived to pass through the mental exercises of an adult convert. But on the other hand, if that duty was purposely neglected, or if baptism was unaccompanied by a proper frame of mind in the parent, there was no reason or hint from revelation to believe that the child was saved. Considering that the infant was justly liable to eternal suffering on account of Adam's sin, it was impossible for the human mind to see how God could be just and yet the justifier of an unbaptized infant. But it was not for the human mind to limit infinite mercy and wisdom, and possibly in His secret councils God had devised a way of salvation even for so desperate a case. So that while hope was not absolutely forbidden to parents who had neglected the baptism of their infants, confidence would be most wicked and presumptuous.

Deacon Edwards fidgeted on his seat at the laxity of this doctrine as well might the son of Jonathan Edwards, and Deacon Nash, who inherited his Calvinism from a father who had moved from Westfield to Stockbridge for the express purpose of sitting under that renowned divine, seemed equally uncomfortable. Parson West, as a young man, had been notoriously affected with Arminian leanings, and although his conversion to Calvinism by Dr. Hopkins of Great Barrington, had been deemed a wonderful work of grace, a tendency to sacrifice the logical development of doctrines to the weak suggestions of the flesh, was constantly cropping out in his sermons, to the frequent grief and scandal of the deacons.

At length the service was at an end and the hum and buzz of voices rose from all parts of the house, as the people passing out of their pews met and greeted each other in the aisles. The afternoon service came in an hour and a half, and only those went home who lived close at hand or could easily make the distances in their carriages. These took with them such friends and acquaintances as they might invite. Others of the congregation spent the brief nooning in the "noon-house," a shed near by, erected for this purpose. There, or on the meeting-house steps, or maybe seated near by on the grass and using the stumps of felled trees, with which it was studded, for tables, they discussed the sermon as a relish to their lunches of doughnuts, cheese, pie and ginger-bread. To converse on any other than religious subjects on the Sabbath, was a sin and a scandal which exposed the offender to church discipline, but in a public emergency like the present, when rebellion was rampant throughout the county, it was impossible that political affairs should not preoccupy the most pious minds. Talk of them the people must and did, of the stopping of the courts, the breaking of the jails, of Squire Woodbridge and Perez Hamlin, of the news from the other counties, and of what would next take place, but it was amusing to see the ingenious manner by which the speakers contrived to compound with their consciences and prevent scandal by giving a pious twist and a Sabbatical intonation to their sentences.

Among the younger people, as might be expected, there was less of this affectation. They were all discussing with eager interest something which had just happened.

"Wal, all I say is I don't want to be a lady if it makes folks so crewel an so deceitful as that," said Submit Goodrich, a black-eyed, bright cheeked wench, old Israel's youngest daughter. "To think o' her pretendin not to know him, right afore all the folks, and she on her knees to him a cryin only four days ago. I don't care if she is Squire Edwards' gal, I hain't got no opinyun o' such doin's."

Most of the girls agreed with Submit, but some of the young men were inclined to laugh at Perez, saying it was good enough for him, and that he who was nothing more

than a farmer like the rest of them was served right for trying
to push in among the big folks.

"I s'pose she's dretful riled to think it's all 'round bout her
goin over to the Hamlins las' week an she thort she'd jess
let folks see she was as proud as ever. Land! How red he
was! I felt reel bad for him, and such a nice bow ez he made,
jess like any gentleman!"

"I callate Jerushy wouldn't a been so hard on him," jeal-
ously snickered a young farmer sitting by the young woman
who last spoke.

"No, I wouldn't," she said, turning sharply to him. "I
s'pose ye thort I wasn't no judge o' hansome men, cause
I let you keep kumpny with me." There was nothing more
from that quarter.

But what is it they are talking about anyway? Why, simply
this: In front of the meeting-house, as they came out from
the service, Perez met Desire face to face. All the people were
standing around, talking and waiting to see the great folks
get into their carriages to drive home. Naturally, everybody
looked with special interest to see the meeting of these two
whose names gossip had so constantly coupled during the
week. Jonathan was with Desire, and looked fiercely at Perez,
but his fierceness was quite wasted. Perez did not see him. He
took off his hat and bowed to her with an air of the most
profound respect. She gave not the faintest sign of recognition, even to the dropping of an eyelid. The people had
stopped talking and were staring. The blood rushed to Perez'
forehead.

"Good day, Miss Edwards," he said, firmly and distinctly,
yet respectfully, his hat still in his hand. Jonathan, in his
indignation, was as red as he, but Desire could not have
appeared more unconscious of being addressed had she been
stone deaf as well as blind. In a moment more she had passed
on and entered the carriage, and the people were left with
something to talk about. Now, Captain Perez Hamlin had

gone to meeting that morning as much in love with Desire
Edwards as four days thinking of little else save a fair face
and charming form might be expected to leave a susceptible
young man, particularly when the manly passion is but the
resurrection of an unforgotten love of boyhood. He walked
home somewhat more angry with the same young woman
than he could remember ever having been with anybody.
If a benevolent fairy had asked him his dearest wish just
then, it would have been that Desire Edwards might be
transformed into a young gentleman for about five minutes,
in order that he might impart to him the confoundedest thrash-
ing that a young gentleman ever experienced, nor did even
the consciousness that no such transformation was possible,
prevent his fingers from tingling with a most ungallant
aspiration to box her small ears till they were as red as his
own face had been at the moment she cut him so coolly.
For he was a very proud man, was Captain Perez Hamlin,
with a soldier's sensitiveness to personal affronts, and none
of that mean opinion of himself and his position in society
which helped the farmers around to bear with equanimity
the snubs of those they regarded as their natural superiors.

The father and mother had fortunately driven on before
the scene took place, and so at least he was spared the added
exasperation of being condoled with on arriving at home.
Prudence had stayed to the afternoon service. Toward twilight, as he was walking to and fro behind the barn, and
indulging an extremely unsanctified frame of mind, she came
to him and blurted out, breathlessly:

"All the girls think she was mean and wicked, and I'll
never do any more work for her or Mis Woodbridge either,"
and before he could answer she had run back into the house
with burning cheeks. He had seen that her eyes were also
full of tears. It was clear she had been struggling hard between the pity which prompted her to tender some form of
consolation, and her fear of speaking to him.

The dreamy habit of the mind induced by love in its first stage, often extends to the point of overspreading all the realities of life and the circumstances of the individual, with a glamour, which for the time being, disguises the hard and rigid outlines of fact. The painful shock which had so sharply ended Perez' brief delusion, that Desire might possibly accept his devotion, had at the same time roused him to a recognition of the critical position of himself and his father's family. What business had he or they lingering here in Stockbridge? Yesterday, in the vague unpractical way in which hopeful lovers do all their thinking he had thought they might remain indefinitely. Now he saw that it would be tempting Providence to postpone any further the carrying out of his original plan, of moving with them to New York State. The present insurrection might last a longer or shorter time, but there was no reason to think it would result in remedying the already desperate financial condition of the family. The house was to have been sold the past week, and doubtless would be as soon as affairs were a little quieter. Reuben was, moreover, liable to re-arrest and imprisonment on his old debt, and as for himself, he knew that his life was forfeit to the gallows for the part he had taken in the rebellion.

Once across the state line, however, they would be as safe as in Europe, for the present Union of the states was not yet formed, and the loose and nerveless bond of the old Federation, then in its last stage of decrepitude, left the states practically foreign countries to each other. His idea was then to get the family over into New York without delay, with such remnants of the farm stock as could be got together, and leaving them for the winter at New Lebanon, just the other side the border, to go on himself, meanwhile, to the western part of the state, to secure a farm in the new tracts being already opened up in that rich region, and rapidly filling with settlers. For the populating of the west, and New York

was then the west, has gone on by successive waves of emigra-
tion, set in motion by periodical epochs of financial and industrial distress in the Atlantic states, and the first of these
impulses, the hard times following the Revolution, was already sending thousands to seek new homes toward the setting
sun.

Busy with preparations for the start, he kept close at home
during the entire week following. Only once or twice did he
even go down street, and then on some errand. Obadiah
dropped around frequently and looked on as he worked,
evidently having something on his mind. One twilight as
Perez was cutting wood for the evening fire, the young man
came into the back yard and opened conversation in this
wise:

"Guess it's gonter rain."

"Looks a little like it," Perez assented.

Obadiah was silent a space, and ground the heel of his bare
foot into the dirt.

"D'you know what's good fer warts?" he finally asked. Perez
said he did not. After a pause, Obadiah remarked critically:

"Them bricks roun' the top o' the chimly be kinder loose,
bean't they?" They were, and Perez freely admitted as much.
Obadiah looked around for some other topic of conversation,
but apparently finding none, he picked up a stone and asked
with affected carelessness, as he jerked it toward the barn:

"Be ye a gonter take George Fennell 'long with ye?"

"No," said Perez. "He will not live long, I fear, and he can't
be moved. I suppose some of the people will take him and
Prudence in, when we go."

Obadiah said nothing, but from the change which instantly
came over his manner, it was evident that the information
obtained with such superfluous diplomacy was a prodigious
relief to his mind. The officiousness with which he urged a
handful of chestnuts on Perez, and even offered to carry in
the wood for him, might moreover be construed as indicating

a desire to make amends to him for unjust suspicions secretly cherished. As for asking Prudence directly whether she was expecting to go away, that would have been a piece of hardihood of which the bashful youth was quite incapable. If he could not have ascertained her intentions otherwise than by such a desperate measure, he would have waited till the Hamlins set out, and then been on hand to see for himself whether she went or not.

AN AUCTION SALE AND
ITS CONSEQUENCES

Squire Woodbridge had not failed to detect the first signs of decrease in the ebullition of the popular mind after the revolt of Tuesday, and when by Friday and Saturday the mob had apparently quite disappeared, and the village had returned to its normal condition, he assured himself that the rebellion was all over, and it only remained for him and his colleagues cautiously to get hold of the reins again, and then — then for the whip. For, the similitude under which the Squire oftenest thought of the people of Stockbridge was that of a team of horses which he was driving. There had been a little runaway, and he had been pitched out on his head. Let him once get his grip on the lines again, and the whip in his hand, and there should be some fine dancing among the leaders, or his name was not Jahleel Woodbridge, Esquire, and the whipping post on the green was nothing but a rosebush.

He was in a hurry for two reasons to get the reins in his hands again. In the first place, for the very natural and obvious reason that he grudged every moment of immunity from punishment enjoyed by men who had put him to such an open shame. The other and less obvious reason was the expected return of Squire Sedgwick from Boston. Sedgwick had been gone a week. He might be absent a week or two weeks more, but he might return any day. One thing was evident to Jahleel Woodbridge. Before this man returned, of whose growing and rival influence he had already so much reason to be jealous, he must have put an end to anarchy in Stockbridge, and once more stand at the head of its government. Sedgwick had warned him of the explosive state of popular feeling: he had resented that warning, and the event had proved his rival right. The only thing now left him was to show Sedgwick that if he had not been able to foresee the rebellion, he had been able to suppress it. Nevertheless he would proceed cautiously.

The red flag of the sheriff had for some weeks waved from the gable end of a small house on the main street, owned by a Baptist cobbler, one David Joy. There were quite a number of Baptists among the Welsh iron-workers at West Stockbridge, and some Methodists, but none of either heresy save David in Stockbridge, which, with this exception was, as a parish, a Congregational lamb without blemish. No wonder then that David was a thorn in the side to the authorities of the church, nor was he less despised by the common people. There was not a drunken loafer in town who did not pride himself upon the fact that, though he might be a drunkard, he was at least no Baptist, but belonged to the "Standing Order." Meshech Little, himself, who believed and practiced the doctrine of total immersion in rum, had no charity for one who believed in total immersion in water.

The date which had been set for the sale of David's goods and house, chanced to be the very Monday following the Sunday with whose religious services and other events the previous chapters have been concerned. It seemed to Squire Woodbridge that David's case would be an excellent one with which to inaugurate once more the reign of law. Owing to the social isolation and unpopularity of the man, the proceedings against him would be likely to excite very little sympathy or agitation of any kind, and having thus got the machinery of the law once more into operation, it would be easy enough to proceed thereafter, without fear or favor, against all classes of debtors and evil-doers in the good old way. Moreover, it had long been the intention of those having the interest of Zion at heart to "freeze out" David by this very process, and to that end considerable sanctified shrewdness had been expended in getting him into debt. So that by enforcing the sale in his case, two birds would, so to speak, be killed with one stone, and the political and spiritual interests of the parish be coincidently furthered, making it altogether an undertaking on which the blessing of Heaven might be reasonably looked for.

At three o'clock in the afternoon the sale took place. Everything worked as the Squire had expected. It being the general popular supposition that there were to be no more sheriffs' sales, there were no persons present at the auction save the officers of the law and the gentlemen who were to bid. Only here and there an astonished face peered out of a window at the proceedings, and a knot of loafers, who had been boozing away the afternoon, stood staring in the door of the tavern. That was all. There was no crowd, and no attempt at interruption. But the news that a man had been sold out for debt spread fast, and by sunset, when the men and boys came home from their farm-work or mechanical occupations, numerous groups of excited talkers had gathered in the streets. There was a very full meeting that night at the tavern.

"I declar for't," said Israel Goodrich, with an air of mingled disappointment and wrath, "I be reel put aout, an disappinted like. I dunno what tew make on't. I callated the trouble wuz all over, an times wuz gonter be good and folks live kinder neighbourly 'thout no more suein an jailin, an sellin aout, same ez long from '74 tew '80. I reckoned sure nuff them times wuz come 'round agin, an here they've gone an kicked the pot over, an the fat's in the fire agin, bad's ever."

"Darn em. Gosh darn em, I say," exclaimed Abner. "Didn't they git our idee what we wuz arter wen we stopped the courts? Did they think we wuz a foolin baout it? That's what I want some feller tew tell me. Did they think we wuz a foolin?"

Abner's usually good humoured face was darkly flushed, and there was an ugly gleam in his eye as he spoke.

"We wuz so quiet like las' week, they callated we'd jess hed our fling an got over it. I guess that wuz haow it wuz," said Peleg Bidwell.

"Did they think we'd been five year a gittin our dander up an would git over it in a week?" demanded Abner, glaring round. "If t'wuz caze we wuz tew quiet, we'll make racket nuff to suit em arter this, hey, boys? If racket's the ony thing they kin understan, they shall hev a plenty on't."

"Israel thought it wuz kingdom come already," said Paul Hubbard, who had hurried down from the iron-works with a gang of his myrmidons, on receipt of the news. "He thought the silk stockings was goin to give right in as sweet as sugar. Not by a darned sight. No sir. They ain't going to let go so easy. They ain't none o' that sort. They mean to have the old times back again, and they'll have em back, too, unless you wake up and show em you're in earnest."

"Not yit awhile, by the everlastin Jocks," shouted Abner. "Ef thar's any vartue in gunpowder them times shan't come back," and there was an answering yell that shook the room.

"That's the talk, Abner. Give us yer paw," said Paul, delighted to find the people working up to his own pitch of bitter and unrelenting animosity against the gentlemen. "That's the talk, but it'll take more'n talk. Look here men, three out of four of you have done enough already to get a dozen lashes on his bare back, if the silk stockings get on top again. It's all in a nutshell. If we don't keep them under they'll keep us under. We've just got to take hold and raise the devil with them. If we don't give them the devil, they'll give us the devil. Take your choice. It's one or the other."

There was a chorus of exclamations.

"That's so." "By gosh we're in for't, an we might's well go ahead." "Ye're right, Paul." "We'll git aout the hoss-fiddles an give em some mewsic." "We'll raise devil nuff fer em ter night." "Come on fellers." "Les give em a bonfire."

There was a general movement of the men out of the bar-room, all talking together, clamorously suggesting plans, or merely, as in the case of the younger men and boys, venting their excitement in hoots and catcalls. It was a close dark night, obscure enough to make cowards brave, and the crowd that surged out of the tavern were by no means cowards, but angry and resolute men, whose exasperation at the action of the authorities, was sharpened and pointed by well-founded apprehensions of the personal consequences to themselves which that action threatened if not resisted. Some one's sug-gestion that they should begin by putting David Joy and his family back into their house, was received with acclamation and they were forthwith fetched from a neighboring shed, under which they had encamped for the night, and without much ceremony thrust into their former residence and ordered to stay there. For though in this case David happened to be identified with their own cause, it went against their grain to help a Baptist.

"Now, boys, les go an see Iry Seymour," said Abner, and with a yell, the crowd rushed off in the direction of the deputy sheriff's house.

Their blood was up, and it was perhaps well for that official that he did not wait to be interviewed. As the crowd surged up before the house, a man's figure was seen dimly flitting across the field behind, having apparently emerged from the back door. There was a yell "There goes Iry," and half the mob took after him, but, thanks to the darkness, the nimble-footed sheriff made good his escape, and his pursuers presently re-turned, breathless, but in high good humor over the novel sport, protesting that they laughed so hard they couldn't run.

The only other important demonstration by the mob that evening, was the tearing up of the fence in front of Squire Woodbridge's house and the construction of an immense bonfire in the street out of the fragments, the conflagration proceeding to the accompaniment of an obligato on the horse-fiddles.

So it came to pass that, as sometimes happens in such cases, Squire Woodbridge's first attempt to get the reins of the runaway team into his hands, had the effect of startling the horses into a more headlong gallop than ever.

If the events of the night, superadded to the armed revolt of the week before, left any doubt in the most sanguine mind that the present disturbances were no mere local and trifling irritations, but a general rebellion, the news which was in the village early the following morning, must have dispelled it. This news was that the week before, an armed mob of several hundred had stopped the courts at their meeting in Worcester and forced an adjournment for two months; that the entire state, except the district close around Boston, was in a ferment; that the people were everywhere arming and drilling and fully determined that no more courts should sit till the distresses of the times had been remedied. As yet the state authorities had taken no action looking toward the suppression of the insurrection, in which, indeed, the great majority of the population appeared actively or sympathetically engaged. The messenger reported that in the lower counties a sprig of hemlock in the hat, had been adopted as the badge of the insurgents, and that the towns through which he had ridden seemed to have fairly turned green, so universally did men, women and children wear the hemlock. The news had not been an hour in Stockbridge before every person on the streets had a bit of hemlock in their hat or hair. I say every person upon the street, for those who belonged to the anti-popular or court party, took good care to keep within doors that morning.

"I'm glad to see the hemlock, agin," said Israel Goodrich. "The old pine tree flag wuz a good flag to fight under. There wuz good blood spilt under it in the old colony days. Thar wuz better times in this 'ere province o' Massachusetts Bay, under the pine tree flag, than this dum Continental striped rag hez ever fetched, or ever will, I reckon."

The dismay which the news of the extent and apparent irresistibleness of the rebellion produced among those attached to the court party in Stockbridge, corresponded to the exultation to which the people gave themselves up. Nor did the populace lose any time in giving expression to their bolder temper by overt acts. About nine o'clock in the morning, Deputy Sheriff Seymour, who had not ventured to return to his house, was found concealed in the corn-bin of a barn near the burying-ground. A crowd instantly collected and dragged the terrified man from his concealment. Some one yelled:

"Ride him on a rail," and the suggestion finding an echo in the popular breast, a three-cornered fence rail was thrust between his legs, and lifted on men's shoulders. Astride of this sharp-backed steed, holding on with his hands for dear life, lest he should fall off and break his neck, he was carried through the main streets of the village, followed by a howling crowd, and pelted with apples by the boys, while the windows of the houses along the way were full of laughing women. Having graced the popular holiday by this involuntary exhibition of himself, Seymour was let go without suffering any further violence, the crowd appearing boisterously jocose rather than embittered in temper. Master Hopkins, a young man who had recently entered Squire Sedgwick's office to study law, was next pounced upon, having indiscreetly ventured on the street, and treated to a similar free ride, which was protracted until the youth purchased surcease by consenting to wear a sprig of hemlock in his hat.

About the middle of the forenoon Squire Woodbridge, Deacon Nash, Dr. Partridge, with Squire Edwards and several other gentlemen were sitting in the back room of the store. It was a gloomy council. Woodbridge quaffed his glass of rum in short, quick unenjoying gulps, and said not a word. The others from time to time dropped a phrase or two expressive of the worst apprehensions as to what the mob might do, and entire discouragement as to the possibility of doing anything to restrain them. Suddenly, young Jonathan Edwards, who was in the outer room tending store, cried out:

"Father, the mob is coming. Shall I shut the door?"

Squire Edwards cried "Yes," and hastily went out to assist, but Dr. Partridge, with more presence of mind than the others seemed to possess at that moment, laid his hand on the storekeeper's arm, saying:

"Better not shut the door. They will tear the house down if you do. Resistance is out of the question."

In another moment a boisterous crowd of men, their faces flushed with drink, all wearing sprigs of hemlock in their hats, came pouring up the steps and filled the store, those who could not enter thronging the piazza and grinning in at the windows. Edwards and the other gentlemen stood at bay at the back end of the store, in front of the liquor hogsheads. Their bearing was that of men who expected personal violence, but in a justifiable agitation did not forget their personal dignity. But the expression on the face of Abner, who was the leader of the gang, was less one of exasperation than of sardonic humor.

"Good mornin," he said.

"Good morning, Abner," replied Edwards, propitiatingly.

"It's a good mornin and it's good news ez is come to taown. I s'pose ye hearn it a' ready. I thort so. Ye look ez ef ye hed. But we didn' come tew talk 'baout that. Thar wuz a leetle misunderstandin yisdy 'baout selling aout David. He ain't nothin but a skunk of a Baptis, an ef Iry hed put him in the stocks or licked him 'twould a sarved him right. But ye see some of the boys hev got a noshin agin heven any more fellers sole aout fer debt, an we've been a explainin our idee to Iry this mornin. I callate he's got it through his head, Iry hez."

Ye see ef neighbors be gonter live together peaceable they've jess got ter unnerstan each other. What do yew s'pose Iry said? He said Squire thar tole him to sell David aout. In course we didn' b'leeve that. Squire ain't no gol darned fool, ez that would make him aout ter be. He knowd the men ez stopped the courts las' week wouldn' be afeard o' stoppin a sherriff. He knows the folks be in arnest 'baout hevin an eend on sewin an sellin an sendin tew jail. Squire knows, an ye all know that thar'll be fightin fore thar's any more sellin."

Abner had grown excited as he spoke, and the peculiar twinkle in his eye had given place to a wrathy glare as he uttered the last words, but this passed, and it was with his former sardonic grin that he added:

"But Iry didn' save his hide by tryin tew lay it orf ontew Squire an I guess he won't try no more sellin aout right away, not ef Goramity tole him tew."

"Yer gab's runnin away with yer. Git to yer p'int, Abner," said Peleg Bidwell.

"Lemme 'lone I'm comin 'roun," replied Abner. "Ye wuz over't the sale yisdy, warn't ye, Squire?" he said, addressing Edwards.

"Yes, Abner."

"Wal, ye see, when we come tew put back David's folks intew the haouse his woman missed the clock, and somebody said ez haow ye'd took et."

"I bid it in," said Edwards.

"I s'pose ye clean furgut t'wuz the on'y clock she hed," suggested Abner with a bland air of accounting for the other's conduct on the most favorable supposition.

Edwards, making no reply save to grow rather red, Abner continued:

"In course ye furgut it, that's what I tole the fellers, for ye wouldn't go and take the on'y clock a poor man hed wen ye've got a plenty, 'nless ye furgut. Ye see we knowed ye'd wanter send it right back soon ez ye thort o' that, and so we jess called in for't, callaten tew save ye the trouble."

"But — but I bought it," stammered Edwards.

"Sartin, sartin," said Abner. "Jess what I sed, ye bought it caze ye clean furgut it wuz David's on'y one, an he poor an yew rich. Crypus! Squire, ye hain't got no call tew explain it tew us. Ye see we knows yer ways Squire. We knows how apt ye be tew furgit jiss that way. We kin make allowances fer ye."

Edwards' forehead was crimson.

"There's the clock," he said, pointing to it where it lay on the counter. Abner took it up and put it under his arm, saying:

"David 'll be 'bliged to ye, Squire, when I tell him how cheerful ye sent it back. Some o' the fellers," he pursued with an affectation of a confidential tone, "some o' the fellers said mebbe ye wouldn't send it back cheerful. They said ye'd got no more compassion fer the poor than a flint stun. They said, them fellers did, that ye'd never in yer life let up on a man as owed ye, an would take a feller's last drop o' blood sooner'n lose a penny debt. They said, them fellers did, that yer hands, wite ez they looks, wuz red with the blood o' them that ye'd sent to die in jail."

Abner's voice had risen to a tremendous crescendo of indignation, and he seemed on the point of quite forgetting his ironical affectation, when, with an effort which added to the effect, he checked himself and resuming his former tone and grin, he added:

"I argyed with them fellers ez said them things bout ye. I tole em haow it couldn't be so, caze ye wuz a deakin, an hed family prayers, and could pray mos' ez long ez parson. But I couldn't do nothin with em, they wuz so sot. Wy them fellers akchilly said ye took this ere clock a knowin that it wuz David's on'y one, wen ye hed a plenty o' yer own tew. Jess think o' that Squire. What a hoggish old hunks they took ye fer, didn't they, naow?" Edwards glared at his tormentor with a countenance red and white with speechless rage, but Abner appeared as unconscious of anything peculiar in his manner as he did of the snickers of the men behind him. Having concluded his remarks he blandly bade the gentlemen good morning and left the store, followed by his gang, the suppressed risibilities of the party finding expression in long continued and uproarious laughter, as soon as they reached the outer air. After leaving the store they called on all the gentlemen who had bidden in anything at yesterday's sale, one after another, and reclaimed every article and returned it to David.

If any of the court party had flattered themselves that this mob, like that of the week before, would, after making an uproar for a day or two, disappear and leave the community in quiet, they were destined to disappointment. The popular exasperation and apprehension which the Squire's ill-starred attempt to regain authority had produced, gave to the elements of anarchy in the village a new cohesive force and impulse, while, thanks to the news of the spread and success of the rebellion elsewhere, the lawless were encouraged by entire confidence of impunity. From this day, in fact, it might be said that anarchy was organized in the village.

There were two main elements in the mob. One, the most dangerous, and the real element of strength in it, was composed of a score or two of men whom the stoppage of the courts had come too late to help. Their property all gone, they had been reduced to the condition of loafers, without stake in the community. Having no farms of their own to work on, and the demand for laborers being limited, they had nothing to do all day but to lounge around the tavern, drinking when they could get drinks, sneering at the silk stockings, and debating how further to discomfit them. The other element of the mob, the most mischievous, although not so seriously formidable, was composed of boys and half-grown youths, who less out of malice against the court party, than out of mere love of frolic, availed themselves to the utmost of the opportunity to play off pranks on the richer class of citizens. Bands of them ranged the streets from twilight till midnight, robbing orchards, building bonfires out of fences, opening barns and letting the cows into the gardens, stealing the horses for midnight races, afterwards leaving them to find their way home as they could, tying strings across the streets to trip wayfarers up, stoning windows, and generally making life a burden for their victims by an ingenious variety of petty outrages. Nor were the persons even of the unpopular class always spared. In the daytime it was tolerably safe for one of them to go abroad, but after dark, let him beware of unripe apples and overripe eggs. For the most part the silk stockings kept their houses in the evening, as much for their own protection as for that of their families, and the more prudent of them sat in the dark until bedtime, owing to the fact that lighted windows were a favorite mark with the boys.

The mob had dubbed itself "The Regulators," a title well enough deserved, indeed, by the extent to which they undertook to reorganize the property interests of the community. For the theory of the reclamation of property carried out in the case of the goods of David Joy, by no means stopped there. It was presently given an ex-post facto application, and made to cover articles of property which had changed hands at Sheriff's sales not only since but also previous to the stoppage of the courts. Wherever, in fact, a horse or a cart, a harness, a yoke of oxen or a piece of furniture had passed from the ownership of a poor man to the possession of a rich man and one of the court party, the original owner now reclaimed it, if so disposed, and so effectual was the mob terrorism in the village that such a claim was, generally, with better or worse grace yielded to.

Nor was the application of this doctrine of the restitution of all things even confined to personal property. Many of the richer class of citizens occupied houses acquired by harsh fore-

closures since the dearth of circulating medium had placed
debtors at the mercy of creditors. A few questions as to when
they were thinking of moving out, with an intimation that the
neighbors were ready to assist them, if it appeared necessary,
was generally hint enough to secure a prompt vacating of
the premises, though now and then when the occupants were
unusually obstinate and refused to "take a joke" there were
rather rough proceedings. Among those thus ejected was
Solomon Gleason, the schoolmaster, who had been living in
the house which George Fennel had formerly owned. In this
case, however, the house remained vacant, George being too
sick to be moved.

When Friday night came round again, there was a tremendous carouse at the tavern, in the midst of which Widow
Bingham, rendered desperate by the demands for rum, demands which she did not dare to refuse for fear of provoking
the mob to gut her establishment, finally exclaimed:

"Why don' ye go over't the store an let Squire Edwards
stan treat awhile? What's the use o' making me dew it all.
He's got better likker nor I hev an more on't, an he ain't a
poor lone widder nuther, without noboddy ter stan up fer
her," and the widow pointed her appeal by beginning to cry,
which, as she was a buxom well-favored woman, made a decided impression on the crowd.

Abner, who was drunk as a king, instantly declared that
"By the everlastin Jehu" he'd break the head o' the "fuss dum
Nimshi" that asked for another drink, which brought the
potations of the company to a sudden check. Presently Meshech Little observed:

"Come long fellersh, lesh go t' the store. Whosh fraid? I
ain't." There was a chorus of thick-tongued protestations of
equal valor, and the crowd reeled out after Meshech. Abner
was left alone with the widow.

"I'm reel beholden to ye Abner Rathbun, fer stannin up

fer me," said she warmly, "an Seliny Bingham ain't one tew ferget a favor nuther."

"I'd a smashed the snout o' the fuss one on em ez assed fer more. I'd a knocked his lights outer him, I don' keer who twuz," declared Abner, his valor still further inflamed by the gratitude which sparkled from the widow's fine eyes.

"Lemme mix ye a leetle rum 'n sugar, Abner. It'll dew ye good," said the widow. "I hope ye didn' take none o' that to yerself what I said tew the res' on em. I'm sure I don' grudge ye a drop ye've ever hed, caze I know ye be a nice stiddy man, an I feels safer like wen ye be raoun. Thar naow, jess try that an see ef it's mixed right."

Abner did try that, and more subsequently and sweet smiles and honeyed words therewith, the upshot of all which was the tacit conclusion that evening of a treaty of alliance, the tacitly understood conditions being that Abner should stand by the widow and see she was not put upon, in return for which the widow would see that he was not left thirsty, and if this understanding was sealed with a kiss snatched by one of the contracting parties as the other leaned too far over the bar with the fourth tumbler of rum and sugar, why it was all the more likely to be faithfully observed. That the widow was a fine woman Abner had previously observed, but any natural feeling which this observation might have excited had been kept in check by the consciousness of a long unsettled score. The woman was merged in the landlady, the sex in the creditor. Seeing that there is no more ecstatic experience known to the soul than the melting of awe into a tenderer sentiment, it will not be wondered at that Abner lingered over his twofold inebriation till at nine o'clock the widow said that she must really shut up the tavern.

His surprise was great on passing the store to see it still lit up, and a crowd of men inside, while from the apartments occupied by the Edwards family came the tinkling of Desire's piano. Going in, he found the store filled with drunken men, and the back room crowded with drinkers, whom young Jonathan Edwards was serving with liquor, while the Squire was walking about with a worn and anxious face, seeing that there was no stealing of his goods. As he saw Abner he said, making a pitiable attempt to affect a little dignity:

"I've been treating the men to a little liquor, but it's rather late, and I should like to get them out. You have some control over them, I believe. May I ask you to send them out?"

In the pressure of the present emergency, the poor man appeared to have forgotten the insults which Abner had heaped upon him a few days before, and Abner himself, who was in high good humor, and really felt almost sorry for the proud man before him, replied:

"Sartin, Sartin. I'll git em aout, but what's the peeanner agoin fer?"

"The men thought they would like to hear it, and my daughter was kind enough to play a little for them," said Edwards, his face flushing again, even after the mortifications of the evening, at the necessity of thus confessing his powerlessness to resist the most insulting demands of the rabble.

Abner passed through the door in the back room of the store, which opened into the living-room, a richly carpeted apartment, with fine oaken furniture imported from England. The parlor beyond was even more expensively furnished and decorated. Flat on his back, in the middle of the parlor carpet, was stretched Meshech Little, dead drunk. In nearly every chair was a barefooted, coatless lout, drunk and snoring with his hat over his eyes, and his legs stretched out, or vacantly staring with open mouth at Desire, who, with a face like ashes and the air of an automaton, was playing the piano.

PLOTS AND COUNTERPLOTS

On the day following, which was Saturday, at about three o'clock in the afternoon, Perez Hamlin was at work in the yard behind the house, shoeing his horse in preparation for the start west the next week. Horse shoeing was an accomplishment he had acquired in the army, and he had no shillings to waste in hiring others to do anything he could do himself. As he let the last hoof out from between his knees, and stood up, he saw Israel Goodrich and Ezra Phelps coming across the yard toward him. Ezra wore his working suit, sprinkled with the meal dust of his gristmill, and Israel had on a long blue-woolen farmer's smock, reaching to his knees, and carried in his hand a hickory-handled whip with a long lash, indicating that he had come in his cart, which he had presumably left hitched to the rail fence in front of the house. After breaking ground by a few comments on the points of Perez' horse, Israel opened the subject of the visit, as follows:

"Ye see, Perez, I wuz over't Mill-Holler arter a grist o' buckwheat, an me 'n Ezry got ter talkin baout the way things wuz goin in the village. I s'pose ye've hearn o' the goins on."

"Very little, indeed," said Perez. "I have scarcely been out of the yard this week, I've been hard at work. But I've heard considerable racket nights."

"Wal," said Israel, "the long an short on't is the fellers be raisin the old Harry, an it's time somebody said whoa. I've been a talkin tew Abner baout it, an so's Ezry, but Abner ain't the same feller he wuz. He's tight mos' o' the time naow, an he says he don' keer a darn haow bad they treats the silk stockins. Turn abaout 's fair play, he says, an he on'y larfed w'en I tole him some o' the mischief the fellers wuz up tew. An you said, Ezry, he talked jess so to yew."

"Sartin, he did," said Ezra. "Ye see," he continued to Perez, "me an Isr'el be men o' prop'ty, an we jined the folks agin' the courts caze we seen they wuz bein 'bused. Thar warn't no sense in makin folks pay debts w'en ther warn't no money in cirk'lashun to pay em. 'Twuz jess like makin them ere chil'ren of Isr'el make bricks 'thout no straw. I allers said, an I allers will say," and the glitter that came into Ezra's eye indicated that he felt the inspiring bound of his hobby beneath him, "ef govment makes folks pay ther debts, govment's baoun ter see they hez sunthin tew pay em with. I callate that's plain ez a pike-staff. An it's jess so with taxes. Ef govment —— "

"Sartin, sartin," interrupted Israel, quietly choking him off, "but less stick tew what we wuz a sayin, Ezry. Things be a goin tew fur, ye see, Perez. We tuk part with the poor folks w'en they wuz bein 'bused, but I declar' for't 't looks though we'd hefter take part with the silk stockins pootty soon, at the rate things be agoin. It's a reg'lar see-saw. Fust the rich folks eend wuz up too fur, and naow et's t'other way."

"They be a burnin fences ev'ry night," said Ezra, "an they'll have the hull town afire one o' these days. I don' b'lieve in destroyin prop'ty. Thar ain't no sense in that. That air Paul Hubbard's wuss 'n Abner. Abner he jess larfs an don' keer, but Paul he's thet riled agin the silk stockins that he seems farly crazy. He's daown from the iron-works with his gang ev'ry night, eggin on the fellers tew burn fences, an stone houses, an he wuz akchilly tryin tew git the boys tew tar and feather Squire, t'uther night. They didn't quite dasst dew that, but thar ain't no tellin what they'll come tew yit."

"Ye see, Perez," said Israel, at last getting to the point, "we callate yew mout dew suthin to kinder stop em ef ye'd take a holt. Abner 'l hear ter ye, an all on em would. I don' see's nobody else in taown kin dew nothin. Ezry an me wuz a talkin baout ye overt' the mill, an Ezry says, 'Le's gwover ter see him.' I says, 'Git right inter my cart, an we'll go,' an so here we be."

"I can't very well mix in, you see," replied Perez, "for I'm going to leave town for good the first of the week."

"Whar be ye goin?"

"I'm going to take father and mother and Reuben over the York line, to New Lebanon, and then I'm going on to the Chenango purchase to clear a farm and settle with them."

"Sho! I wanter know," exclaimed Israel, scratching his head. "Wal, I swow," he added, thoughtfully, "I don't blame ye a mite, arter all. This ere state o' Massachusetts Bay, ain't no place fer a poor man, sence the war, an ye'll find lots o' Stockbridge folks outter Chenango. They's a lot moved out thar."

"Ef I war ten year younger I'd go long with ye," said Ezra, "darned ef I wouldn't. I callate thar muss be a right good chance fer a gristmill out thar."

"Wal, Ezry," said Israel, after a pause, "I don' see but wat we've hed our trouble fer nothin, an I declar I dunno wat's gonter be did. The silk stockins be a tryin tew fetch back the ole times, an the people be a raisin Cain, an wat's a gonter come on't Goramity on'y knows. Come 'long, Ezry," and the two old men went sorrowfully away.

It seems that Israel and Ezra were not the only persons in Stockbridge whose minds turned to Perez as the only available force which could restrain the mob, and end the reign of law-lessness in the village. Scarcely had those worthies departed when Dr. Partridge rode around into the back yard and approached the young man.

"I come to you," he said, without any preliminary beating about the bush, "as the recognized leader of the people in this insurrection, to demand of you, as an honest fellow, that you do something to stop the outrages of your gang."

"If I was their leader the other day, I am so no longer," replied Perez, coldly. "They are not my followers. It is none of my business what they do."

"Yes, it is," said Dr. Partridge, sharply. "You can't throw off the responsibility that way. But for you, the rebellion here in Stockbridge would never have gained headway. You can't drop the business now and wash your hands of it."

"I don't care to wash my hands of it," replied Perez, sternly. "I don't know what the men have done of late for I have stayed at home, but no doubt the men who suffer from their doings, deserve it all, and more too. Even if I were to stay in Stockbridge, I see no reason why I should interfere. The people have a right to avenge their wrongs. But I am going away the coming week. My only concern in the rebellion was the release of my brother, and now I propose to take him and my father and mother out of this accursed Commonwealth, and leave you whose oppression and cruelties have provoked the rebellion, to deal with it."

"Do you consider that an honorable course, Captain Hamlin?" The young man's face flushed, and he answered angrily:

"Shall I stay here to protect men who the moment they are able will throw my brother into jail and send me to the gallows? Have you, sir, the assurance to tell me that is my duty?"

The doctor for a moment found it difficult to reply to this, and Perez went on, with increasing bitterness:

"You have sown the wind, you are reaping the whirlwind. Why should I interfere? You have had no pity on the poor, why should they have pity on you? Instead of having the face to ask me to stay here and protect you, rather be thankful that I am willing to go and leave unavenged the wrongs which my father's family has suffered at your hands. Be careful how you hinder my going." The doctor, apparently inferring from the bitter tone of the young man, and the hard, steely gleam in his blue eyes, that perhaps there was something to be considered in his last words turned his horse's head, without a word, and went away like the two envoys who had preceded him.

The doctor was disappointed. Without knowing much of Perez, he had gained a strong impression from what little he had seen of him, that he was of a frank, impulsive temperament, sudden and fierce in quarrel, perhaps, but incapable of a brooding revengefulness, and most unlikely to cherish continued animosity toward enemies who were at his mercy. And as I would not have the reader do the young man injustice in his mind, I hasten to say that the doctor's view of his character was not far out of the way. The hard complacency with which he just now regarded the calamities of the gentlemen of the town, had its origin in the constant and bitter brooding of the week past over Desire's treatment of him. The sense of being looked down on by her, as a fine lady, and his respectful passion despised, had been teaching him the past few days a bitterness of caste jealousy, which had never before been known to his genial temper. He was trying to forget his love for her, in hatred for her class. He was getting to feel toward the silk stockings a little as Paul Hubbard did.

Probably one of this generation of New Englanders, who could have been placed in Stockbridge the day following, would have deemed it a very quiet Sabbath indeed. But what, by our lax modern standards seem very venial sins of Sabbath-breaking, if indeed any such sins be now recognized at all, to that generation were heinous and heaven-daring. The conduct of certain reckless individuals that Sabbath, did more to shock the public mind than perhaps anything that had hitherto occurred in the course of the revolt. For instance, divers young men were seen openly walking about the streets with their sweethearts during meeting-time, laughing and talking in a noisy manner, and evidently bent merely on pleasure. It was credibly reported that one man, without any attempt at concealment, rode down to Great Barrington to make a visit of recreation upon his friends. Several other persons, presumably for similar profane purposes, walked out to Lee and Lenox furnaces, to the prodigious scandal of the dwellers along those roads. As if this were not enough iniquity for one day, there were whispers that Abner Rathbun and Meshech Little had gone a fishing. This rumor was not, indeed, fully substantiated, but the mere fact that it found circulation and some to credit it, is in itself striking evidence of the agitated and abnormal condition of the public mind.

Toward sunset, the news reached Stockbridge of yet another rebel victory in the lower counties. The Monday preceding, 300 armed farmers had marched into the town of Concord, and prevented the sitting of the courts of Middlesex county. The weakness of the government was shown by the fact that, although ample warning of the intentions of the rebels had been given, no opposition to them was attempted. The governor had, indeed, at first ordered the militia to arms, but through apprehension of their unfaithfulness had subsequently countermanded the order. The fact that the rebellion had manifested such strength and boldness within a few hours' march of Boston, the capital of the state, was an important element in the elation which the tidings produced among the people. It showed that the western counties were not alone engaged in the insurrection, but that the people all over the state were making common cause against the courts and the party that upheld them.

The jubilation produced by this intelligence, combining with the usual reaction at sunset after the repression of the day, caused that evening a general pandemonium of tin-pans, bonfires, mischief of all sorts, and the usual concomitant of unlimited drunkenness. In the midst of the uproar, Mrs. Jahleel Woodbridge, Squire Edward's sister, died. The violence of the mob was such, however, that Edwards did not dare to avail himself of even this excuse for refusing to furnish liquor to the crowd.

The funeral took place Tuesday. It was the largest and most imposing that had taken place in the village for a long time. The prominence of both the families concerned, procured the attendance of all the gentry of Southern Berkshire. I employ an English phrase to describe a class for which, in our modern democratic New England, there is no counterpart. The Stoddards, Littles, and Wendells, of Pittsfield, were represented. Colonel Ashley was there from Sheffield, Justices Dwight and Whiting from Great Barrington, and Barker from Lanesborough, with many more. The carriages, some of them bearing coats of arms upon their panels, made a fine array, which, not less than the richly attired dames and gentlemen who descended from them, impressed a temporary awe upon even the most seditious and democratically inclined of the staring populace. The six pall-bearers, adorned with scarves, and mourning rings, were Chief Justice Dwight, Colonel Elijah Williams of West Stockbridge, the founder and owner of the iron-works there, Dr. Sergeant of Stockbridge, Captain Solomon Stoddard, commander of the Stockbridge militia, Oliver Wendell of Pittsfield, and Henry W. Dwight of Stockbridge, the county treasurer. There were not in Stockbridge alone enough families to have furnished six pall-bearers of satisfactory social rank. For while all men of liberal education or profession, or such as held prominent offices were recognized as gentlemen in sharp distinction from the common people, yet the generality of even these were looked far down upon by the county families of long pedigree and large estate. The Partridges, Dr. Sergeant, the Dwights, the Williamses, the Stoddards, and of course his brother-in-law Edwards, were the only men in Stockbridge whom Woodbridge regarded as belonging to his own caste. Even Theodore Sedgwick, despite his high public offices, he affected to consider entitled to social equality chiefly by virtue of his having married a Dwight.

After the funeral exercises, Squire Woodbridge managed to whisper a few words in the ear of a dozen or so of the gentlemen present, the tenor of which, to the great surprise of those addressed, was a request that they would call on him that evening after dark, taking care to come alone, and attract as little attention as possible. Each one supposed himself to have been alone invited, and on being met at the door by Squire Woodbridge and ushered into the study, was surprised to find the room full of gentlemen. Drs. Partridge and Sergeant and Squire Edwards were there, Captain Stoddard, Sheriff Seymour, Tax-collector Williams, Solomon Gleason, John Bacon, Esquire, General Pepoon and numerous other lawyers, County Treasurer Dwight, Deacon Nash, Ephraim Williams, Esquire, Sedgwick's law-partner, Captain Jones, the militia commissary of Stockbridge, at whose house the town stock of arms and ammunition was stored, and some other gentlemen.

When all had assembled, Woodbridge, having satisfied himself there were no spies lurking about the garden, and that the gathering of gentlemen had not attracted attention to the house, proceeded to close the blinds of the study windows and draw the curtains. He then drew a piece of printed paper from his pocket, opened it, and broached the matter in hand to the wondering company, as follows:

"The awful suggestions with which the recent visitation of God has invested my house for the time being, has enabled us to meet to-night without danger that our deliberations will be interrupted, either by the curiosity or the violence of the rabble. For this one night, the first for many weeks, they have left me in peace, and I deem it is no desecration of the beloved memory of my departed companion, that we should avail ourselves of so melancholy an opportunity to take counsel for the restoration of law and order in this sorely troubled community. I have this day received from his excellency, the governor, and the honorable council at Boston, a proclamation, directed to all justices, sheriffs, jurors, and citizens, authorizing and strictly commanding them to suppress, by force of arms, all riotous proceedings, and to apprehend the rioters. I have called you privately together, that we might arrange for concerted action to these ends." In a low voice, so that no chance listener from without might catch its tenor, the Squire then proceeded to read Governor Bowdoin's proclamation, closing with that time-honored and impressive formula, "God save the Commonwealth of Massachusetts." Captain Stoddard was first to break the silence which followed the reading of the document.

"I, for one, am ready to fight the mob to-morrow, but how are we to go about it. There are ten men for the mob to one against it. What can we do?"

"How many men in your company could be depended on to fight the mob, if it came to blows?" asked Woodbridge.

"I'm afraid not over twenty or thirty. Three-quarters are for the mob."

"There are a dozen of us here, and I presume at least a score more gentlemen in town could be depended on," said Dr. Partridge.

"But that would give not over three score, and the mob could easily muster four times that," said Gleason.

"They have no leaders, though," said Bacon. "Such fellows are only dangerous when they have leaders. They could not stand before us, for methinks we are by this time become desperate men."

"You forget this Hamlin fellow will stop at nothing, and they will follow him," remarked Seymour.

"He is going to leave town this week, if he be not already gone," said Dr. Partridge.

"What?" exclaimed Woodbridge, almost with consternation.

"He is going away," repeated the doctor.

"Perhaps it would be expedient to wait till he has gone," was Gleason's prudent suggestion.

"And let the knave escape!" exclaimed Woodbridge, look-

ing fiercely at the schoolmaster. "I would not have him get
away for ten thousand pounds. I have a little reckoning to
settle with him. If he is going to leave, we must not delay."

"My advices state that Squire Sedgwick will be home in
a few days to attend to his cases at the October term of the
Supreme Court at Barrington. His co-operation would no
doubt strengthen our hands," suggested Ephraim Williams.

If the danger of Hamlin's escape had not been a sufficient
motive in Woodbridge's mind for hastening matters, the
possibility that his rival might return in time to share the
credit of the undertaking would have been. But he merely
said, coldly:

"The success of our measures will scarcely depend on the
co-operation of one man more or less, and seeing that we have
broached the business, as little time as possible should inter-
vene ere its execution lest some whisper get abroad and warn
the rabble, for it is clear that it is only by a surprise that we
can be sure of beating them."

He then proceeded to lay before them a scheme of action
which was at once so bold and so prudent that it obtained
the immediate and admiring approval of all present. Just
before dawn, at three o'clock in the morning of Thursday,
the next day but one, that being the hour at which the village
was most completely wrapped in repose, the conspirators were
secretly to rendezvous at Captain Jones' house, and such as
had not arms and ammunition of their own were there to be
supplied from the town stock. Issuing thence and dividing
into parties the arrest of Hamlin, Abner Rathbun, Peleg
Bidwell, Israel Goodrich, Meshech Little, and other men
regarded as leaders of the mob, was to be simultaneously
effected. Strong guards were then to be posted so that when
the village woke up it would be to find itself in military
possession of the legal authorities. The next step would be
immediately to bring the prisoners before Justice Woodbridge
to be tried, the sentences to be summarily carried out at the

whipping-post on the green, and the prisoners then remanded to custody to await the further action of the law before higher tribunals. It might be necessary to keep up the military occupation of the village for some time, but it was agreed among the gentlemen that the execution of the above program would be sufficient to break the spirit of the mob entirely. The excesses of the rabble during the past week had, it was believed, already done something to produce a reaction of feeling against them among their former sympathizers, and there would doubtless be plenty of recruits for the party of order as soon as it had shown itself the stronger. The intervening day, Wednesday, was to be devoted by those present to secretly warning such as were counted on to assist in the project. It was estimated that including all the able-bodied gentlemen in town as well as some of the people known to be disaffected to the mob, about seventy-five sure men could be secured for the work in hand.

Now Lu Nimham, the beautiful Indian girl whom Perez had noticed in meeting sitting beside Prudence Fennell, had another lover besides Abe Konkapot, no other in fact than Abe's own brother Jake. Abe had been to the war and Jake had not, and Lu, as might have been expected from a girl whose father and brother had fallen at White Plains in the Continental uniform, preferred the soldier lover to the other. But not so the widow Nimham, her mother, in whose eyes Jake's slightly better worldly prospects gave him the advantage. It so happened that soon after dusk, Wednesday evening, Abe, drawn by a tender inward stress betook himself to the lonely dell in the extreme west part of the village, now called Glendale, where the hut of the Nimham family stood. His discomfiture was great on finding Jake already comfortably installed in the kitchen and basking in Lu's society. He did not linger. The widow did not invite him to stop; in fact, not to put too fine a point upon it, she intimated that it would be just as well if he were to finish his call some other time.

Lu indeed threw sundry tender commiserating glances in his direction, but her mother watched her like a cat, and mothers in those times were a good deal more in the way than they are nowadays.

How little do we know what is good for us! As he beat an ignominious retreat, pursued by the scornful laughter of his brother, Abe certainly had apparent reason to be down on his luck. Nevertheless the fact that he was cut out that particular evening proved to be one of the clearest streaks of luck that had ever occurred in his career, and a good many others besides he had equal reason ere morning dawned to be thankful for it. The matter fell out on this wise:

A couple of hours later, a little after nine in fact, the Hamlin household was about going to bed. Elnathan and Mrs. Hamlin had already retired to the small bedroom opening out of the kitchen. Reuben, George Fennell and Perez slept in the kitchen, and Prudence in the loft above. The two invalids were already abed, and the girl was just giving the last attentions for the night to her father before climbing to her pallet. Perez sat at the other end of the great room before the open chimney, gazing into the embers of the fire. The family was to start for New York the next morning, and as this last night in the old homestead was closing in the young man had enough sad matter to occupy his thoughts. Her loving cares completed, Prudence came and stood silently by his side. Taking note of her friendly presence, after awhile he put out his hand without looking up and took hers as it hung by her side. He had taken quite a liking to the sweet-tempered little lassie, and had felt particularly kindly towards her since her well-meaning, if rather inadequate effort to console him that Sunday behind the barn.

"You're a good little girl, Prudy," he said, "and I know you will take good care of your father. You can stay here if you want, you know, after we're gone. I don't think Solomon Gleason or the sheriff will trouble you. Or you can go to your father's old house. Obadiah says Gleason has left it. Obadiah will look after you and do any chores you may want about the house. He'll be very glad to. He thinks a good deal of you, Obadiah does. I s'pose he'll be wanting you to keep house for him when you get a little older," and he looked cheerily up at her. But evidently his little jest had struck her mind amiss. Her eyes were full of tears and the childish mouth quivered.

"Why what's the matter Prudy?" he asked in surprise.

"I wish you wouldn't talk so to me, now," she said, "as if I didn't care anything when you're all going away and have been so good to me and father. And I don't care about Obadiah either, and you needn't say so. He's just a great gumph."

At this point, the conversation was abruptly broken off by the noise of the latchstring being pulled. Both turned. Lu Nimham was standing in the doorway, her great black eyes shining in the dusk like those of a deer fascinated by the night-hunter's torch. Prudence, with a low exclamation of surprise, crossed the room to her, and Lu whispering something drew her out. Immediately, however, the white girl reappeared in the doorway, her rosy face pale, her eyes dilated, and beckoned to Perez, who in a good deal of wonderment at once obeyed the gesture. The two girls were standing by a corner of the house, out of earshot from the window of Elnathan's bedroom. Both looked very much excited, but the Indian girl was smiling as if the stimulus affected her nerves agreeably rather than otherwise. Abe Konkapot, looking rather sober, stood near by.

"Oh, what shall we do?" exclaimed Prudence in a terrified half-whisper. "She says the militia are coming to take you!"

"What is it all?" demanded Perez of the Indian girl, as he laid his hand soothingly on Prudence's shoulder.

"Jake Konkapot, he come see me tonight," said Lu, still smiling. "Jake no like Abe, cause Abe like me too. Jake he ask me if I like Abe any more after he git whip on back by constable man. I say no. Indian gal, no like marry man what

been whip. Jake laugh and say I no marry Abe sure nuff, cause
Abe git whip to-morrow. He no tell me what he mean till I
say I give him kiss. Man all like kiss. Jake he says yes, an I give
him kiss. Ugh! Arter that he say Squire an Deacon Edwards,
and Deacon Nash, an Cap'n Stoddard an heap more, an Jake
he go too, gonter git up arly, at tree o'clock to-morrer, with
guns; make no noise go roun creepy, creepy, creepy." Here
she expressed by pantomime the way a cat stealthily ap-
proaches its prey, culminating by a sudden clutch on Perez'
arm that startled him, as she added explosively, "Catch you so,
all abed, an Abe an Abner an heap more! Then when mornin
come they whip all on yer to the whippin-post. When Jake
go home I wait till mammy go sleep, slip out winder an go
tell Abe so he no git whip. Then I tink come here tell Prudence, for I tink she no like you git whip."

Perez had listened with an intense interest that lost not a
syllable. As the girl described the disgrace which his enemies
had planned to inflict on him, if their plan succeeded, his
cheek paled and his lips drew tense across his set teeth. As
Prudence looked up at him there was a suppressed intensity
of rage in his face which checked the ejaculations upon her
lips. There was a silence of several seconds, and then he said
in a low suppressed voice, hard and unnatural in tone:

"Young woman, I owe you more than if you had saved me
from death." Lu smilingly nodded, evidently fully appreciat-
ing the point.

"Three o'clock, you said?" muttered Perez presently, half
to himself, as the others still were silent.

"Tree 'clock, Jake say. Jake an all udder man meet to Cap'n
Jones' tree 'clock to git um guns."

"It's nine now, six hours. Time enough," muttered Perez.

"Yes, there's time for you to get away," said Prudence
eagerly. "You can get to York State by three o'clock, if you
hurry. Oh, don't wait a minute. If they should catch you!"

He smiled grimly.

"Yes, there's time for me to get away, but there's no time for them, my sirs."

"Abe," he added, abruptly changing his tone, "you've heard what they're going to do? What are you going to do?"

"I tink me go woke up fellers. Heap time, run clean 'way 'fore tree 'clock," said the Indian. "Mlishy come tree 'clock, no find us. 'Fraid have to leave Abner. Abner heap drunk to-night. No can walk. Too big for carry. Heap sorry, but no can help it."

"But you don't want to leave home, Abe. You don't want to leave Lu here for Jake to get."

Abe shook his head gloomily.

"No use stay," he said. "If I get whip, Lu no marry me."

"Abe," said Perez, stepping up to the disconsolate Indian and clapping him sharply on the shoulder, "you were in the army. You're not afraid of fighting. We'll stay and beat these fine gentlemen at their own game. By three o'clock we'll have every one of them under guard, and, by the Lord God of Israel, by noon to-morrow, every man of them shall get ten lashes on his bare back with all Stockbridge looking on. We'll see who's whipped."

"Ha! you no run. You stay fight em. What heap more better as run. You, great brave, ha! ha!" cried Lu dancing in front of Perez and clapping her hands in noiseless ecstasy, while her splendid eyes rested on him with an admiration of which Abe might have been excusably jealous.

Her Mohegan blood was on fire at the prospect of a scrimmage, and her lover's response, if more laconic, was quite as satisfactory.

"Me no like to run. Me stay fight. Me do what you say."

"Wait here till I get my sword and pistols. We've plenty of time, but none to lose," and Perez went into the house, followed by Prudence. Mrs. Hamlin, with something hastily thrown over her nightdress, had come out of her bedroom.

"I heard voices. What is it, Perez?" she said.

"Abe has come to get me to go off on a coon hunt. He thinks he's treed several," replied Perez, strapping on his accoutrements. He had no notion of leaving his mother a prey to sleepless anxiety during his absence.

"You're not telling me the truth, Perez. Look at Prudence."

The girl's face, pale as ashes and her eyes full of fear and excitement, had betrayed him, and so he had to tell her in a few words what he was going to do. The door stood open. On the threshold, as he was going out, he turned his head, and said in confident, ringing tones:

"You needn't be at all afraid. We shall certainly succeed."

No wonder the breath of the night had inspired him with such confidence. It was the night of all nights in the year which a man would choose if he were to stake his life and all on the issue of some daring stake, assured that then, if ever, he could depend to the uttermost on every atom of nerve and muscle in his body. The bare mountain peaks overhanging the village were tipped with silver by the moon, and under its light the dense forests that clothed their sides, wore the sheen of thick and glossy fur. The air was tingling with that electric stimulus which characterizes autumn evenings in New England about the time of the first frosts. A faint, sweet smell of aromatic smoke from burning pine woods somewhere off in the mountains, could barely be detected. The intense vitality of the atmosphere communicated itself to the nerves, stringing them like steel chords, and setting them vibrating with lust for action, reckless, daring emprise.

CHAPTER EIGHTEENTH

LEX TALIONIS

The plan which Perez had formed for forestalling his adversaries and visiting upon their own heads the fate they had prepared for him, was very simple. He proposed to go down into the village with Abe and Lu and with their assistance, to call up, without waking anybody else, some forty or fifty of the most determined fellows of the rebel party. With the aid of these, he intended as noiselessly as possible, to enter the houses of Woodbridge, Edwards, Deacon Nash, Captain Stoddard and others, and arrest them in their beds, simultaneously seizing the town stock of muskets and powder, and conveying it to a guarded place, so that when the conspirators' party assembled at three o'clock, they might find themselves at once without arms or officers, their leaders hostages in the hands of the enemy, and their design completely set at naught. Thanks to the excesses of the past week or two, there were many more than forty men in the village who, knowing that the restoration of law and order meant a sharp reckoning for them, would stop at nothing to prevent it, and Perez could thus command precisely the sort of followers he wanted for his present undertaking.

For generations after, in certain Stockbridge households, the story in grandmother's repertoire most eagerly called by the young folks on winter evenings, was about how the "Regulators" came for grandpa; how at dead of night the heavy tramp of men and the sound of rough voices in the rooms below, awoke the children sleeping overhead and froze their young blood with fear of Indians; how at last mustering courage, they crept downstairs, and peeking into the living-room saw it full of fierce men, with green boughs in their hats, the flaring candles gleaming upon their muskets and bayonets, and the drawn sword of their captain; while in the midst, half-dressed and in his nightcap, grandpa was being hustled about.

Leaving these details to the imagination, suffice it to say that Perez' plan, clearly-conceived and executed with prompt, relentless vigor, was perfectly successful, and so noiselessly carried out, that excepting those families whose heads were arrested by the soldiers, the village as a whole, had no suspicion that anything in particular was going on, until waking up the next morning, the people found squads of armed men on guard at the street corners, and sentinels pacing up and down before the Fennell house, that building left vacant by Gleason's ejection, having been selected by Perez for the storage of his prisoners and the stores he had confiscated. As the people ran together on the green, to learn the reason of these strange appearances, and the story passed from lip to lip what had been the plot against their newly-acquired liberties, and the persons of their leaders, and by what a narrow chance, and by whose bold action the trouble had been averted, the sensation was prodigious. The tendency of public opinion which had been inclining to sympathize a little with the abuse the silk stockings had been undergoing the past week, was instantly reversed, now that the so near success of their plot once more made them objects of terror. The exasperation was far more general and profound than had been excited by the previous attempt to restore the old order of things, in the case of the sale of David Joy's house. This was more serious business. Every man who had been connected with the rebellion, felt in imagination the lash on his back, and white faces were plenty among the stoutest of them. And what they felt for themselves, you may be sure their wives and children and friends felt for them, with even greater intensity. As now and then the wife or child of one of the prisoners in the guard house, with anxious face, timidly passed through the throng, on the way to make inquiries concerning the welfare of the husband or father, black looks and muttered curses followed them, and the rude gibes with which the sentinels responded to their anxious, tearful questionings, were received with hoarse laughter by the crowd.

As Perez, coming forth for some purpose, appeared at the door of the Fennell house, there was a great shout of acclamation, the popular ratification of the night's work. But an even more convincing demonstration of approval awaited him. As he began to make his way through the throng, Submit Goodrich, Old Israel's buxom, black-eyed daughter, confronted him, saying:

"My old daddy 'd a been in the stocks by this time if it hadn't been for you, so there," and throwing her arms around his neck she gave him a resounding smack on the lips. Meshech Little's wife followed suit, and then Peleg Bidwell's and a lot of other women of the people, amid the uproarious plaudits of the crowd, which became deafening as Resignation Ann Poor, Zadkiel's wife, elbowed her way through the pack and clasping the helpless Perez against her bony breast in a genuine bear's hug, gave him a kiss like a file.

"Well, I never," ejaculated Prudence Fennell, who was bringing some breakfast to Perez, and had observed all this kissing with a rather sour expression.

Unluckily for her, Submit overheard the words.

"You never, didn't you? an livin in the same haouse long with him too? Wal it's time you did," she exclaimed loudly, and seizing the struggling girl she thrust her before Perez, holding down her hands so that she could not cover her furiously blushing face, and amid the boisterous laughter of the bystanders she was kissed also, a proceeding which evidently pleased Obadiah Weeks, who stood near, as little as the other part had pleased Prudence. As Submit released her and she rushed away, Obadiah followed her.

"Haow 'd ye like it?" he said, with a sickly grin of jealous irony. "I see ye didn' cover yer face very tight, he! he! Took keer to leave a hole, he! he!"

The girl turned on him like a flash and gave him a re-sounding slap on the cheek.

"Take that, you great gumph!" she exclaimed.

"Wha'd ye wanter hit a feller fer?" whined Obadiah, rubbing the smitten locality. "Gol darn it, I hain't done nothin to ye. Ye didn' slap him wen he kissed ye, darn him. Guess t'ain't the fuss time he's done it, nuther."

Prudence turned her back to him and walked off, but Obadiah, his bashfulness for the moment quite forgotten in his jealous rage, followed her long enough to add:

"Oh ye needn' think I hain't seen ye settin yer cap fer him all 'long, an he ole nuff tew be yer dad. S'pose ye thort ye'd git him, bein in the same haouse long with him, but ye hain't made aout. He's goin tew York an he don' keer no more baout yew nor the dirt unner his feet. He ez good 's tole me so."

"Thar comes Abner Rathbun," said some one in the group around Perez. With heavy eyes, testifying to his debauch over night, and a generally crestfallen appearance, the giant was approaching from the tavern, where he had presumably been bracing up with a little morning flip.

"A nice sorter man you be Abner, fer yer neighbors to be a trustin ter look aout fer things," said an old farmer, sarcastically.

"Ef 't hadn't been fer Cap'n Hamlin thar, the constable would 'a waked ye up this mornin with the eend of a gad," said another.

"You'll have to take in your horns a little, after this, Abner. It won't do to be putting on any more airs," remarked a third.

"Go ahead," said Abner, ruefully, "I hain't got nothin ter say. Ye kin sass me all ye wanter. Every one on ye kin take yer hack at me. I'm kinder sorry thar ain't any on ye big nuff ter kick me, fer I orter be kicked."

"Never mind, Abner," said Perez, pitying his humiliated condition. "Anybody may get too much flip now and then. We missed you, but we managed to get through with the job all right."

"Cap'n," said Abner, "I was bleeged ter ye w'en ye pulled them two Britshers or'fer me tew Stillwater, but that ain't a sarcumstance to the way I be bleeged to ye this mornin, fer it's all your doins, and no thanks ter me, that I ain't gittin ten lashes this very minute, with all the women a snickerin at the size o' my back. I hev been kinder cocky, an I hev put on some airs, ez these fellers says, fer I callated ye'd kinder washed yer hands o' this business, an leff me tew be capin, but arter this ye'll fine Abner Rathbun knows his place."

"You were quite right about it, Abner. I have washed my hands of the business. I am going to take my folks out to York State. I meant to start this morning. If the silk stockings had waited till to-night they wouldn't have found me in their way."

"I callate twuz Providenshil they did'n wait, fer we'd 'a been gone suckers sure ez ye hedn't been on hand to dew wat ye did," said one of the men. "Thar ain't another man in town ez could a did it, or would dast try."

"But ye ain't callatin ter go arter this be ye, Perez?" said Abner.

"This makes no difference. I expect to get off to-morrow," replied Perez.

"Ye shan't go, not ef I hold ye," cried Mrs. Poor, edging up to him as if about to secure his person on the spot.

"Ef ye go the res' on us mout 's well go with ye, fer the silk stockins 'll hev it all ther own way then," remarked a farmer, gloomily.

"I don't think the silk stockings will try any more tricks right off," said Perez, grimly. "I propose to give em a lesson this morning, which they'll be likely to remember for one while."

"What be ye a gonter dew to em?" asked Abner, eagerly.

"Well," said Perez, deliberately, as every eye rested on him. "You see they had set their minds on havin some whipping done this morning, and I don't propose to have em disappointed. I'm going to do to them as they would have done to us. The whipping will come off as soon as Abe can find Little Pete to handle the gad. I sent him off some time ago. I don' see what's keeping him."

His manner was as quiet and matter-of-course as if he were proposing the most ordinary sort of forenoon occupation, and when he finished speaking he walked away without so much as a glance around to see how the people took it. It was nevertheless quite worth observing, the fascinated stare with which they looked after him, and then turned to fix on each other. It was Abner who, after several moments of dead silence, said in an awed voice, like a loud whisper:

"He's a gonter whip em." And Obadiah almost devoutly murmured, "By Gosh!"

The men who stood around, were intensely angry with the prisoners, for their plot to arrest and whip them, but the idea of retaliating in kind, by whipping the prisoners themselves, had not for an instant occurred to the boldest. The prisoners were gentlemen, and the idea of whipping a gentleman just as if he were one of themselves, was something the most lawless of them had never entertained. Education, precedent, and innate caste sentiment had alike precluded the idea. But after the first sensation of bewilderment had passed, it was evident that the shock which the popular mind had received from Perez' words, was not wholly disagreeable, but rather suggestive of a certain shuddering delight. The introspective gleam which shone in everybody's eye, betrayed the half-scared pleasure with which each in his own mind was turning over the daring imagination.

"Wy not, arter all?" said Meshech Little, hesitatingly, as

if his logic didn't convince himself. "They wuz gonter lick us. They'd a had us licked by this time. It's tit for tat."

"I s'pose Goramity made our backs as well as theirn," observed Abner. "The on'y odds is in the kind o' coats we wears. Ourn ain't so fine ez theirn, but it's the back an not the coat that gits licked. Arter Pete has tuk orf ther coats thar won't be no odds."

The chuckle with which this was received, showed how fast the people were yielding to the awful charm of the thought.

"Dew yew s'pose Cap'n really dass dew it?" asked Obadiah.

"Dew it? Yes he'll dew it, you better b'lieve. Did yer see the set of his jaw w'en he wuz talkin so quiet-like baout lickin em? I wuz in the army with Perez, an I know his ways. W'en he sets his jaw that air way I don' keer to git in his way, big ez I be. He'll dew it ef he doos it with his own hands. He's pison proud, Perez is, an I guess the idee they wuz callatin tew hev him licked, hez kinder riled him."

As the people talked, their hearts began to burn. The more they thought of it, the more the idea fascinated them. Jests and hilarious comments, which betrayed a temper of delighted expectancy, soon began to be bandied about.

In ten minutes more, this very crowd which had received in shocked silence the first suggestion of whipping the gentlemen, had so set their fancy on that diversion that it would have been hard balking them. It must be remembered that this was a hundred years ago. The weekly spectacle of the cruel punishment of the lash, and the scarcely less painful and disgraceful infliction of the stocks and the pillory left in their minds no possibility for any revolt of mere humane sentiment against the proposed doings, such as a modern assembly would experience. To men and women who had learned from childhood to find a certain brutish titillation in beholding the public humiliation and physical anguish of their acquaintances and fellow-townsmen, the prospect of seeing the scourge actually applied to the backs of envied and hated social superiors, could not be otherwise than delightfully agitating.

Nor were there lacking supplies of Dutch courage for the timid. Among the town stores seized and conveyed to the Fennell house the night before, had been several casks of rum. One of these had been secretly sequestrated by some of the men and hidden in a neighboring barn. The secret of its whereabouts had been, in drunken confidence, conveyed from one man to another, with the consequence that pretty much all the men were rapidly getting drunk. Shortly after Perez had communicated his intention to the people, Paul Hubbard, with thirty or forty of the iron-workers, armed with bludgeons, arrived from West Stockbridge. Some rumor of the doings of the previous night had reached there, and he had hastily rallied his myrmidons and come down, not knowing but there might be some fighting to be done.

"Paul 'll be nigh tickled to death to hear of the whippin," said Abner, seeing him coming. "If he had his way he'd skin the silk stockins, an make whips out o' their own hides to whip em with. He don't seem to love em somehow 'nuther, wuth a darn." Nor was Paul's satisfaction at the news any less than Abner had anticipated. Presently he burst into the room in the Fennell house, which Perez had appropriated as a sort of headquarters, and wrung his rather indifferent hand with an almost tremulous delight.

"Bully for you, Hamlin, bully for you, by the Lord I didn't s'pose you had the mettle to do it. Little Pete is just the man for the business, but if he don't come, you can have one of my Welshmen. I s'pose most of the Stockbridge men wouldn't quite dare, but just wait till after the whipping. They won't be afraid of the bigwigs any longer. That'll break the charm. Little Pete's whip will do more to make us free and equal than all the swords and guns in Berkhire." And Hubbard went out exultant.

As he was leaving, he met no less an one than Parson West coming in, and wearing rather a discomfited countenance. The parson had been used, as parsons were in those days, to a good deal of deference from his flock, and the lowering looks and covered heads of the crowd about the door were disagreeable novelties. No institution in the New England of that day was, in fact, more strictly aristocratic than the pulpit. Its affiliations were wholly with the governing and wealthy classes, and its tone with the common people as arrogant and domineering as that of the magistracy itself. And though Parson West was personally a man of unusual affability toward the poor and lowly, it was impossible in a time like this that one of his class should not be regarded with suspicion and aversion by the popular party.

"I would have word with your captain," he said to the sentinel at the door.

"He's in thar," said the soldier, pointing to the door of the headquarters' room. Perez, who was walking to and fro, turned at the opening door and respectfully greeted the parson.

"Are you the captain of the armed band without?"

"I am."

"You have certain gentlemen in confinement, I have heard. I came to see you on account of an extraordinary report that you had threatened to inflict a disgraceful public chastisement upon their persons. No doubt the report is erroneous. You surely could not contemplate so cruel and scandalous a proceeding?"

"The report is entirely true, reverend sir. I am but waiting for a certain Hessian drummer who will wield the lash."

"But man," exclaimed the parson, "you have forgotten that these are the first men in the county. They are gentlemen of distinguished birth and official station. You would not whip them like common offenders. It is impossible. You are beside yourself. Such a thing was never heard of. It is most criminal, most wicked. As a minister of the gospel I protest! I forbid such a thing," and the little parson fairly choked with righteous indignation.

"These men, if they had succeeded in their plan last night, would have whipped me, and a score of others to-day. Would you have protested against that?"

"That is different. They would have proceeded against you as criminals, according to law."

"No doubt they would have proceeded according to law," replied Perez, with a bitter sneer. "They have been proceeding according to law for the past six years here in Berkshire, and that's why the people are in rebellion. I'm no lawyer, but I know that Perez Hamlin is as good as Jahleel Woodbridge, whatever the parson may think, and what he would have done to me, shall be done to him."

"That is not the rule of the gospel," said the minister, taking another tack. "Christ said if any man smite you on the right cheek, turn to him the other also."

"If that is your counsel, take it to those who are likely to need it. I am going to do the smiting this time, and it's their time to do the turning. They need not trouble themselves, however. Pete will see that they get it on both sides."

"And now sir," he added, "if you would like to see the prisoners to prepare them for what's coming, you are welcome to," and opening the door of the room he told the sentinel in the corridor to let the parson into the guard room, and the silenced and horrified man of God mechanically acting upon the hint went out and left him alone.

The imagination of the reader will readily depict the state of mind in which the families of the arrested gentlemen were left after the midnight visit of Perez' band. That there was no more sleep in those households that night will be easily understood. In the Edwards family the long hours till morning passed in praying and weeping by Mrs. Edwards and Desire, and the younger children. They scarcely dared to doubt that the husband and father was destined to violence or death at the hands of these bloody and cruel men. At dawn Jonathan, who, on trying to follow his father when first arrested, had been driven back with blows, went out again, and the tidings which he brought back, that the prisoners were confined in the Fennell house and as yet had undergone no abuse, somewhat restored their agitated spirits. An hour or two later the boy came tearing into the house, with white face, clenched fists and blazing eyes.

"What is it?" cried his mother and sister, half scared to death at his looks.

"They're going," — Jonathan choked.

"They're going to have father whipped," he finally made out to articulate.

"Whipped!" echoed Desire, faintly and uncomprehendingly.

"Yes!" cried the boy hoarsely, "like any vagabond, stripped and whipped at the whipping-post."

"What do you mean?" said Mrs. Edwards, as she took Jonathan by the shoulder.

"They're going to whip father, and uncle, and all the others," he repeated, beginning to whimper, stout boy as he was.

"Whip father? You're crazy, Jonathan, you didn't hear right. They'd never dare! It can't be! Run and find out," cried Desire, wildly.

"There ain't any use. I heard the Hamlin fellow say so himself. They're going to do it. They said it's no worse than whipping one of them, as if they were gentlemen," blubbered Jonathan.

"Oh no! no! They can't, they won't," cried the girl in an anguished voice, her eyes glazed with tears as she looked appealingly from Jonathan to her mother, in whose faces there was little enough to reassure her.

"Don't, mother, you hurt," said Jonathan, trying to twist

away from the clasp which his mother had retained upon his arm, unconsciously tightening it till it was like a vise.

"Whip my husband!" said she, slowly, in a hollow tone. "Whip him!" she repeated. "Such a thing was never heard of. There must be some mistake."

"There must be. There must be," exclaimed Desire again. "It can never be. They are not so wicked. That Hamlin fellow is bad enough, but oh he isn't bad enough for that. They would not dare. God would not permit it. Some one will stop them."

"There is no one to stop them. The people are all against us. They are glad of it. They are laughing. Oh! how I hate them. Why don't God kill them?" and with a prolonged, inarticulate roar of impotent grief and indignation, the boy threw himself flat on the floor, and burying his face in his arms sobbed and rolled, and rolled and sobbed, like one in a fit.

"I will go and have speech with this Son of Belial, Hamlin. It may be the Lord will give me strength to prevail with him," said Mrs. Edwards. "And if not, they shall not put me from my husband. I will bear the stripes with him, that he may never be ashamed before the wife of his bosom," and with a calm and self-controlled demeanor, she bestirred herself to make ready to go out.

"Let me go mother," said Desire, half hesitatingly.

"It is not your place my child. I am his wife," replied Mrs. Edwards.

"Yes mother, but Desire's so pretty, and this Hamlin fellow stopped the horse-fiddles just to please her, the other time," whimpered Jonathan. "Perhaps he'd let father off if she went. Do let her go mother."

The allusion to the stopping of the horse-fiddle was Greek to Mrs. Edwards, to whose ears the story had never come. But the present was not a time for general inquiries. It sufficed that she saw the main point, the persuasive power of beauty over mankind.

"It may be that you had better go," she said. "If you fail I will go myself to my husband, and meantime I shall be in prayer, that this cup may pass from us."

Hastily the girl gathered her beautiful disheveled hair into a ribbon behind, removed the traces of tears from her wild and terror-stricken eyes, and not stopping even for her hat, in her fear that she might be too late, left the house and made her way through the throng before the Fennell house. At sight of her pallid cheeks and set lips, the ribald jeer died on the lips even of the drunken, and the people made way for her in silence. It was not that they had ever liked her, or now sympathized with her. She had always held herself too daintily aloof from speech or contact with them for that, but they guessed her errand, and had a certain rude sense of the pathos of such a humiliation for the haughty Desire Edwards.

PEREZ GETS HIS TITLE

As Desire entered the headquarters room, which Parson West had barely left, Perez was sitting at a table with his back to the door. He turned at the noise of her entrance and seeing who it was gave a great start. Then he rose slowly to his feet and confronted her. It was the first time he had seen her since that Sunday when she cut him dead before all the people, coming out of meeting. For a moment the two stood motionless gazing at each other. Then she came quickly up to him and laid her hand upon his arm. Her dark eyes were full of terrified appeal.

"What are you going to do to my father?" she cried in poignant tones. After a pause he repeated stammeringly, as if he had not quite taken in the idea.

"Your father?"

"Yes, my father! What are you going to do to him?" she repeated more insistently.

His vacant answer had been no affectation. Her beauty, her distress, the touch of her hand on his arm, her warm breath on his cheek, her face so near to his, left him capable in that moment of but one thought, and that was that he loved her wildly, with a love which it had been madness for him to think he could ever overcome or forget. But it was not with soft and melting emotions, but rather in great bitterness, that he owned the mastery of the passion which he had tried so hard to throw off. He knew that if she despised him before, she must hate and loathe him now. Knowing this it gave him a cruel pleasure to crush her, and to make her tears flow, and even while his glowing eyes devoured her face he answered her in a hard, relentless voice.

"What am I going to do with your father? I am going to whip him with the others."

She started back, stung into sudden defiance, her eyes flashing, her bosom tumultuously heaving.

"You will not! You dare not!"

He shrugged his shoulders and replied coldly:

"If you are so sure of that, why did you come to me?"

"Oh, but you will not! You will not!" she cried again, her terror returning with a rush of tears.

Weeping she was even more beautiful than before. But conscious of her loathing her beauty only caused him an intolerable ache. In the self-despite of an embittered hopeless love he gloated over her despair, even while every nerve thrilled with wildering passion. She caught that look, at once so passionate and so bitter, and perhaps by her woman's instinct interpreting it aright, turned away as in despair, and with her head bent in hopeless grief walked slowly across the room, laid her hand on the latch and there paused. After a moment she turned her head quickly and looked at him, as he stood gazing after her, and shuddered perceptibly. Her left hand, which hung at her side, clenched convulsively. Then after another moment she removed her hand from the latch and came back a few steps toward him and said:

"You kissed me once. Would you like to do it now? You may if you will let my father go."

His gaze, before so glowing, actually dropped in confession before her cold, hard eyes, and for a moment it seemed as if such supreme and icy indifference had been able quite to chill his ardor. But as he lifted his eyes again, and looked upon her, the temptation of so much submissive beauty proved too great. He snatched her in his arms and covered her lips and cheeks and temples with burning kisses, for one alone of which he would have deemed it cheap to give his life if he could not have won it otherwise. He kissed her, passive and unresisting as a statue, till in very pity he was fain to let her go. Even then she did not start away, but standing there before him, pallid, rigid, with compressed lips and clenched hands, said faintly:

"You will release my father?" He bowed his head, unable to speak, and she went out.

The people whispered to each other as she passed through the crowd, that she had failed in her mission, she looked so white and anguish-stricken. And when she reached home and throwing herself into a chair, covered her face with her hands, her mother said:

"The Lord's will be done. You have failed."

"No, mother, I have not failed. Father will be released, but I had liefer have borne the whipping for him."

But that was all she said, nor did she tell any one at what price she had delivered him.

Desire had scarcely gone when the door opened and Hubbard and Abner came in. Perez was sitting staring at the wall in a daze.

"Little Pete's come, an the people want to know when the whipping's going to begin. Shall I bring em out?" said Hubbard.

"I've made up my mind that it will be better to have no whipping," replied Perez, quietly.

"The devil, you have!" exclaimed Hubbard, in high dudgeon.

"I knowd haow 'twoud be w'en I see that air Edwards gal goin in. Ef I'd been on guard, she'd never a got in," said Abner, gloomily.

"Who'd have supposed Hamlin was such a milksop as to mind a girl's bawling?" said Hubbard, scornfully.

"The fellers is kinder sot on seein the silk stockins licked, now ye've got em inter the noshin on't, an I dunno haow they'll take it ter be disappointed," continued Abner.

There was a shout of many voices from before the house. "Bring em out! Bring out the silk stockins."

"Do you hear that?" demanded Hubbard, triumphantly. "I tell you, Hamlin," he went on in a bolder tone, "you can't stop this thing, whether you want to, or not, and if you know what's best for you, you won't try. I tell you that crowd won't stand any fooling. They're mad, and they're drunk, and they're bound to see a silk stocking whipped for once in their lives, and by God they shall see it, too, for all you or any other man. If you won't order em brought out, I will," and he went out.

Without a word, Perez took his pistols from the table, and followed him, and Abner, who seemed irresolute and demoralized, came slowly after. The report that Perez, in a sudden whim, now proposed to deprive them of the treat he had promised them, had produced on the drunken and excited crowd, all the effect which Hubbard had counted on, and as Perez reached the front door of the house, a mass of men with brandished clubs and muskets, were pressing around it, and the sentinel, hesitating and frightened, in another moment would have given way and let them into the building. As Perez, a pistol in either hand, appeared on the threshold, the crowd recoiled a little.

"Stand back," he said. "If any one of you tries to enter, I'll blow his brains out. The men in here, are my prisoners, not yours. I took them when most of you were snoring in bed, and I'll do what I please with them. As for Hubbard and these West Stockbridge men, who make so much noise, this is none of their business, anyway. If they don't like the way we manage here in Stockbridge, let them go home."

As he finished speaking, Abner shouldered his way by him, from within, and stepped out between him and the crowd. Deliberately taking off his coat and laying it down, and pitching his hat after it, he drawlingly observed:

"Look a here, fellers. I be ez disapp'inted ez any on ye, not ter see them fellers licked. But ye see, 'twuz the Cap'n that saved my back, an it don't nohow lie in my mouth no more'n doos yourn to call names naow he's tuk a noshin tew save theirn. So naow, Cap'n," he continued, as he drew his immense bulk squarely up, "I guess you won't need them shooters. I'll break ther necks ez fass ez they come on."

But they didn't come on. Perez' determined attitude and words, especially his appeal to local prejudice, perhaps the most universal and virulent of all human instincts, would have of themselves suffered to check and divide the onset, and Abner's business-like proposal quite ended the demonstration.

A couple of hours later, when the people had largely gone home to dinner, the prisoners were quietly set free, and went to their homes without attracting special attention. About twilight a carriage rolled away from before Squire Woodbridge's door, and took the road to Pittsfield. The next day it was known all over the village that the Squire had left town, without giving out definitely when he would return.

"Squire's kinder obstinit, but arter all he knows w'en he's licked," observed Abner, which was substantially the view generally taken of the magnate's retirement from the field.

That night, Perez set a guard of a dozen men at the Fennell house, to secure the town military stores against any possibility of recapture by another silk stocking conspiracy, and to still further protect the community against any violent enterprise, he organized a regular patrol for the night. If any of the disaffected party were desperate enough still to cherish the hope of restoring their fortunes by force, it must needs have died in their breasts, as looking forth from their bedroom windows, that night, they caught the gleam of the moonlight upon the bayonet of the passing sentinel. But there was no need of such a reminder. Decidedly, the spirit of the court party was broken. Had their leaders actually undergone the whipping they had so narrowly escaped, they would

have scarcely been more impressed with the abject and powerless situation in which they were left by the miscarriage of
their plot. The quasi military occupation of the town, the
night after the attempted revolution, was indeed welcomed
by them and their terrified families as some guarantee of
order. So entirely had the revolution of the past twenty-four
hours changed their attitude toward Perez, that they now
looked on him as their saviour from the mob, and only possible protector against indefinite lengths of lawlessness. It
was among them, rather than among the people, that the
knowledge of his intended speedy departure for New York,
now produced the liveliest apprehensions. And the most timid
of the popular party were not more relieved than they, when
the next day it became known that he had declared his resolve to give up going west, and remain in Stockbridge for the
present.

It would sound much better if I could make out that this
abrupt change in his plans was on account of concern for the
welfare of the community, but such was not the case. His
motive was wholly selfish. The key to it was the discovery that
as responsible chief of the mob, holding the fate and fortunes of her friends in his power, he had a hold on Desire.
Unwilling brides were not the most unhappy wives. Yes, even
to that hight had his hopes suddenly risen from the very dust
in which they had lain quite dead a few hours ago. As the
poor ex-captain and farmer she had held him afar off in
supercilious scoorn; as the chief of the insurgents she had
come to him in tears and entreaty, had laid her hand on his
arm, had even given him her lips. With that scene in the
guardhouse to look back on, what might he not dare to hope.

His fate was in his own hands. Who could foresee the end
of the epoch of revolution and anarchy upon which the state
now seemed entering. These were times when the sword
carved out fortunes and the soldier might command the most
brilliant rewards.

No sooner then had he resolved to stay in Stockbridge, than he set about strengthening his hold on his followers, and imparting a more regular military organization to the insurgent element in the town. The Fennell house was adopted as a regular headquarters, and a young hemlock tree, by way of rebel standard, planted before the door. Night and day patrols, with regular officers of the day, were organized, and about a hundred men formed into a company and drilled daily on the green. A large proportion of them having served in the revolution, they made a very creditable appearance after a little practice. In their hats they wore jauntily hemlock plumes, and old Continental uniforms being still quite plentiful, with a little swapping and borrowing, enough army coats were picked up to clothe pretty much the entire force.

One afternoon, as the drill was going on, a traveling carriage turned in from the Boston road, drove across the green in front of the embattled line, and turning down toward the Housatonic, stopped before the Sedgwick house, and Theodore Sedgwick descended. The next day, as Perez was walking along the street, he saw Dr. Partridge, Squire Edwards, and a gentleman to him unknown, conversing. As he approached them, the doctor said, in the good-humored, yet half-mocking tone characteristic of him:

"Squire Sedgwick, let me introduce to you the Duke of Stockbridge, Captain Perez Hamlin, to whose gracious protection we of the court party, owe our lives and liberties at present."

Sedgwick scanned Perez with evident curiosity, but merely bowed without speaking, and the other passed on. Either somebody overheard the remark, or the doctor repeated it elsewhere, for within a day or two it was all over town, and henceforth, by general consent, half in jest, half in recognition of the aptness of the title under the circumstances, Perez was dubbed Duke of Stockbridge, or more briefly referred to as "The Duke."

The conversation which his passing had momentarily interrupted, was a very grave one. Sedgwick had passed through Springfield in his carriage on the twenty-seventh of September, and reported that he had found the town full of armed men. The Supreme Judicial Court of the Commonwealth was to have met on the twenty-sixth, but 1200 insurgents, under Captain Daniel Shays himself, were on hand to prevent it, and were confronted by 800 militia under General Shepard, who held the courthouse. The town was divided into hostile camps, with regular lines of sentinels. At the time Sedgwick had passed through, no actual collision had yet taken place, but should the justices persist in their intention to hold court, there would certainly be fighting, for it was justly apprehended by Shays and his lieutenants that the court intended to proceed against them for treason, and they would stop at nothing to prevent that. It was this news which Sedgwick was imparting to the two gentlemen.

"We have a big business on our hands," he said gravely, "a very big and a very delicate business. A little bungling will be enough to turn it into a civil war, with the chances all against the government."

"I don't see that the government, as yet, has done anything," said Edwards. "Do they intend to leave everything to the mob?"

"Between us, there is really nothing that can be done just now," replied Sedgwick. "The passiveness of the government results from their knowledge that the militia are not to be depended on. Why, as I passed through Springfield, I saw whole companies of militia that had been called out by the sheriff to protect the court, march, with drums beating, over to the insurgents. No, gentlemen, there is actually no force that could be confidently counted on against the mob save a regiment or two in Boston. Weakness leaves the government no choice but to adopt a policy of conciliation with the rascals, for the present, at least. His Excellency has called the

Legislature in extra session the twenty-sixth, and a number of measures will at once be passed for relief. If these do not put an end to the mobs, they will, it is hoped, at least so far improve the public temper that a part of the militia will be available.

"It is a mysterious Providence, indeed," he continued, "that our state, in the infancy of its independence, is left to undergo so fearful a trial. Already there are many of the Tories who wag the head and say 'Aha, so would we have it,' averring that this insurrection is but the first fruits of our liberty, and that the rest will be like unto it."

"God grant that we may not have erred in throwing off the yoke of the King," said Edwards, gloomily. "I do confess that I have had much exercise of mind upon that point during the trials of the past weeks."

"I beg of you, sir, not to give way to such a frame," said Sedgwick earnestly, "for it is to gentlemen of your degree that the well disposed look for guidance and encouragement in these times. And yet I am constrained to admit that in Boston at no time in the late war, no, not when our fortunes were at the lowest ebb, has there been such gloom as now. And verily I could not choose but to share it, but for my belief that the convention, which is shortly to sit in Philadelphia to devise a more perfect union for the thirteen states, will pave the way for a stronger government of the continent, and one that will guarantee us not only against foreign invasion but domestic violence and insurrection also."

"We had best separate now," said Partridge in a low voice. "If the populace see but two or three of us having our heads together, they straightway imagine that we are plotting against them, and I see those fellows yonder are sending black looks this way already.

"I shall do myself the honor," he added, to Sedgwick, "to call upon you at your house for further consultation, since under the pretext of a physician's duty, I am allowed by their high mightinesses, the rabble, to go about more freely than is prudent for other gentlemen."

The next day the news from Springfield, which Sedgwick had privately brought, reached the village from other sources, together with the developments since his passage through the town. It seemed that there had indeed been no collision between the militia and the rebel force, but it was because the Supreme Court had, after demurring for two days, finally yielded to the orders of Captain Shays and adjourned, after which the rebels took triumphant possession of the court-house. The elation which the news produced among the people was prodigious. Perez doubled the patrols, and even then had to wink at a good many acts of lawlessness at the expense of the friends of the courts. Nothing but his personal interposition prevented a drunken gang from giving Sedgwick a tin-pan serenade. As for Squire Edwards, he was glad to purchase immunity at the expense of indiscriminate treating of the crowd.

Whether the Supreme Court would attempt to hold its regular session the first week in October, at Great Barrington, was a point on which there was a diversity of opinion. Before adjourning at Springfield, it had indeed passed resolutions that it would not be expedient to go to Berkshire, but it was loudly declared by many that this was a mere trick to put the people off their guard, and prevent their assembling in arms to stop the proceedings. Accordingly, when the time came, although the justices did not put in an appearance, a mob of several hundred men did, and a very ugly mob it turned out to be, in fact the worst hitherto in the entire course of the insurrection. Finding no court to stop, and the empty jail affording no opportunity for another jail delivery, the crowd, after loafing around town for a while and getting thirsty, began to break into houses to get liquor. A beginning once made, this was found to be such an amusing recreation that it was gone into generally, and when liquor could not be found the men contented themselves with appropriating other articles. The fun growing fast and furious, they next began to hustle and stone prominent citizens known to be friendly to the courts, as well as such as objected to having their houses entered and gutted. When their victims broke away from them and fled, being too drunk to overtake them it was quite natural that they should fire their muskets after them, and if the bullets did not generally hit their marks it was merely because the hands of the marksmen were as unsteady as their legs. Some of the most prominent citizens of Great Barrington passed the day hid in outhouses and garrets, while others, mounted on fleet steeds, escaped amid a peltering of bullets, and took refuge in neighboring towns, some going as far as Pittsfield before they halted.

Squire Sedgwick chanced to be at Great Barrington, that day, at the house of his brother-in-law, Justice Dwight. As a lawyer, an aristocrat, and a member of the detested State Senate, he not only shared the general unpopularity of those classes, but as prosecuting attorney for the county, was in particularly evil odor with the lewd fellows of the baser sort, who were to-day on the rampage. When the uproar was at its height, word got around that he was in town, and immediately the mob dropped whatever was in hand, and rushed in a body toward Dwight's house. As they came in sight of the house a servant was holding Sedgwick's gray by the bridle before the gate. Fearing that their prey might yet escape them, the crowd burst into a run, brandishing cudgels, guns and pitchforks, and yelling, "Kill him," "Hang him," "Shoot him." They were not fifty yards away when Sedgwick came out and deliberately mounted his horse. The beast was a good one, and the distance was enough to make his rider's escape perfectly secure. But instead of galloping off, Sedgwick turned his horse's head toward the onrushing, hooting multitude, and rode at a gentle trot directly toward them. It seemed like madness, but the effect fully justified the cool daring that had prompted the action. With the first forward step of the animal, the moment the rider's intention became evident, the mob stopped dead, and the uproar of execrations gave place to a silence of perfect astonishment, in which you could have heard the swish of a bird's wing. As the horse's head touched the line of men, they slunk aside as if they knew not what they did, their eyes falling abashed before Sedgwick's quiet glance and air, as devoid of a trace of fear as it was of ostentatious defiance. The calm, unquestioning assumption that no one would presume to stop him, was a moral force which paralyzed the arm of the most reckless ruffian in the crowd. And so, checking his horse when he would have gone faster, his features as composed as if he were sitting in the Senate, and his bearing as cool and matter of course as if he were on a promenade, he rode through the mob, and had passed out of musket shot by the time the demoralized ruffians had begun to accuse each other of cowardice, and each one to explain what he would have done if he had been in somebody else's place, or would do again.

TWO CRITICAL INTERVIEWS

The news of the riot at Great Barrington, brought by Sedgwick, excited a ferment of terror among the gentlemen's families in Stockbridge. Later in the day when the report got around that the mob intended to visit the latter place, and treat it in like manner, there was little less than a panic. The real facts of the Great Barrington outrages, quite bad enough in themselves, had been exaggerated ten-fold by rumor, and it was believed that the town was in flames and the streets full of murder and rapine. Some already began to barricade their doors, in preparation for the worst, while others who had horses and vehicles prepared to convey a part at least of their families and goods out of reach of the marauders. There were some in Stockbridge who well remembered the alarm, "The Indians are coming," that summer Sunday, when the Schaghticokes came down on the infant settlement, one and thirty years before. There was scarcely wilder terror then, but one point of difference sadly illustrated the distinction between a foreign invasion and a civil war. Then all the people were in the same fright, but now the panic was confined to the well-to-do families and those conscious of being considered friendly to the courts. The poorer people looked on their agitation with indifference, while some even jeered at it.

The afternoon wore away, however, and the expected mob failed to make its appearance, whereupon the people gradually took heart again. Those who had put their furniture into carts unloaded it, and those who had buried their silver in their cellars dug it up to use on the tea table. Nevertheless, along about dusk, a good many men living in Stockbridge, who had been down to Great Barrington all day, came home drunk and flushed with victory and these, with the aid of some of the same kidney in the village, kept up a lively racket all the evening, varied with petty outrages which Perez thought best to ignore, knowing too well the precarious tenure of his authority, to endanger it by overstrictness. Perhaps, indeed, he was not wholly averse to such occasional displays by the mob, as would keep before the gentlemen of the town a vivid impression of what would be in store for them if but for his guardianship.

It was about eight o'clock in the evening that, coming in sight of the store, he saw it besieged by a gang of men, whom Squire Edwards, visible against the background of the lighted doorway, was expostulating with. The men were drunk and reckless. They wanted rum and were bound to have it, and on the other hand the Squire had evidently made up his mind that if they got into his store in their present mood, they would be likely to plunder him of whatever he had, and drawing valor from desperation, was opposing, a resistance which involved no small personal peril. The crowd, besides being drunk, was composed of the very men who had grudged him his escape from the whipping-post a few days previous, and was by no means disposed to stand on ceremony with him. Already he was being hustled, his wig had been displaced, and his cane struck out of his hand, and in another minute he would have been knocked down and the store thronged. The light of a blazing bonfire on the green, threw glimmering reflections upon the crowd before the store, and Edwards catching sight of Perez' three-cornered hat cried in desperation:

"Captain Hamlin, will you let them kill me?"

In another moment Perez was up on the piazza in full view of the crowd, which abashed a little by his presence, for a moment drew back a little.

"What do you want, men? You ought not to break into people's houses! You musn't disgrace the hemlock."

"Tha's all mighty fine, Cap'n," said Meshech Little, "but we want suthin tew drink."

"Why don't you get it at the tavern?"

"The widder won't treat no more, an she's kinder got Abner bewitched like, so's he backs her up, an we can't git nothin thar 'thout fightin Abner, darn him."

"I say Cap'n 'tain't fa'r fer yew ter be a interferin with all our fun," spoke up another.

"That's so," said others. "Cap'n," remarked Meshech, "yew jess let us 'lone, we hain't a techin yew, an we're baoun tew hev a time ter night."

Perez knew well enough that to attempt to wholly thwart the intentions of this excited and drunken crowd, would be beyond his power, or at least involve a bloody riot, and so he replied, good-naturedly:

"That's all right, boys, you shall have your time, but it won't do to break into houses. Go over to the guardhouse and tell Abe Konkapot that I say you may have a couple of gallons of the town rum we seized the other night." This compromise was tumultuously accepted, the entire crowd starting on a run toward the Fennell house, each hoping to get the first advantage of the largess.

"Come in, Captain," said Edwards, and Perez entered.

Mrs. Edwards, Desire and Jonathan were in the store, having hurried thither from the inner living-rooms at the noise of the crowd, to share if they could not repel, the danger which threatened the head of the house. As Jonathan quickly closed and barred the door, Edwards said:

"Wife, I owe my property and perhaps my life, also, to Captain Hamlin."

Mrs. Edwards dropped a stately curtsey, and said with a grand air which made Perez feel as if her acknowledgments were a condescension quite dwarfing his performance:

"I truly thank you for your succor." He mumbled something, he could not have said what, and then his eyes sought

Desire, who stood a little aside. As he met her eye, he found himself blushing with embarrassment at thought of their last interview. He had supposed that it would be she who would be confused and self-conscious when they met, but it was all on his side. She looked cool, dignified and perfectly composed, quite as if he were a stock or a stone. He could but wonder if he had remembered the incidents correctly. What with Mrs. Edwards' grand air of condescending politeness, and Desire's icy composure, he began to feel that he needed to get outdoors again, where he could review the situation and recover his equanimity. But on his making a movement in that direction, Squire Edwards, who had no notion of parting with the protection of his presence just at present, insisted that he should first go into the parlor, and Mrs. Edwards dutifully and crushingly seconding the invitation, he found himself without choice. The education of the camp, while it may adapt a man to command other men, does not necessarily fit him to shine in the salon. Perez stepped on his toes once or twice in passing through the store, and in the parlor doorway, to his intense mortification, jostled, heavily against Desire. He plumped down in the easiest chair in the room, before being invited to sit at all, and changing hastily from that to a stool too small for him, at the third attempt settled in a chair of the right size. It was then that he remembered to take off his hat, and having crossed and uncrossed his legs several times, and tried numerous postures, finally sat bolt upright, gripping the lapels of his coat with his hands. As for any tender emotions on account of the girl who sat near him, he was scarcely conscious of her presence, save as an element of embarrassment.

"I understand that you have served at the south, Captain Hamlin," said Mrs. Edwards.

"Yes, I thank you," he replied.

"You were with General Green, perhaps?"

"Yes — that is — yes m'am."

"How is your mother's health?"

"Very well indeed, — that is, when — when she isn't sick. She is generally sick."

"Indeed."

"Yes, but she's pretty well otherwise. How are you?" this last, desperately.

"Oh, thanks, I'm quite well," Mrs. Edwards replied, with a slight elevation of the eyebrows. Somehow he felt that he ought not to have asked that, and then he made another desperate resolution to go home.

"I think they'll be looking for me at home," he said, tentatively rising halfway from his chair. "Father isn't well, you see." He had a vague feeling that he could not go unless they formally admitted the adequacy of his excuse.

At that moment there came the noise of an axe from the green, with shouts.

"What is that?" asked Mrs. Edwards of her husband, who entered from the store at that moment.

"The rascals — that is — " he corrected himself with a glance at Perez, "the men are chopping down the whipping-post to put on the bonfire. You were not thinking of going so soon, Captain Hamlin?" he added with evident concern.

"Yes, I think I will go," said Perez, straightening up and assuming a resolute air.

"I beg you will not be so hasty," said Mrs. Edwards, taking her husband's cue, and Perez abjectly sat down again.

"You must partake of my hospitality," said Edwards. "Jonathan, draw a decanter of that old Jamaica. Desire, bring us tumblers."

The only thought of Perez was that the liquor would, perhaps, brace him up a little, and to that end he filled his tumbler well up and did not refuse a second invitation. The result answered his expectations. In a very few moments he began to feel much more at ease. The incubus upon his faculties seemed lifted. His muscles relaxed. He recovered the

free control of his tongue and his eyes. Whereas he had previously been only conscious of Mrs. Edwards, and but vaguely
of the room in which they were and its other inmates, he now
began to look around, and take cognizance of persons and
things and even found himself complimenting his host on the
quality of the rum with an ease at which he was surprised.
He could readily have mustered courage enough now to take
his leave, but he no longer felt in haste. As I observed above,
he had heretofore but vaguely taken notice of Desire, as she
had sat silently near by. Now he became conscious of her. He
observed her closely. He had never seen her dressed as she was
now, in a low-necked, white dress with short sleeves. As he
was a few moments before, such new revelations of her beauty
would have daunted him, would have actually added to his
demoralization, but now he contemplated her with an intense,
elated complacency. It was easier talking with Mr. Edwards
than with Madam, and half an hour had passed, when Perez
rose and said, this time without trying to excuse himself, that
he must go. Mrs. Edwards had some time before excused herself from the room. Jonathan had also gone. Desire bade him
good evening, and Squire Edwards led the way into the store
to show him out. But Perez, after starting to follow him,
abruptly turned back, and crossing the room to where Desire
stood, held out his hand. She hesitated, and then put hers in
it. He raised it to his lips, although she tried to snatch it away,
and then, as if the touch had maddened him, he audaciously
drew her to him and kissed her lips. She broke away, shivering
and speechless. Then he saw her face crimson to the roots of
her hair. She had seen her mother standing in the doorway,
looking at her. But Perez, as he turned and went out through
the store, did not perceive this. Had he turned to look back,
he would have witnessed a striking tableau.

Desire had thrown herself into a chair and buried her face
in her arms, against whose rounded whiteness the crimsoned
ear tips and temples testified to the shameful glow upon the

hidden face while her mother stood gazing at her, amazement and indignation pictured on her face. For a full half minute she stood thus, and then said:

"My daughter, what does this mean?"

There was no answer, save that, at the voice of her mother, a warm glow appeared upon the nape of the girl's neck, and even spread over the glistening shoulders, while her form shook with a single convulsive sob.

"Desire, tell me this instant," exclaimed Mrs. Edwards.

The girl threw up her head and faced her mother, her eyes blazing with indignant shame and glistening with tears, which were quite dried up by her hot cheeks ere they had run half their course.

"You saw," she said in a low, hard, fierce tone, "the fellow kissed me. He does it when he pleases. I have no one to protect me."

"Why do you let him? Why didn't you cry out?"

"And let father be whipped, let him be killed! Don't you know why I didn't?" cried the girl in a voice hoarse with excitement and overwhelming exasperation that the motive of the sacrifice should not be understood, even for a moment. She had sprung to her feet and was facing her mother.

"Was it for this that he released your father the other day?"

Desire looked at her mother without a word, in a way that was an answer. Mrs. Edwards seemed completely overcome, while Desire met her horrified gaze with a species of desperate hardihood.

"Yes, it is I," she said, in a shrill, nervously excited tone. "It is your daughter, Desire Edwards, whom this fellow has for a sweetheart. Oh, yes. He kisses me where he chooses, and I do not cry out. Isn't it fine, ha! ha!" and then her overstrained feelings finding expression in a burst of hysterical laughter, she threw herself back into her chair, and buried her face in her arms on the table as at first.

"What's the matter? What ails the girl?" said Edwards,

coming in from the store, and viewing the scene with great surprise.

"The matter?" replied Mrs. Edwards slowly. "The matter is this: as that fellow was leaving, and your back was turned, he took our girl here and hugged and kissed her, and though she resisted what she could, she did not cry out. I stood in that door and saw it with my own eyes. When I called her to account for this scandal, she began vehemently to weep, and protested that she dared not anger him by outcry, fearing for your life if he were offended. And she further hinted that it was not the first time he had had the kissing of her. Nay, she as good as said it was with kisses that she ransomed you out of his hands the other day."

Edwards listened with profound interest, but with more evidence of curiosity than agitation, and after thinking a few moments, said thoughtfully:

"I have marvelled much by what manner of argument she compassed our deliverance, after the parson, a man mighty in persuasion and rebuke, had wholly failed therein. Verily, the devices of Providence for the protection of his saints in troublous times are past understanding. To this very intent doubtless, was the gift of comeliness bestowed on the maiden, a matter wherefore I have often, in much perplexity, inquired of the Lord, seeing that it is a gift that often brings the soul into jeopardy through vain thoughts. But now is the matter made plain to my eyes."

It was no light thing in those days for a wife to reproach her lord, but Mrs. Edwards' eyes fairly lightened as she demanded with a forced calm:

"Will you, then, give up your daughter to these lewd fellows as Lot would have given up his daughters to save his house?"

"Tut! tut!" said Edwards, frowning. "Your speech is unbridled and unseemly. I am not worthy to be likened to that holy man of old, for whose sake the Lord well nigh saved

Sodom, nor am I placed in so sore a strait. You spoke of nothing worse than kissing. The girl will not be the worse, I trow,
for a buss or two. Women are not so mighty tender. So long
as girls like not the kissing, be sure t'will do them no harm,
eh, Desire?" and he pinched her arm.

She snatched it away, and rushing across the room, threw
herself upon the settle, with her face in the cushion.

"Pish!" said her father, peevishly, "she grudges a kiss to save
her father from disgrace and ruin. It is a sinful, proud wench!"

"Proud!" echoed the girl, raising her tear-stained face from
the cushion and sitting up. "I was proud, but I'm not any
more. All the rabble are welcome to kiss me, seeing my father
thinks it no matter."

"Pshaw, child, what a coil about a kiss or two, just because
the fellow smells a little, maybe, of the barn! Can't you wash
your face after? Take soap to 't, and save your tears. Bless me!
you shall hide in the garret after this, but for my part, I shall
still treat the fellow civilly, for he holds us, as it were, in the
hollow of his hand," and he went into the store in a pet.

There was one redeeming feature about the disturbances
in Stockbridge. The early bedtime habits of the people were
too deeply fixed to be affected by any political revolution, and
however noisy the streets might be soon after dusk, by half
past nine or ten all was quiet. As Perez crossed the green,
after leaving the store, the only sound that broke the stillness
of the night, was the rumble of wheels on the Boston road. It
was Sedgwick's carriage, bearing him back to the capital, to
take his seat in the already convened State Senate. If his flying visit home had been a failure so far as his law business before the Supreme Court was concerned, it had at least enabled him to gain a vivid conception of the extent and virulence of the insurrection.

There was really a good deal more than a joke in calling
Perez, Duke of Stockbridge. The antechamber of the headquarters room, at the guardhouse, was often half full of a

morning with gentlemen, and those of lower degree as well, waiting to see him with requests. Some wanted passes, or authority to go out of town, or carry goods away. Others had complaints of orchards robbed, property stolen, or other injuries from the lawless, with petitions for redress. The varieties of cases in which Perez' intervention as the only substitute for law in the village was being constantly demanded, it would quite exceed my space to enumerate. In addition to this, he had the military affairs of the insurgent train-band to order, besides transacting business with the agents of neighboring towns, and even with messengers from Shays, who already had begun to call on the Berkshire towns for quotas to swell the rebel forces, of which a regular military organization was now being attempted.

An informal sort of constitutional convention at the tavern had committed the general government of the town, pending the present troubles, to a Committee of Correspondence, Inspection and Safety, consisting of Perez, Israel Goodrich and Ezra Phelps, but the two latter practically left everything to Perez. There was not in this improvised form of town government, singular as it strikes us, anything very novel or startling to the people of the village, accustomed as they were all through the war to the discretionary and almost despotic sway in internal as well as external affairs, of the town revolutionary committees of the same name. These, at first irregular, were subsequently recognized alike by the Continental and state authorities, and on them the work of carrying the people through the war practically and chiefly fell. In Berkshire, indeed, the offices of the revolutionary committees had been even more multifarious and extensive than in the other counties, for owing to the course of Berkshire in refusing to acknowledge the authority of the state government from 1775 to 1780, and the consequent suppression of courts during that period, even judicial functions had often devolved upon the committees, and suits at law had been heard and determined, and the verdicts enforced by them. To the town meeting alone did the revolutionary committees hold themselves responsible. The effect of the outbreak of the revolutionary war had been, indeed, to reduce democracy to its simplest terms. The Continental Congress had no power, and only pretended to recommend and advise. The state government, by sundering its relations with the crown, lost its legal title, and for some time after the war began, and as regards Berkshire, until the county voted to accept the new state constitution in 1780, its authority was not recognized. During that period it may be properly said that, while the Continental Congress advised and the state convention recommended, the town meeting was the only body of actual legislative powers in the Commonwealth. The reader must excuse this brief array of dry historical details, because only by bearing in mind that such had been the peculiar political education of the people of Berkshire, will it appear fully credible that revolt should so readily become organized, and anarchy assume the forms of law and order.

From the extent of his property interests and the popular animosity which endangered them, no gentleman in Stockbridge had more necessity to keep the right side of Perez Hamlin than Squire Edwards, and it was not the storekeeper's fault if he did not. Comparatively few days passed in which Perez did not find himself invited to take a glass of something, as he passed the store, and without touching the point either of servility or hypocrisy Edwards knew how to make himself so affable that Perez began actually to think that perhaps he liked him for his own sake, and even cherished the wild idea of taking him into confidence concerning his passion and hope as to Desire. Had he done so Edwards would certainly have found himself in a very awkward predicament. Meanwhile, day after day and even week after week passed, and save for an occasional glimpse of her passing a window, or the shadow on her bedroom curtain with which his long night watches were sometimes rewarded, he saw nothing of Desire. She never went on the street, and for two Sundays had stayed at home from meeting. He could not muster courage to ask Edwards about her, feeling that it must be that she kept within doors merely to avoid him. One evening, however, late in October, as he was sitting over some rum with the storekeeper, the latter remarked, in a casual way, that the doctor had advised that his daughter Desire, who had not been well of late, should take a trip to Pittsfield for her health, and as if it were something quite casual, asked Perez to have the kindness to make out a pass for her to go the next day. As the Squire made this request, speaking as if it were a mere matter of course, Perez was in the act of raising a glass of liquor to his lips. He gave Edwards one glance, very slowly set down the untasted beverage, and without a word of reply or of parting salutation, got up and went out. The moment he was gone the door connecting the living-rooms with the back of the store, softly opened, and Mrs. Edwards and Desire entered.

"Did you get it?" asked the latter.

"Get it," replied Edwards in disgust, "I should think not. He looked at me like a wolf when I spoke of it. I had some notion that he would stick his hanger through my stomach, but he thought better of that and got up and stalked out without so much as winking at me. He's a terrible fellow. I doubt if he does not some outrage to us for this."

"Dear! Dear! What shall I do?" cried Desire, wringing her hands. "I must go. I can't stay here, shut up like a prisoner, I shall be sick and die."

"Who knows," said Mrs. Edwards, "what this ruffian may do next? He will stop at nothing. He will not much longer respect our house. He may force himself in any day. She is not safe here. I dare not have her stay another day."

"I don't know what can be done, she can't get away without a pass," replied Edwards. "It would do no good for me to ask him again. Perhaps the girl herself might coax a pass out of him. It's the only chance."

"I coax him! I see him again! Oh I can't, I can't do that," cried Desire with an air of overwhelming repugnance.

"I could leave the door ajar you know, Desire, and be ready to come into the room if he were unmannerly," said her mother. "I think he's rather afraid of me. I'm afraid it's the only chance, as your father says, if you could but bring yourself to it."

"Oh it doesn't seem as if I could. It doesn't seem as if I could," cried the girl.

Perez did not come near the store for some days and it was on the street that Edwards next met him. The storekeeper was very cordial and made no further allusion to the pass. In the course of conversation he managed to make some reference to Desire's piano, and the curiosity the people seemed to feel about the novel instrument. He asked Perez if he had ever seen it, and Perez saying no, invited him to drop in that evening and hear Desire play a little. It is needless to say that the young man's surprise at the invitation did not prevent his accepting it. It would have melted the heart of his worst enemy to have seen how long he toiled that afternoon trying to refurbish his threadbare coat so white in the seams, and the rueful face with which he contemplated the result. On presenting himself at the store soon after dusk, Edwards at once ushered him into the parlor, and withdrew, saying that he must see to his business.

Desire sat at the piano, no one else being in the room. She looked rather pallid and thinner than when he had seen her last, but all the more interesting for this delicacy. There was, however, a far more striking alteration in her manner, for to his surprise she rose at his entrance, and came forward with a smile to greet him. He was delightfully bewildered.

"I scarcely know how to greet a Duke, for such I hear you are become," said Desire with a profound curtsy and a bewitching tone of badinage.

Entirely taken aback, he murmured something inarticulate, about her piano.

"Would your grace like to have me play a little?" she asked, gaily.

He intimated that he would, and she at once sat down before the little instrument. It was scarcely more to be compared with the magnificent machines of our day than the flageolets of Virgil's shepherds with the cornet-a-piston of the modern star performer, but Mozart, Haydn, Handel, or Beethoven never lived to see a better. It was only about two feet across by four and a half in width, with a small square sounding board at the end. The almost threadlike wires, strung on a wooden frame, gave forth a thin and tinny sound which would instantaneously bring the hands of a modern audience to its ears. But to Perez it seemed divine, and when, too, Desire opened her mouth and sang, tears of genuine emotion filled his eyes. She was more richly dressed than he had ever seen her before, wearing a cherry colored silk bodice, low necked, and with bell mouthed sleeves reaching to her elbows only, while the rounded white arms were set off with coral bracelets, a necklace of the same material encircling her throat. Upon one cheek, a little below the outside corner of the eye she wore a small black patch, according to a fashion of the time, by way of heightening by contrast the delicacy of her complexion. The faint perfume with which she had completed her toilet, seemed less a perfume than the very breath of her beauty, the voluptuous effluence which it exhaled. Having played and sung for some time she let her hands drop by her side and raising her eyes to meet Perez' fascinated gaze, said lightly:

"Do you like it?" The most exacting performer would have been satisfied with the manner in which after a husky attempt to say something in reply, he bowed his head in silence.

"I'm glad you came in to-night," she said, "for I want to ask something of you. Since you are Duke of Stockbridge we all have to ask favors of you, you see."

"What is it?" he asked.

"Oh, dear me," she said, laughing. "That's not the way people ask favors of kings and dukes. They make em promise to grant the favor first, and then tell em what it is. This is the way," and with the words she dropped lightly on one knee before Perez, and with her clasped hands pressed against her bosom, raised her face up toward his, her eyes eloquent, of intoxicating submissiveness.

"If thine handmaiden has found grace in the sight of my lord, the duke, let my request be done even according to the prayer of my lips."

Perez leaned forward toward the beautiful upward turning face.

"Whatever you want," he murmured.

"To the half of my dukedom, you must say."

"To the half of my dukedom," he repeated, in a mechanical voice, not removing his eyes from hers.

"Do you pledge your honor?" she demanded, still retaining her position.

If he had known that she intended asking him to blow his own brains out the next moment, and had expected to keep his promise, he must needs, with her kneeling so before him, have answered "yes," and so he did in fact reply.

"Thanks," she said, rising lightly to her feet, "you make a very good duke indeed, and to reward you I shall not ask for anything like half your dukedom, but only for a scrap of paper. Here is ink and paper and a pen. Please write me a pass to go to Pittsfield. Dr. Partridge says I must have change of air, and I don't want to be stopped by your soldiers."

A ghastly pallor overspread his face. "You're not going away," he stammered, rising slowly up.

"To be sure I am. What else should I want of the pass? Come, you're not going to make me do all that asking over again. Please sit right down again and write it. You know you promised on your word of honor."

She even put her hand smilingly on his shoulder, as if to push him down, and as he yielded to the light but irresistible pressure, she put a pen in his nerveless fingers, saying gayly:

"Just your name at the bottom, that's all. Father wrote the rest to save you trouble. Now, please." Powerless against an imperious magnetism which would have compelled him to sign his own death-warrant, he scrawled the words. As she took up the precious scrap of paper, and hid it in her bosom, the door opened, and Mrs. Edwards entered with stately formality, and the next moment Perez found himself blunderingly answering questions about his mother's state of health, not having the faintest idea what he was saying. The next thing he was conscious of was the cold frosty air on his face as he walked across the green from the store to the guard-house.

THE HUSKING

Scarcely had Perez left, when Edwards entered the parlor.

"Did you get it?" he asked of Desire.

"Yes, yes," cried the girl. "Oh, that horrible, horrible fellow! I am sick with shame all through, sick! sick! But if I can only get away out of his reach, I shall not mind. Do let Cephas harness the horse into the chaise at once. He may change his mind. Oh, hurry, father, do; don't, oh, don't lose a minute."

Half an hour later, Cephas, an old freedman of Edwards, drove the chaise up to the side door, and a few bundles having been put into the vehicle, Desire herself entered, and was driven hastily away toward Pittsfield.

To go back to Perez, on reaching the guardhouse, coming from the store, he went in and sat down in the headquarters room. Presently, Abe Konkapot, who was officer of the day, entered and spoke to him. Perez making no reply, the Indian spoke again, and then went up to him and laid his hand on his shoulder.

"What is it?" said Perez, in a dull voice.

"What matter with you, Cap'n? Me speake tree time. You no say nothin. You seek?" Perez looked up at him vacantly.

"He no drunk?" pursued Abe, changing from the second to the third person in his mode of speech, as he saw the other paid no attention. "Seem like was heap drunk, but no smell rum," and he scratched his head in perplexity. Then he shook Perez' shoulder again. "Say, Cap'n, what ails yer?"

"She's going away, Abe. Desire Edwards is going away,"

replied Perez, looking up at the Indian in a helpless, appealing way.

"You no like have her go, Cap'n? You like better she stay? What for let her go then?"

"I gave her a pass, Abe. She was so beautiful I couldn't help it."

Abe scratched his head.

"If she so preety, me s'pose you keep her all more for that. No let her go."

Perez did not explain this point, but presently said:

"Abe, you may let the men go home, if you want. It's nothing to me any more what happens here in Stockbridge. The silk stockings are welcome to come and hang me as soon as they please," and his head dropped on his breast like one whose life has suddenly lost its spring and motive.

"Look a here, Cap'n," said Abe, "you say to me, Abe, stop that air gal, fetch her back. Good. Me do it quick. Cap'n feel all right again."

"I can't, Abe, I can't. I promised. I gave her my word. I can't. I wish she had asked me to cut my throat instead," and he despairingly shook his head.

Abe regarded him with evident perplexity for some moments, and then with an abrupt nod of the head turned and glided out of the room. Perez, in his gloomy preoccupation did not even note his going. His head sunk lower on his breast, and he murmured to himself wild words of passion and despair.

"If she only knew. If she knew how I loved her. But she would not care. She hates me. She will never come back. Oh, no, never. I shall never see her again. This is the end. It is the end. How beautiful she was!" and he buried his face in his arms on the table and wept miserable tears.

There were voices and noises about and within the guard-house, but he took no note of them. Some one came into the room, but he did not look up, and for a moment Desire

Edwards, for she it was, in hat and cloak, stood looking down on him. Then she said, in a voice whose first accent brought him to his feet as if electrified:

"No wonder you hide your head."

There was a red spot as big as a cherry in either cheek, and her eyes scintillated with concentrated scorn and anger. Over her shoulder was visible Abe Konkapot's swarthy face, wearing a smile of great self-satisfaction.

"I was foolish enough to think even a rebel might keep his word," Desire went on, in a voice trembling with indignation. "I did not suppose even you would give me a pass and then send your footpads to stop me."

It was evident from his dazed look, that he did not follow her words. He glanced inquiringly at Abe, who responded with lucid brevity:

"Look a' here, Cap'n, me see you feel heap bad cause gal go away. You make fool promise; no can stop her. Me no make promise. Gal come long in cart. Show pass. Pass good, but no good for gal to go. Tear up pass; fetch gal back. Cap'n no break no promise, cause no stop gal. Abe no break promise, cause no make none. Cap'n be leetle mad with Abe for tear up pass, but heap more glad for git gal back," and having thus succinctly stated the matter the Indian retired.

"I beg your pardon, Captain Hamlin," said Desire, with an engaging smile. "I was too hasty. I suppose I was angry. I see you were not to blame. If you will now please tell your men that I am not to be interfered with again, I will make another start for Pittsfield."

"No, not again," he replied slowly.

"But you promised me," she said, with rising apprehension, nervously clasping the edge of her cloak with her fingers as she spoke. "You promised me on the word of a duke you know," and she made another feeble attempt at a smile.

"I promised you," replied he, "I don't know why I was so mad. I was bewitched. I did not break the promise, but I will not make it again. God had pity on me, and brought you back. What have I suffered the last hour, and shall I let you go again? Never! never! None shall pluck you out of my hand.

"Don't let me terrify you, my darling," he went on passionately, in a softened voice, as she changed countenance and recoiled before him in evident fright. "I will not hurt you. I would die sooner than hurt a hair of your head." He tried to take her hand, and then as she snatched it away, he caught the hem of her cloak, and kneeling quickly, raised it with a gesture of boundless tenderness and reverence, to his lips. She had shrunk back to the wall, and looked down on him in wide-eyed, speechless terror, evidently no longer thinking of anything but escape.

"Oh, let me go home. Let me go home. I shall scream out if you don't let me go," she cried.

He rose to his feet, walked quickly across the room and back, and then having in some measure subdued his agitation, replied:

"Certainly, you shall go home. It is dark; I will go with you," and they walked together across to the store without speaking. Returning, Perez met Abe, and taking him by the hand, gave it a tremendous grip, but said nothing.

Whatever resentment Squire Edwards cherished against Perez on account of Desire's recapture and return, he was far too shrewd to allow it to appear. He simply ignored the whole episode and was more affable than ever. Whenever he met the young man, he had something pleasant to say, and was always inviting him into the store to take a drop when he passed. Meanwhile, however, so far as the latter's opportunities of seeing or talking with Desire were concerned, she might just as well have been in Pittsfield, so strictly did she keep the house. A week or ten days passed thus, every day adding fuel to his impatience, and he had already begun to entertain plans worthy of a brigand or a kidnapper, when cir-

cumstances presented an opportunity of which he made
shrewd profit.

During the Revolutionary war it had been a frequent policy
with the town authorities to attempt to correct the high and
capricious prices of goods, always incident to war times, by
establishing fixed rates per pound, bushel, yard or quart, by
which all persons should be compelled to sell or barter their
merchandise and produce. It had been suggested in the Stockbridge Committee of Correspondence, Inspection, and Safety
that the adoption of such a tariff would tend to relieve the
present distress and promote trade. Ezra Phelps proposed the
plan, Israel Goodrich was inclined to favor it, and Perez'
assent would have settled the matter. He, it was, whom Squire
Edwards approached with vehement protestations. He might
well be somewhat agitated, for being the only merchant in
town, the proposed measure was little more than a personal
discrimination against his profits, which, it must be admitted,
had been of late years pretty liberal, thanks to a dearth of
money that had made it necessary for farmers to barter produce for tools and supplies, at rates virtually at the merchant's
discretion. If the storekeeper had been compelled to trade at
the committee's prices for awhile, it would perhaps have been
little more than a rough sort of justice; but he did not take
that view. It is said that all is fair in love and war, and this
was the manner in which Perez proceeded selfishly to avail
himself of the Squire's emergency. He listened to his protestations with a sympathetic rather than a hopeful air, admitting
that he himself would be inclined to oppose the new policy,
but remarking that the farmers and some of the committee
were so set on it that he doubted his ability to balk them. He
finally remarked, however, he might possibly do something,
if Edwards, himself, would meantime take a course calculated
to placate the insurgents and disarm their resentment. Being rather anxiously inquired of by the storekeeper as to what
he could consistently do, Perez finally suggested that Israel

Goodrich was going to have a husking in his barn the following night, if the warm weather held; and if Desire Edwards
should attend, it would not only please the people generally,
but possibly gain over Israel, a member of the committee.
Edwards made no reply, and Perez left him to think the
matter over, pretty confident of the result.

That evening in the family circle, after a gloomy account
of the disaster threatening to engulf the family fortunes if
the proposed policy of fixing prices were carried out, Edwards spoke of Hamlin's disposition to come to his aid, and
his suggestion concerning Desire's presence at the husking.

"These huskings are but low bussing-matches," said Mrs.
Edwards with much disgust. "Desire has never set a foot in
such a place. I suspect it is a trick of this fellow to get her in
his reach."

"It may be so," said her husband, gloomily. "I thought of
that myself, but what shall we do? Shall we submit to the
spoiling of our goods? We are fallen upon evil times, and the
most we can do is to choose between evils."

Desire, who had sat in stolid silence, now said in much
agitation:

"I don't want to go. Please don't make me go, father. I'd
rather not. I'm afraid of him. Since that last time I'm afraid.
I'd rather not."

"The child is well nigh sick with it all," said Mrs. Edwards,
sitting down by her and soothingly drawing the head of the
agitated girl to her shoulder, which set her to sobbing. It was
evident that the constant apprehensions of the past several
weeks as well as her virtual imprisonment within doors, had
not only whitened her cheek but affected her nervous tone.

Edwards paced to and fro with knitted brow. Finally he
said:

"I will by no means constrain your will in this matter,
Desire. I do not understand all your woman's megrims, but
your mother shall not again reproach me with willingness to

secure protection to my temporal interests at the cost of your peace and quiet. You need not go to this husking. No doubt I shall be able to bear whatever the Lord sends," and he went out.

Soon after, Desire ceased sobbing and raised her head from her mother's shoulder. "Mother," she said, "did you ever hear of a maiden placed in such a case as mine?"

"No, my child. It is a new sort of affliction, and of a strange nature. I scarcely have confidence to advise you as to your duty. You had best seek the counsel of the Lord in prayer."

"Methinks in such matters a woman is the best judge," said the girl naively.

"Tut, tut, Desire!"

"Nay, I meant no harm, mother," and then with a great sigh, she said: "I will go. Poor father feels so bad."

The next evening when, dressed for the husking, she took a last look in her mirror she was fairly scared to see how pretty she was. And yet despite the dismay and sinking of heart with which she apprehended Perez' attentions, she did not brush down the dark ringlets that shadowed her temples so bewitchingly, or choose a less becoming ribbon for her neck. That is not a woman's way. It was about seven o'clock when she and Jonathan, who went as her escort, reached Israel Goodrich's great barn, guided thither by the light which streamed from the open door.

The husking was already in full blast. A dozen tallow dips, and half as many lanterns, consisting of peaked cylinders of tin, with holes plentifully punched in their sides for the light of the candle to trickle through, illumined the scene. In the middle of the floor was a pile of full a hundred bushels of ears of corn in the husk, and close around this, their knees well thrust into the mass, sat full two-score young men and maidens, for the most part duly paired off, save where here and there two or three bashful youths sat together. The young men had their coats off, and the round white arms of the girls twinkled distractingly as with swift deft motions they freed the shining yellow ears from their incasements and tossed them into the baskets. The noisy rustling of the dry husks, the chatter and laughter of the merry workers, ever and anon swelling into uproarious mirth as some protesting maiden redeemed a red ear with a pair of red lips, made altogether a merry medley that caused the cows and horses munching their suppers in the neighboring stalls to turn and stare in wonder.

Some of the huskers, looking up, caught sight of Desire and Jonathan at the door, and by a telegraphic system of whispers and nudges, the information was presently carried to Israel Goodrich.

"Glad to see ye. Come right in," he shouted in a broad, cheery voice. "More the merrier's, the sayin is. Glad to see ye. Glad to see ye. Look's kinder neighborly."

As Desire entered the barn, some of the girls rose and curtsied, the most merely looking bashful and avoiding her eye, as the rural mode of greeting continues to be to this day. Perez was the first person whom Desire had seen on entering the barn. Her eyes had been drawn to him by a sort of fascination, certainly not a pleasant sort, the result of her having thought so much about him. Nor was this fascination without another evidence. There was a vacant stool by Perez, and as she passed it, and he rose and bowed, she made as if she would seat herself there.

"Don't ye sit thar," said Israel, "that ain't nothin but a stool. Thar's a chair furder along."

The offer to sit by Perez was almost involuntary on her part, merely a sign of her sense of powerlessness against him. She had had the thought that he meant to have her sit there, and in her nervously abject mood she had not thought of resisting. Her coming to the husking at all had been a surrender to his will, and this seemed but an incident and consequence of that. At Israel's words she blushed faintly, but not in a way to be compared with the red flush that swept over Perez' face.

"Thar," said Israel, good-humoredly, as she seated herself in the promised chair, "naow I guess we'll see the shucks begin to fly."

"For the land sakes, Miss Edwards, you ain't a gonter go ter shuckin with them ere white hands o' yourn," exclaimed Submit Goodrich. "Lemme git yer some mittins, an an apron tew. Deary me, yew mustn't dew the fuss thing till yew've got an apron."

"Guess yew ain't uster huskin, or yew woulden come in yer bes gaown," said Israel cheerfully.

"Come naow, father," Submit expostulated, "tain't likely she's got nothin poor nuff fer sech doins. Ez if this ere wuz Miss Edwards' bes gaown. Yew've got a sight better'n this, hain't yew?"

Desire smiled vaguely. Meanwhile the husking had been pretty much suspended, the huskers either staring in vacant, open mouthedness at Desire, or communicating whispered comments to each other. And even after she had been duly provided with mittens and apron, and begun on the corn, the chatter and boisterous merriment which her arrival had interrupted, did not at once resume its course. Perhaps in a more modern assembly the constraint might have been lasting, but our forefathers did not depend so exclusively as we upon capricious and uncompellable moods, which, like the winds, blow whence and when they list, for the generation of vivacity in social gatherings. For that same end they used most commonly a force as certain as steam in its action; an influence kept in a jug.

Submit whispered to her father, and the old man merely poured a double portion of rum into the cider flip, with which the huskers were being regaled, and soon all went prosperously again. For rum in those good old days was recognized as equally the accompaniment of toil and recreation, and therefore had a double claim to the attention of huskers. From a sale of meeting-house pews or an ordination, to a ball or a general training, rum was the touch of nature that made the whole world of our forefathers kin. And if Desire did but wet her lips with the flip to-night, it was because the company rather than the beverage offended her taste. For even at risk of alienating the sympathies of my teetotal readers, I must refrain from claiming for the maiden a virtue which had not then been invented.

The appearance of Uncle Sim's black and smiling countenance, as he entered bowing and grinning, his fiddle under his arm, was hailed with uproar and caused a prodigious accession of activity among the huskers, the completion of whose task would be the signal for the dancing to begin. The red ears turned up so rapidly as to suggest the theory that some of the youths had stuffed their pockets with a selected lot from the domestic corn bin before coming. But though this opinion was loudly expressed by the girls, it did not seem to excite that indignation in their bosoms which such unblushing duplicity should have aroused. Half a dozen lively tussles for kisses were constantly going on in various parts of the floor and the uproar was prodigious.

In the midst of the hurly-burly, Desire sat bending over the task of which her unused fingers made slow work, replying now and then with little forced smiles to Submit's good natured efforts to entertain her, and paying no attention to the hilarious confusion around. She looked for all the world to Perez like a captive queen among rude barbarian conquerors, owing to her very humiliation, a certain touching dignity. It repented him that he had been the means of bringing her to the place. He could not even take any pleasure in looking at her, because he was so angry to see the coarse stares of admiration which the bumpkins around fixed on her. Paul Hubbard, who sat opposite him had been particularly free with his eyes in that direction, and all the more so after he perceived the discomfort it occasioned Perez, toward whom since their collision concerning the disposition to be made of the prisoners, he had cherished a bitter animosity. The last husks were being stripped off, and Sim was already tuning his fiddle, when Hubbard sprang to his feet with a red ear in his hand. He threw a mocking glance toward Perez, and advanced behind the row of huskers toward Desire. Bending over her lap, with downcast face, she did not observe him till he laid his hand on the rich kerchief of India silk that covered her shoulders. Looking up and catching sight of the dark, malicious face above her, its sensual leer interpreted by the red ear brandished before her eyes, she sprang away with a gasp. There was not one of the girls in the room who would have thought twice about a kiss, or a dozen of them. One of their own number who had made a fuss about such a trifle would have been laughed at. But somehow they did not feel inclined to laugh at Desire's terror and repugnance. They felt that she was different from them, and the least squeamish hoyden of the lot experienced a thrill of sympathy, and had a sense of something tragic. And yet no one interfered. Hubbard was but using his rights according to the ancient rules of the game. A girl might defend herself with fists and nails from an unwelcome suitor, but no third party could interfere. As Jonathan, who sat some way from his sister was about to run to her aid, a stout farmer caught him around the waist crying, good naturedly:

"Fair play youngster! fair play! No interferin!"

Perez had sprung up, looking very white, his eyes congested, his fists clenched. As Desire threw an agonized look of appeal around the circle, she caught sight of him. With a sudden impulse she darted to him crying:

"Oh, keep me from that man."

"Get out of the way, Hamlin," said Hubbard, rushing after his prey. "God damn you, get out of my way. What do you mean by interfering?"

Perez scarcely looked at him, but he threw a glance around upon the others, a glance of appeal, and said in a peculiar voice of suppressed emotion:

"For God's sake, some of you take the fellow away, or I shall kill him."

Instantly Israel Goodrich and half a dozen more had rushed between the two. The twitching muscles of Perez' face and that strange tone as of a man appealing to be saved from himself, had suddenly roused all around from mirthful or curious contemplation of the scene to a perception that a terrible tragedy had barely been averted.

Meanwhile the floor was being cleared of the husks and soon the merry notes of the fiddle speedily dissipated the sobering influence of the recent fracas. Desire danced once with her brother and once with old Israel, who positively beamed with pleasure. But Hubbard, who was now pretty drunk, followed her about, every now and then taking the red ear out of his pocket and shaking it at her, so that between the dances and after them, she took care not to be far from Perez, though she pretended not to notice her pursuer. As for Perez, he was far enough from taking advantage of the situation. Though his eyes followed her everywhere, he did not approach her, and seemed very ill at ease and dissatisfied. Finally he called Jonathan aside and told him that the last end of a husking was often rather uproarious, and Desire perhaps would prefer to go home early. He would, himself, see that they reached home without molestation. Desire was glad enough to take the hint, and glad enough, too, in view of Hubbard's demonstration, to accept the offered escort. As the three were on the way home, Perez finally broke the rather stiff silence by expressing with evident distress his chagrin at the unpleasant events of the evening; and Desire found herself replying quite as if she felt for, and wished to lessen, his self-reproach. Then they kept silent again till just before the store was reached, when he said:

"I see that you do not go out doors at all. I suppose you are afraid of me. If that is the reason, I hope you will not stay in after this. I give you my word you shall not be annoyed, and I hope you'll believe me. Good night."

"Good night."

Was it Desire Edwards' voice which so kindly, almost softly, responded to his salutations? It was she who, in astonishment, asked herself the question.

BRACE OF PROCLAMATIONS

Perez profited by the fact that, however a man may have abused a woman, that is all forgotten the moment he protects her against another man, perhaps no worse than himself. Ever so little gratitude is fatal to resentment, and the instinct of her sex to repay protection with esteem is so deep, that it is no wonder Desire found her feelings toward Perez oddly revolutionized by that scene at the husking. Try as she might to resume her former resentment, terror, and disgust toward the young man, the effort always ended in recalling with emotions of the liveliest thankfulness how he had stood between her and that hateful fellow, whom otherwise she could not have escaped. All that night she was constantly dreaming of being pursued by ruffians and rescued by him. And the grateful sense of safety and protection which, in her dreams, she associated with him, lingered in her mind after she awoke in the morning, and refused to be banished. She was half ashamed, she would not have had anybody know it, and yet she had to own that after these weeks of constant depression and apprehension, the change of mood was not wholly disagreeable.

She had quite a debate with herself as to whether it would be consistent with her dignity to accept Perez' assurance that she would not be annoyed, and go out to walk. Without fully determining the question, she concluded to go anyway, and a beginning having been thus made, she thereafter resumed her old habit of long daily walks, to the rapid improvement of her health and spirits. For some days she did not chance to meet

Perez at all, and it annoyed the high-spirited girl to find that she kept thinking of him, and wondering where she would meet him, and what he would say or do, and how she ought to appear. And yet it was perfectly natural that such should be the case. Thanks to his persecution, he had preoccupied her mind with his personality for so long a time that it was impossible the new phase of her relations toward him should not strongly affect her fancy. The first time they actually did meet, she found herself quite agitated. Her heart beat oddly when she saw him coming, and if possible she would have turned aside to avoid him. But he merely bowed and passed on with a word of greeting. After that he met her oftener, but never presumed to stop — or say more than "Good morning," or "Good afternoon," the result of which was that, after having at first welcomed this formality as a relief, after awhile she came to think it a little overstrained. It looked as if he thought that she was childishly afraid of him. That seemed absurd. One day, as they met, and with his usual courteously curt salutation he was passing by, she observed that it was delightful weather. As her eye caught his start of surprise, and the expression of almost overpowering pleasure that passed over his face at her words, she blushed. She unquestionably blushed and hurried on, scarcely waiting for his reply. Some days later, as she was taking a favorite walk over a path among the thickets on the slope of Laurel Hill, whence the hazy Indian Summer landscape could be seen to perfection beneath the thin but wonderfully bland sunshine of November, she again met him face to face. Perhaps it was the color in her cheeks which reminded him to say:

"You don't look as if you needed to go to Pittsfield for your health now."

"No," she said, smiling. "When I found I could not go, I concluded I would get well here."

"I suppose you are very angry with me for stopping you that night, though it was not I that did it."

"If I were angry, I should not dare tell you, for fear of bringing down your vengeance on me."

"But are you angry?" he asked anxiously.

"I told you I did not dare say," she replied, smiling at him with an indomitable air.

"Please forgive me for it," he said, not jestingly or lightly, but in deepest earnest, with a look almost of tears in his eyes. She wondered she had never before noticed what beautiful blue eyes they were. She rather liked the sensation of having him look at her so.

"Won't you stop me if I try to go again?" she demanded, with an audacious impulse. But she repented her boldness as the passion leaped back into his eyes, and hers fell before it.

"I can't say that," he said. "God knows I will stop you so long as I have power, and when I can no longer stop you, the wheels of your carriage shall pass over my body. I will not let you go."

It was strange that the desperate resolution and the inexorable set of his jaws, which, as he had made a similar declaration on the night of her recapture, had caused her heart to sink, now produced a sensation of rather pleasant excitement. Instead of blanching with fear or revolting in defiance, she replied, with a bewitching air of mock terror:

"Dear me, what a terrible fellow!" and, with a toss of the head, went on her way, leaving him puzzling his heavy masculine wits over the fact that she no longer seemed a particle afraid of him.

The Laurel Hill walk, as I observed before, was an old favorite with Desire, and in her present frame of mind it seemed no sufficient reason to forsake it, that after this she often met Perez there. It is a pleasant excitement, playing with lions or other formidable things. Especially when one has long been in terror of them, the newly gained sense of fearlessness is highly exhilarating. Desire enjoyed playing with her lion, calming and exciting him, making his eyes now

half fill with tears, and now flash with passion. The romantic
novelty of the situation, which might have terrified a more
timid maiden, began to be its most attractive feature to her.
Besides, he was really very good-looking, come to observe
him closely. How foolish it had been of her to be so frightened of him at first! The recollection of her former terror actually amused her; as if it were not easy enough to manage
such a fellow. She had not been in such high spirits for a long
time. She began to think that instead of being a hateful,
terrible, revolting tragedy, the rebellion was rather jolly,
providentially adapted, apparently, for the amusement of
young ladies doomed to pass the winter in dismal country
towns. One day her mother, commenting on the fact that the
patrol and pass system of the insurgents had been somewhat
relaxed, suggested that Desire might go to Pittsfield. But she
said she did not care to go now. The fact was she preferred to
play with her lion, though she did not mention that reason to
her mother. When from time to time she heard of the fear
and apprehension with which the gentlemen's families in
town regarded Perez, she even owned to being a little complacent over the fact that this lawless dictator was her humble
adorer. She finally went so far as occasionally to ask him as a
favor to have this or that done about the village. It was such
fun to feel that through him she could govern the community. One afternoon, being in a particularly gracious mood,
she took a pink ribbon from her neck, knotted it about the
hilt of his sword as an ornament.

The hillside path among the laurel thickets where they so
often chanced to meet, was a lonely spot, beyond the reach of
spectators or eavesdroppers; but, while their meetings were
thus secret, nothing could be more discreet than the way she
managed them. She kept him so well in hand that he did not
even dare to speak of the love of which his whole manner was
eloquent. Since she had ceased to fear him, he had ceased to
be at all fear-inspiring. The rude lover whose lawless attempts
had formerly put her in such fear, was now respectful to the

point of reverence, and almost timid in his fear of offending her. The least sign of anything like tenderness on her part sufficed to stir him with a passion of humility which in turn touched her more deeply sometimes than she would have liked to admit. Now that she had come to see how the poor fellow loved her, she could not cherish the least anger with him for what he had done to her.

Sometimes she led him on to speak of himself and his present position, and he would tell her of his dream and hope, in this present period of anarchy to make himself a name. She was somewhat impressed by his talk, though she would not tell him so. She had heard enough political discussion at her father's and uncle's tables to know that the future political constitution and government of the colonies were wholly unsettled, and that even a royal and aristocratic form, with Washington, or some foreign princeling, at the head, was advocated by many. Especially here in Massachusetts, just now, almost anything was possible. And so when he said one day, "They call me Duke of Stockbridge in jest, but it may be in earnest yet," she did not laugh, but owned to herself that the tall, handsome fellow would look every inch a duke, if he only had some better clothes. She did not let him tell her in so many words that the motive of his ambition was to win her, but she knew it well enough, and the thought did not excite her indignation, though she knew it ought to.

The nearest she would let him come to talking love to her, was to talk of their childhood and how he had adored her then. Her own remembrance of those days of budding girlhood was dim, but he seemed to remember everything about her, and she could but be touched as he reminded her of scores of little incidents and scenes and words which had quite escaped her memory. The doting tenderness which his tone sometimes took on as he dwelt on these reminiscences, made her heart beat rather fast, and in her embarrassment she had some ado to make light of the subject.

But now Indian Summer, by whose grace the warm weather

had been extended nearly through November, came abruptly to a close. New England weather was as barbarous in its sudden changes then as now. One day was warm and pleasant, the next a foot of snow covered the ground and the next after that the thermometer, had there been one at that date in Berkshire, would have recorded zero. The Sunday before Thanksgiving was bitterly cold, "tejus weather" in the farmer's phrase. There was of course no stove or other heater in the meeting-house and the temperature within differed very slightly from that without, a circumstance aggravated by the fact that furs were as yet almost unknown in the wardrobes even of the wealthiest of the people. A small tippet of Desire's, sent from England, was the only thing of the kind in Stockbridge. Parson West wore his gown and bands outside an overcoat and turned his notes with thick woolen mittens, now and then giving a brisk rub to his ears. Like so many clouds of incense rose the breath of the auditors, as they shivered on their hard board seats. The wintry wind blew in gusts through the plentifully broken window panes — for glass was as brittle then as now and costlier to replace, — and every now and then sifted a whiff of snow down the backs of the sitters in the gallery. Fathers and mothers essayed to still their little one's chattering teeth by taking them in their laps and holding them tight, and where a woman was provided with the luxury of a foot-stove or hot-stone, children were squatted round it in the bottom of the pew quarreling with each other to get their tingling toes upon it. A dreadful sound of coughing rose from the audience, mingled with sneezing from such as were now first taking their all-winter colds and diversified from time to time by the wail of some child too miserable and desperate to have any fear of the parental knuckles before its face.

Struggling with these noises and sometimes wholly lost to those in the back part of the house, when some tremendous gust of wind shook and strained the building, the voice of

Parson West flowed on and on. He was demonstrating that seeing it was evident some souls would be lost it must be for the glory of God that they should be lost, and such being the case all true saints must and should rejoice in the fact, and praise God for it. But in order that their approval of the Divine decree in this matter should be genuine and sincere it must be purely disinterested, and therefore they must be willing, if God in his inscrutable wisdom should so will, to be themselves among the lost and forever to hate and blaspheme him in hell, because thus would his glory be served. The parson warmly urged that all who believed themselves to have been born again, should constantly inquire of their own souls whether they were so resigned, for if they did not feel that they were, it was to be feared they were still dead in trespasses and sins.

The sermon ended, the parson proceeded to read the annual Thanksgiving Day proclamation of the governor. To this magic formula, which annually evoked from the great brick oven stuffed turkey, chicken pie, mince pie and plum pudding galore, the children listened with faces of mingled awe and delight, forgetful of their aching toes. The mothers smiled at the children, while the sheepish grins and glances exchanged between the youth and maidens in their opposite galleries, showed them not unmindful of the usual Thanksgiving ball, and, generally speaking, it is to be feared the thoughts of the congregation were quite diverted, for the time being, from the spiritual exercise suggested by the parson. But now the people lift faces of surprise to the pulpit, for instead of the benediction the parson begins to read yet another proclamation. It is no less than an offer by His Excellency, the Governor and the honorable Council, of pardon to those concerned in the late risings against the courts provided they take the oath of allegiance to the state before the first of January, with the warning that all not availing themselves in time of this offer will be subject to arrest without bail at the governor's discretion, under the recent act suspending the Habeas corpus. Added to which is a recital of the special act of the Legislature, that all persons who do not at once disperse upon reading of the riot act are to receive thirty-nine lashes and one year's imprisonment, with thirty-nine more lashes at the end of each three months of that period.

There was little enough Thanksgiving look on the people's faces by the time the parson had made an end, and it is to be feared that in many a heart the echo of the closing formula, "God save the Commonwealth," was something like "May the devil take it."

"Pardon fer wot I sh'd like ter know," blurted out Abner on the meeting-house steps. "I dunno nothin baout the res' on ye, but I hain't done nothin I'm shamed on."

And Israel Goodrich, too, said: "Ef he's gonter go ter pardinin us for lettin them poor dyin critters outer jail tew Barrington t'other day, he's jess got the shoe onter the wrong foot. It's them as put em in needs the pardinin cordin tew my noshin."

"An I guess we don' want no pardon fer stoppin courts nuther. Ef the Lord pardons us fer not hangin the jedges an lawyers, it'll be more'n I look fer," observed Peleg Bidwell.

"Here comes the Duke," said another. "Wat dew yew say ter this ere proclamashin, Cap'n?"

Perez laughed.

"The more paper government wastes on proclamations, the less it'll have left for cartridges," he replied.

There was a laugh at this, but it was rather grim sort of talk, and a good many of the farmers got into their sleighs and drove away with very sober faces.

"It is the beginning of the end," said Squire Edwards, in high good humor, as he sat in his parlor that evening. "From my seat I could see the people. They were like frightened sheep. The rebellion is knocked on the head. The governor won't have to call out a soldier. You see the scoundrels have bad consciences, and that makes cowards of them. This Hamlin here will be running away to save his neck in a week, mark my words."

"I don't believe he is a coward, father, I don't believe he'll run away," said Desire, explosively, and then quickly rose from the chair and turned her back, and looked out the window into the darkness.

"What do you know about him, child?" said her father, in surprise.

"I don't think he seems like one," said Desire, still with her back turned. And then she added, more quietly: "You know he was a captain in the army, and was in battles."

"I don't know it; nobody knows it. He says so, that's all," replied Edwards, laughing contemptuously. "All we know about it is, he wears an old uniform. He might have picked it up in a gutter, or stolen it anywhere. General Pepoon thinks he stole it, and I shouldn't wonder."

"It's a lie, a wicked lie!" cried the girl, whirling around, and confronting her father, with blazing cheeks and eyes.

She had been in a ferment ever since she had heard the proclamation read that afternoon at meeting, and her father's words had added the last aggravation to the already explosive state of her nerves. Squire Edwards looked dumbfounded, and Mrs. Edwards cried in astonishment:

"Desire, child, what's all this?"

But before the girl could speak, there was an effectual diversion. Jonathan came rushing in from outdoors, crying:

"They're burning the governor!"

"What!" gasped his father.

"They've stuffed some clothes with straw, so's to look like a man, and put that hat of Justice Goodrich they fetched back from Barrington, on top and they're burning it for Governor Bowdoin, on the hill," cried Jonathan. "See there! You can see it from the window. See the light!"

Sure enough, on the summit of Laurel Hill the light of a big bonfire shone like a beacon.

"It's just where they burned Benedict Arnold's effigy in

the war," continued Jonathan. "There's more'n a hundred men up there. They're awful mad with the governor. There was some powder put in the straw, and when the fire came to't, it blew up, and the people laughed. But Cap'n Hamlin said 'twas a pity to waste the powder. They might need it all before this business was through with. And then they cheered again. He meant there'd be fighting, father."

In the new excitement there was no thought of resuming the conversation which Jonathan's advent had broken off so opportunely for Desire, and the latter was able without further challenge to escape to her own room. Scarcely had she reached it when there was a sound of fife and drum, and presently a hundred men or more with hemlock in their hats came marching by on their way from Laurel Hill, and Perez Hamlin was riding ahead. They were singing in rude chorus one of the popular songs of the late war, or rather of the stamp act agitation preceding it:

> "With the beasts of the wood, we will ramble for food,
> And lodge in wild deserts and caves;
> And live as poor Job on the skirts of the globe,
> Before we'll submit to be slaves, brave boys,
> Before we'll submit to be slaves."

Such was the rebels' response to the governor's proclamation of mingled mercy and threats. Desire had thrown open her window at the sound of the music, and, carried away with excitement, as Perez looked up and bowed, she waved her handkerchief to him. Yes, Desire Edwards actually waved her handkerchief to the captain of the mob. In the shining winter night her act was plainly seen by the passing men, and her parents and brother, who having first blown out the candle, were looking out from the lower windows, were astonished beyond measure to hear the ringing cheer which the passing throng sent up. Then Desire cried a little and went to bed feeling very reckless.

Squire Edwards had clearly been mistaken in thinking that

the proclamation had made an end of the rebellion. Its first effect had been rather intimidating, no doubt, but upon reflection the insurgents found that they were more mad than scared. It was indeed just opposition enough to exasperate those who were fully committed and stimulate to more vigorous demonstrations; and an express from Shays having summoned a Berkshire contingent to join in a big military demonstration at Worcester, fifty armed men under Abner marched from Stockbridge Thanksgiving Day amid an excitement scarcely equalled since the day when Jahleel Woodbridge's minute men had left for Bennington. But the return of the party about the middle of December, threw a damper on the enthusiasm. The demonstration at Worcester had been indeed a brilliant success in some respects. One thousand well armed men headed by Shays himself with a full staff of officers and a band of music had held the town for several days in full military occupation, overawing the militia, preventing the sitting of the courts, and even threatening to march on Boston. But on the other hand the temper of the population had been lukewarm and often hostile. The soldiers had been half starved through the refusal to supply provisions and nearly frozen. Some indeed had died. In coming back a number of the Berkshire men had been arrested and maltreated in Northampton. Formidable military preparations were being made by the government, and parties of Boston cavalry were scouring the eastern counties and had taken several insurgent leaders prisoners, who would probably be hung. The men had been demoralized by the spread of a well substantiated report that Shays had offered to desert to the other side if he could be assured of pardon. In the lower counties indeed all the talk was of pardon and terms of submission. The white paper cockade which had been adopted in contradistinction to the hemlock as the badge of the government party, predominated in many of the towns through which Abner's party had passed.

"That air proclamashin 's kinder skeert em more'n did us Berkshire folks." Abner explained to a crowd at the tavern. "They all wanter be on the hangman's side wen it comes tew the hangin. They hain't got the pluck of a weasel, them fellers daown east hain't. This ere war'll hev tew be fit aout in this ere caounty, I guess, ef wuss comes to wuss."

"They've got a slew o' men daown Bosting way," said a farmer. "I callate we couldn' hole aout agin' em long ef it come tew fightin, an they should reely tackle us."

"I dunno baout that nuther," declared Abner with a cornerwise nod of the head. "Thar be plenty o' pesky places long the road wen it gits up intew the mountings an is narrer and windin like. I wouldn' ass fer more'n a kumpny tew stop a regiment in them places. I wuz talkin tew the Duke baout that tidday. He says the hull caounty's a reglar fort, an ef the folks 'll hang tewgether it can't be tuk by the hull res' o' the state. We kin hole aout jist like the Green Mounting boys did agin the Yorkers an licked em tew, and got shet of em an be indypendent tidday, by gol, same ez Berkshire orter be."

"Trew's Gospel Abner," averred Israel Goodrich, "thar ain't no use o' the two eends o' the state tryin tew git on tewgether. They hain't never made aout tew gree, an I guess they never would nuther ef they tried it a hundred year more. Darn it, the folks is differn folks daown east o' Worcester. River folks is more like us but git daown east o' Worcester, an I hain't no opinyun on em."

"Yer right thar Isr'el," said Abner with heartiness, "I can't bear Bosting fellers no more'n I kin a skunk, and I kin tell em baout ez fer orf. I dunno wat tiz baout em, but I can't git up no more feller feelin fer em nor I kin fer Britishers. Seems though they wern't ezzackly human, though I s'pose they be, but darn em anyhaow."

"I callate thar's suthin in the mountain air changes men," said Peleg, "fer it's sartain we be more like the Green Mounting boys in aour noshins an ways an we be like the Bosting chaps."

"I'd be in favor o' jinin onter Vairmount, an mebbe that'll be the upshot on't all," observed Ezra Phelps. "Ye see Vairmount hain't a belongin tew the cussed Continental federashin, an it hain't got none o' them big debts ez is hangin round the necks o' the thirteen states, and so we sh'd git rid o' the biggis part o' our taxes all kerslap. Vairmount is an indypendent kentry, an I callate we'd better jine. Ef they'd a made aout with that air noshin folks hed a spell ago, baout raisin up a new state, made aout o' Hampshire caounty an a track o' land tew the northard, 'twould a been jess the sorter thing fer us Berkshire fellers to a hitched on tew."

"I never hearn nothin baout that idea" said Peleg.

"I s'pose ye hain't," replied Ezra. "I wuz livin in Hampshire them times, an so I wuz right in the way o' the talk. They wuz gonter call the state New Connecticut. But the idee never come ter nothin. The war come on an folks hed other fish ter fry."

But Israel declared that he was not in favor of joining on to anything. Berkshire was big enough state for him, and he did not want to see any better times than along from '74 to '80, when Berkshire would take no orders from Boston.

SNOW-BOUND

All through the first half of December one heavy snow storm had followed another. The roads about Stockbridge were often blocked for days together. In the village the work of digging paths along the sidewalks, between the widely-parted houses, was quite too great to be so much as thought of, and the only way of getting about was in sleighs, or wading mid-leg deep. Of course, for the women, this meant virtual imprisonment to the house, save on the occasion of the Sunday drive to meeting. In these days, even the disciplinary tedium of a convict's imprisonment is relieved by supplies of reading matter gathered by benevolent societies. But for the imprisoned women of whom I write there was not even this recreation. Printing had, indeed, been invented some hundreds of years, but it can scarcely be said that books had been as yet, and especially the kinds of books that ladies care to read. A bible, concordance, and perhaps a commentary, with maybe three or four other grave volumes, formed the limit of the average library in wealthy Berkshire families of that day.

It is needless to say then, that Desire's time hung very heavy on her hands, despite the utmost alleviations which embroidery, piano-playing, and cakemaking could afford. For her, isolated by social superiority, and just now, more than ever, separated from intercourse with the lower classes by reason of the present political animosities, there was no participation in the sports which made the season lively for the farmers' daughters. The moonlight sledding and skating expeditions, the promiscuously packed and uproarious sleigh-

ing-parties, the candy-pulls and "bees" of one sort and another, and all the other robust and not over-decorous social
recreations in which the rural youth and maidens of that day
delighted, were not for the storekeeper's fastidious daughter.
The gentlemen's families in town did, indeed, afford a more
refined and correspondingly duller social circle, but naturally enough in the present state of politics, there was very
little thought of jollity in that quarter.

And so, as I said, it was very dull for Desire, in fact terribly
dull. The only outside distraction all through the livelong
day was the occasional passage of a team in the road, and her
mother, too, usually occupied the chair at the only window
commanding the road. And when the aching dullness of the
day was over, and the candles were lit for the evening, and
the little ones had been sent to bed, there was nothing for
her but to sit in the chimney corner, and look at the blazing
logs and brood and brood, till, at bedtime her father and
Jonathan came in from the store. Then her mother woke up,
and there was a little talk, but after that yawned the long
dead night — sleep, sleep, nothing but sleep for a heart and
brain that cried out for occupation.

Up to the time when the sudden coming of the winter put
an abrupt end to her meeting with Perez, she was merely
playing, or in more modern parlance, "flirting" with him, as
a princess might flirt with a servitor. She had merely allowed
his devotion to amuse her idleness. But now, thanks to the
tedium which made any mental distraction welcome, the
complexion of her thoughts concerning the young man
suffered a gradual change. Having no other resource, she
gave her fancy *carte blanche* to amuse her, and what materials
could fancy find so effective as the exciting experiences of
the last Autumn? Sitting before the great open fireplace in
the evenings, while her mother dozed in the chimney corner,
and the silence was only broken by the purring of the cat, the
crackling of the fire, the ticking of the clock, and the low

noise heard through the partition, of men talking over their cups with her father in the back room of the store, she fell into reveries from which she would be roused by the thick, hot beating of her heart, or wake with cheeks dyed in blushes at the voice of her mother. And then the long, dreamful nights. Almost two-thirds of each twenty-four hours in this dark season belonged to the domain of dreams. What wonder that discretion should find itself all unable to hold its own against fancy in such a world of shadows. What wonder that when, after meeting on Sundays she met Perez as she was stepping into her father's sleigh at the meeting-house door, she should feel too confused fairly to look him in the face, much as she had thought all through the week before of that opportunity of meeting him.

One day it chanced that Mrs. Edwards who was sitting by the window, said abruptly:

"Here comes that Hamlin fellow."

Desire sprang up with such an appearance of agitation that her mother added:

"Don't be scared, child. He won't come in here. It's only into the store he's coming."

She naturally presumed that it was terror which occasioned her daughter's perturbation. What would have been her astonishment if she could have followed the girl as she presently went up to her room, and seen her cowering there by the window in the cold for a full half-hour, so that she might through a rent in the curtain have a glimpse of Perez as he left the store! I am not sure that I even do right in telling the reader of this. Indeed her own pride did so revolt against her weakness that she tingled scarcely less with shame than with cold as she knelt there. Once or twice she did actually rise up and leave the window, and start to go downstairs, saying that she was glad she had not seen him yet, for she could still draw back with some self-respect. But even as she was thus in the act of retiring, some noise of boots in the store below suggesting that now he might be going out, brought her hurriedly back to the window. And when at last he did go, in her eagerness to see him, she forgot all about her scruples. Her heart sprang into her throat as she caught sight of him. She could have cried at a fleck in the miserable glass which spoiled her view. Then when he turned and looked up, a wave of color rushed all over her face, and she jumped back in such fear at the thought he might see her, although she was well hidden, that he had passed out of sight ere she dared look out again. But that upward glance and the eager look in his eyes consoled her for the loss. Had he not looked up, she would no doubt have yielded to a revulsion of self-contempt for her weakness, which would have been a damper on her growing infatuation. But that glance had made her foolishly, glowingly elated, and disposed to make light of the reproaches of her pride.

"I suppose you were waiting for that Hamlin fellow to go away, before coming down," said her mother as Desire re-ëntered the living-room. The girl started and averted her face with a guilty terror, saying faintly, "What?" How did her mother know? Her fears were relieved, though not her embarrassment, as her mother added:

"You needn't have been so much frightened, although I really can't blame you for it, after all you've been through at his hands. Still he would scarcely dare, with all his impudence, to try to force a way in here. You would have been quite safe, had you staid downstairs."

The good lady could not understand why, in spite of this reassurance, Desire should thereafter persist, as she did, in retiring to her own room whenever Hamlin came into the store. As the better informed reader will infer from this fact the girl's infatuation was on the increase. She had become quite shameless and hardened about using her point of es-pionage to see, without being seen, the lover who so occupied her thoughts. The only events of the slow, dull days for her were now his visits to the store. She no longer started back when, in going, his eager glance rose to her window, but panting, yet secure behind her covert, looked into his eyes and scanned his expression. Sometimes a quick rush of tears would rob her of her vision as she read in the sad hunger of those eyes how he longed for a glimpse of her face. But for very shame's sake she would have pulled the curtains up. It was so unfair of her, she thought self-reproachfully, to sate her own eyes while cheating his. She knew well enough that all which brought him to the store so often was the hope of seeing and speaking with her. And finally, about the middle of January, she made a desperate resolution that he should. For several days she managed to occupy her mother's usual seat by the window commanding the approach to the store, and finally was rewarded by seeing Hamlin go in. She said nothing at first, but soon remarked carelessly:

"I wonder if father hasn't got some other dimity in the store."

"Perhaps. I think not, though," replied Mrs. Edwards. Desire leaned back in her chair, stifled a yawn and presently said:

"I believe I'll just run in and ask him before I get any further on this." She rose up leisurely, stole a glance at the mirror in passing — how pale she was — opened the connecting door and went into the store.

She saw Perez, out of the corner of her eye, the instant she opened the door. But not taking any notice of him, in fact holding her head very stiffly, and walking unusually fast, she went across to her father and asked him about the dimity. Receiving his reply she turned, still without looking at Perez, and began mechanically to go back. So nervous and cowardly had she been made by the excessive preoccupation of her mind with him, that she actually had not the self-possession to carry out her boldly begun project of speaking to him, now that he was so near. It seemed as if she were actually afraid of looking at him. But when he said in a rather hurt tone, "Good afternoon, Miss Edwards," she stopped, and turned abruptly toward him and without speaking held out her hand. He had not ventured to offer his, but he now took hers. Her face was red enough now, and what he saw in her eyes made him forget everything else. They stood for several seconds in this intensely awkward way, speechless, for she had not even answered his greeting. Squire Edwards, in the act of putting back the roll of dimity on the shelf, was staring over his shoulder at them, astounded. She knew her father was looking at them, but she did not care. She felt at that moment that she did not care who looked on or what happened.

"How cold the weather is!" she said, dreamily.

"Yes, very," replied Perez.

"I hope it will be warmer, soon, don't you?" she murmered.

Then she seemed to come to herself, slowly withdrew her hand from his, and walked slowly into the living-room and shut the door, and went upstairs to her chamber. As soon as Hamlin had gone Edwards came in and spoke with some indignation of his presumption.

"If he had not let go her hand, I should have taken him by the shoulder in another second," he said angrily.

"Whatever made her shake hands with him?" demanded Mrs. Edwards.

"I suppose she thought she had to, or he would be murdering us all. The girl acted very properly, and would not have noticed him if he had not stopped her. But by the Providence of God matters now wear a better look. This fellow is no longer to be greatly feared. The rebels lose ground daily in town as well as in the county and state, and this Hamlin is losing control even over his own sort. If he does not leave the village he will be arrested soon. There is no need that we should humble ourselves before him any longer."

All of which was quite true. For while we have been following the dreams of a fancy-fevered girl, secluded in her snow-bound home among the hills of Berkshire, the scenes have shifted swiftly in the great drama of the rebellion, and a total change has come over the condition and prospects of the revolt. The policy of conciliation pursued by the state government had borne its fruit, better and more speedy fruit than any other policy could have borne. Any other would have plunged the state into bloody war and been of doubtful final issue. The credit for its adoption is due primarily to the popular form of the government which made it impossible for the authorities to act save in accordance with popular sentiment. There was no force save the militia, and for their use the approval of the two houses of the Legislature was needful. The conservative and aristocratic Senate might alone have favored a harsh course, but it could do nothing without the House, which fully sympathized with the people. The result was a compromise by which the Legislature at its extra session, ending the middle of November, passed laws giving the people the most of what they demanded, and then threatened them with the heavy arm of the law if they did not thereafter conduct themselves peaceably.

To alleviate the distress from the lack of circulating medium, the payment of back taxes in certain specified articles other than money was authorized, and real and personal estate at appraised value was made legal tender in actions for debt and in satisfaction for executions. An act was also passed and others were promised reducing the justly complained of costs of legal processes, and the fee tables of attorneys, sheriffs, clerks of courts and justices, for, according to the system then in vogue, most classes of judges were paid by fees from litigating parties instead of by salary. The complaint against the appropriation of so large a part of the income from the import and excise taxes to the payment of interest on the state debt was met by the appropriation of one-third of those taxes to government expenses. To be sure the Legislature had refused to provide for the emission of any more paper money, and this, in the opinion of many, was unpardonable but it had shown a disposition to make up in some degree for this failure by passing a law to establish a mint in Boston. These concessions practically cut the ground out from under the rebellion, and the practical minded people of the state, reckoning up what they had gained, wisely concluded that it would not be worth while to go to blows for the residue, especially as there was every reason to think the Legislature at the next sitting would complete the work of reform it had so well begun. A convention of the Hampshire County people at Hadley, on the second of January, gave formal expression to these views in a resolution advising all persons to lay aside arms and trust to peaceable petition for the redress of such grievances as still remained.

Indeed, even if the mass of the people had been less satisfied than they had reason to be with the Legislature's action, they had had quite enough of anarchy. The original stopping of the courts and jail deliveries, had been with their entire approval. But, as might be expected, the mobs which had done the business had been chiefly recruited from the idle and shiftless. Each village had furnished its contingent of tavern loafers, neerdowells, and returned soldiers with a distaste for industry. These fellows were all prompt to feel their importance and responsibility as champions of the people, and to a large extent had taken the domestic police as well as military affairs into their own hands. Of course it was not long before these self-elected dictators, began to indulge themselves in unwarrantable liberties with persons and property, while the vicious and criminal classes generally, taking advantage of the suspension of law, zealously made their hay while the sun shone. In fact, whatever course the government had taken, this state of things had grown so unbearable in many places that an insurrection within the insurrection, a revolt of the people against the rebels, must presently have taken place. But as may readily be supposed these rebel bands, both privates and officers, were by no means in favor of laying down their arms and thereby relapsing from their present position of importance and authority to their former state of social trash, despised by the solid citizens whom now they lorded it over. Peace, and the social insignificance it involved had no charms for them. Property for the most part they had none to lose. Largely veterans of the Revolution, for eight years more used to camp than house, the vagabond military state was congenial to them and its license sufficient reward. The course of the Shays' rebellion will not be readily comprehensible to any who leave out of sight this great multitude of returned soldiers with which the state was at the time filled, men generally destitute, unemployed and averse to labor, but inured to war, eager for its excitements, and moreover feeling themselves aggrieved by a neglectful and thankless country. And so though the mass of the people by the early part of winter had grown to be indifferent to the rebellion, if not actually in sympathy with the government, the insurgent soldiery still held together wonderfully and in a manner that would be impossible to understand without taking into account the peculiar material that composed it. Not a man of the lot took advantage of the governor's proclamation offering pardon, and instead of being intimidated by the crushing military force sent against them in January, the rebel army at the Battle of Springfield the last day of that month was the largest body of insurgents that had been assembled at any time.

The causes described which had been at work in the lower counties, to weaken popular sympathy with the insurgents, had simultaneously operated in Berkshire. The report brought back from Worcester by Abner's men, with the subsequent action of the Hadley convention in advising the laying aside of arms, had strengthened the hands of the conservatives in Stockbridge. The gentlemen of the village who had been so quiet since Perez' relentless suppression of the Woodbridge rising in September, found their voices again, and cautiously at first, but more boldly as they saw the favorable change of popular feeling, began to talk and reason with their fellow-citizens. If the insurrection had had no other effect, it had at least taught these somewhat haughty aristocrats the necessity of a conciliatory tone with the lower classes. The return home of Theodore Sedgwick in the latter part of December, gave a marked impulse to the government party, of whom he was at once recognized as the leader. He had the iron hand of Woodbridge, with a velvet glove of suavity, which the other lacked. To command seemed natural to him, but he could persuade with as much dignity as he could command, a gift at once rare and most needful in the present emergency. He it was who wore into the village the first white paper cockade which had been seen there, though within a week after, they were full as plenty as the hemlock sprigs. The news which came in the early part of January, that the government had ordered 4,400 militia under General Lincoln to march into the disaffected counties, and put down the rebellion, produced a strong impression. People who had thought stopping a court or two no great matter, and indeed quite an old fashion in Berkshire, were by no means ready to go to actually fighting the government. But still it should be noted that the majority of those who took off the green did not put on the white. The active furtherance of the government interests was left to a comparatively small party. The mass of the people contented themselves with withdrawing from open sympathy with the insurrection, and maintaining a surly neutrality. They were tired of the rebellion, without being warmly disposed toward the government. Neither the friends of government nor the insurgents who still withstood them, could presume too much on the support of this great neutral body, a fact which prevented them from immediately proceeding to extremities against each other.

It was fortunate that there was some such check on the animosity of the two factions. For the bitterness of the still unreconciled insurgents against the friends of the government was intense. They derided the white cockade as "the white feather," denounced its wearers as "Tories," every whit as bad as those who took King George's part against the people, and deserving nothing better than confiscation and hanging. Outrages committed upon the persons and families of government sympathizers in outlying settlements were daily reported. Against Sedgwick especial animosity was felt, but though he was constantly riding about the county to organize and encourage the government party, his reputation for indomitable courage, protected him from personal molestation under circumstances where another man would have been mobbed. In Stockbridge itself, there were no violent collisions of the two parties save in the case of the children, terrific snowball fights raging daily in the streets between the "Shayites" and the "Boston Army." Had Perez listened to the counsels of his followers, the exchange of hard knocks in the village would have been by no means confined to the children. But he well knew that the change in public opinion which was undermining the insurrection would only be precipitated by any violence towards the government party. Many of the men would not hear reason, however, and his attitude on this point produced angry murmurs. The men called up his failure to whip the silk stockings in September, his care for Squire Edwards' interests, and his veto of the plan for fixing prices on the goods at the store. It was declared that he was lukewarm to the cause, no better than a silk stocking himself, and that it would have been better to have had Hubbard for captain. Even Abner Rathbun, as well as Meshech Little, joined in this schism, which ended in the desertion of the

most of the members of the company Perez had organized, to
join Hubbard up at the iron-works. About the same time,
Israel Goodrich withdrew from the committee of safety. He
told Perez he was sorry to leave him, but the jig was plainly
up, and he had his family to consider. If his farm was confiscated, they'd have to go on the town. "Arter all, Perez,
we've made somethin by't. I hain't sorry I gone intew it.
Them new laws ull be somethin of a lift; an harf a loaf be
considabul better nor no bread." He advised Perez to get out
of the business as quick as possible. " 'Tain't no use kickin
agin' the pricks," he said. Ezra, who was disgusted at the
failure of the Legislature to print more bills, stuck awhile
longer, and then he too withdrew. Peleg Bidwell and other
men who had families or a little property at stake, rapidly
dropped off. They owed it to their wives and children not to
get into trouble, they said, and Perez could not blame them.
And so day by day all through the month of January he saw
his power melting away by a process as silent, irresistible and
inevitable as the dissolving of a snow bank in spring; and he
knew that if he lingered much longer in the village, the constable would come some morning and drag him ignominiously away to the lockup. It was a desperate position, and yet he
was foolishly, wildly happy. Desire was not indifferent to him.
That awkward meeting in the store, those moments of silent
hand-clasp, with her eyes looking with such bold confession
into his, had told him that the sole end and object of his
strange role here in Stockbridge was gained. She loved him.
Little indeed would he have recked that the role was now at
an end; little would he have cared to linger an hour longer on
this scene of his former fantastic fortunes, if but he could have
borne her with him on his flight. How gayly he would have
laughed at his enemies then. If he could but see her now,
could but plead with her. Perhaps he might persuade her.
But there was no opportunity. Even as far back as December,
as soon as the rebellion began evidently to wane, Edwards had

began to turn the cold shoulder to him on his visits to the store. He had put up with insults which had made his cheek burn, merely because at the store was his only chance of seeing Desire. But Edwards' tone to him after that meeting with her, had been such that he knew it was only by violence that he could again force an entrance over the storekeeper's threshold. The fact was, Edwards, now that the danger was over, blamed himself for an unnecessary subservience to the insurgent leader, and his mortified pride expressed itself in a special virulence toward him. There was then no chance of seeing Desire. She loved him, but he must fly and leave her. One moment he said to himself that he was the happiest of men. In the next he cursed himself as the most wretched. And so alternately smiling and cursing, he wandered about the village during those last days of January like one daft, too much absorbed in the inward struggle to be more than half conscious of his danger.

THE BATTLE OF WEST STOCKBRIDGE

One day, three days before the end of January, as Perez, returning from a walk, approached the guardhouse, he saw that it was in possession of Deputy Sheriff Seymour and a posse. The rebel garrison of three or four men only, having made no resistance, had been disarmed and let go. Perez turned on his heel and went home. That same afternoon about three o'clock, as he was sitting in the house, his brother Reuben, who had been on the watch, came in and said that a party of militia were approaching.

"I've saddled your horse, Perez, and hitched him to the fence. You've got a good start, but it won't do to wait a minute." Then Perez rose up, bade his father and mother and brother good-bye, and went out and mounted his horse. The militia were visible descending the hill at the north of the village, several furlongs off. Perez turned his horse in the opposite direction, and galloped down to the green. He rode up in front of the store, flung himself from his horse, ran up the steps and went in. Dr. Partridge was in the store talking to Edwards, and Jonathan was also there. As Perez burst in, pale, excited, yet determined, the two gentlemen sprang to their feet and Jonathan edged toward a gun that stood in the corner. Edwards, as if apprehending his visitor's purpose, stepped between him and the door of the living-rooms. But Perez' air was beseeching, not threatening, almost abject, indeed.

"I am flying from the town," he said. "The hue and cry is out after me. I beg you to let me have a moment's speech with Miss Desire."

"You impudent rascal," cried Edwards. "What do you mean by this. If you do not instantly go, I will arrest you myself. See my daughter, forsooth! Get out of here, fellow!" and he made a threatening step forward, and then fell back again, for though Perez' attitude of appeal was unchanged, he looked terribly excited and pertinacious.

"Only a word," he cried, his pleading eyes fixed on the storekeeper's angry ones. "A sight of her, that's all I ask, sir. You shall stand between us. Do you think I would harm her? Think, sir, I did not treat you ill when I was master. I did not deny you what you asked."

There was something more terrifying in the almost whining appeal of Perez' voice than the most violent threat could be, so intense was the repressed emotion it indicated. But as Edwards' forbidding and angry face plainly indicated that his words were having no effect, this accent of abjectness suddenly broke off in a tremendous cry:

"Great God, I must see her!"

Edwards was plainly very much frightened, but he did not yield.

"You shall not," he replied between his teeth. "Jonathan! Dr. Partridge! Will you see him murder me?"

Jonathan, gun in hand, pluckily rallied behind his father, while the doctor laid his hand soothingly on Perez' shoulder, who did not notice him. But at that moment the door into the living-rooms was flung open, and Desire and her mother came in. The loud voices had evidently attracted their attention and excited their apprehensions, but from the start which Desire gave as she saw Perez, it was evident she had not guessed he was there. At sight of her, his tense attitude and expression instantly softened, and it was plain that he no longer saw or took account of any one in the room but the girl.

"Desire," he said, "I came to see you. The militia are out

after me at last, and I am flying for my life. I couldn't go without seeing you again."

Without giving Desire a chance to reply, which indeed she was much too confused and embarrassed to do, her mother interposed.

"Mr. Edwards," she exclaimed indignantly, "can't you put the fellow out? I'm sure you'll help, Doctor. This is an outrage. I never heard of such a thing. Are we not safe in our own house from this impudent loafer?" Perez had not minded the men, but even in his desperation, Mrs. Edwards somewhat intimidated him, and he fell back a step, and his eye became unsteady. Dr. Partridge walked to the window, looked out, and then turning around, said coolly:

"I suppose it is our duty to arrest you, Hamlin, and hand you over to the militia, but hang me if I wish you any harm. The militia are just turning into the green, and if you expect to get away, you have not a second to lose."

"Run! Run!" cried Desire, speaking for the first time.

Perez glanced out at the window and saw his pursuers not ten rods off.

"I will go," he said, looking at Desire. "I will escape, since you tell me to, but I will come again some day," and opening the door and rushing out, he leaped on his horse and galloped away on the road to Lee, the baffled militiamen satisfying themselves with yelling and firing one or two vain shots after him.

Sedgwick, aware that in the ticklish state of public opinion, the government party could not afford to provide the malcontents with any martyrs, had postponed the attempt to arrest Perez until affairs were fully ripe for it. The militia company of Captain Stoddard had been quietly reorganized, so that the very night of Perez' flight, patrols were established, and a regular military occupation of the town began. The larger part of the old company having gone over to the insurgents, the depleted ranks had been filled out by the enlistment as privates of the gentlemen of the village. The two Dwights, Drs. Sergeant and Partridge, Deacons Nash and Edwards, and many other silk stockinged magnates carried muskets, and a dozen gentlemen besides had organized themselves into a party of cavalry, with Sedgwick himself as captain. Even then the difficulty in finding men enough to fill out the company was so great that lads of sixteen and seventeen, gentlemen's sons, were placed in line with the gray fathers of the settlement. There was need indeed of every musket that could be mustered, for up at West Stockbridge, only an hour's march away, Paul Hubbard had a hundred and fifty men about him, from whom a raid might at any moment be expected.

But Stockbridge was now to become the center of military operations, not only for its own protection, but for that of the surrounding country. Hampshire County, as well as the eastern counties, had been called on for quotas to swell General Lincoln's army, but upon Berkshire no requisition had been made. The peculiar reputation of that county for an independent and insubordinate temper, afforded little reason to hope such a requisition would be regarded if made. And indeed the county promptly showed itself quite equal to the independent role which the Governor's course conceded to it. An effective plan for the suppression of the rebellion in the county had been concerted between Sedgwick and the leading men of the other towns. It had been agreed upon to raise five hundred men, and concentrate them at Stockbridge, using that town as a base of operations against the rebel bands in Southern Berkshire. Captain Stoddard's company had scarcely taken military possession of Stockbridge, when it was reënforced by companies from Pittsfield, Great Barrington, Sheffield, Lanesboro, Lee and Lenox. It was under escort of the Pittsfield company, that Jahleel Woodbridge returned to Stockbridge, after an absence of nearly four months. General

Patterson, one of the major-generals of militia in the county, and an officer of revolutionary service, assumed command of the battalion, and promptly gave it something to do.

Far from appearing daunted by the presence of so large a body of militia in Stockbridge, Hubbard's force at the iron-works had increased to two hundred men who boldly threatened to come down and clean out Patterson's "Tories," a feat to which, if joined by some of the smaller insurgent bands in the neighborhood, they might ere long be equal. For this Patterson wisely decided not to wait. And so at noon of one of the first days of February, about three hundred of the government troops, with half a dozen rounds of cartridges per man, set out to attack Hubbard's camp.

There had been tearful farewells in the gentlemen's households that morning. Most had sent forth father and sons together to the fray and some families there were which had three generations in the ranks. For this was the gentlemen's war. The mass of the people held sullenly aloof and left them to fight it out. It was all that could be expected of themselves if they did not actively join the other side. There were more friends of theirs with Hubbard than with Patterson, and the temper in which they viewed the preparations to march against the rebels was so unmistakably ugly that as a protection to the families and property in the village one company had to be left behind in Stockbridge. It was a muggy overcast day, a poor day to give men stomach for fighting; drum and fife were silent that the enemy might have no unnecessary warning of their coming; and so with an ill-wishing community behind their backs and the foe in front, the troops set out under circumstances as depressing as could well occur. And as they went, mothers and daughters and wives climbed to upper windows and looked out toward the western mountain up whose face the column stretched, straining their ears for the sound of shots with a more quaking apprehension than if their own bosoms had been their marks. It is bad enough to send friends to far-off wars, sad enough waiting for the slow tidings, but there is something yet more poignant in seeing loved ones go out to battle almost within sight of home.

The word was that Hubbard was encamped at a point where the road running directly west over the mountain to West Stockbridge met two other roads coming in from northerly and southerly directions. Accordingly, in the hope of catching the insurgents in a trap the government force was divided into three companies. One pushed straight up the mountain by the direct road, while the others made respectively a northern and a southern detour around the mountain intending to strike the other two roads and thus come in on Hubbard's flanks while he was engaged in front. The center company did not set out till a little after the other two, so as to give them a start. When it finally began to climb the mountain Sedgwick with his cavalry rode ahead. A few rods behind them came a score or two of infantry as a sort of advance guard, the rest of the company being some distance in the rear. The gentlemen in that little party of horsemen had nearly all seen service in the late war and knew what fighting meant, but that was a war against their country's foes, invaders from over the sea, not like this, against their neighbors. They had no taste for the job before them, resolute as they were to perform it. The men they were going to meet had most of them smelled powder, and knew how to fight. They were angry and desperate and the conflict would be bloody and of no certain issue. So far as they knew, it would be the first actual collision of the insurrection, for the news of the battle at Springfield had not yet reached them. No wonder they should ride along soberly and engrossed in thought.

Suddenly a man stepped out from the woods into the road and firing his musket at them turned and ran. Thinking to capture him the gentlemen spurred their horses forward at a gallop. Other shots were fired around them, indicating clearly that they had come upon the picket line of the enemy. But their blood was up and they rode on pell-mell after the fugitive sentry. There was a turn in the road a short distance ahead. As they dashed around it, now close behind the flying man, they found themselves in the clearing at the crossing of the roads. Why do they rein in their plunging steeds so suddenly? Well they may! Not six rods off the entire rebel line of two hundred men is drawn up. They hear Hubbard give the order "Present!" and the muskets of the men rise to their cheeks.

"We're dead men. God help my wife!" says Colonel Elijah Williams, who rides at Sedgwick's side. Advance or retreat is alike impossible and the forthcoming volley can not fail to annihilate them.

"Leave it to me," says Sedgwick, quietly, and the next instant he is galloping quite alone toward the line of levelled guns. Seeing but one man coming the rebels withhold their fire. Reining up his horse within a yard of the muzzles of the guns he says in a loud, clear, authoritative voice:

"What are you doing here, men? Laban Jones, Abner Rathbun, Meshech Little, do you want to hang for murder? Throw down your arms. You're surrounded on three sides. You can't escape. Throw down your arms and I'll see you're not harmed. Throw away your guns. If one of them should go off by accident in your hands, you couldn't be saved from the gallows."

His air, evincing not the slightest perturbation or anxiety on his own part, but carrying it as if they only were in peril, startled and filled them with inquietude. His evident conviction that there was more peril at their end of the guns than at his, impressed them. They lowered their muskets, some threw them down. The line wavered.

"He lies. Shoot him! Fire! Damn you, fire!" yelled Hubbard in a panic.

"The first man that fires hangs for murder!" thundered Sedgwick. "Throw down your arms and you shall not be harmed."

"Kin yew say that for sartin, Squire?" asked Laban, hesitatingly.

"No, he lies. Our only chance is to fight!" yelled Hubbard, frantically. "Shoot him, I tell you."

But at this critical moment when the result of Sedgwick's daring experiment was still in doubt, the issue was determined by the appearance of the laggard infantry at the mouth of the Stockbridge road, while simultaneously shots resounding from the north and south showed that the flanking companies were closing in.

"We're surrounded! Run for your lives!" was shouted on every side, and the line broke in confusion.

"Arrest that man!" said Sedgwick, pointing to Hubbard, and instantly Laban Jones and others of his former followers had seized him. Many, throwing down their arms, thronged around Sedgwick as if for protection, while the rest fled in confusion, plunging into the woods to avoid the troops who were now advancing in plain sight on all three roads. A few scattered shots were exchanged between the fugitives and the militia, and the almost bloodless conflict was over.

"Who'd have thought they were such a set of cowards?" said a young militia officer, contemptuously.

"They are not cowards," replied Sedgwick reprovingly. "They're the same men who fought at Bennington, but it takes away their courage to feel they're arrayed against their own neighbors and the law of the land."

"You'd have had your stomach full of fighting, young man," added Colonel Williams, "if Squire Sedgwick had not taken them just as he did. Squire," he added, "my wife shall thank you that she's not a widow, when we get back to Stockbridge. I honor your courage, sir. The credit of this day is yours."

Those standing around joining heartily in this tribute, Sedgwick replied quietly:

"You magnify the matter over much, gentlemen. I knew the men I was dealing with. If I could get near enough to fix them with my eye before they began to shoot I knew it would be easy to turn their minds."

The reëntry of the militia into Stockbridge was made with screaming fifes, and resounding drums, while nearly one hundred prisoners graced the triumph of the victors. The poor fellows looked glum enough, as they had reason to do. They had scorned the clemency of the government and been taken with arms in their hands. Imprisonment and stripes was the least they could expect, while the leaders were in imminent danger of the gallows. But considerations other than those of strict justice according to law determined their fate, and made their suspense of short duration. It was well enough to use threats to intimidate rebels, but in an insurrection with which so large a proportion of the people sympathized partly or fully, severity to the conquered would have been a fatal policy. As a merely practical point, moreover, there was not jail room in Stockbridge for the prisoners. They must be either forthwith killed or set free. The upshot of it was that excepting Hubbard and two or three more they were offered release that very afternoon, upon taking the oath of allegiance to the state. The poor fellows eagerly accepted the terms. A line of them being formed they passed one by one before Justice Woodbridge, with uplifted hand took the oath, slunk away home, free men, but very much crestfallen. As if to add a climax to the exultation of the government party, news was received, during the evening, of the rout of the rebels under Shays at Springfield, in their attack on the militia defending the arsenal there, the last day of January.

Now it must be understood that not alone in Captain Stoddard's Stockbridge company had gentlemen filled up the places of the disaffected farmers in the ranks, but such was equally the case with the companies which had come in from the other towns, the consequence of which was that the present muster represented the wealth, the culture, and aristocracy of all Berkshire. There are far more people in Berkshire now than then; far more aggregate wealth, and far more aggregate culture, but with the decay of the aristocratic form of society which prevailed in the day of which I write, passed away the elements of such a gathering as this, which stands unique in the social history of Stockbridge. The families of the county gentry here represented, though generally living at a day or two's journey apart, were more intimate with each other than with the farmer folk, directly surrounded by whom, they lived. They met now like members of one family, the sense of unity heightened by the present necessity of defending the interests of their order, sword in hand, against the rabble. The gentlemen's families of Stockbridge had opened wide their doors to these gallant and genial defenders, whose presence in their households, far from being regarded as a burden, required by the public necessity, was rather a social treat of rare and welcome character; and, unless tradition deceives, more than one happy match was the issue of the intimacies formed between the fair daughters of Stockbridge and the knights who had come to their rescue.

Previous to the conflict at West Stockbridge and the news of the battle at Springfield, the seriousness of the situation availed indeed to put some check upon the spirits of the young people. But no sooner had it become apparent that the suppression of the rebellion was not likely to involve serious bloodshed than there was such a general ebullition of fun and amusement as might be expected from the collection of such a band of spirited youths. Not to speak of dances, teas, and indoor entertainments, gay sleighing parties, out to the scene of "battle" of West Stockbridge, as it was jokingly called, were of daily occurrence, and every evening Mahkeenac's shining face was covered with bands of merry skaters, and screaming, laughing sledge-loads of youths and damsels went whizzing down Long Hill to the no small jeopardy of their own lives and limbs, to say nothing of such luckless wayfarers as might be in their path. To provide partners for so many gentlemen the cradle was almost robbed, and many a farmer's daughter of Shayite proclivities found herself, not unwillingly, conscripted to supply the dearth of gentlemen's daughters, and provided with an opportunity for contrasting the merits of silk-stockinged and worsted-stockinged adorers, an experience possibly not redounding to their after contentment in the station to which Providence had called them.

But even with these conscripts there was still such an excess of beaux that every girl had half a dozen. As for Desire Edwards, she had the whole army. If I have hitherto spoken of her in a manner as if she were the only "young lady" in Stockbridge, that is no more than the impression which she gave. Although there were several families in the village which had a claim to equal gentility, their daughters somehow felt that they failed to make good that claim in Desire's presence. They owned, though they found less flattering terms in which to express it, the same air of distinction and dainty aloofness about her, which the farmers' daughters, too humble for jealousy, so admiringly admitted. The young militia officers and gentlemen privates found her adorable, and the three or four young men whom Squire Edwards took into his house, as his share in quartering the troops, were the objects of the most rancorous envy of the entire army. These favored youths had too much appreciation of their fortune to be absent from their quarters save when military duty required, and what with the obligation of entertaining and being entertained by them, and keeping in play the numerous callers who dropped in from other quarters in the evening, Desire had mighty little time to herself. It was of course very exciting for her and very agreeable to be the sole queen of so gallant and devoted a court. She enjoyed it as any sprightly, beautiful girl fond of society and well nigh starved for it might be expected to. Provided here so unexpectedly in remote winter-bound Stockbridge, it was like a table spread in the wilderness, whereof the Psalmist speaks.

And in this whirl of gayety, did she quite forget Perez, did she so soon forget the secret flame she had cherished for the Shayite captain? Be sure she had not forgotten, but she would have been willing to give anything in the world if she could.

After the conventual seclusion and mental vacancy of the preceding months, the sudden, almost instantaneous change in her surroundings, had been like a burst of air and sunlight which dissipates the soporific atmosphere of a sleeping-room. It had brought back her thoughts and feelings all at once to their normal standards, making her recollection of that infatuation seem like a fantastic, grotesque dream; unreal, impossible, yet shamefully real. Every time she entered her chamber, and her eye caught sight of the little hole in the curtain whence she had spied upon Perez, shame and self-contempt overcame her like a flood. How could she, how ever could she be left to do such a thing! What would the obsequious, admiring gallants she had left in her parlor say if they but knew what that little pin-hole in her curtain reminded her of? She could not believe it possible herself that the girl whose fine-cut haughty beauty confronted her gaze from the mirror could have so lost her self-respect, could have actually — Oh! and tears of self-despite would rush into her eyes as her remorseless memory set before her those scenes. And had she been utterly beside herself that day in the store, when she gave him that look and that hand-clasp? But for that the only fruit of her folly would have been the loss of her own self-respect, but now she was guilty toward him. This wretched business was dead earnest to him, if not to her. With what a pang of self-contemptuous self-reproach she recalled his white, anguished face as he rushed into the store to bid her farewell when the soldiers were coming to take him. If he at first, by his persecution of her, had left her with a right to complain, she had given him such a right by that glance. She writhed as she admitted to herself that by that she had given him a sort of claim on her.

The village gossip about Perez' infatuation for her, although of her own weakness none guessed, had naturally come to the ears of the visitors, and some of the young men at Edwards' good naturedly chaffed her about it, speaking of it as an amusing joke. She had to bear this without wincing, and worse still, she had to play the hypocrite so far as to reply in the same jesting tone, joining in turning the laugh on the poor, shabby mob captain, when she knew in her heart it ought to be turned against her.

There was nothing else she could do, of course. She could not confess to these gay bantering young gentlemen the incredible weakness of which she had been guilty. But if the self-contempt of the doer can avenge a wrong done to another, Perez was amply avenged for this. And the worst of it was that the thought that she had wronged him here also, and meanly taken advantage of him, added to that horrid sense of his claim on her. He began to occupy her mind to a morbid and most painful extent, really much affecting her enjoyment. His sad and shabby figure, with its mutely reproachful face, haunted her. All that might have been to his disadvantage compared with the refined and cultivated circle about her, was overcome by the pathos and dignity with which her sense of having done him wrong invested him. Such was her unenviable state of mind, when one evening, a week or ten days after the affair at West Stockbridge, one of the young men at the house said to her gayly:

"May I hope, Miss Edwards, not to be wholly forgotten if I should fall on the gory field to-morrow?"

"What do you mean?" she asked.

"What, didn't you know? General Patterson is fearful the Capuan delights of Stockbridge will sap our martial vigor, and is going to lead us against the foe in his lair at dawn to-morrow."

"Where is his lair this time?" asked Desire, carelessly.

"We've heard that two or three hundred of the rascals have collected out here at Lee to stop a petty court, and we're going to capture them."

"By the way, too, Miss Edwards," broke in another, "your admirer, Hamlin, is at the head of them, and I've no doubt his real design is to make a dash on Stockbridge, and carry you off from the midst of your faithful knights. He'll have a chance to repent of his presumption to-morrow. Squire Woodbridge told me this afternoon that if he does not have him triced up to the whipping-post in two hours after we bring him in, it will be because he is no justice of the quorum. It's plain the Squire has no liking for the fellow."

"I hope there'll be a little more fun this time than there was last week. I'm sick of these battles without any fighting," doughtily remarked a very young man.

"I'm afraid your blood-thirstiness won't be gratified this time," answered the first speaker. "The General means to surprise them and take every man-jack of them prisoner before they're fairly waked up. We shall be back to breakfast to receive your congratulations, Miss Edwards."

But Miss Edwards had left the room.

A GAME OF BLUFF

Had Perez Hamlin been her sweetheart, her brother, her dearest friend, the announcement that he was to be captured and brought to Stockbridge for punishment would not have come upon her with a greater effect of consternation. After hearing that news it would have been impossible for her to have retained her composure sufficiently to have avoided remark had she remained in the parlor. But there were other reasons why she had fled to the seclusion of her chamber. It was necessary that she should think of some plan to evade the humiliation of being confronted by him, of being reminded by his presence, by his looks, and maybe his words even, of the weak folly of which she was so cruelly ashamed, and which she was trying to forget about. Desperately, she resolved to make some excuse to fly to Pittsfield, to be away from home when Perez was brought in. But no, she could think of no excuse, not even the wildest pretense for thus precipitately leaving a house full of guests, and taking a journey by dangerous roads to make an uninvited visit. Perez must be warned, he must escape, he must not be captured. Thus only could she see any way to evade meeting him. But how could word be got to him? They marched at dawn. There were but a few hours. There was his family. Surely, if they were warned, they would find a way of communicating with him. She had heard that he had a brother. Whatever she did she must do quickly, before she was missed from the parlor and her mother came to her door to ask if she were sick. There was no time to change her dress, or even her shoes. Throwing a big shawl over her head, which quite concealed

her figure, she noiselessly made her way downstairs, and out
into the snowy street, passing, as she went, close under the
lighted windows of the parlor, whence came the sound of the
voices and laughter of guests who, no doubt, were already
wondering at her absence.

Thanks to the amount of travel of late weeks, the snow in
the street had been trodden to a passable condition. But
blinded by the darkness every now and then, with a gasp and
a flounder, she would step out of the path into the deep snow
on either side, and once hearing a sleigh coming along, she
had to plunge into a drift nearly as high as her waist, and
stand there till the vehicle had passed, with the snow freezing
her ankles, and also ruining, as she well knew, her lovely
morocco shoes. Suddenly a tall figure loomed up close before
her, there was a rattle of accoutrements, and a rough voice
said sharply:

"Halt!"

She stopped, all in a tremble. She had quite forgotten that
the streets were now-a-days guarded by regular lines of
sentries.

"Advance and give the countersign," said the soldier.

At first she gave herself quite up for lost. Then she remembered that by the merest chance in the world she knew the
countersign for that night. The officer of the day had play-
fully asked her to name it, and in honor of the patriotic citizens of the capital who had lent to the empty treasury the
money needed to equip and supply the force of militia the
governor had ordered out, she had given "The Merchants of
Boston." Scarcely believing that so simple a formula could
remove this formidable obstacle from her path, she repeated
it in a tremulous voice. "Pass on," said the sentry, and the
way was clear. Now turning out of the main street, she made
her way slowly and pantingly, rather wading than walking
up the less trodden lane leading to the Hamlins' house,
through whose windows shines the flickering light of the fire

on the hearth within, the only species of evening illumination afforded in those days save in the households of the rich. She pulls the latchstring and enters. The miserable fittings of the great kitchen denote extreme poverty, but the great fire of logs in the chimney is such as the richest, in these days of wasted forests, cannot afford, and the ruddy light illumines the room as all the candles in Stockbridge scarcely could do. Before it sit Elnathan and his wife and Reuben. The shawl which Desire wears is thickly flecked with the snow, through which she has stumbled, and instinctively her first motion on entering the room is to open and shake it, thereby revealing to the eyes of the astonished family the toilet of a fashionable beauty. Her hair is built up over a toupee with a charming effect of stateliness, the dusting of powder upon the dark strands bringing out the rich bloom of her brunette complexion. The shoulders gleam through the meshes of the square of ancient yellow lace that covers them, while the curves of the full young figure and the white roundness of the arms, left bare by the elbow sleeves, are set off in charming contrast by the stiff folds of the figured crimson brocade.

"Miss Edwards!" murmurs Mrs. Hamlin, as Elnathan and Reuben gape in speechless bewilderment.

"Yes, it is I," replied Desire, coming forward a few steps, but still keeping in the back of the room. "I came to tell you that the army is going to march at dawn to-morrow to Lee, to take your son, and all who are with him prisoners, and bring them back here to be punished." There was a moment's silence, then Mrs. Hamlin said:

"How do you know it?"

"I was told so ten minutes since by the officers at my father's house," replied Desire.

"And why do you tell us?" asked Mrs. Hamlin again, regarding her keenly from beneath her bushy grey eyebrows, and speaking with a certain slight hardness of tone, as if half suspicious of a warning from such a source.

"I thought if I told you in time, you might get some word to him so he could get away. The countersign is 'The Merchants of Boston.' "

Mrs. Hamlin's face suddenly changed its expression, and she answered slowly, in a tone of intense, suppressed feeling:

"And so you left them gay gentlemen, and waded through the snow all alone half a mile way out here, all in your pretty clothes, so that no harm might come to my boy. God bless you, my child! God bless you with his choicest blessings, my sweet young lady! My son does well to worship the ground you walk on."

It was an odd sensation, but as the gray-haired woman was speaking, her face aglow with tenderness, and her eyes wet with a mother's gratitude, Desire could not help half wishing she had deserved the words, even though that wish implied her being really in love with this woman's son. It was not without emotion, and eyes to which a responsive wetness had sprung that she exclaimed, with a gesture of deprecation:

"No, no, do not thank me. If you knew all, you would not thank me. I am not so good as you think," and, throwing the door open she sprang out into the snow.

When she reëntered the parlor at home, the silver-dialed clock, high upon the wall, accused her of only an hour's absence, and since nobody but herself knew that her feet were quite wet through, there were no explanations to make. But for the first time she wearied a little of her courtiers. She found their compliments insipid and her repartees were slow. Her thoughts were wandering to that poor home where all undeservedly she had been received as an angel of light; and her anxieties were with the messenger stumbling along the half broken road to Lee to carry the warning. When, at last, Squire Edwards proposed that all should fill their punch-glasses and drain to the success of the morrow's expedition, she set down hers untasted, passing off her omission with some excuse. That night toward morning, though it was yet pitch dark, she was awakened by the noise of opening doors and men's boots, and loud talk; and afterwards hearing a heavy, jarring sound, she looked out the window and descried in the road, a long black column moving rapidly along, noiseless save for now and then a hoarse word of command. It was the expedition setting out for Lee. The impressiveness of this silent, formidable departure gave her a new sense of the responsibility she had taken on herself in frustrating the design of so many grave and weighty men, and interfering with issues of life and death. And then for the first time a dreadful thought occurred to her. What if after all there should be a battle? She had only thought of giving Perez warning, so he might fly with his men, but what if he should take advantage of it to prepare an ambush and fight? She had not thought of that. Jonathan was with the expedition. What if she should prove to be the murderer of her brother? What had she done? Sick at heart, she lay awake trembling till dawn. Then she got up and dressed, and waited about miserably, till toward eight o'clock the news of the result came. Then she laughed till she cried and ended by saying that she would go to bed, for she thought she was going to be sick. And she was right. Her mother wondered how she could have taken such a terrible cold.

But leaving Dr. Partridge to cure her cold with calomel and laudanum, after the manner of the day, let us inquire in a historical spirit what it was in the news of the result at Lee which should cause a young woman to laugh so immoderately.

It had been nearly midnight of the preceding evening, when Reuben wearily and slowly making his way along the dark and difficult road, reached Lee, and was directed at the rebel outposts to the house of Mrs. Perry as the place which Perez occupied as a headquarters. Although it was so late, the rebel commander, too full of anxious and brooding thoughts to sleep, was still sitting before the smouldering fire in the kitchen chimney when Reuben staggered in.

"Reub," he cried, starting up as he recognized his brother, "what's the matter? Has anything happened at home?"

"Nothing bad. I've brought you news. Have you got some rum? I'm pretty tired."

Perez found a demijohn, poured out a mug, and watched his brother with anxious eyes as he gulped it down. Presently, a little color came back to his white face, and he said:

"Now I feel better. It was a hard road. I felt like giving out once or twice. But I'm all right now."

"What made you come, Reub? You're not strong yet. It might have killed you."

"I had to, Perez. It was life or death for you. The army at Stockbridge are going to surprise you at sunrise. I came to warn you. Desire Edwards brought us word."

"What!" exclaimed Perez, his face aglow. "She brought you word? Do you mean that?"

"Jess hole on, and I'll tell you how it was," said Reub, with a manner almost as full of enthusiasm as his brother's. "It was nigh bedtime, and we were setting afore the fire a talking 'bout you, and a hopin you'd get over the line into York, when the door opened, an in come Desire Edwards, all dressed up in a shiny gaown, an her hair fixed, an everything like as to a weddin. I tell yew, Perez, my eyes stood out some. An afore we could say nothing, we wuz so flustered, she up an says as haow she hearn them ossifers tew her haouse tellin haow they wuz gonter s'prise ye in the mornin, an so she come ter tell us, thinkin we mout git word ter ye."

"Did she say that, Reub? Did she say those words? Did she say that about me? Are you sure?" interrupted Perez, in a hushed tone of incredulous ecstasy, as he nervously gripped his brother's shoulder.

"Them wuz her words, nigh es I kin reckullec," replied Reub, "an that 'bout yew she said for sartin. She said we wuz ter sen' word ter ye, so's ye mout git away, an then she guv me the countersign for ter say tew the sentries, so's I could git by ter fetch ye word."

"To think of her doing all that for me, Reub. I can't believe it. It's too much. Because you see, Reub, if she'd take all that trouble for me, it shows — it shows — I think it must be she" — he hesitated, and finally gulped out — "cares for me, Reub," and his eyes filled with tears.

"Ye may say so, for sartin, Perez," replied his brother with sympathetic enthusiasm. "A gal wouldn' dew what she did for no feller, unless she sat store by him, naow. It's a sign fer sure."

"Reub," said Perez, in a voice uneven with suppressed emotion, "now I know she cares for me that much, I don't mind a snap of the finger what happens to me. If they came to hang me this minute, I should laugh in their faces," and he sprang up and paced to and fro, with fixed eyes and a set smile, and then, still wearing the same look came back and sat down by his brother, and said: "I sort of hoped she cared for me before, but it seemed most too much to believe. You don't know how I feel, Reub. You can't think, nohow."

"Yes I can," said Reuben, quietly; "I guess ye feel suthin ez I uster baout Jemimy, sorter light inside an so pleased like ye don't keer a copper ef ye live or die. Yes, I know mor'n ye think I dew baout the feelin's a feller hez long o' women, on'y ye see it didn't come ter nothin with Jemimy, fer wen my fust crop failed, an I was tuk for debt, Peleg got her arter all."

"I didn't think 'bout Jemimy, Reub," said Perez, softly. In the affluence of his own happiness, he was overwhelmed with compassion for his brother. He was stricken by the patient look upon his pale face. "Never mind, Reub," he said. "Don't be downhearted. You and me 'll stand by each other, an mebbe it 'll be made up to ye some time," and he laid his arm tenderly on the other's shoulder.

"I on'y spoke on't 'cause o' what ye said 'bout my not under-
standin," said Reuben, excusing himself for having made
a demand on the other's compassion. "She never guv me no
sech reasin ter think she set store by me ez ye've hed ter night
'long o' Desire Edwards. I wuzn't a comparin on us, nohow."
There was a space of silence finally disturbed by a noise of
boots in an adjoining room and presently Abner Rathbun
stumped out. Abner had escaped at the West Stockbridge
rout and having made his way to Perez, at Lee, had been
forgiven his desertion by the latter and made his chief lieutenant and adviser.

"Hello, Reub," he exclaimed. "Whar'd ye drop from?
Heard so much talkin, callated suthin must a happened, an
turned out ter see what it wuz. Fetched any news, hev ye
Reub? Spit it aout. Guess it muss be pooty good, or the
cap'n would'n be lookin so darned pleased."

"The news I fetched is that the army in Stockbridge is
going to attack you to-morrow at dawn."

Abner's jaw fell. He looked from Reuben to Perez, whose
face as he gazed absently at the coals on the hearth still wore
the smile which had attracted his attention. This seemed to
decide him, for as he turned again to Reub, he said, shrewdly:

"Yew can't fool me with no gum-game o' that sort. I guess
Perez wouldn't be grinnin that ar way ef he callated we wuz
gonter be all chawed up afore mornin."

"Reuben tells the truth. They are going to attack us in
the morning," said Perez, looking up. Abner stared at him a
moment, and then demanded half-sullen, half-puzzled:

"Wal, Cap'n, wat dew ye see tew larf at in that? Derned ef
I see nothin funny."

"Your glum mug would be enough to laugh at if there was
nothing else Abner," said Perez, getting up and gayly slapping the giant on the shoulder.

"I s'pose ye must hev got some plan in yer head fer gittin
the best on em," suggested Abner, at last, evidently racking

his brains to suggest a hypothesis to explain his commander's untimely levity.

"No, Abner," replied Perez, "I have not thought of any plan yet. What do you think about the business?"

"I'm afeard thar ain't no dependin on the men fer a scrimmage. I callate they'll scatter ez soon's the news gits raound that the white feathers be comin, 'thout even waitin fer em tew git in sight," was Abner's gloomy response.

"I shouldn't be at all surprised if they did. I don't believe there's a dozen in the lot we could depend on," said Perez cheerfully.

"Wat's the matter with ye, Cap'n," burst out Abner, in desperation. "I can't make aout wat's come over ye. Ye talk 's though ye didn' keer a Bungtaown copper wether we fit or run, or stayed an got hung, but jess set thar a grinnin tew yerself ez if ye'd loss yer wits."

Perez laughed again, but checking himself, replied: "I s'pose I do seem a little queer, Abner, but you mustn't mind that. I hope I haven't lost my wits quite. Let's see, now," he went on in a businesslike tone, with the air of one abruptly enforcing a new direction upon his thoughts. "We could get up the men and retreat to the mountains by morning, but two-thirds would desert before we'd marched two miles, and slink away home, and the worst of it is the poor chaps would be arrested and abused when they got home."

"That's sartin so, Cap'n," said Abner, his anxiety for Perez' sanity evidently diminishing.

"It's a shame to retreat, too, with such a position to defend. Why, Abner, just look at it. The snow is three to four feet deep in the fields and woods, and the enemy can only come in on the road. That road is just like a causeway through a swamp or a bridge. They can't go off it without snowshoes. With half a company that I could depend on, I'd defend it against a regiment. If I wanted breastworks all I've got to do is to dig paths in the snow. I could hold Lee till the snow melts or till they took it by zig-zags and parallels through the drifts. But there's no use talking about any such thing, for there's no fight left in the men, not a bit. If they had ever so little grit left, we might hold out long enough at least to get some sort of fair terms, but, Lord they haven't. They'll just run like sheep."

"Ef we on'y hed a cannon naow, ef 'twan't but a three-pounder!" said Abner, pathetically. "We could jess sot it in the middle of the road, and all creation couldn't get intew Lee. Yew an I could stop em alone then. Gosh naow wat wouldn't I give fer a cannon the size o' Mis Perry's yarn-beam thar. Ef the white feathers seen a gun the size o' that p'inted at em an a feller behind it with a hot coal, I callate they'd be durn glad tew 'gree tew a fa'r settlement. But Lordomassy, gosh knows we hain't got no cannon, and we can't make one."

"I don't know about that, Abner," replied Perez, deliberately. His glance had followed Abner's to the loom standing in the back of the kitchen, and as he answered his lieutenant he was fixedly regarding the very yarn-beam to which the other had alluded, a round, smooth, dark colored wooden roller, five or six feet long and eight or ten inches through.

But perhaps it will be better to let Dr. Partridge tell the rest of the story as he related it nearly three weeks later for the amusement of Desire during her convalescence from the cold and fever through which he had brought her.

"It was pitch dark when we left Stockbridge," said the doctor, "and allowing a good hour for the march owing to the state of the road, the General calculated we should reach Lee about dawn and catch the rascals taking their beauty sleep. It was excessively cold and our fingers began to grow numb very soon, and if anybody touched the iron part of his gun without the mittens he would leave a piece of skin behind. But you see we had just heard of General Lincoln's thirty-mile night march from Hadley to Petersham in even worse weather, and for the credit of Berkshire, we had to keep on if we froze to death. We met nobody until we were within half a mile of Lee. Then we overhauled one of the rebel sentries, and captured him, though not till he had let off his gun. Then we heard the drum beating in the town. There was nothing to do but to hurry on as fast as we could. And so we did for about ten minutes more when somebody said, 'There they are.' Sure enough, about twenty rods off, where the road enters the village was a black mass of men occupying its entire breadth with a man on horseback in front whom I took for Hamlin. We kept on a little longer and then the General ordered us to halt, and Squire Wood-bridge rode forward within easy speaking distance of the rebels and began to read the riot act. But he had no sooner begun than Hamlin made a gesture, and a drum struck up lustily among the rebels, drowning the Squire's voice. Nevertheless he made an end of the reading so that we might proceed legally and thereupon the General ordered the men to fix bayonets and gave the order to march. Then it seemed that the rebels were about to retire, for their line fell back a little and already our men had given a cheer when a sharp-eyed fellow in the front rank sang out:

"'They've got a cannon!' And when we looked, sure enough the slight falling back of the rebels we had noted, had only been to uncover a piece of artillery which was planted squarely in the middle of the road, pointing directly at us. A man with a smoking brazier of coals stood by the breech, and another, whom by his size I took to be Abner Rathbun, with a pair of tongs held a bright coal which he had taken from it. It being yet rather dark, though close on sunrise, we could plainly see the redness of the coal the fellow held in the tongs above the touchhole of the gun, and ticklish near, it seemed, I can say. I know not to this day, and others say the same, whether any one gave the order to halt or not, but it is certain we stopped square, nor were those behind at all disposed to push forward such as were in front, for there is this about cannon balls that is different from musket balls. The front rank serves the rear rank as a shield from the bullets, but the cannon ball plows the whole length of the file and kills those behind as readily as those before. And, moreover, we had as soon expected to see the devil in horns and tail leading the rebels, as this cannon, for no one supposed there was a piece of artillery in all Berkshire. You must know the place we were in, was, moreover, as bad as could be; for we could only march by the road, by reason of the deep snow on either hand, which was like walls shutting us in, and leaving room for no more than eight men to go abreast. If the cannon were loaded with a ball, it must needs cut a swathe like a scythe from the first man to the last, and if it were loaded with small balls, all of us who were near the front must needs go down at once. The General asked counsel of us who were riding with him at the front what had best be done, whereupon Squire Sedgwick advised that half a dozen of us with horses should put spurs to them and dash suddenly upon the cannon and take it. 'Ten to one,' he said, 'the rascal with the tongs will not dare touch off the gun, and if he does, why, 'tis but one shot.' But this seemed to us all a foolhardy thing; for, though there were but one shot, who could tell whom it might hit? It might be one of us as well as another. Your uncle Jahleel, as it seemed, lest any should deem Squire Sedgwick braver than he, declared that he was ready, but the others of us, by no means fell in with the notion and General Patterson said flatly that he was responsible for all our lives and would permit no such madness. And then, as no one had any other plan to propose, we were in a quandary, and I noted that each one had his eyes, as it were, fastened immovably upon the cannon and the glowing coal which the fellow held in the tongs. For, in order to keep it clear of ash, he kept waving it to and fro, and once or twice when he brought it perilously close to the touchhole, I give you my word I began to think in a moment of all the things I had done in my life. And I remember, too, that if one of us was speaking when the fellow made as if he would touch off the gun, there was an interruption of a moment in his speech, ere he went on again. It must be that not only civilians like myself, but men of war also do find a certain discomposing effect in the stare of a cannon. Meanwhile the wind drew through the narrow path wherein we stood, with vehemence, and, whereas we had barely kept our blood in motion by our laboring through the snow, now that we stood still, we seemed freezing. Our horses shivered and set their ears back with the cold, but it was notable how quietly the men stood packed in the road behind us, though they must have been well nigh frost-bitten. No doubt they were absorbed in watching the fellow swinging the coal as we were. But if we did not advance, we must retreat, that was plain. We could not stay where we were. It was, I fancy, because no one could bring himself to propose such an ignoble issue to our enterprise, that we were for a little space all dumb.

"Then it was when the General could no longer have put off giving the order to right about march, that Hamlin tied a white rag to his sword and rode toward us holding it aloft. When he had come about half way, he cried out:

" 'Will your commander and Dr. Partridge, if he be among you, ride out to meet me? I would have a parley.'

"Why he pitched on me I know not, save that, wanting a witness, he chose me as being a little more friendly to him than most of the Stockbridge gentlemen. When we had ridden forward, he saluted us with great cordiality and good humor, as if forsooth, instead of being within an ace of murdering us all, he had but been trying us with a jest.

" 'I see,' said he to the general, 'that your fellows like not the look of my artillery, and I blame them not, for it will be a nasty business in that narrow lane if we have to let drive, as assuredly we shall do if you come another foot further.

But it may be we can settle our difference without bloodshed. My men have fled together to me to be protected from arrest and prosecution, for what they have heretofore done, not because they intend further to attack the government. I will agree that they shall disperse and go quietly to their homes, provided you give me your word that they shall not be arrested or injured by your men, and will promise to use your utmost influence to secure them from any arrest hereafter, and that at any rate they shall have trial before a jury of their neighbors.'

"The General is a shrewd bargainer, I make no doubt, for though I knew he was delighted out of measure to find any honorable escape from the predicament in which we were, he pulled a long face, and after some thought, said that he would grant the conditions, provided the rebels also surrendered their arms, and took the oath of allegiance to the state. At this Hamlin laughed a little.

" 'I see, sir, we are but wasting time,' he said, with a mighty indifferent air. 'You have got the boot on the wrong foot. It is we who are granting you terms, not you us. You may thank your stars I don't require your men to surrender their arms. Look you, sir, my men will not give up their guns, or take any oath but go as free as yours, with your promise of protection hereafter. If you agree to those terms, you may come into Lee, and we will disperse. If not let us lose no more time waiting, but have at it.'

"It was something to make one's blood run cold, to hear the fellow talk so quietly about murdering us. The General hemmed and hawed a little, and made a show of talking aside with me, and presently said that to avoid shedding the blood of the misguided men on the other side, he would consent to the terms, but he added, the artillery must at any rate be surrendered.

" 'It is private property,' said Hamlin.

" 'It is forfeited to its owner by its use against the government,' replied the General sturdily.

" 'I will not stickle for the gun,' said Hamlin, 'but will
leave you to settle that with the owner,' and, as he spoke, he
looked as if he were inwardly amused over something.

"Thereupon we separated. The announcement of the
terms was received by our men with a cheer, for they had
made up their minds that there was nothing before them but
a march back to Stockbridge in the face of the wind and to
meet the ridicule of the populace. As we now approached the
cannon at quick-step Abner Rathbun came around and
stood in front of it, so we did not see it till we were close
upon it. He was grinning from ear to ear. The road just
behind was packed with rebels all likewise on the broad grin,
as if at some prodigious jest. As we came up Hamlin said to
the General:

" 'Sir, I now deliver over to you the artillery, that is if you
can settle it with Mrs. Perry. Abner stand aside.'

"Rathbun did so and what we saw was a yarn-beam
mounted on a pair of oxcart wheels with the tongue of the
cart resting on the ground behind."

THE RESTORATION

As was remarked in the last chapter, it was some three weeks after the famous encounter at Lee that Dr. Partridge entertained Desire one afternoon with the account of the affair which I have transcribed for the information of my readers. The interval between the night before the Lee expedition, when she had taken her sickness, and the sunny afternoon of expiring February, when she sat listening to the doctor's story, had for her been only a blank of sickness, but in the community around, it had been a time of anxiety, of embitterment, and of critical change. The gay and brilliant court, of which she had for a brief period been the center, had long ago vanished. Hamlin's band at Lee had been the last considerable force of rebels embodied in Southern Berkshire, and a few days after its dispersal the companies from other towns left Stockbridge to return home, leaving the protection of the village to the home company. Close on this followed the arrival at Pittsfield of General Lincoln with a body of troops called into Berkshire by the invitation of General Patterson, to the disgust of some gentlemen who thought the county quite capable of attending to its own affairs. These forces had completed the pacification of Northern Berkshire, where, among the mountain fastnesses rebel bands had till then maintained themselves, so that now the entire county was subdued and the insurrection, so far as concerned any overt manifestation, was at an end. In Stockbridge Tax-collector Williams once more went his rounds. Deputy Sheriff Seymour's red flag floated again from the gable ends of the houses whence the mob had torn it last September, foreclosure sales were made, processes were served, debtors taken to jail, and the almost forgotten sound of the lash was once more heard on the green of Saturday afternoons as the constable executed Squire Woodbridge's sentences at the reërected whipping-post and stocks. Sedgwick's return to Boston to his seat in the Legislature early in February, had left Woodbridge to resume unimpeded his ancient autocracy in the village, and with as many grudges as that gentleman had to pay off, it may well be supposed the constable had no sinecure. The victims of justice were almost exclusively those who had been concerned in the late rebellion. For although the various amnesties, as well as the express stipulations under which a large number had surrendered, protected most of the insurgents from penalties for their political crimes, still misdemeanors and petty offenses against property and persons during the late disturbances were chargeable against most of them, and tried before a magistrate whom, like Woodbridge, they had mobbed. A charge was as good as a proof.

Nor if they appealed to a jury, was their chance much better, for the Legislature coming together again in February, had excluded former rebels from the jury box for three years, binding them to keep the peace for the same time, and depriving them of the elective franchise in all forms for a year, while on the other hand complete indemnity was granted to the friends of government for all offences against property or persons, which they might have committed in suppressing the rebellion. Without here controverting the necessity of these measures, it is easy to realize the state of hopeless discouragement to which they reduced the class exposed to their effect. Originally driven into the rebellion by the pressure of a poverty which made them the virtual serfs of the gentlemen, they now found themselves not only forced to resume their former position in that respect, but were in addition, deprived of the ordinary civil rights and guarantees of citizens. In desperation many fled over the border into New York and Connecticut, and joined bands of similar refugees which were camped there. Others, weaker spirited, or bound by ties they could not or would not break, remained at home, seeking to propitiate their masters by a contrite and circumspect demeanor, or sullenly enduring whatever was put upon them. A large number prepared to emigrate to homes in the West as soon as spring opened the roads.

Of the chief abettors of Perez, the fortunes may be briefly told. Jabez Flint had sold all he had and escaped to Nova Scotia to join one of the numerous colonies of deported Tories which had been formed there. Jabez was down on his luck.

"I've hed enough o' rebellin," he declared. "I've tried both sides on't. In the fust rebellion I wuz agin' the rebels, an the rebels licked. This ere time I tuk sides agin' the govment, an the govment hez licked. I'm like a feller ez is fust kicked behind an then in the stummick. I be done on both sides, like a pancake."

Israel Goodrich and Ezra Phelps, being excepted from the amnesties as members of the rebel committee, had only escaped jailing because, as men of some substance they had been able to give large bonds to await the further disposition of the Boston government.

"I didn' mind so much 'bout that," said Israel, "but what come kinder tough on me wuz a seein them poor white-livered pulin chaps tew my house tuk back ter jail."

For the debtors whom the mob had released from Great Barrington jail, including those to whom Israel had given asylum, had now been recaptured and returned to the charge of Cephas Bement and his pretty wife. Reuben Hamlin had been taken with the rest, though his stay in jail this time did not promise to be a long one, for he had overdone his feeble strength in that night walk through the snow to Lee, and since then had declined rapidly. He was so far gone that it would scarcely have been thought worth while to take him to jail if he could have remained at home. But as the sheriff had now sold the Hamlin house at auction, and Elnathan and his wife had been separated and boarded out as paupers, this was out of the question.

There was one man in Stockbridge, however, who was more to be pitied than Reuben. Peleg Bidwell found himself at the end of the rebellion as at the opening of it, the debtor and thrall of Solomon Gleason, save that his debt was greater, his means of paying it even less, while by his insolent bearing toward Solomon during the rebellion, he had made him not only his creditor but his enemy. The jail yawned before Peleg, and of the jail he, as well as the people generally, had acquired a new horror since the day when the mob had brought to light the secrets of that habitation of cruelty. He felt that, come what might, he could not go to a jail. And he did not. But his pretty wife stayed at home and avoided her former acquaintances, and those who saw her said she was pale and acted queer, and Peleg went about with a hangdog look, and Solomon Gleason was a frequent caller, and the women of the neighborhood whispered together.

Abner Rathbun and Meshech Little had fled across the border, and Abe Konkapot would have done so but for the fact that he could not leave his sweetheart Lu to be secured by his rival and brother, Jake. Jake, having out of enmity to his brother sided with the government party, was now in favor with the powers that were, and more preferred than ever by Lu's mother. But Abe knew the girl liked him rather the better, and did not let himself be discouraged. Jake, observing that he made little progress in spite of his advantages, laid a plot against his brother. The latter had acquired in the army a tendency to use profane language in moments of excitement, and it was of this weakness that Jake took advantage. Picking an opportunity when there were witnesses, he provoked Abe to wrath, and having made him swear profusely, went straightway to Squire Woodbridge and complained of him for blasphemy. Abe was promptly arrested and brought before the magistrate. The Squire, not unwilling to get a handle against so bad a rebel, observed that it was high time for the authorities to make a head against the tide of blasphemy which had swept over the state since the war, and to advertise to the rabble that the statute against profanity was not a dead letter and thereupon sentenced Abe to ten lashes at the whipping-post, to be at once laid on, it chancing to be a Saturday afternoon. While Abe, frantic with rage, was struggling with the constable and his assistants, Jake ran away to the Widow Nimham's cottage and asking Lu to go to walk, managed to bring her across the green in time to see the sentence carried into execution. Jake had understood what he was about. There were no doubt white girls in Stockbridge who might have married a lover whom they had seen publicly whipped, but for Lu, with an Indian's intense sensitiveness to a personal indignity, it would have been impossible. Abe needed no one to tell him that. As he was unbound and walked away from the post, his blood-shotten eyes had taken her in standing there with Jake. He did not even make an effort to see her afterwards and next Sunday Jake's and Lu's banns were called in meeting. Abe had been drunk pretty much all the time since, lying about the tavern floor. Widow Bingham said she hadn't a heart to refuse him rum, and in truth the poor fellow's manhood was so completely broken down, that he must have been a resolute teetotaler, indeed, who would not have deemed it an act of common humanity to help him temporarily to forget himself.

Such then are the events that were taking place in the community about her while Desire was lying on her sick bed, or making her first appearances as a convalescent downstairs. Only faint and occasional echoes of them had reached her ears. She had been told, indeed, that the rebellion was now all over and peace and order restored, but of the details and incidents of the process she knew nothing. To be precise it was during the latter part of the afternoon of the twenty-sixth day of February, that Dr. Partridge was entertaining her as aforesaid with his humorous version of the Lee affair. The Dr. and Mrs. Partridge had come to tea, and to spend the evening, and just here, lest any modern housewife should object that it is not a New England country practice to invite company on washing-day, I would mention that in those days of inexhaustible stores of linen, washing-day rarely came over once a fortnight. After tea in the evening the Doctor and Squire Edwards sat talking politics over their snuff-boxes, while Mrs. Partridge and Mrs. Edwards discussed the difficulty of getting good help, now that the negroes were beginning to feel the oats of their new liberty, and the farmers' daughters, since the war and the talk about liberty and equality, thought themselves as good as their betters. Now that the insurrection had still further stirred up their jealousy of gentlefolk, it was to be expected that they would be quite past getting on with at all, and for all Mrs. Edwards could see, ladies must make up their minds to do their own work pretty soon.

Desire sat in an armchair, her hands folded in her lap, musingly gazing into the glowing bed of coals upon the hearth, and listening half absently to the talk about her. She had been twice to meeting the day before, and considered herself as now quite well, but she had not disused the invalid's privilege of sitting silent in company.

"I marvel," said Squire Edwards, contemplatively tapping his snuff-box, "at the working of Providence, when I consider that so lately the Commonwealth, and especially this county, was in turmoil, the rebels having everything their own way, and we scarcely daring to call our souls our own, and behold them now scattered, fled over the border, in prison, or disarmed and trembling, and the authority of law and the courts everywhere established."

"Yes," replied the Doctor, "we have reason to be thankful indeed, and yet I cannot help compassionating the honester among the rebels. It is the pity of an uprising like this, that while one must needs sympathize with the want and suffering of the rebels, it is impossible to condemn too strongly the mad plans they urge as remedies. Ezra Phelps was telling me the other day, that their idea, had they succeeded, was to cause so many bills to be printed and scattered abroad, that the poorest could get enough to pay all their debts and taxes. Some were for repudiating public and private debts altogether, but Ezra said that this would not be honest. He was in favor of printing bills enough so everything could be paid. I tried to show him that one plan was as dishonest as the other; that they might just as well refuse payment, as pay in worthless bits of printed paper, and that the morality of the two schemes being the same, that of refusing outright the payment of dues, was preferable practically, because at least, it would not further derange trade by putting a debased and valueless currency in circulation. But I fear he did not see it at all, if he even gave me credit for sincerity, and yet he is an honest, well-meaning chap, and more intelligent than the common run of the rebels."

"That is the trouble nowadays," said Edwards, "these numskulls must needs have matters of government explained to them, and pass their own judgment on public affairs. And when they cannot understand them, then forsooth comes a rebellion. I think none can deny seeing in these late troubles the first fruits of those pestilent notions of equality, whereof we heard so much from certain quarters, during the late war of independence. I would that Mr. Jefferson and some of the other writers of pestilent democratic rhetoric might have been here in the state the past winter, to see the outcome of their preaching."

"It may yet prove," said Dr. Partridge, "that these troubles are to work providentially to incline the people of this state to favor a closer union with the rest of the continent for mutual protection, if the forthcoming convention at Philadelphia shall devise a practicable scheme. By reason of the preponderant strength of our Commonwealth we have deemed ourselves less in need of such a union than are our sister colonies, but this recent experience must teach us that even we are not strong enough to stand alone."

"You are right there, sir," said Edwards. "It is plain that if we keep on as we are, Massachusetts will ere long split into as many states as we have counties, or at least into several. What have these troubles been but a revolt of the western counties against the eastern, and had we gentlemen gone with the rebels, the state would have been by this time divided, and you know well," here Edwards' voice became confidential, "we have in the main, no great cause to be beholden to the Bostonians. They treat our western counties as if they were but provinces."

Desire's attention had lapsed as the gentlemen's talk got into the political depths, but some time after it was again aroused by hearing the mention of Perez Hamlin's name. The doctor was saying:

"They say he is lurking just over the York border at Lebanon. There are four or five score ruffians with him, who breathe out threatenings and slaughter against us Stockbridge people but I think we need lose no sleep on that account for the knaves will scarcely care to risk their necks on Massachusetts soil."

"It is possible," said Edwards, "that they may make some descents on Egremont or Sheffield or other points just across the line, but they will never venture so far inland as Stockbridge for fear of being cut off, and if they do our militia is quite able for them. What mischief they can do safely they will do, but nothing else for they are arrant cowards when all's said."

The talk of the gentlemen branched off upon other topics,

but Desire did not follow it further, finding in what had just been said quite enough to engross her thoughts. Of course there could be no real danger that Hamlin would venture a visit to Stockbridge, since both her father and the doctor scouted the idea; but there was in the mere suggestion enough to be very agitating. To avoid the possibility of a meeting with Hamlin, as well as to acquit her conscience of a goading conviction of unfairness to him, she had already once risked compromising herself by sending that midnight warning to Lee, nor did she grudge the three weeks' sickness it cost her, seeing it had succeeded. Nor was the idea of meeting him any less terrifying now. The result of her experiences in the last few months had been that all her old self-reliance was gone. When she recalled what she had done and felt, and imagined what she might have gone on to do, she owned in all humility that she could no longer take care of herself or answer for herself. Desire Edwards was after all capable of being as big a fool as any other girl. Especially at the thought of meeting Hamlin again, this sense of insecurity became actual panic. It was not that she feared her heart. She was not conscious of loving him but of dreading him. Her imagination invested him with some strange, irresistible magnetic power over her, the magnetism of a tremendous passion, against which, demoralized by the memory of her former weakness, she could not guarantee herself. And the upshot was that just because she chanced to overhear that reference to Perez in the gentlemen's talk, she lay awake nervous and miserable for several hours after going to bed that night. In fact she had finally to take herself seriously to task about the folly of scaring herself to death about such a purely fanciful danger, before she could go to sleep.

She woke hours after with a stifled scream, for her mother was standing in the door of the room, half dressed, the candle she held revealing a pale and frightened face, while the words Desire heard were:

"Quick, get up and dress, or you'll be murdered in bed! An army of Shayites is in the village."

"Four o'clock in the morning courage," that steadiness of nerve which is not shaken when, suddenly roused from the relaxation and soft languor of sleep, one is called to face pressing, deadly, and undreamed of peril in the weird and chilling hour before dawn, was described by Napoleon as a most rare quality among soldiers, and such being the case it is hardly to be looked for among women. With chattering teeth and random motions, half-distraught with incoherent terrors, Desire made a hasty, incomplete toilet in the dark of her freezing bedroom, and ran downstairs. In the living-room she found her mother and the smaller children with the negro servants and Keziah Pixley, the white domestic. Downstairs in the cellar her father and Jonathan were at work burying the silver and other valuables, that having been the first thought when a fugitive from the tavern where the rebels had first halted, brought the alarm. There were no candles lit in the living-room lest their light should attract marauders, and the faint light of the just breaking dawn made the faces seem yet paler and ghastlier with fear than they were. From the street without could be heard the noise of a drum, shouts, and now and then musket shots, and having scraped away the thick frost from one of the panes, Desire could see parties of men with muskets going about and persons running across the green as if for their lives. As she looked she saw a party fire their muskets after one of these fugitives, who straightway came back and gave himself up. In the room it was bitterly cold, for though the ashes had been raked off the coals no wood had been put on lest the smoke from the chimney should draw attention.

The colored servants were in a state of abject terror, but the white "help" made no attempt to conceal her exultation. They were her friends the Shayites, and her sweetheart she declared was among them. He'd sent her a hint that they were coming, she volubly declared, and yesterday when Mrs. Edwards was "so high 'n mighty with her a makin her sweep the kitchen twicet over she was goodamiter tell her ez haow she'd see the time she'd wisht she'd a kep the right side on her."

"I've always tried to do right by you Keziah. I don't think you have any call to be revengeful," said the poor lady, trembling.

"Mebbe I hain't and mebbe I hev," shrilled Keziah, tossing her head disdainfully. "I guess I know them ez loves me from them ez don't. I s'pose ye think I dunno wat yer husbun an Jonathan be a buryin daown stairs."

"I'm sure you won't betray us, Keziah," said Mrs. Edwards. "You've had a good place with us, Keziah. And there's that dimity dress of mine. It's quite good yet. You could have it made over for you."

"Oh yes," replied Keziah, scornfully. "It's all well nuff ter talk bout givin some o' yer things away wen yer likely to lose em all."

With that, turning her back upon her terrified mistress, with the air of a queen refusing a petition, she patronizingly assured Desire that she had met with more favor in her eyes than her mother, and she would accordingly protect her. "Though," she added, "I guess ye won't need my helpin for Cap'n Hamlin 'll see nobuddy teches ye cept hisself."

"Is he here?" gasped Desire, her dismay suddenly magnified into utter panic.

"Fer sartain, my sweetheart ez sent me word 's under him," replied Keziah.

A noise of voices and tramp of feet at the outside door interrupted her. The marauders had come. The door was barred and this having been tested, there was a hail of gunstock blows upon it with orders to open and blasphemous threats as to the consequences of refusal. There was a dead silence within, but for Mrs. Edwards' hollow whisper, "Don't open." With staring eyes and mouths apart the terrified women and children looked at one another motionless, barely daring to breathe. But as the volley of blows and threats was renewed with access of violence, Keziah exclaimed:

"Ef they hain't yeur frens they be mine, an I hain't gonter see em kep aout in the cold no longer fer nobuddy," and she went to the door and took hold of the bar.

"Don't you do it," gasped Mrs. Edwards springing forward to arrest her. But she had done it, and instantly Meshech Little with three or four followers burst into the room, wearing the green insignia of rebellion in their caps and carrying muskets with bayonets fixed.

"Why didn' ye open that ar door, afore?" demanded Meshech, angrily.

"What do you want?" asked Mrs. Edwards tremblingly confronting him.

"Wat dew we want ole woman?" replied Meshech. "Wal, we want most evrything, but I guess we kin help oursels. Hey boys?"

"Callate we kin make aout tew," echoed one of his followers, not a Stockbridge man, and then as his eye caught Desire, as she stood pale and beautiful, with wild eyes and disheveled hair, by her mother, he made a dive at her saying: "Guess I'll take a kiss tew begin with."

"Let the gal 'lone," said Meshech, catching him by the shoulder. "Hands orfen her. She's the Duke's doxy, an he'll run ye through the body ef ye tech her."

"Gosh, she hain't, though, is she?" said the fellow, refraining from further demonstration but regarding her admiringly. "I hearn baout she. Likely lookin gal, tew, hain't she? On'y leetle tew black, mebbe."

"Did'n ye know, ye dern fool, it's along o' her the Duke sent us here, tew see nobuddy took nothin till he could come raoun?" said Meshech. "But I callate the on'y way to keep other fellers from takin anything tidday is ter take it yerself.

We'll hev suthin tew drink, anyhaow. Hello, ole cock," he added as Edwards, coming up from down cellar, entered the room. "Ye be jess'n time. Come on, give us some rum," and neither daring nor able to make resistance, the storekeeper was hustled into the store. Keziah's sweetheart had remained behind. In the midst of their mutual endearments, she had found opportunity to whisper to him something, of which Mrs. Edwards caught the words, "cellar, nuff tew buy us a farm an a haouse," and guessed the drift. As Keziah and her young man, who responded to her suggestion with alacrity, were moving toward the cellar door, Mrs. Edwards barred their way. The fellow was about to lay hands on her, when one of the drinkers, coming back from the store, yelled: "Look out, thar's the cap'n," and Perez entered.

SOME REAL FIGHTING

At sight of his commander the soldier who had been about to lay hands on Mrs. Edwards to thrust her out of his path to the cellar, giving over his design, slunk into the store to join his comrades there, and was followed by the faithful Keziah. Mrs. Edwards, who had faced the ruffian only in the courage of desperation, sank trembling upon a settle, and the children throwing themselves upon her, bawled in concert. Without bestowing so much as a glance on any other object in the room Perez crossed it to where Desire stood, and taking her nerveless hand in both his, devoured her face with glowing eyes. She did not flush or show any confusion; neither did she try to get away. She stood as if fascinated, unresponsive but unresisting.

"Were you frightened?" he asked.

"Yes," she replied in a mechanical tone corresponding with her appearance.

"Didn't you know I was here? I told you I would come back for you, and I have come. You have been sick. I heard of it. Are you well now?"

"Yes."

"Reuben told me you came on foot through the snow to bring word so he might warn me the night before the Lee battle. Was it that made you sick?"

"Yes."

"What is that, Desire? What do you mean about sending him warning?" cried Mrs. Edwards amazedly. Desire made no reply but Perez did:

"It is thanks to her I was not caught in my bed by your

men that morning. It is thanks to her I am not in jail today, disgraced by the lash and waiting for the hangman. Oh my dear, how glad I am to owe it to you," and he caught the end of one of the long strands of jetty hair that fell down her neck and touched it to his lips.

"You are crazy, fellow!" cried Mrs. Edwards, and starting forward and grasping Desire by the arm she demanded, "What does this wild talk mean? There is no truth in it, is there?"

"Yes," said the girl in the same dead, mechanical voice, without turning her eyes to her mother or even raising them.

Mrs. Edwards opened her mouth, but no sound came forth. Her astonishment was too utter. Meanwhile Perez had passed his arm about Desire's waist as if to claim her on her own acknowledgement. Stung by the sight of her daughter in the very arms of the rebel captain, Mrs. Edwards found her voice once more, righteous indignation overcoming her first unmingled consternation.

"Out upon you for a shameless hussy. Oh, that a daughter of mine should come to this! Do you dare tell me you love this scoundrel?"

"No," answered the girl.

"What?" faltered Perez, his arm involuntarily dropping from her waist.

For all reply she rushed to her mother and threw herself on her bosom, sobbing hysterically. For once at least in their lives Mrs. Edwards' and Perez Hamlin's eyes met with an expression of perfect sympathy, the sympathy of a common bewilderment. Then Mrs. Edwards tried to loosen Desire's convulsive clasp about her neck, but the girl held her tightly, crying:

"Oh, don't, mother, don't."

For several moments Perez stood motionless just where Desire had left him, looking after her stupefied. The pupils of his eyes alternately dilated and contracted, his mouth opened and closed; he passed his hand over his forehead. Then he went up to her and stood over her as she clung to her mother, but seemed no more decided as to what he could do or say further.

But just then there was a diversion. Meshech and his followers who had passed through from the living-room into the store in search of rum had thrown open the outside door, and a gang of their comrades had poured in to assist in the onset upon the liquor barrels. The spigots had all been set running, or knocked out entirely, and yet comparatively little of the fiery fluid was wasted, so many mugs, hats, caps, and all sorts of receptacles were extended to catch the flow. Some who could not find any sort of a vessel, actually lay under the stream and let it pour into their mouths, or lapped it up as it ran on the floor. Meanwhile the store was being depleted of other than the drinkable property. The contents of the shelves and boxes were littered on the floor, and the rebels were busy swapping their old hats, boots and mittens for new ones, or filling their pockets with tobacco, tea or sugar, while some of the more foresighted were making piles of selected goods to carry away. But whatever might be the momentary occupation of the marauders, all were drunk, excessively yet buoyantly drunk, drunk with that peculiarly penetrating and tenacious intoxication which results from drinking in the morning on an empty stomach, a time when liquor seems to pervade all the interstices of the system and lap each particular fibre and tissue in a special and independent intoxication on its own account. Several fellows, including Meshech, had been standing for a few moments in the door leading from the store into the living-room, grinningly observing the little drama which the reader has been following. As Desire broke away from Perez and rushed to her mother, Meshech exclaimed:

"Wy in time did'n yer hole ontew her, Cap'n? I'd like ter seen her git away from me."

"Or me nuther," seconded the fellow next him.

Perez paid no heed to this remonstrance, and probably did not hear it at all, but Mrs. Edwards looked up. In her bewilderment and distress over Desire the thought of her husband and Jonathan had been driven from her mind. The sight of Meshech recalled it.

"What have you done with my husband?" she demanded anxiously.

"He's all right. He an the young cub be jess a gonter take a leetle walk with us fellers 'cross the border," replied Meschech jocularly.

"What are you going to take them away for? What are you going to do to them?" cried Mrs. Edwards.

"Oh, ye need'n be skeert," Meshech reassured her. "He'll hev good kumpny. Squire Woodbridge an Ginral Ashley an Doctor Sergeant, Cap'n Jones an schoolmaster Gleason, an a slew more o' the silk stockins be a goin' tew."

"Are you going to murder them?" exclaimed the frantic woman.

"Wal," drawled Meshech, "that depends. Ef govment hangs any o' our fellers wat they've got in jail, we're gonter hang yewr husban' an the res' on em, sure's taxes. Ef none o' aourn ain't hurt, we shan't hurt none o' yourn. We take em fer kinder hostiges, ye see, ole lady."

"Where have you got my husband? I must go to him. God help us!" ejaculated Mrs. Edwards; and loosing herself from her daughter, now in turn forgotten in anxiety for husband and son, the poor woman hurried past Meshech through the confused store and so out of the house.

At the same moment the drum at the tavern began to beat the recall to the plundering parties of insurgents scattered over the village, and the men poured out of the store.

Save for the presence of the smaller children and the negro servants cowering in a corner, Desire and Perez were left alone in the room. With no refuge to fly to, she stood where her mother had left her, just before Perez, with face averted, trembling, motionless, like a timid bird which seeing no escape struggles no longer, but waits for its captor's hand to close upon it. But in his nonplused, piteously perplexed face, you would have vainly looked for the hardened and remorseless expression appropriate to his part. The roll of the rebel drum kept on.

"See here, Cap'n," said Abner Rathbun, suddenly appearing at the outside door of the living-room, "we've got the hostiges together, an we'd better be a gittin along, for the 'larm's gone ter Pittsfield an all roun' an we'll hev the milishy ontew us in no time. An besides that the fellers tew the tavern be a gittin so drunk, some on em can't walk a' ready."

Aroused by Abner's insistent words, Perez took Desire's hand, and said desperately:

"Won't you come, my darling? You shall have a woman to go with you, and we'll be married as soon as we're over the border. I know it's sudden, but you see I can't wait, and I thought you liked me a little. Won't you come, now?"

"Oh, no! Oh, no! I don't want to," she said, shuddering and drawing her hand away.

Abner was silent a moment, and then he broke out vehemently:

"Look a' here, Cap'n, we hain't got no time fer soft sawder naow, with the milishy a comin daown on us. I kin hear em a drummin up ter Lee a'ready, an every jiffey we stay means a man's life an hangin fer them as is tuk. Ye've hed fuss nuff 'long o' that gal fust and last, an this ain't no time fer ye ter put up with any more o' her tantrums."

"She don't want to come, Abner. She don't like me and I thought she did," said Perez, turning his eyes from the girl to Abner, with an expression of despairing, appealing helplessness, almost childlike.

"Nonsense," replied Abner, with contemptuous impatience. "She likes ye, or she'd never a sent ye that warnin.

Akshins speaks louder'n words. She's kinder flustered an dunno her own mind, that's all. Gals don't, genally. Ye'd be a darnation fool ter let her slip through yer fingers naow, arter riskin yer neck an all aour necks in this ere job jess ter git a holt of her, an a settin sech store by her ez ye allers hev. Take a fool's advice, Cap'n. Don' waste no more talk, but jess grab her kinder soft like, an fetch her aout ter the sleigh, willy nilly. She'll come roun' in less 'n an hour, an thank ye for't. Gals allers does. They likes a masterful man. There, that's the talk. Fetch her right along."

As the last words indicated, Perez, apparently decided by Abner's words, had thrown his arm about Desire's waist and drawing her to him and half lifting her from her feet had begun with gentle force to bear her away. She made no violent resistance which indeed would have been quite vain in his powerful clasp, but burst into tears, crying poignantly:

"Oh, don't! Please! Please don't! Don't! Oh, don't!" Had there been a trace of defiance or of indignant pride in her tone, it would have been easy for him to carry out his attempt. But of the proud, high-spirited Desire Edwards there was no hint in the tear-glazed eyes turned up to his in wild dismay. She was but a frightened girl quite broken up with terror.

And yet if the thought of leaving her had been dreadful before, now the pressure of his arm upon her pliant waist, the delicious sensation of her weight, made it maddening, and thrilled him with all sorts of reckless impulses. Still clasping her, he whispered hoarsely, "I love you, I love you," as if that mighty word left nothing further needed as excuse or explanation for his conduct. "Let me go, then, if you love me. Let me go," she cried, frantically, catching at his plea and turning it against him.

"Ef ye let her go, ye'll never set eyes on her agin, Cap'n," said Abner.

"I can't. I can't. Have pity on me," groaned Perez. "I can't let you go."

"Oh, for pity's sake, do! If you loved me, you would. Oh, you would," she cried again. He took her by the shoulders and held her away from him, and looked long at her. There was something in his eyes which awed her so that she quite forgot her former terror. Then he dropped his hands to his side, and turned away as if he would leave her without another word. But half way to the door he turned again and said huskily:

"You know I love you now. You believe it, don't you?"

"Yes," she answered in a small, scared voice, and without another word he went out. As he went out, Mrs. Edwards, who had been standing in the open doorway of the store a silent spectator of the last scene, came forward, and at sight of her Desire started from the motionless attitude in which she had remained, and cried out, pressing her hands to her bosom:

"Oh, mother, mother, I wish he'd taken me. He feels so bad."

"Nonsense, child," said Mrs. Edwards, in a soothing, sensible voice. "That would have been a pretty piece of business indeed. You're all upset, and don't know what you're saying, and no wonder, either, with no breakfast and all this coil. There, there, mother's little girl," and she drew her daughter's head down on her shoulder and stroked her hair till the nervous trembling and sobbing ceased, and raising her head she asked:

"Where are father and Jonathan?"

"Hush! I gave one of the rebels my silver shoe-buckles, and he turned his back while Mrs. Bingham hid them in the closet behind the chimney at the tavern. They're safe."

The rebel column having only awaited the arrival of Perez and Abner, at once set off at quick step on the road to Great Barrington, the prisoners, thirty or forty in number, marching in the center. Perez rode behind, looking neither to the right hand or the left, and taking heed of nothing, and

Abner seeing his condition, tacitly assumed command. Two or three fellows, too utterly drunk to walk, had been perforce left behind on the tavern floor, destined to be ignominiously dragged off to the lockup by the citizens before the rebel force was fairly out of sight. Two or three others nearly as drunk as those who were left behind, but more fortunate in having friends, by dint of leaning heavily upon a man on either side, were enabled to march. But the pace was rapid, and at the first or second steep hill these wretches had to be left behind unless their friends were to be sacrificed with them. There was no danger of their freezing to death by the wayside. The pursuing militia would come along soon enough to prevent that, never fear.

Nor were these poor chaps the only sort of burdens that were speedily rejected by their bearers. As the rebels marched out of Stockbridge, nearly every man was loaded with miscellaneous plunder. Some carried bags of flour, or flitches of bacon, some an armful of muskets, others bundles of cloth or clothing, hanks of yarn, a string of boots and shoes, a churn, an iron pot, a pair of bellows, a pair of brass andirons, while one even led a calf by a halter. Some, luckier than their fellows, carried bags from which was audible the clink of silverware. Squire Woodbridge, lagging a little, was poked in the back by his own gold-headed cane to remind him to mend his pace, while Dr. Sergeant, as a special favor from one of the rebels whose wife he had once attended, was permitted to take a drink out of his own demijohn of rum. In their eagerness to carry away all they could, the rebels had forgotten that loads which they could barely hold up when standing still, would prove quite too heavy to march under, and accordingly before the band had got out of the village the road began to be littered with the more bulky articles of property. At the foot of the first hill there was a big pile of them, and two miles out of Stockbridge the rebels were reduced once more to light marching order, and not much richer than when they entered the village an hour or two before. Besides the hostages, they had under their escort several sleighs containing old men, women and children, the families of members of the band, or of sympathizers with the rebellion, who were taking this opportunity to elude their creditors and escape out of bondage across the New York border. As the rebels crossed Muddy Brook, just before entering Great Barrington, Abner Rathbun came up to Perez and said: "I don' see yer father'n mother nowhar in the sleighs."

"My father and mother?" repeated Perez vacantly.

"Yes," rejoined Abner. "Ye know ye wuz a gonter bring em back ter York with ye, but I don' see em nowhar." Perez stared at Abner, and then glanced vaguely at the row of sleighs in the line.

"I must have forgotten about them," he finally said.

As the rebels entered Great Barrington, a company of militia was drawn up as if to defend the tavern-jail, but upon the approach of the rebels, who were decidedly more numerous, they retired rapidly on the road to Sheffield. Halting in front of the building, a guard was left with the prisoners, and then the rebels swarmed into the tavern, with the double purpose of emptying the jail of debtors, and filling themselves with Cephas Bement's rum, for the hard tramp from Stockbridge had sobered them and given them fresh thirst. Perez did not go in, but sat on his horse in the road. Presently Abner came out with a very sober face and slowly approached him. He looked around.

"What are we stopping here for, Abner?" he asked, a little peevishly.

"Wy, it's the caounty jail, ye know, an we're lettin aout the debtors. Reub's in here, ye know."

"So he is; I'd forgotten," replied Perez, and then after a pause, "Why don't he come out?"

"Cap'n," said Abner, taking off his cap and looking at it,

as he fingered it. "I've got kinder tough news fer ye. Reub's dead. He died this mornin. I thort mebbe ye'd like ter see him."

"Is he in there?"

"Yes."

Perez got off his horse, and went in at the door, Abner leading the way. In the barroom of the tavern there was a crowd of drinking, carousing men, and among them a number of the white-faced debtors, already drunk with the bumpers their deliverers were pouring down their throats. Bement was not visible, but as Abner and Perez entered the jail, they saw Mrs. Bement in the corridor. She was not making any fuss or trouble at all over the breaking of the jail this time. With apparent complaisance she was promptly opening cells, or answering questions in response to the demands of Meshech Little and some companions. But there was a vicious glint in her pretty blue eyes, and she was softly singing the lugubrious hymn, beginning with the significant words,

> Ye living men, come view the ground
> Where ye shall shortly lie.

Abner pushed open the door of one of the cells that had been already opened, and went in, Perez following. He knelt by the body of his brother, and Abner turned his back. It was the same cell in which Perez had found Reuben and George Fennell, six months before. Several minutes passed, and neither moved. The drum began to beat without, summoning the men to resume their march.

"Cap'n," said Abner, "we'll hev ter go. We can't do the poor chap no good by stayin, an they can't do him no more harm."

Then Perez rose up, and leaned on Abner's shoulder, looking down on the patient face of the dead. The first tears gathered in his eyes, and trickled down, and he said:

"I never was fair to Reub. I never allowed enough for his losin Jemima. I was harder on him than I should have been."

"Ye warn't noways hard on him, Perez. Ye wuz a good brother tew him. I never hearn o' no feller hevin a better brother nor he hed in yew," protested Abner, in much distress.

Perez shook his head.

"I was hard on him. I never allowed as I'd ought for his losin his girl. I'd a been kinder to him if I'd known. Ye must a thought I was hard an unfeelin, Reub, dear, often's the time, but I didn't know, I didn't know. We'll go now, if you want, Abner."

The rebels had not left Stockbridge a moment too soon. Captain Stoddard was rallying his company before they had got out of the village, and messengers had been sent to Lee, Lenox, Pittsfield, Great Barrington, Egremont and Sheffield, to rouse the people. Within an hour or two after the rebels had marched south, the Stockbridge and Lenox companies were in pursuit. Among the messengers to Great Barrington, was Peleg Bidwell. For Peleg, since he had bought his safety by such a shameful surrender, was embittered above all against those of his former comrades who had been too brave to yield. And having brought word to Great Barrington, he took his place in the ranks of the militia of that town, and though the men among whom he stood, eyed him askance, knowing his record, not one of them was really so eager to empty his gun into the bosom of the rebel band as Peleg Bidwell.

As previously stated, the Great Barrington company, in which Peleg carried a musket, had retired toward Sheffield, when the rebels entered the former town. At Sheffield they were joined by the large company of that populous settlement, and Colonel Ashley of the same village, taking command of the combined forces, ordered a march on Great Barrington, to meet the rebels. Now Great Barrington is but four or five miles from the New York border, while Sheffield is about six, and as many south of Great Barrington, the road between the two towns running nearly parallel to the state line. There was nothing to hinder the rebels, after they had gained their main objects, the capture of hostages and the release of the debtors, from turning west from Great Barrington, and placing themselves in an hour's march across the town of Egremont, beyond the reach of the militia, in neutral territory. Becoming apprehensive that this would be their course, Colonel Ashley, instead of keeping on the road from Sheffield to Great Barrington, presently left it and marched his men along a back road running northwest toward the state line in a direction that would intercept the rebels if they struck across Egremont to New York.

He adopted, however, the precaution of leaving a party at the junction of the main road with the road he took, so that if after all instead of retreating westward the rebels had boldly kept on the main road to Sheffield word might be sent after him. It so happened that this was just what the rebels had done. Not having the fear of the Sheffield company before their eyes, instead of trying to escape to New York by the shortest cut, they had kept on toward Sheffield, marching south by the main road. And not only this, but when they came to the junction of the main road with that which Colonel Ashley had taken, and learned by capturing the guard what plan the Colonel had devised, they became so enraged that instead of keeping on to Sheffield and leaving the militia to finish their wild goose chase, they turned into the back road after them, and so the hunters became the hunted. In this way it happened that while the militia were pressing on at full speed, breathlessly debating their chances of heading off the flying rebels, "bang," "bang," came a volley in their rear, and from the stragglers who had been fired upon arose a cry, "The Shayites are after us."

It is greatly to the credit of the militia officers that the result of this surprise was not a hopeless panic among their men. As it was, for several minutes utter confusion reigned. Then one of the companies took to the woods on the right, the other entering the woods on the left, and marching back they presently came in sight of their pursuers, still pushing on pell-mell in the road. The militia now had every advantage, and Colonel Ashley ordered them to open fire. But the men hesitated. There, intermingled with the rebels, their very lineaments plainly to be seen, were the prisoners, the first gentlemen of Stockbridge and of the county. To pour a volley in upon the rebels would endanger the lives of the prisoners as much as those of the enemy. Meanwhile the rebels themselves were rapidly deploying and opening fire. The militia were in danger of losing all their advantage, of being shot down defenseless, of perhaps losing the day, all owing to the presence of the prisoners in the enemy's ranks. Again Colonel Ashley gave the order to fire. Again not a man obeyed.

"We can't kill our friends," said an officer.

"God have mercy on their souls, but pour in your fire!" roared the commander, and the volley was given. The prisoners broke from the ranks of the enemy and ran; the firing became general. For five or ten minutes a brisk engagement was kept up, and then the rebels broke and fled in every direction. The Stockbridge and Lenox companies after having followed the rebels through Great Barrington and on toward Sheffield had also turned in after them on the back road, and coming up behind in the nick of time had attacked their rear and caused their panic.

Only two of the militia had been wounded, one mortally. One also of the prisoners had proved in need of Colonel Ashley's invocation. Solomon Gleason had fallen dead at the first volley from his friends. It was generally supposed that his death was the result of a chance shot, but Peleg Bidwell was never heard to express any opinion on the subject, and Peleg was a very good marksman.

As the smoke of the last shot floated up among the tops of the gloomy pines along the road, some thirty killed and wounded rebels lay on the trampled and blood-stained snow. Abner Rathbun, mortally wounded, writhed at the foot of a tree, and near by lay Perez Hamlin quite dead.

THE JOHN HARVARD LIBRARY

*The intent of
Waldron Phoenix Belknap, Jr.,
as expressed in an early will, was for
Harvard College to use the income from a
permanent trust fund he set up, for "editing and
publishing rare, inaccessible, or hitherto unpublished
source material of interest in connection with the
history, literature, art (including minor and useful
art), commerce, customs, and manners or way of
life of the Colonial and Federal Periods of the United
States . . . In all cases the emphasis shall be on the
presentation of the basic material." A later testament
broadened this statement, but Mr. Belknap's interests remained constant until his death.*

*In linking the name of the first benefactor of
Harvard College with the purpose of this later,
generous-minded believer in American culture the
John Harvard Library seeks to emphasize the importance of Mr. Belknap's purpose. The John Harvard
Library of the Belknap Press of Harvard University
Press exists to make books and documents
about the American past more readily
available to scholars and the
general reader.*